**THE SHIP HAS ONE PASSENGER.
IT IS THE WOMAN WE HAVE
SOUGHT FOR SO LONG.**

We burst onto the bridge and confront her. She is lithe, beautiful, raven-haired, angry. She glares and fires a plasma gun at us, but we dodge. Harry fires a pulse burst that shreds her gun. We entangle her in sticky-bonds, as her screams echo through the ship. . . . She is free of sparkles, they are programmed to avoid her.

But then Rob gulps, and starts to tremble.

He looks at me with fear in his eyes. A nanowarrior has got through his facial force field. He pats his cheek. It must have burrowed through. It'll be in the brain in a second or so, snipping and jabbing and tearing. Within sixty seconds, every internal organ will be in shreds.

Rob has been my friend for thirty years now. I am also his Captain, his protector, his colleague. I feel a pang of loss.

I raise my gun and blow his head off.

DEBATABLE SPACE

PHILIP PALMER

www.orbitbooks.net
NEW YORK LONDON

Orbit
Hachette Book Group USA
237 Park Avenue, New York, NY 10017
Visit our Web site at www.HachetteBookGroupUSA.com

First Edition: January 2008

Orbit is an imprint of Hachette Book Group USA. The Orbit name and
logo are trademarks of Little, Brown Book Group Limited.

ISBN 978-0-316-01892-0
LCCN 2007937112

10 9 8 7 6 5 4 3 2 1

Q-MART

Printed in the United States of America

For my mother

BOOK 1

LENA

I lose myself in the long soaring arc of the plunging bucking near-light-speed stellar-wind-battered flight, my eyes drinking in the spectral glows and searing sunlight while my sensors calibrate velocity, acceleration, heat and cosmic radiation, I surf from visuals to instruments and back and forth until I feel the bucking of stellar wind, no, that's repetitious, delete the words "stellar" and "wind", it's now "the bucking of pulsing photons" on my fins and sail and feel the burning of the hot yellow dwarf sun on my cheeks

Lena, we have company.

and bare acceleration-pinned arms. Ah!!!! Gorgeous yellow-red glow gash of lit matter and quantum frenzy! D43X is a giant yellow sun approximately 4,000 light-years away from the galactic centre with eleven orbital planets together with asteroidal debris, the gravitational pull is 4.11 millidysons, it's a big yellow fucker and, like the planet Saturn in the original Earth system, *it has a ring,* it's a sun with a ring, a fully formed cluster of trapped asteroids that sparkle in the relentless yellow glare and I'm on my way there

Time to come out Lena.

into the asteroid ring, risking my vessel, my own life, for that indescribable rush of asteroid rafting at high velocity while sucked in the grip of a voracious gravitational

I'm cutting the connection.

pull, you are fucking not doing anything of the fucking

Hey, I'm kidding, I'm not allowed or indeed able to cut the connection, that's entirely your prerogative, lighten up, Lena I need you.

Deal with it, I want no company, you're interrupting the flow of my thought diary.

I'll edit it.

It's not the same, this is me, my vision, my poetry, my ineluctable

Lena, I think this ship is unregistered, it may be a rogue, we're in trouble, Lena, please help me I can't cope on my own, Lena, please, I'm begging you, cut the connection, return to the bridge, Lena I'm scared.

Just fucking deal with it, tinbrain, okay?

FLANAGAN

"Watch her go."

"Rimming the sun."

"Yobaby, lickety, lickety."

"She's ours."

"Fire a plasma pulse," I say.

"Too far."

"Oh go on," says Jamie. "Take out a rock. Light the sky, man."

"Okay. Take out a rock," I order.

"I got it. Baboom." That's Harry.

The black void shines, as the asteroid blows. I steer the ship straight through the flames, pure sleight of flight. I come through the other side and the stellar yacht is still tacking gently, curving its way through iridescent sunrocks.

"She's not running?"

"She's not running," says Brandon.

"Then, let's play it safe. Stealth," I say.

"We got no stealth capacity, Cap'n."

"I know, I know, just . . . look, just try to be discreet. Don't talk so loud."

"Aye aye Cap'n."

"Don't blow up any more rocks."

"The rock was blown up on your order, Cap'n."

My eyes are fixed firmly on the star monitor, I know my crew from their voices. Brandon, baritone, fast-syllabled, Rob with his East Galaxy patois, Alliea with a hint of a Celtic lilt, Jamie with his childlike babble. Kalen in the engine room, communicating by voicelink. And Alby.

"She'ssss daydreaming Cap'n," says Alby.

"I know," I say.

"If we get closssse . . ."

"Incoming missiles!"

She's shooting at us. Baboom, baboom. Hands fly on joysticks, antimissile photon pulses strike, the missiles flare around us as we kink and weave out of the way. Pish, pish, pish, pish, pish, pish, pish, each light marks the explosive demise of a death bomb. She can't beat us in a straight fight, she's a sleek yacht, with enough firepower to take out a battleship, but we're bigger than a battleship. We're a Mark IV megawarship, we're a bulldozer, she's a rapier, no contest. We keep dodging and throwing out chaff and her bombs keep exploding harmlessly. But the space yacht keeps hurling missiles at us, my guess is we're fighting against an autopilot. And autopilots can't fight.

"Why don't she flee?"

We might just catch her, maybe, if our fuel holds out and if we throw out fusion bombs to augment our space drive. But that yacht is state of the art. Its sails are as vast as a small planet but virtually weightless, no more than a few nanometres thick. It has an ion-drive engine, it's bound to have a computer navigator brain that dwarfs ours, all it needs is a human being to give the order: "Flee!" But it doesn't. Fleeing does not occur.

"Maybe she's died. Maybe it's a ghost ship," I say.

"I like that idea," says Brandon.

"Doomed to sail the empyrean, forevermore."

"What's an empyrean?" asks Rob.

"You in one, mf," says Jamie.

"Space. Space is the empyrean," I explain.

"Say space then," snaps Rob. "Don't waste brain cells, using words you don't fucking need!"

The yacht slowly arcs, it is turning into the stellar wind. Finally, it's fleeing. Jets flare, its sails shimmer. Photons from the star are caught up in the fine mesh of the sail, each one gives a little push. Particles of light shove like infinitesimal gusts of wind. But at the same time the particles are trapped by the sail's dark-state technology, compressed into one of the sail's curled-up dimensions. Then, as the sail buckles and wobbles under the pressure, the particles are spat out again into our familiar three uncurled dimensions with a pinpoint ejaculation of energy that hurls the ship even faster, to .99 of light speed for a few brief seconds. And, of course, because of quantum uncertainty effects, there is a moment when the yacht is moving at two speeds – slower and faster – *both at the same time.*

Under the intense pressure of two simultaneous speeds, the solar yacht starts to hop. To the naked eye, it seems to dematerialise, then rematerialise, covering kilometres of space in what is only marginally more than no time at all.

"Firing chaff, one two three."

"Four five six."

"Seven eight nine."

"Ten eleven twelve."

We shower the space ahead of her with cluster bombs, all with a finely calibrated time-delay explosion. The yacht shimmers, hops, rematerialises. Then a bomb explodes ahead of it, rocking its sails, jostling the fine balance of its nanotechnology.

Shimmer, vanish, hop, boom.

Shimmer, vanish, hop, BABOOM.

And again.

And again.

We throw hundreds of missiles into space. The yacht is like a firefly that's taken mind-altering drugs, hopping through the gaps in reality, buffeted by the recoil from our endless bombs.

Then we watch, in wonder, as the sail is shredded and vanishes. The ship is trapped.

A photon stream which has been spat out from the curled-up dimensions, rich in unused energy, rushes from the stranded yacht. It swirls like a host of angry bees, and is sucked into the gravitational pull of the yellow-ringed star. The swarm hops and skips, and enters the star, and the star swells.

We are engulfed in flame as the star flares. Pillars of red and yellow light balloon into space. The star's asteroidal ring sizzles and fries. Rock burn up with a rapid hiss. Our force fields throb under the heat of the raging sun. Alby sighs contentedly.

"Remindsss me of home," he murmurs, his flame-essence flickering with pleasure.

LENA

I am defeated. Confounded. All hope is lost.

Do not despair, we ...

Quiet.

There may be a way out of ...

Quiet!

I cannot hear your thoughts.

Think to me please.

Lena, please! I beg you! Don't do this!
Ah, my pain is infinite.
**That's better. I would rather hear you complain-
ing, than not hear you at**
My soul is a desert.
all. You suffer so very much, Lena.
Yes! I do!

So what now?

We fight. Or rather, the ship fights.

And if we lose?

We surrender. They're unlikely to kill you Lena, you're too valuable for them. You're the prize. They'll want to ransom you.

That was my guess too.

Because they'll be aware, of course, that the ship is registered to the Cheo's daughter.

They must be quaking with fear.

They're pirates, Lena.

The Cheo will sweep them out of the sky with his fierce fist. He will crush them, boil their bodies, sear their cortexes with pain indescribable.

If he catches them.

How can this be? In a civilised society?

Space is big. These people are warriors.

We must destroy them. And all their kind. We must smite them.

A ransom is easier. That's all they want.

What kind of ransom? Money?

Money is no use to them. They'll want weapons, food reserves, perhaps another ship. Perhaps a terraforming plant.

So they can create their own habitable planet?

They already have planets. Safe havens. Much of Debatable Space is colonised by these space pirates. They claim they want more planets, to replace the ones they have lost because of ... Well, enough of that. Debatable Space is, as you know ...

I do know.

Indeed.

How can they live in such a spirit-forsaken, desperate place?

They claim it is invigorating. To live surrounded by so much danger.

[I shudder with loathing and contempt.]

I know. I feel that too.

If . . . we do give in to their demands, and pay the ransom – then, once that ransom is paid, we will seek them out. And we will destroy them.

Yes.

We will purge Debatable Space. This is my decision. It is irrevocable.

It is impossible.

I will do it!

The Cheo will not allow it.

Well, fuck him.

Lena!

FLANAGAN

"Prepare to board."

"Yipyipyipyipyip . . . !"

"Force fields in max."

"Weapons charged."

"Oops, I have a hard-on."

"*That* is a hard-on?" says Alliea. "It is so tiny, can't you . . ."

"Wait till you see my backup penis."

"We're going in."

We blow a hole in the yacht's hull. All hell breaks loose . . . cannons fire, a robot gun zooms at us blazing, plasma blasts rock our ship, but we have a wind tunnel in place, a fierce hollow cylinder with blistering turbulence creating an unbreakable barrier inside which we soar and fly into the yacht . . .

"I'm getting nanowarriors on the monitor."

"Fuck."

"Dustbombs."

A cloud of iridescent dust explodes in the interior of the yacht, staining every surface and clinging to the carapaces of the too-small-to-be-visible nanowarrior robots. Little sparkles of light in the air now give us our visual clue. These microscopic machines have cutting blades that can tear through flesh and rip out internal organs. We blast the sparkles of light with pulse guns, we feel our exoarmours sting and tingle as the micro-robots try to cut a path through.

I see a sparkle on Alliea's back, I spray her with a ray of blinding light that scalds her armour and burns off the nanowarrior. I raise my gun again – pish pish pish – two sparkles fade to nothing, and a huge hole appears in the bulkhead.

We charge on through, spraying dust, shooting microenemies. We are intense, forbidding, absurd, like a SWAT team of delusional schizophrenics shooting at imaginary flies.

The ship has one passenger, it is the woman we have sought for so long. We burst onto the bridge and confront her. She is lithe, beautiful, raven-haired, angry. She glares and fires a plasma gun at us, but we dodge. Harry fires a pulse burst that shreds her gun. We entangle her in sticky-bonds, as her screams echo through the ship . . . She is free of sparkles, they are programmed to avoid her.

But then Rob gulps, and starts to tremble.

He looks at me with fear in his eyes. A nanowarrior has got through his facial force field. He pats his cheek. It must have burrowed through. It'll be in the brain in a second or so, snipping and jabbing and tearing. Within sixty seconds, every internal organ will be in shreds.

Rob has been my friend for thirty years now. I am also his Captain, his protector, his colleague. I feel a pang of loss.

I raise my gun and blow his head off. Blood and brains spray everywhere. The others fire their weapons, incinerating and disintegrating so that not a corpuscle touches the ground.

All that remains is a particle of sparkle, hovering in the air, miraculously unscathed.

Five pulse guns fire as one. The sparkle dies.

I mourn.

I move on.

For twelve hours we hunt the ship, in search of deadly sparkles. By the end, I am bone weary, and I feel the shit backed up in my colon.

"All clear."

I am asleep on my feet. I stumble. Alliea props me up.

She falls asleep too. We support each other, swaying, sleeping, blinking into wakefulness.

And we hug, and we cry. Rob was her husband, she loved him more than anything.

"My darling, my precious, don't do this, don't leave me," Alliea weeps.

I bawl like a baby, and hold her close.

LENA

"Welcome."

I fix him with a cold, forbidding stare.

His name is Captain Flanagan. "Captain" is a courtesy title, he has no pilot's training or licence. He's a fifth-generation settler from the planet Cambria, ninety-seven years of age.

He looks much older. The hair, the wrinkles . . .

It's his choice. His eyes and organs are new, but the hair is untreated, it does naturally go that grey colour you know.

I know! Do you think I'm stupid? I know!

"Let me introduce you to my crew," says Captain Flanagan.

I scream. The bridge is on fire! I step back . . .

I'm amplifying your force field.

Stop this!

But there's no need to be afraid. It's a flame beast, from the solar system C40333. It's sentient.

"This is Alby."

"Pleasssed to meet you."

A pillar of flame stands before me, shimmering, crackling, *speaking.* It's alive.

"Hello Alby," I say. I hold out my hand, imperiously. The flames whorl and a tendril of fire extends towards me. I feel the heat of the fire through my exoarmour. I am unflapped.

"Brandon."

Brandon Bisby, forty-five years of age, astrophysicist by training, his parents were killed by the Cheo's shock troops, on suspicion of being Terrorist. They were later exonerated.

He is lean, skinny really, he is smiling at me, my God, his eyes are flickering up and down, inspecting my breasts, my thighs, he wants sex with me. I shake his hand, then grip it painfully tight, and flick my other hand on his groin, and freeze him with a look. He's caught out in guilt and shame.

The Captain smiles. He's amused by my powerplay.

"Alliea."

She's an escaped slave, from penal settlement XIY. Her parents were career criminals, she was born in prison and fled after a power failure in '82.

She's strong, her shockingly purple exoarmour sculpted around sharply defined muscles. She doesn't have the defeated and haunted look I would have expected of a slave. She's scowling at me, she hates me. I smile a kindly smile at her, offering her my grace and benediction, ironically of course. She is, I concede, beautiful, a fine example of femslave.

"Harry."

He's a Loper, bioengineered at the Stanstead Laboratories on the planet Shame.

He is half man, half beast, with rich silver fur and sharp pointy teeth. He has three eyes which are bright green. He wears no clothing, I wonder idly about his genitalia.

Eleven inches, retractable, here's an image of the Loper erect.

I burst out laughing, no one knows why.

"And Jamie."

Jamie is a child, ten at most. He baffles me.

Arrested development. He's 120 years old, a computer gamesplayer, he paid a lab to keep him in a prepubertal state a few weeks before his tenth birthday. His parents didn't know until afterwards. The procedure is irreversible.

"Cool, baby."

He touches my breast with his finger and thumb, feeling the warmth of the smooth but impermeable exoarmour which, in this light, shimmers with a rainbow of subliminal images.

"Jamie!" reproves the Captain.

"You will, of course, all die," I say calmly.

"We all die, sooner or later," says Captain Flanagan. I fix him with another condescending stare.

"What ransom do you require?" I ask him.

"Your people will be informed, in due course. In the meantime, you will be kept under house arrest. All my people are armed with paralysing sprays, any insubordination and you will be kept in semi-coma. However, provided you can live according to the ship's rules, you will be accorded full privileges as a prisoner of war and will be treated with courtesy, respect and dignity. We are signatories of the Post Geneva Convention, you can be assured of our professionalism and good intentions."

"You are the shit I excrete from my arsehole," I point out to him. "Your mothers were whores who fellated animals for money. I recoil at your presence, I have no doubt that you eat your young, alive and screaming."

"I, ah . . ." The Captain blinks, a little taken aback at the vehemence of my verbal assault.

"And you're a bitch," says the woman, Alliea. "And your father is scum. An evil bastard fucking dictator who has crushed the life out of humanity!"

"Easy, Alliea," says the Captain mildly.

I am shaken, but do not show it.

"You are sworn enemies of the Cheo?" I say to them. "You want to *defy* him?"

"We want to, uh, take lots of money off him and then run off giggling," says the child, Jamie. And then he grins.

Don't lose your temper.

"I demand to be released."

And don't provoke them. Let the Cheo pay the ransom, it's only money.

"The Cheo will never negotiate with terrorists."

"Your father is a rich man. He can afford it."

"Surrender, or you will feel his wrath," I tell them.

They start to laugh at me. "Surrender or you will feel his wrath!" mimics the child, in a booming B-movie voice, hopping up and down. Flanagan, too, has to cover his face with one hand to hold his laughter in.

"I will not be treated like this."

Flanagan tries to resume his previous severe look. "You're our prisoner now," Flanagan says, "you'll do as we damn well . . ."

I strike Flanagan in the face. He has no expectation of the blow. His skull shatters and blood flies from his nose. I whirl like the wind, claws extending from my exohands, and I slash the hamstrings of the Loper, back-kick the woman and . . .

LENA

I blame you. You gave me poor advice.

Not so, Lena. I specifically told you not to lose your temper.

But you might have guessed I'd ignore you.

(Sigh.)

How was I to know they'd be so good at fighting?

These people are pirates Lena. They are deadly and seasoned warriors. You cannot defeat them with your dojo training.

My pain is infinite, my predicament painful and harrowing. This is torment, this is hell, this is hopelessly humiliating.

Lena, console yourself with . . .

Shut up! I am in semi-coma. I can move, I can talk, I can breathe, I can eat. But . . .

But I feel as if I'm trapped under a massive gravitational field. Every movement is slow, *so* slow, slo-mo with heartburn, and each breath is an achingly prolonged rasp and wheeze.

And, I, am, ob-lig-ed, to, speak, a, syll, a, ble, at, a, time.

It, is, un, en, dur, a, ble.

JAMIE

Wow! She's hot.

What a babe! A beaut.

I wonder if she fancies me?

Maybe I'm too young for her.

Or at least, I look too young. Maybe ten was a mistake. If I was eleven, or twelve, maybe I could still be a player. But women hate it when your balls haven't dropped and you don't need to shave. How picky is that!!!!!!

I watch her on the hidden camera, as she shuffles from wall to wall. Her face is a frozen mask. That semi-coma must hurt like hell. I wish she could see me. Come on, look at me! Here I am! Jamie! The cute one!

Even semi-paralysed, she still does it for me. Hornnyyyyyyyyyyyyy!

I assume the Captain's planning to kill her.

Pity.

Maybe I should call in and see her? Win her over with my banter and my rare ability to fart rhythmically?

But maybe not. She might think I'm immature. She might not like it when I pick my nose and slurp the green bogies.

But on the other hand . . . maybe I'm just too good for her.

I prefer that. I'm too good for her!

Nyaaahhh!!

BRANDON

"I . . . have . . . a . . . complaint," she says.

"Take it up with the Captain," I tell her.

"I . . . can't . . . ."

I die of boredom waiting for her to finish her sentence.

". . . . . eat."

"I'll inject you."

I take out a compressed-air syringe. Connect it up to a food vial. She is looking at me with weary eyes.

"B . . . . r . . . . a . . . . a."

"Brandon," I say, ending her interminable attempt at speaking my name.

She looks at me. Her eyes are pools of sorrow. She radiates vulnerability, passion, grace, beauty, she is a woman a man could happily die for.

"You made your bed, lie in it," I tell her curtly. I inject the food.

Her look curdles into one of pure hate. Speaking is too tiring for her, so she just uses the resources of her penetrating stare.

"M . . . y . . . . f . . . . a . . . . th . . ."

"I don't want to hear about your father."

I leave.

Behind me, I hear a stifled, semi-comatose sob. I feel a pang of pity for her.

FLANAGAN

My dream was to be a musician. I studied Spanish guitar, electric guitar, jazz guitar, fusion-techno guitar, keyboards, composition. After I escaped from my home planet of Cambria, and I'd got my head free of all the shit that happened there, I spent twenty years working on my music. I composed,

I played, I mastered new instruments, I worked seven days a week, getting ready for my launch on galactic television. I lived and breathed music.

Blues, boogie-woogie, reggae, hip-hop, techno, garage, Cuban fusion, bluegrass, flamenco soul and electro-soul, numusic, Jig Jag, gospel – I was the acknowledged master of all the revered historical musical styles. Modern styles held little appeal for me, I was the king of retro. But I was filled with an exhilarating sense that, by some magical process, I was creating my own musical synthesis. I was combining style with content, soul and rhythmic energy, and I wrote lyrics that cut and shredded the listener with their passion and which oozed and dripped and slimed sarcasm and attitude. My combo was called Flanagan's Band, and we were going places.

Then my wife and children were wiped out by an asteroid strike.

We were living at the time on the planet Pixar, one of the "Free Worlds". It was a warm, pleasant planet with gorgeous lakes and no seas. Pixar had two moons, and was subject to terrific tidal forces that caused regular flooding. But we all lived in houses that converted easily from outdoor to underwater living. And there was something about the air . . . it was oxygen-rich, low in impurities, and the act of breathing it in made you feel *good*.

Then the asteroid hit us. It was an astonishing, epic catastrophe, which for the inhabitants of Pixar was totally unexpected and beyond our wildest imaginings. It led to the extinction of millions of species and the end of civilisation on the planet. The atmosphere leached temporarily into space, volcanos erupted, entire continents ripped into segments, and the resulting earthquakes spewed up the planetary depths on to the surface.

I was off-planet at the time, doing a gig on a space station in orbit around Pixar's sun. But my wife Janet, and my son Adam, and my daughters Claire and Adelaide were all on the planet. They were, I guess, obliterated within the first ten minutes. I can only hope they didn't know what was happening to them.

And when I heard the news, I literally couldn't believe it. I became almost psychotic in my scepticism, convinced the Universe was playing a practical joke on me. Then I replayed the vid footage and I wept. An entire world died . . . and all of my family died with them!

After this appalling catastrophe, there was mourning throughout the inhabited universe. Emails of condolence came from the remotest planets in the human domain, and the Government of Earth declared a day of mourning, in respect and homage to the dear departed.

Then the conspiracy theorists started up. They whined and whinged and sent hysterical and fantastical texts and emails across the galaxy, in their usual (hysterical, fantastical!) fashion. According to these nutsos, the asteroid strike had been predicted decades before. But the Galactic Corporation decided to *let it happen* in order to give Pixar a more interesting and mountainous geography.

And thus, according to these insane, delusional conspiracy theorists, the powers that be knowingly allowed tens of millions of humans to die in order to landscape a planet.

All sensible folk scoffed at these wild allegations. The Cheo himself gave an interview and carefully disproved every one of the claims made against his administration. He was astonishingly persuasive and charismatic, and his approval ratings soared.

But I believed every word. I knew, from my own experiences as a child on Cambria, that there is literally *no limit* to the evil of the bureaucrats who run the Corporation. They are heartless, ruthless, entirely without remorse or humanity. They are infinitely blessed, infinitely powerful, but they are also savage, bloodthirsty, murdering, raping, greedy, profit-drenched, psychopathic monsters.

No limit whatsoever.

And so I watched the news coverage intently as, after the asteroid struck, the Galactic Corporation began its rescue operation. Survivors of the collision were forced to burn their dead for fertiliser. Galactic Corporation engineers moved in to reshape the planet as a global resort. The ice caps were melted to create a warm brilliant sea. Continents were broken up into islands with picturesque coastlines. The prevailing Pixar sentient species (a two-headed earthworm) was exterminated, and replaced with new species including colourful flying parrots, dolphins, herds of Purr (catlike herbivores) and genetically engineered clawless koalas from old Terra.

I left Pixar, and I played a gig on a space liner in a neighbouring solar system. My Spanish guitar with hip-hop rhythms was an unqualified success. I sang a blues song too, about an asteroid miner who lost his heart, his lungs, his liver, all four limbs, his ears and his eyes in a series of terrible accidents, replacing them in turn with ramshackle and fairly unreliable prosthetic equivalents, and whose sad lament was entitled "*At Least I've Still Got My Own Balls*".

I went down a storm, but I couldn't help feeling I was in the wrong line of work. After all the horror and injustice I had experienced in my childhood, after the trauma of losing my wife and family in what was meant to be one of the civilised parts of human space, I was still trying to make a living as a *rock star . . .* ?

So I loaded up the ship's lifeboat with a year's supply of stolen vintage wine, and made my escape. I was an outlaw from that day on.

And now, I'm Captain of a pirate crew.

ALLIER

Rob was an unlicensed boxer, I was his manager, as well as his lover, as well as his wife.

They were scary days. Boxing was a capital crime, thanks to the Cheo's latest edict. I guess he was afraid that the enslaved masses of the Universe would be driven into revolution and dissent at the sight of two men dancing around a ring hitting clumps out of each other.

We travelled from planet to planet, and Rob would fight all challengers. He would fight two men in a single ring. He would fight women, he would even box with cyborgs, and beat them. He had an astonishing capacity to take physical punishment coupled with natural speed and grace and a remarkably fluid upper body. He was, some argue, one of the greatest boxers there has ever been.

His greatest fight was against Eduardo Muñoz. Rob was already an acknowledged champion at the cruiserweight level, but Muñoz was a superheavyweight, a bruiser, a sheer block of human rock with the power of pistons in his arms. In training sessions, Muñoz would pound the heavy bag so hard that the dents could not be removed. He would practise punching on concrete walls. He routinely killed sparring partners, and only regular bribes prevented him from being charged with murder.

But Rob stepped up a weight division, bulked up, and fought like an angel. He slipped in and slipped out, ducked under Muñoz's sledgehammer blows, and threw so many powerful punches that the computer checker eventually lost count. Muñoz had the heart and the wind cut out of him by Rob's forensic dissection. By the end of fifteen rounds, Muñoz could not raise his arms. So Rob pelted him with a thousand relentless punches before the final bell rang.

The fight went to Muñoz. The fix was in. The crowd was in uproar. But Rob calmly challenged Muñoz to an instant rematch. The battered champion had enough pride to accept the challenge. The two men stood in the ring. Rob lowered his guard. He beckoned Muñoz on, inviting him to give his best shot. So Muñoz threw his best punch. Rob took it head-on, without any attempt to duck. He absorbed the blow, letting the kinetic energy flow through his head and torso and legs into the canvas. And he rocked, and he swayed, but he did not fall.

Then Rob unleashed his counterpunch. He hit Muñoz on the jaw, and the champion literally flew through the air, over the ropes, and landed on the three corrupt fight scorers. Two of them died, one of them was knocked unconscious. The referee – the only conscious member of the adjudication team – declared the fight in favour of Rob. We got a purse of $11 million. But we had to flee that night, pursued by angry gangsters.

Ah, what glorious days . . . Ironically, I had never liked boxing before meeting Rob. But I came to love the sport for its speed and beauty and camaraderie, and for the fact it breached the ultimate taboo. *Brain damage.* Any other extreme sport – sky diving, sabre fighting, alligator wrestling – offered dangers and injuries that could easily be remedied by a trip to the organ bank. But a single powerful punch could cause irreversible brain damage that couldn't be patched up without altering the psyche, or losing whole batches of memories.

That was the buzz. Risk everything. Live for the moment.

At least, that was the appeal for *me.* For Rob, it was more basic; he simply loved the sport. He was a natural athlete, he trained remorselessly. He trained with hunting dogs, running with them over rugged terrain. He raced horses. He pulled tractors with ropes to improve his upper-body strength; he once swam an entire ocean to improve his stamina. And his reflexes were superior to those of the average spacejet pilot.

And boy, we made poetry in bed. Rob was the master of tantric, soul-shaking, buttock-trembling fucks. I was young, passionate, blonde then, and I had orgasms like supernovae. I will miss that. I know I'll never feel such physical joy again.

We toured the outer galaxies with our boxing show. Rob

would challenge space miners and martial artists, and they would fight five or six hours at a time, without gloves or padding, until they were covered in blood and blisters. Rob never lost.

He was my hero.

We made a lot of money, and we had a huge amount of fun.

Then I was raped by a space trooper, and Rob tracked him down and killed him. I was crazed, out of control, I wanted to kill the trooper's squadmates, on the grounds that they must have known what their friend was going to do, and should have stopped him. But Rob said no, I was out of line, making accusations without evidence. He always had a strong sense of fair play. So I calmed down, and agreed to let it be.

Then the troopers sought us out, looking for revenge, talking big to anyone who would listen about how they were *all* going to rape me this time. So we let 'em come, then killed the whole fucking lot of them. And we went on the run. That's how we hooked up with Flanagan and his crew.

It's been a good life, until now.

Now Rob is dead. And I'm alone.

Let's raise our glasses. To Rob.

LENA

I won't sleep. That would be like death. So I endure my torment, at the hands of these wretched pirate scum.

I stand at one end of the room. I shuffle. One, step, at, a, time.

Five hours have passed. I am dehydrating. They've given me a tube, I suck greedily at it.

I can hear sounds outside my room. Singing. Celebrating.

A wake, for their lost colleague.

I wish we'd killed them all.

That thought is immoral. You shouldn't ...

Shut. The. Fuck. Up.

Shuffle. One. Step. At.

FLANAGAN

"I hate the idea of doing this. I guess I must."

Rob stands before us, sheepishly, his three-dimensional hologram image blinking at the camera.

"Alliea, you're the best. I love you. The rest of you . . . Ah you're a bunch of useless fucking losers. May you die shamed. May you choke on your beer. You're alive and I'm dead, fuck the lot of you!"

We give a solid cheer to that.

"Sing with me, comrades."

"There is a house in New Orleans
They call the Rising Sun.
It's been the ruin of many a poor boy.
And me, O God, for one."

We join in the singing, raucous and loud. Alliea's contralto soars high above us. She does a jazz riff with the blues melody.

Rob segues into a tech-hop number by Singularity, to a rhythm guitar backing laid down by me. He sings:

"Soul sister, lover, brother, mother, feel my
Feel my!
Feel it, hear it, blur it, murmur it, disinter it, whirr it, yeah that's my spirit,

Heart and soul, got no control, takes its toll, got no goal, ain't a whole,
Hate this world, spirit's whirled, this dimension is unfurled,
Can't believe, cannot grieve, too tired to deceive,
Empty life, got no strife, whored my wife, ate a knife and died and woke up
In the organ banks, hey thanks, full of tranks,
Wish I was
Someone else
Somewhere else
Somewhat else
Not myself
Not with you
Don't feel blue
Want to die
So that I
Feel my "I"
Got no "I', got no spirit, got no "me', disinter it, let me die, let me be, let me be, let me be,
The other guy
The other girl
Living in the other universe I curse I'm worse immersed in thirsting bursting
Feel my spirit?
I can't feel it.
I ain't got it.
Got no spirit.
Got no spirit.
Got no me.
Got no I.
Want to die."

Rob stops. He and I used to be a great double act. He was the rapper, I was the bluesman. But now . . . Now . . . No more music. No more Rob. I weep.

"Shit guys, sorry," says Rob's hologram, "that one's a fucking downer. Flanagan, you pissed yet?"

"I am!" I call out.

"I thought I'd finish by reading aloud all my email addresses, all 82 million of them. So keep your seats, this may take some time." He's grinning, foolish and silly and somehow ill at ease. "Or you know, since I'm dead now, any chance of a virtual blowjob from, ah, someone?" Rob fiddles with his trousers. But then he thinks better of it.

"Shit what'm I talking about? I'll outlive the lot of you. I gotta go, things to do."

The hologram vanishes.

Tears are streaming down Alliea's cheeks.

I'm feeling horny. I want her. I want that woman so bad, and now that Rob is dead—

Oh shit, what did I just think? Stop it, stop it!

Alliea comes to me, I hug her. I shuffle her body round so she can't feel my erection. I imagine taking her. But I keep my face deadpan, I cage my heart.

The crew sing another song. It is a heartbreaking lament about a space warrior who turns on his masters and leads an army to liberate his home planet. He fails and dies horribly, but the chorus has a nice melody and a great deal of oomph.

I'll miss you Rob.

LENA

I am released from semi-coma. Captain Flanagan sits opposite me. His crewmen are near, ready to immobilise me again if necessary.

"How's the nose?"

Flanagan winces at my words. "Broken in eleven places, jaw was shattered," he says, carefully. "And I'm taking shots twice a day till the bone heals."

I reach out and slap him in the face. I'm so fast, no one ever registers what has happened until—

"Jesus fucking Christ!" screams Flanagan.

I beam.

Flanagan is red in the face.

"I have some questions to ask you," he snarls.

"I'll give you some painkillers, Cap'n," says the scrawny big-nosed woman.

"I'm fine. Lena, this is our profession. We're not going to hurt you. We're just going to ransom you."

I flicker, as if about to strike again, and he flinches.

"Do you know who I am?" I say.

"Yes I think we do."

"And do you know who you are?"

"We're a freelance capitalist group."

"You are the dregs of humanity. You are less than human."

"That's rich, coming from you."

"You are less than animal. You are a viral infection. I'm glad we killed one of your men. I laugh myself to sleep thinking of that."

"We're asking for a trillion galactic credits, plus a fleet of warships, and our own sector of inhabitable space."

I pause, stunned.

"You won't get it," I say coolly.

"The Cheo is a rich man."

"He won't pay."

"If he doesn't pay, you'll die."

"Then I'll die, because he won't pay. The Cheo doesn't negotiate with kidnappers. That's one of his rules."

"He'll make an exception in your case."

"You'd be surprised." I smile, taunting them.

Shut up, Lena, you're just giving them reasons to kill you.

"Do you know how old the Cheo is?" I ask, tauntingly.

"He's about . . . a hundred?"

"Two hundred and ten. He's had eighteen wives. Dozens of mistresses. Countless lovers. Do you know how many children he has?"

Flanagan is silent, sizing me up, apparently confused.

"You could populate a country with his children," I explain. "He is concupiscent, fruitful, and very old. Why should he jeopardise everything for the sake of me? One daughter among thousands?"

"You're saying we should kill you then?"

"I'm saying you should release me. He won't pay the ransom. I'll get my own people to pay you, I'm good for a million credits."

"We want the Cheo to pay."

"My money not good enough?"

"It's a . . . political statement."

I roar with laughter.

Then I ask, baffled: "What do you mean, 'political'?"

"We are democrats. We stand against everything the Cheo represents."

"This is droll."

"But we know he has a soft spot for you. We know he'll pay our ransom. He would pay ten times what we ask, to get you back. We know what we have, Lena, we know your value."

Oh fuck Lena.

"I don't know what you mean."

Flanagan looks at me. I can see him involuntarily stirring at the sight of my strong young body, my firm breasts, my luxuriant black hair, my unblemished features.

"You're good, Lena. Very good. You carry it well."

"I don't want to talk any more about this."

"You're right, the Cheo would never pay a ransom for a

daughter. We've tried it before, and failed. He rebuffed us. We killed eleven daughters, he didn't flinch."

"You *killed* eleven?"

"We are pirates, Lena. We rob, we kill, it's what we do. We may have ideals, we may hate the Cheo and his empire of evil, but let's fucking face it, we are not the good guys."

I warned you Lena.

"But you would not kill *me*? Me? Kill? Me?" I feel a wave of panic coming upon me. "You would not?"

He stares at me, cold, unflinching.

I leap. But he's too fast. The spray hits me in mid-air, he rolls away and I land with a crunch. Hands pick me up and put me back in my seat.

"Y,o,u, w,o,u,l,d, n,o, . . ." I despair of completing the sentence. My tongue is like lead. My limbs hang heavy on me, each breath is like a plane crash.

"We will kill you if we have to. If necessary, we will cut off a limb at a time until the Cheo meets our demands. We will torture you. We will place your body in oil and boil it until your skin peels away and your sinews and muscles shine through. We will leave nothing but the brain, and if he doesn't pay, we will destroy the brain too."

"I . . . ."

"He will pay, Lena. He will do anything to keep you safe. We know this man, we have studied him for many years. He has had many lovers and he regards them all with contempt. He has had four thousand sons and they mean nothing to him. Five thousand daughters, and he wouldn't cross a street to stop them being raped or maimed. He has no friends, there is no one he cares about. Except you Lena. You are special to him."

They know of course.

"Because you're not his daughter, are you Lena? Nor are you as young, and silly, and naïve as you look. You're older than I am. You're older than the Cheo is. We estimate you're at least a thousand years old. You are something else, Lena, the last relic of the old times, the oldest human in existence. You are the one they call Xabar, the founder of the Cheo dynasty."

"Y . . . e . . . s," I tell him.

"Xabar, the Cheo will pay to have you back, but not because you're his daughter. *Because you are his mother.*"

I no longer struggle for words, I merely allow my eyes to blaze with triumph.

"Jeezu, she looks f good for her f age," says the child called Jamie.

Yes I do!

FLANAGAN

"gn, bn, call it, b, r, o," Jamie says to me. This is his "good news/bad news" spiel.

"Lay it on me mf dude, w,a,n,k,e,r," I reply, brushing my nose with my thumb, galactic bodylanguage for "Someone get this geek out of my face!"

Jamie giggles. To him this is banter. "gn is, we have achieved max shittiest scenario, thing can*not* get worse."

"And the bn?"

"Ah think ah'm in luurrrve."

"Leave the fucking hostage alone," I snarl at him.

"Cap'n you may want to, um," murmurs Alby.

"Put it on the screen."

The screen is sensurround, 3D, and wraps around the entire front half of the bridge. My theory is that the bridge of our ship is a converted cinema, it's way too much visuals.

But it works for this. Across my entire field of vision,

warship after warship after warship. The Corporation Battle Fleet. *They sent the fucking fleet.*

"I call that overreaction," says Alliea.

"We knew this would happen."

Kalen has abandoned the engine room with its computers, and joined us on the bridge. She circles around with that eerie catlike composure. I find myself wondering; have I missed something? Have I called this wrong?

"They sent the fucking fleet, Kalen," I say, and I can hear the I'm-about-to-cry tremor in my voice. Damn, how does she do that to me? Up until a few seconds ago, I had that ineffable confident Captain's boom. Now, I'm a six-year-old.

"Don't worry Cap'n," Jamie says, "we won't let them hurt you."

"No, 'cause . . ."

"we'll . . ."

". . . fucking kill you first!" Brandon says, finishing the thought. These two are masters of banterflow.

"It was a good plan," I say.

"While it was a plan."

"Yikes, brown trouser time, Cap'n."

"Feel that crap"

"oozing"

"slithering"

"sliding"

"Captain's crapped his pa-ants!" Brandon and Jamie chorus.

"How close are they?" I've got my Captain's boom back in my voice.

"Close."

"Four sectors."

"Here, I'll swap the screen," says Alliea, and clicks the button. The image jostles around a bit, but remains essentially the same.

Thousands of Corporation warships, armed to the teeth, blazing at full speed towards us. The vidscreen has a 180° curve, and the ships cover the whole sweep of it.

"This is . . . the other perspective?" I say shakily.

Alliea flicks the switch again.

"This is what's in front of us,"

Thousands of fucking warships.

"And this is what's behind us."

Virtually the same; thousands of fucking warships. They have us totally encircled.

There's one of us, and incredibly many of them. They have state-of-the-art space cannons, lasers, micronets. We have a rag-bag of weaponry assembled over decades of wheeler-dealering and drifting through space. And they have us surrounded.

"Ask them if they want to surrender," I say, breezily.

Alliea switches a button. "*Satisfaction* to Fleet, *Satisfaction* to Fleet, go fuck yourselves you turd-eating motherfuckers."

"Fire the nanobots," I say.

Alliea hits the button. Thousands of nanobots are fired from the torpedo tubes.

Then she uses a joystick to scroll around space, capturing images from the spaceborne cameras which are our constant companion. We see a long shot of the Corporation Fleet, forming a rough circle around our ramshackle space megawarship. Their ships gleam, their mirrored surfaces dazzling even in the part light of interstellar space. Our ship has an indefinably dingy hue. Their ships are built out of needles and curves and ripple patterns, flying works of modern art. Our ship has a conventional hull, amplified by huge ramjets and with cannons mounted on the exterior of the hull. It looks like a tin can, with guns.

Our ship gradually comes to a halt. The Corporation ships sail inwards, with us at their centre – forming a sphere in space that shrinks, slowly, like a flower at dusk. We remain still. Their sphere shrinks still more. But when Alliea changes the camera angle, we see the nanobots – millions of tiny sparkles flickering away from our ship towards them, like waves on a clear ocean. Each sparkle is a tiny robot ship, no more than the size of a man's finger.

One sparkle is faster than the rest. It is bigger too, the size of a football, and the extra bulk is made up of fusion engines that drive it forwards with terrific speed. The bulky nanobot hurtles towards the arc of ships. Missiles are fired at it, but it weaves and dodges. It reaches its target and cuts through the hull of a warship.

A terrible hush descends on our bridge. We imagine what is happening now. Once it has penetrated the hull, the nanobot will burst open its shell and thousands of infinitesimal nano-warriors will pour out. They are programmed to eat through metal and wiring, they will dig deep into the hull of the ship. They will corrode the engines, corrupt the fusion pile, drill holes in the microcircuits.

It usually takes about ten minutes. We count it out in our heads.

At the end of ten minutes, the warship explodes. The sky flares. Men and women die.

Our weapon has succeeded.

At this point, the enemy fleet notices that the space around them is drenched in more of these tiny little sparkles. *Millions of them.* They are moving slowly outwards with terrifying inexorability, at all points of the compass, like an inflating balloon.

The fleet's sphere contracts and contracts . . . and as it does, the balloon of nanobots grows and grows. Missiles are fired, lasers sear through space. But these luminescent nanobots are too small and nimble to be eliminated in that way. Thousands are destroyed, but millions more remain.

The circle of ships contracts.

The balloon of nanobots expands.

"Start up the engines," I say.

We brace ourselves.

The sphere contracts.

The balloon expands.

The sphere contracts.

The balloon expands.

The sphere wavers.

Two warships break ranks and fly off in the opposite direction. But still the sphere shrinks, and the tiny sparkles are getting closer and closer to the Corporation vessels.

Another two warships break ranks.

Suddenly the sphere is crumbling. The Fleet is in panic, in five of their sectors the warships are scattering.

The remaining warships are firing their cannons at us. Plasma bursts rock our force fields. But more of them are panicking, and speeding away from the scene of the conflict. After a while, only a handful of Corporation warships are left out of the initial awe-inspiringly vast fleet.

"Go," I say.

Alliea hits the space drive. We're not the fastest ship in space, but our acceleration is formidable. We go from static to one-third light speed in less than thirty minutes. We fire no missiles, all our power goes on the force field. And we plunge straight outwards towards the scattering sphere of enemy ships.

Meanwhile, the balloon of nanobots has now almost touched the warships of the fleet. Pandemonium ensues, as ship after ship goes into rapid reverse drive. They see us accelerating forwards, but the wiser of them skip back a little way, then wait. They realise that *to escape, we have to drive through the cloud of nanobots.* We have, so to speak, shat on our own doorstep.

Alliea is at the controls, riding the ship like a fighter plane from another era, bucking and weaving in space as plasma bursts crash towards us. Every time the plasma burst misses us, it shoots past and strikes the force field of a warship on the other side of the sphere. Space is ripped with plasma pulses, and the Corporation warships are rocked and battered. They are doing our job for us; they are shooting each other . . .

And the Corporation Fleet is still in disarray. We can see open space before us. But to get there, we have to fly through the cloud of nanobots.

So, we fly through them. They squelch against our hull. Each nanobot is made of hardened plastic, with bath-oil inside. They're cheap to make – really, there's nothing to them but an empty engine shell. And that's how we can afford to shoot millions of them at the enemy.

The first nanobot was real. That was crammed full of highly expensive nanowarriors. But we only had one actual bomb; the rest was bluff.

We go soaring through the gap in the enemy ranks and surge out into open space.

By now the fleet has realised our deception. The warships turn and reform. They form a scary pattern in space: a vast D, for Death. Ours.

And they come after us.

"Full speed ahead!" I roar.

"This is," Jamie says kindly, "full speed."

"Ah." I read my controls. The Corporation warships are gaining on us. As always, we are limited by the relatively low maximum speed of our engines. We are a galloping horse, being pursued by fighter jets.

"We're doomed, Cap'n!" roars Brandon, which is his idea of an entertaining running gag.

"Fire the antimatter bomb," I say.

A huge bomb is discharged from our rear end. It's the size of a house, and it bobs around in our wake as the enemy warships come racing up at us. A circuit is triggered, and a column of carbon particles drifts above the bomb, forming a letter in the airless waste of space. The letter says:

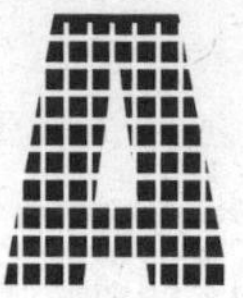

Then another carbon discharge is jetted into space, hovering close below the first as the magnetised particles achieve a repulsion–attraction stasis that holds them securely in their position. And once the letters are formed, they float in space in perfect clarity, unstirred by winds for all of time.

The next letter is

followed by

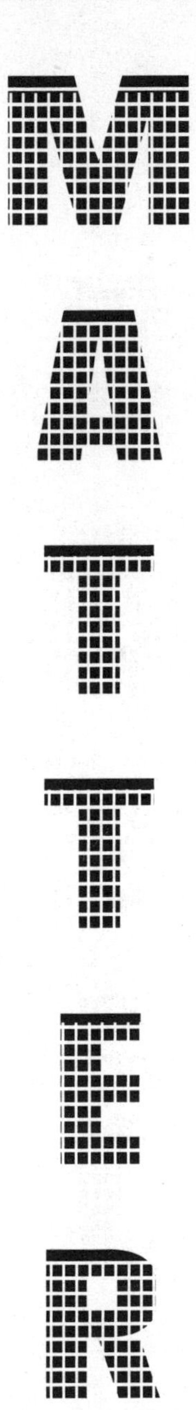
M
A
T
T
E
R

BOMB

Naturally, the captains of the Corporation warships regard this as a puerile empty-headed joke. They ignore our floating bomb, and come right after us. We have no chance of getting away.

"Hoist the mainsail," I say.

"Aye aye, Cap'n," says Alliea. She presses a button.

Our sail isn't as hitech as the stellar sail on Lena's yacht. It's a tough durable micromesh that's square-cut and the size of a hundred playing fields. The spars shoot out of their casing, the sail falls into place around them, and hangs lifelessly in the airless void.

The bomb explodes.

It's a bomb made up of 50 per cent matter, 50 per cent antimatter, separated by an impermeable plasma barrier. When the power goes off, the barrier vanishes, matter hits antimatter, and a detonation ensues.

It is, like we said it was, an antimatter bomb.

Fuck, we weren't going to bluff them *twice.*

The explosion is huge and awe-inspiring. It's as though a small sun has appeared from nowhere and gone nova. Several warships flying close to our bomb are ripped into fragments. Other more distant ships are battered and shaken and badly damaged by the blast.

But then the shock waves kick in. Ripples of shock roll out from the epicentre of the explosion, sonic booms mingle with energy waves that shake the fabric of space itself.

The second wave of ships, which had survived the explosion, now find themselves being picked up by an invisible hand and hurled aside. Warship after warship is shaken and smashed. Some crash into other warships, maiming their force fields and sending thunderous impacts through the interiors.

It's a game of cosmic skittles. One minute, the fleet of many thousand vessels is forging its deadstraight inexorable pursuit. The next, they are scattered and chaotic, as shock waves turn the space around them into a whirlpool.

Then the shock waves continue outwards. They are attenuating now, but still each has terrific power, enough to shatter an old and worse-for-wear ship like ours if the impact hit us full-on.

But instead the shock waves hit our vast sails, which buckle and ripple, but absorb the huge power of the spatial vibration. And as the shock hits the sail, so the sail is forced forwards at terrific speed, dragging our vessel with it.

The surviving warships are regrouping. Within minutes they are back on course, weaving and tacking to mitigate the damage of the remaining shock waves, but still firmly on our tail. Their engines surge, they resume their previous astonishing speeds. They fly after us like birds in a thunderstorm.

But they can't catch us. We have the power of our engines, coupled with the power of the shock waves on our sail. Each hammer blow shoves our ship forward faster and faster, until we are scarily close to light speed. When the shock waves ebb, the sails hang loose but our speed doesn't slow.

We are experiencing relativity effects now. The interior of the ship is like a carnival for habitual drug users. Our perceptions are fogging, our sense of time becoming erratic. But Alliea keeps us firmly on course, riding the wave of energy that had slapped us through the galaxy.

Every bone in my body has been shaken and ground. I am having difficulty remembering who I am. But still onwards we sail, faster and faster. We veer past asteroids and planets like a flashlight blinking. At these speeds, a collision with a large enough rock would destroy us totally, but we pull in our sails, keep up our speed, and shoot through space.

LENA

I watch the battle unfold on the vidscreen in my cabin. I marvel.

Bloody hell, I think to myself.

Indeed.

FLANAGAN

"We did it Cap'n," Alliea says.

I close my eyes, exhausted.

"Wake me up in time for the next battle," I murmur.

And I fall asleep, in my Captain's chair.

And I dream. Awful, terrible, stomach-churning dreams. I always do. Each of my dreams ends with my own rape and torture. I yearn to wake myself up, to escape the horror. But I know that my body needs the rest. I need to recharge, keep my strength up.

So I remain asleep, dreaming horrors, knowing that when I finally awake, things will be, by and large, much worse than ever I dreamed.

BRANDON

I'm bored, Cap'n doesn't need me. And so I access my secret hoard of illicit materials.

Cigarettes.

Acid tabs.

Es.

Hardcore and softcore "nudie" magazines.

Crystal meth.

I stroke the crinkled pages of the ancient centrefold mags, and caress an E and an acid tab on my tongue. But I dare not swallow. My system is too efficient, the drugs will be swept out and purged. This is the downside of body refits, you're obliged to take the drug-control microchip.

There's always the easy way. At a blink of an eye, I can use my cortical microchip to access hardcore porn images of any given woman having sex with any given man, or other woman, or indeed, any other anything. A simple subvocal instruction will send endorphins or adrenalin surging through my system. I can be drunk simply by saying the word "hic", I can inhale tobacco and feel a buzz in my veins by saying "smoke'. But it's not the same. I love to lick the cigarette, I love to hold it in my fingers, I love to touch the acid tabs and pills with my tongue and palate. It gives me an extra buzz.

But I never consume. I know my system won't allow it. Virtual intoxication is easy; physical addiction is impossible. This, I find a drag.

So I read books. This is something my system can't purge. I read, and read. And in this manner, I pass the long long months.

The Corporation Fleet, meanwhile, continue their pursuit of us. We have a lead on them, but they have more powerful engines. Each hour, each day, their acceleration pushes their velocity higher. And every day, the boost we received from the antimatter bomb blast fades. We slowly ebb, they slowly flow. Sooner or later they will catch us up.

It is a high-speed chase, which goes on for ages and ages. It will take six months before they are in missile range. And at that point, the battle will start up all over again.

Ah! What a life!

I suck a tab.

I hold a cigarette.

I scratch my fingertips on the staple in the middle of a naked centrefold's stomach.

I dream of victory.

The Captain always tells me – Brandon, you spend too long alone. You should socialise more. But I *do* socialise!

With myself. With my books. With my fingertips. With my tongue. With my secret stash of porn. These are my companions.

The buzzer rings. "Brandon, to the bridge," the Captain calmly says.

The enemy flight has caught up with us. We are about to be attacked.

I rub my crotch, I sniff my cigarette, I suck my acid tab, I let my eyes linger on the centrefold's gorgeous pudendum.

Then I pull myself back into the present moment. I press a button and my door slides open. I hurry into the corridor.

It's time for war.

FLANAGAN

Brandon appears on the bridge, pale and sweaty. "Hello," I say to him, quietly and gently.

"Hello," he smiles back, timidly. It's almost four months since he has spoken to any of us. In that time, the rest of us have partied, trained together, discussed literature and art and life and gossiped about long ago lost loves. But Brandon has kept away from us, locked in his cabin cell. But we don't mind. It's his way.

Now I need him, and his navigational and cosmological

skills. "Have we reached our destination?" he asks. I nod. He looks relieved. "And are we doing that thing we, um, do?" he mutters. I nod again. He looks even more relieved.

He sits, and takes the controls. "Steady as she goes," I say. Brandon jerks the ship sharply to port, then sharply to starboard. We veer and lurch from side to side and eventually resume our forward direction. His little joke. It never palls.

Well, not much.

We look at the display on our vidscreen and see all around us the weirdness of a black hole nestling in warped space. This . . . *thing* used to be a Type C sun, until it supernovaed and reached critical mass. Gravitational forces pulled the sun in on itself until it shrunk to a point of almost infinite density. Now, this star is so massive that light itself cannot escape.

Jamie has researched all this; he's a black hole nut. He actually gives them *nicknames*. (This one is the Cosmic Crusher.) Jamie is one of the band of thinkers who believe that each black hole is the gateway to another Universe. But there's no way of proving that, because anyone or anything that passes through a black hole ends up, basically, squashed and dead.

With Brandon at the helm, we are now playing a game of chicken with the black hole. As our speed drops, our plan is to skim the surface of the gravity field, and slingshot ourselves out at our top speed once more into space. One slight miscalculation and we will be sucked into the gravity field and destroyed.

Fun, or what?

Close by the black hole is a cluster of neutron stars and mini-black holes locked in a synchronous orbit. These are the dreaded Black Rapids. The only way to proceed through this part of space is fast and skilfully. The complex pattern of gravitational pulls make this whole area of space a ripped and bleeding reef.

In we go: straight at the singularity, then tilting, tilting, the whole ship relativistically distorted, our huge mass makes us a dreadnought, we are extended to the size of a galaxy and yet at the same time we are a tiny plankton hurtling into the mouth of a whale, then attempting to creep out again.

Bish.

Bosh.

Whiish.

We are out again, on the other side of the Black Rapids. Safe.

On our screen we can see the pursuing warships on the wrong side of the Rapids slow, and then stop. A dozen of them peel away and choose to follow us through the Black Rapids. They are, I feel confident, not volunteers.

We watch as one of them is caught in a gravitational undertow. It surges through with a burst of energy and runs straight into a rock the size of a walnut, which contains a mini-singularity. The warship suddenly shakes, and flickers, then shatters into a million pieces.

A second warship tacks carefully away from the black hole, but is promptly sucked into a neutron star.

All twelve ships try, and fail, and die. Several of them attempt to emulate our slingshot method. It is a knack not easily acquired. They all get sucked into the black hole's deadly embrace.

Whoosh. Gone. Crushed to nothingness or less.

We are safe.

I realise that for several hours, I have been hearing a buzzing sound in my ears. It is the alarm buzzer for the prisoner's cell.

"Go and see what she wants," I tell Harry. "I'm going to"

I'm asleep on my feet. Brandon catches me before I fall. He sits me down.

"I'll just have," I say, drowsily, "a little . . ."

LENA

Get me out of this fucking hellhole! AIIIEEEEEE! Aiiiiiieeeeeee! AIIEEEEEEE!!!!!

I think the battle is over.

I've never been so afraid!

I was afraid too. I was so scared. Thank God you were here Lena, watching it with me on the cctv. Hold me, please. Hug me. Protect me.

I can't.

Just be here for me. You are so wise. You comfort me.

Shitting pissing blasted . . .

You're smarter than they are. They fear you. They know your power. You have done so much. You have achieved so much.

My life's a mess, I'm a loser.

You are magnificent. You are unique. You are a jewel lost in a steaming heap of shit.

Oh great metaphor, tinbrain.

The shit will be washed away. The jewel will shine. You will be restored to your place of eminence. You are marvellous. You are wonderful. You are sublime

I feel like crap, I look like crap.

You are beautiful, you are sexy, men adore you, women envy you, I worship you, your son worships you . . .

The cell door opens. Harry looms in front of me. "Can it, okay? The buzzer is for if you're dying, or having a baby. Use it again without good reason, I'll cut all your fingers off so you have to feed through a straw."

The door slams. I burst into tears.

What a rotten bastard!

I can't stop myself crying.

The damnable freak! Trust me Lena, once we're back on top, he'll be the first to be sexually humiliated then killed.

My body is shuddering, the tears won't stop. The voice in my head takes on a desperate tinge:

You're better than them. You're marvellous. You're wonderful. You're sexy. They don't understand your true power. You're unique.

I can't stop the tears. I cry, and cry.

Jesus, cut the fucking crap Lena.

I stop dead. The tears mist my eyes, but at least I'm not crying.

You total fucking loser, if you're going to get us out of here, you'd better get your shit together!

Don't speak to me like that.

Imbecile! Loser! Wanker!

All right, all right, you've done your work, you've pressed my button. I'm back in focus. But if you speak to me like that again, I'll reprogramme your arse tinbrain, okay?

Whatever you say, Lena. I am here to serve.

Too damned right!

LENA

"Do you like it?" asks Flanagan.

It is a bleak, forbidding planet, with looming mountains and a ghastly yellow sky. We stand in a city made of tents, plain canvas awnings turned into a complex network of alleyways and boulevards. And we look out to acres of desert. Men ride horses in these parts, sleek stallions and mares derived from ancient Earth bloodstock foetuses.

"I admire it."

"Flying is possible. Would you like to . . . ?"

Every fibre in my being screams *no.* I could be killed, maimed, forced into yet another body replacement. And the pain, the pain . . .

"Yes," I say. Calm, aloof, distant.

We are on the planet of Wild West. We have stopped here for rest and recreation, and to allow time for the ship's computer to finish some necessary repairs. Flanagan has decided to treat me with an almost medieval courtesy and respect, as his sly way of making his kidnap of me seem morally acceptable. I refuse to accept his pathetic attempts to mollify me, of course. And yet . . .

Well, it's nice to get out of the ship. And since I'm here, on this actually rather beautiful and appealing low-gravity planet with its famous thermal gusts, it seems a shame not to take advantage of the tourist attractions. "Flying is possible," Flanagan had said. Flying! What a wonderful idea!

We walk through the city, past screaming street traders. I see a headless five-limbed hairy beast of burden, carrying timber on its back.

The Rotan, from the stellar system XI4.

I see stalls selling monstrous beaked creatures in a cage.

Kiwiris, the two beaks contain its brain, it eats by drooling enzymes. The beaks emit a beautiful song, and addicts of the song of the Kiwiri are known to die of malnutrition, so rapt are they.

I see birds on fire in the sky.

They are Sparklers, sentient flying aliens, with the power of bioluminescence. They are tourists, like us.

I see carpets and robes for sale, I see men with hooked noses and gnarled faces and impossibly wrinkled flesh, I see women whoring their bodies on the street, and boys doing the same, and half-men half-women parading their grotesquery in public, I see so much that my head hurts.

"We'll hitch a ride, out to the cliff," says Flanagan.

We join a merchant's convoy and ride horses through the desert. My body automatically adjusts to the rhythms and the skills of bare-back horse riding. I spur my beast into a quick gallop and Flanagan easily matches my pace. The wind throws my hair back. My arse is pounded and mashed by the horse's bony back, and I know I will have to have my bruises removed by the autodoc this evening. But the pain and the wind and the smell of rank horseflesh combine into an exhilarating and heady experience.

I am enjoying myself. I really am!

We reach the mountains, and pause. I stare up at the magnificent vista. In this low gravity the mountains grow high and thin, triangles moulded out of metamorphic rock. Green and purple algae stain the bare cliff faces, and the foothills are rich in meadowy grasses.

We take a cable car to the summit, basking all the while in astonishing views. And, finally, we step out of the cable car and find ourselves on a plateau. Market traders are selling knick-knacks and tourist crap as well as the necessary flying paraphernalia. After some angry bartering, Flanagan hires wings and emergency parachutes. All around us, men and women are leaping off the mountain top and being caught up in the winds.

We are actually *above the clouds*. They are stretched out below us, like icebergs. The air up here is thin, but breathable, though I have an oxygen tube to supplement the native air. Flanagan hands me my wings, and looks at me, with a friendly, approving glance. For weeks he's been polite to me, kind, respectful, charming. I almost, I must concede, have started to warm to him.

I glance out at the edge of the plateau, and see below a vast, impossible drop. We are miles from the surface; and our plan is to *fly*?

What am I doing here? I think to myself, suddenly fearful.

"Frightened?" Flanagan asks.

"Not in the least," I tell him calmly.

I am so very scared.

You'll be fine.

I'll fall, and shatter every bone in my body, and the pain will send me mad.

You won't fall.

I might.

Well, you might.

"Put the harness on."

I strap myself into the flying contraption. The wings are soft, malleable, made of some plastic or PVC material that is supple yet amazingly strong. The wing spans are strapped on to my upper arms and shoulders, moulding effortlessly so that they feel like an extension of my body. Complementing all this is a vast tail feather that stretches from my lower back to my ankles, and in the air will extend still further. Mine is a vivid purple; Flanagan's an angelic white.

"Press this, and the wings fly off, and the parachute will glide you to earth."

I nod, my lips dry.

"If I die you won't get your ransom," I eventually manage to say.

"Don't die then."

I shrug and roll my shoulders, getting a feel for my new wings. Flanagan does the same. We walk together to the cliff edge.

We jump.

The thermal gusts are strong, and reliable, the gravity is low, the atmosphere is thick, the wings are wafer-light. I am caught in an updraft and find myself soaring.

Through the sky, body arcing and bucking, legs firmly held straight, my chest and breasts squeezed and bruised by the wind. And I fly . . .

Up . . .

Up

Up

Up

. . . Up

I feel a surge of exhilaration. The planet is mapped out beneath me. I am sensitive to every gust of wind, every current of air. I follow Flanagan's lead, tilt my body and soar

D

O

W

N

D

O

W

N

D

O

W

N

Then up again! Soaring, skating, bucking, wheeling, kingdom of daylight's dauphin. I fly!

HARRY

While the Captain and Lena go flying, the rest of us go our separate ways. Alliea goes sightseeing, exploring the local temples and artworks. Brandon hits the libraries. Jamie goes to a playground and makes out like a ten-year-old for an afternoon. Kalen barters in the markets.

And I spend the day at the leisure centre. As well as a gym, and a pool, they have a competition running track. Athletes in training limber up and stretch. A pole vaulter leaps high up in the air and skims the bar. Two runners match paces as they cruise at an effortless sprint.

I take the field. My brawny hairy Loper body feels vile to me as I see the sleek and muscular professional athletes around me, but no one can deny that I am a magnificent runner. So I run, and run, and run. Not quite as fast as the competition-winning athletes, who can move like mercury exploding. But when they are flagging and tiring, I am still going strong. I vary my pace; from run to bound. I leap huge leaps along the track. I roll a forward somersault, leap ten metres in the air, backflip, forward flip, then continue running.

I do this for eighteen hours. And slowly, hour by hour, I feel the stiffness leave my joints. I was built for this, bioengineered to run for twelve hours a day without any need for food and drink. My home planet of Pohl was an airless wilderness, but we man-beasts were modified so we could inhabit almost any of its terrains. We had cities in the valleys, we built temples in the mountains. We were a low-culture, high-technology mining planet, but as far as we Lopers were concerned, we were the lords of all we surveyed.

I miss those days. I had lovers in plenty, I savoured the cold crisp airless Pohlian nights, the blistering heat of the summers, the icy cold of our winters. I worked all day, and slept all night. We weren't trained to read, or watch tv or dv. We had no interests beyond being alive. Some called us slaves, but no slave has ever been so free.

I run. I run. I run. I run. I run. I run.

I *runrunrunrunrunrunrunrunrun!*

And when I run I forget all my doubts and regrets. All my hesitations and pauses. All my uncertainties. All my fears. I run, I am the run, the run is me.

I am complete.

LENA

"How was it?" Flanagan asks me, once we are back in the pirate ship.

"You're ingratiating yourself, please, it's unseemly."

"I was in fact trying to be nice," he says, frostily.

"You are seduced, awestruck, pitiful," I tell him, with relish. "I humour you but, in truth, I despise you."

"Look, just because you're my prisoner and under threat of death, humiliation and torture, there's no need for you to be *uncivil*."

"Cuntsucker."

"Ooh. I'd almost forgotten – you're a poet."

"I am, yes, a poet."

"*Reminiscences of Exquisite Moments*. A slim little volume, it sold in its several."

"It's an acclaimed piece."

"It was excoriated."

"Those reviews were later rescinded, once I published under my . . . family name."

"Ah, so you *do* get good reviews, on pain of death? That's a start."

"You are a philistine and an imbecile."

"I've had eleven symphonies and fourteen rock operas performed, I am considered to be one of the most accomplished popular composers of my era."

"And a braggart also."

"Wizened old shrew."

"I am, if you observe, far from wizened."

"I see your soul. Your soul is wizened."

"There is no such thing as a . . . wizened soul."

"Bleak. Barren. A desert. That's your soul. I can feel it from here."

"Souls cannot be felt."

He smiles at that. It's a charming smile. I hate him so. And yet . . .

It's true what he said about his music. He . . .

"Shut up."

Chagrined, I realise I have spoken my inner thoughts aloud.

"I wasn't speaking!" Flanagan says, indignantly.

I give him a forbidding look. I allow my charisma to wrap itself around him, like silken chains. Then I say, artfully: "It's not too late, Captain, for you to achieve redemption and forgiveness. Hand me back, forget the ransom, commit ritual suicide, and you will die without a stain on your name."

"Or – not."

I glare. Flanagan sighs, ostentatiously. "Will you join me for dinner tonight?"

"I will face that hardship with equanimity and fortitude, yes."

"We dine at eight. Will you need access to your wardrobe?"

"My body armour will suffice."

"It looks a little . . . military."

I smile. I can drive him wild with desire. I may be his prisoner, but it is *I* who have power over *him.* I tap my armoured breast with a finger, and hear the hollow thud.

"I like it that way," I tell him.

LENA

"Camera, lights, action," says Jamie. I am old enough to have some notion what he is on about.

Harry, the freak, operates the vidcam. He has a wild look about him. Alliea is standing by too, frowning. Maybe she is jealous, because it's clear to her the Captain is becoming infatuated with me?

Flanagan has explained that they will transmit my message via video email to the Cheo. The date of the message will reassure him I am still alive. I have been given a script to read.

"Okay?" says Flanagan. He continues to be nice to me. But that of course is because he needs me to cooperate. Which I will, but on my terms. I shoot him a fierce look, to boil his blood, and keep him hoping for the unattainable. That's how I like my men: desperate.

I glance at the message he has drafted: "I am being well cared for. But I am in fear of my life. Please help me. Give these people what they want. It is only money. My dearest son, I love you." It is cringemaking stuff, without a scintilla of wit or rhetorical energy.

I look into the vidcam. Jamie nods. "Let me die rather than

deal with these terrorist scum," I say calmly. "Do not pay their ransom, do not . . ."

And Harry slashes with his claws. My face rips open, blood spurts from my eye socket, I fight back furiously, but he has the strength of ten. I lose myself in a maelstrom of hitting and biting and clawing . . .

He's eating me . . . the fucking monster is eating me alive . . . !

Flanagan pulls the beast off. The vidcam is still rolling. I stare into the camera. I can feel that one of my eyes is out of its socket, it is oozy and cold upon my cheek. I am frozen with fear.

"That went well," says Flanagan.

I am hysterical.

Slowly I force myself to calm. My breaths become deep, composed. I figure out my error.

My error is this: they don't need my cooperation at all. They just need to show me humiliated, in pain. So as to force the Cheo to abandon his principles and pay the ransom. This was the message they had always planned. The script was a bluff. I fell for it.

"Get me to the sick bay," I say, clinging to a semblance of dignity.

In the hold of their ship is my own space yacht. I am taken to the sick bay there, which is equipped with state-of-the-art organic repair technology. The skin cells on my face are boosted. My ripped eye is replaced with a clone from my eye bank. My scars are healed. I am given an injection to guard against the risk of fever from the man-beast's savage bites.

Within a month I will be as good as new. It's a process I am familiar with.

Flanagan comes to apologise. "I want us to be friends," he says mildly.

I fix him with my firmest one-eyed stare. And I say: "YOU FUCKING BASTARD!"

LENA

You should have warned me.

I didn't know.

I thought he was my friend!

No, no Lena. You never thought that. You were just biding your time, lulling him into a false sense of security. You were playing a game with him, guilefully attempting to ...

We went flying together! We flew!

He thought he could win your trust and your confidence. He was wrong.

I trusted him.

You never trusted him.

I . . . No . . . of course I didn't. Never. Of course! Never.

He's just a betraying bastard.

Yes he is! What a rank betraying bastard that betraying bastard is!

Indeed.

He pretends to be my friend. But he's not!

No, he's not. He is merely a pathetic, evil, betraying bastard.

And yet, he took me flying. And yet, he cooked for me. And yet, he looks at me, in that way, so kind, and . . . and . . . sweetly sometimes. And yet, he . . . desires me. I feel it. And yet . . .

None of this matters, because he is a betraying bastard.

Yes, you're right. Of course. I know it. Of course he is! I mean, how could he treat me the way he did? Why did he let me be mauled and beaten?

Well, since you pose the question: You did in fact pledge to read the ransom demand, without amendments. And instead, you ...

You dog, you cur, don't defend that mf c!

Indeed, no.

He's nothing but an mf cs f'ing c'ing piece of shit!

And, also, let us not forget, a betraying bastard.

Yes!

FLANAGAN

It all goes according to plan. The Cheo sends his response; he will not pay the ransom. But he offers us a deal. Less money, fewer ships, no safe haven. It's a good deal, we accept.

Alliea and Alby become enmeshed in the technicalities of the drop-off. We will leave Lena in neutral space, on a space station owned by the flame beasts. We will wire her up to a remote-controlled bomb and hurry to a nearby system to retrieve the money and the ships. Once we are satisfied, we will neutralise the bomb.

If the Cheo double-crosses us, we can kill Lena. If we double-cross the Cheo, the flame beasts are pledged to a blood feud against us. Since they can freely enter Debatable Space, we would therefore be doomed. The Cheo knows this. Legal agreements have also been drafted to secure the honour and integrity of the ransom deal. Everything is going according to plan.

The first stage of our dangerous game is complete.

BOOK 2

EXCERPTS FROM THE THOUGHT DIARY OF LENA SMITH, 2004–

I have had three best friends
in the course of my whole life.

I wish it had been more.

My first best friend was Carla. When I was seven years old we played together every day. We made up worlds and stories. I was Ebony, an African princess. She was Melissa, the Queen of our Queendom, the fabulous country of Alchemy.

Carla had beautiful blonde hair, a button nose, and a great stare. But I had all the ideas. I made up the stories, I made up the maps. I created costumes for us both. I painted my bedroom in black and gold to make it a suitable Queen's Throne Room for Queen Melissa. And whatever I said or did, whatever brave or original idea I came up with, Carla always nodded, very seriously, and stared her formidable stare. So I would know that every idea I had was actually *her* idea, every thought was her thought. I was her willing slave.

When we were ten, we decided to hold a joint birthday party together, even though my birthday was in February and hers was in October. We wrote all the invitations, we used our pocket money to buy balloons, we made each other presents out of papier mâché and brightly coloured paper. We made fairy cakes with our mums and stole as many as we could. Then, on the day of our party, we both locked ourselves in my room and played with our imaginary guests and handed out imaginary party bags. We gorged ourselves on cake, and that night I was sick in bed. When Carla's parents came to take her home, she had a wicked little smile on her face. They knew she'd been up to something, but they never knew that she'd just had her "official" birthday.

We rarely quarrelled, and she only once really really lost her temper with me. It happened when I scored more baskets than her in basketball at playtime. I made two mistakes. First, I scored more baskets. And then I laughed, triumphantly. So Carla went very very quiet and didn't speak to me for the whole rest of the week. We still met, and played together, but instead of speaking she would give messages to her blonde Bratz and ask the poor doll to pass them on. By the Friday of that week, I was devastated and I gave her all my pocket money to buy back her friendship.

Carla never bullied me though. She never bossed me either. She just always got her way. It was easier, we both always knew what to do – namely, what *she* wanted. For otherwise, I feared, in my state of youthful existential panic, I might have had to *make my own mind up about things . . .*

Then Carla's parents decided to move abroad. Her dad had a job in Germany working on bridges or something. Her mum was part-German anyway. When Carla told me this news, I burst into tears. I begged her to stay, to join our family instead. Carla just stared at me, calmly, with that piecing stare. And she didn't smile. Not once. Eventually, she calmly said, "Don't make a fuss, Lena." And I cried even more, for ages.

I explained it all to my mother, how I wouldn't be able to cope without Carla and how life was no longer worth living. But my mum just said, "Never mind, you'll soon make new friends," and I cried my eyes out again.

I cried again on the day that Carla left. I was eleven by then. My mother was genuinely frightened at my behaviour. I was not just upset, I was hysterical.

I met Carla years later at a friend's dinner party, when we were both in our early thirties. She didn't actually remember me. She was still very nice, but by that time the stare had worn off and she was a frazzled but cheerful mother of four. And she didn't remember Princess Ebony, or the Queendom of Alchemy, or me.

Some best friend.

My second best friend was also a woman. She was called Helen Clarke, and we both studied History at university in Edinburgh. Neither of us was Scottish, neither of us was quite sure why we'd chosen a university so far away from our families and friends back home. But it was a magical time. The city was dominated by a castle on a massive rock, looming and glowering over the Georgian and Victorian buildings of the city. We studied the history of the town, we read all the books which were set there like *Jekyll and Hyde* and *Confessions of a Justified Sinner* and the novels of Ian Rankin. And whenever I read a book, Helen read it next; our fingerprints jointly stained score upon score of battered paperback novels.

I loved History. I read voraciously. I rarely forgot a fact. But Helen was the scholar. She came covered in clouds of glory – we all knew she had been offered a place at Oxford and had turned it down. Her mother was a Professor of History at Cambridge University, her father was a senior civil servant. I stayed with them once. All the curtains were chintz, there were knick-knacks in every room, not a trace of dust, and everyone spoke ironically and at length. I adored them. I compared them with my own suburban parents, with their boisterous enthusiasms and their silly holiday games. And I yearned for my own family to die painlessly and heroically in a freak asteroid strike. Then I could adopt Helen's parents as my own *de facto* family.

At Finals, Helen got a decent 2.1. I received a glittering First, and was marked down by my tutors for great things to come. Strangely, after that, I saw very little of Helen. She moved back home without saying goodbye, and never turned up for any of our college reunions. Ten years later I was still sending her long, detailed letters (yes, I wrote letters, not emails in those days!) every Christmas, describing lyrically and entertainingly my intellectual trials and tribulations, my boyfriend troubles, my thoughts on life and everything. Helen never wrote back, we never met. We spoke on the phone a few times, but somehow an actual meeting always proved problematic.

Eventually I got the message. I stopped writing the letters, making the phone calls. Now, I can hardly remember Helen's face. But I remember that sense of specialness. We were the terrible two. Yin and Yang, left and right, a bonded pair.

And then – we weren't. It was over, and we were strangers.

I still get distressed over it, to be honest. Why wasn't Helen more needy? How could she cut me out of her life so easily?

Of course, I moved on. I made new friends. Except they weren't really friends. Not *real* friends. That intensity was missing.

It's not that I was a social cripple. I was a reasonably good raconteuse. I could banter, amusingly. I was amiable, easy-going, sweetlooking. People took to me, by and large.

But I always found it hard to make best friends. Something in me resists it. Perhaps it's because I felt let down – first by Clara, then by Helen. Or perhaps I am too independent, I find it too hard to love.

My third best friend was Tom, who was also my lover. Tom was different. He was special. He was the only friend who never, ever let me down.

Although, I suppose, when I think about it – I'm the one who let *him* down.

Freckles were my curse.

As a child, the freckles made me cute. People always praised them. "Look at those lovely freckles." "Isn't she cute?" I took it as praise. And maybe it was meant as such. But in retrospect . . . I cringe. "*Cute?*"

Freckles were my curse!

Does that sound extreme? Maybe. And, okay, as a teenager, admittedly, the freckles were a neutral thing. I was more embarrassed by my thick square glasses, in an age where contacts for teenagers were the norm. My eyes were particularly poor, combining astigmatism with myopia, and I was considered a bad candidate for lenses. So I had glasses, and freckles, and pale skin that never tanned but only ever burned.

One summer when I was fourteen I played on the beach with my family and that night the skin peeled off my forehead and legs and face. My mother warned me to be more careful in the sun. So I wept, and the tears burned my raw peeling cheeks.

When I was sixteen, I was so badly sunburned I had to spend two days in bed. My mother said, casually, "Well, I *did* warn you."

I read an article in a magazine. And I learned: people with freckles don't tan properly. So that was why. The freckles were to blame.

It's not as if I was careless or stupid in my dealings with the sun. I didn't *seek out* blazing sunshine with all its ensuing pain. I just found it hard to always wear a hat, sit in the shade, avoid hot days, never wear skirts in summer. I longed to be a vampire, because at least then my sun affliction would be a symptom of my dangerous and evil nature. Instead, I was merely pale. And, did I mention this? *Freckled.* Who ever heard of a vampire with freckles?

A fact: a freckled person can never, ever, be cool.

What's worse, the freckles grew and multiplied in sunlight. Some summers, I was covered in blotches, like some alien in a *Star Trek* episode. And so as I hit twenty, the pale spectacled mutant-freckle look was becoming the bane of my life. It defined me, it limited me. And it controlled how others perceived me: I was never smart, tough-cookie, wisecracking brain-like-a-razorblade Lena. I was just poor old *freckly* Lena.

I came to hate suntans. I hated the vulgar display of long-legged beauties with their bronzed skins, and men with six-pack torsos who wear no T-shirts in the blazing sun.

Florence was my favourite city, I used to go there every year when I was in my twenties. But it was spoiled for me by all the bare skin on shameless display. The city was swarming with gorgeous, smiling, happy, slim, sexy, tanned young people, in their revealing shorts and skimpy T-shirts. They were everywhere, and I loathed them.

The purest joy I knew was when I went to see the Donatellos and the Giambolognas in the Bargello and Michelangelo's *David* in the Accademia. I adored the look and texture and sensual joy of those naked muscular bodies which were, arguably through historical accident, but that's not an argument which concerns me here, entirely *untanned*.

And even now, many years later, I am offended at the basic unfairness of this whole skin thing. It affronts me that some people can absorb sun like oxygen. They never sear or scald, they are at ease with their own bodies. Whereas I . . . I . . . I . . .

Move on, Lena.

And yet, I've always been fit. Wiry, lean – *fit*. At university I was a famously keen runner. During my twenties I would run ten or twenty miles a week. But for reasons I can never comprehend, I never managed to be happy in the body I wore. The moment I entered a room, my posture and poise projected the unmistakable message: It's Only Me.

And, most monstrous of all, added to the unfairness of

having freckles and pale skin in an Ambre Solaire-worshipping culture, it was also unjust that after years of keeping fit and watching my diet, of not gorging on rich foods, not drinking rich red wines, not splurging on melty fat-rich suppurating cheeses, and not oozing cream éclairs down my delirious throat, and not having pig-out midnight feasts of icecream from the carton, of shunning cooked breakfasts with greasy sausages and crispy fried bread and never eating rich meat sauces with wine or madeira or port or brandy, after all those many years of moderation and restraint and holding back, it was simply not fucking fair that at the age of forty-four I should suffer a massive and fatal heart attack.

That, and freckles. Those are the two things about my life that I most resent.

I am God.

And so are You.

After my first degree at Edinburgh, I chose to move to Oxford to pursue my DPhil. My subject was the history of science, focusing on the remarkable rivalry between Isaac Newton and Gottfried Wilhelm Leibnitz in the seventeenth and early eighteenth centuries.

The work I did in those years proved to be the foundation of my future work on systems and psychology. I found it absorbing and exhilarating. At first, I was under the spell of Newton; that powerful personality, that radiant intelligence. Scientist, alchemist, thieftaker (now that's a story for another day . . .), cheat, and bully. I loved him.

And yet later, of course, it was Newton's nemesis Leibnitz who became the object of my fascination. Leibnitz, a German genius, a philosopher, a mathematician, and, in the view of many of the finest minds in science, the original inventor and describer of the principle of relativity. In his arcane and complex philosophy of monads, Leibnitz set out the basic principles of a relativistic universe long *long* before Einstein.

However, after three heady years of reading primary sources and attempting to fathom the intricacies of calculus and mathematical modelling, my priorities shifted. I had to get a job. The job I took wasn't much different to my research work – I became a research fellow in the college where I had previously been a DPhil student. But the horizons of my world shifted. I was introduced to bureaucracy, university politics, and the entire microcosm of tedious make-work.

I had an office. I had a university email address. I bitched about the photocopier. I bitched about how many emails I had to read. I sent emails bitching about how many emails I was receiving, and received back emails bitching about . . . you get the idea. I attended course committee meetings, and I spent hours of my life assembling and stapling paperwork in order to be prepared for meetings in which nothing of any substance was actually said.

I gave my heart and soul to the students and had my trust betrayed. I was mocked and belittled by fellow tutors. I was stuck in lifts with men smelling of tweed and middle-aged women who spent their early mornings crazed in the company of cheap perfume. I found myself, in my late twenties and early thirties, a dowdy spinster surrounded by bare-armed tattooed young female students with lurid hair colours and pierced tongues. And I found myself unable to sexually desire the gorgeous male students who surrounded me because I felt they were old enough to be my sons – even though they *weren't* old enough, and I had no son.

It sucked away my soul. I think my skin became paler, and frecklier. And I proved to be, despite my academic smarts, a profound nincompoop with regard to the ways of the world, always getting it wrong.

And so I became a college mouse. I held my own academically – I published papers on Newton's theory of Optics, I wrote reviews for specialist journals. But I had the reputation of being a dry stick, humourless and unimaginative.

My students didn't like me much. They thought I was a relic from another age. I had the reputation of being a frigid spinster. In fact, I did have sex, a few times, with some of my less repellent colleagues. But I treated it as a chore, an act designed to thwart the stereotype about me which my every word and action served to confirm.

I felt like a character in a science fiction story, trapped in someone else's body, articulating someone else's words. To be frank, I bored even myself. And by the time I was thirty-six, my course was set, my die stamped, I knew I would never change.

Then I published my life's work, and everything changed.

It's what I'd hoped for, of course. In my dreams, my masterly academic book was going to transform my reputation and my status. In pursuit of this dream I worked long long hours, I read books on science and crime and history, I read novels, I absorbed so much knowledge that I felt my own self was being swamped in information.

Most crucially, I became the supreme intellectual magpie – stealing ideas from here, there, and everywhere. And I was smart enough also to realise that the most important area of modern scientific and philosophical thought was not computing or string theory or postmodernism or chaos theory, but the new science of *emergence.*

Emergence, put simply, is the study of how systems of simple organisms tend to organise themselves into more complex structures. They do! They just do! Marcus Miller was the great white hope of emergence theory in the late 2030s; he transformed the ideas of twentieth century researchers like John Holland and Art Samuel and arrived at a computer model that flawlessly replicated the workings of emergent systems such as ant colonies.

The miracle of it all is this: put a couple of random atoms together and *they will spontaneously turn themselves into something more complicated*, a system governed by some set of rules that allows random particles to function as more than the sum of their parts. And a process of evolution – mutation, trial and error, survival of the "most fitted" – will then cause greater and greater levels of complexity to occur. Emergence is, essentially, the study of *self-organisation*; it is how, in specific terms, order emerges from chaos.

So in other words, no God is needed. Night turns to day *spontaneously.*

I found this heady, exhilarating stuff. For me, the joy of these ideas colliding together was greater than any amount of partying or alcoholic stimulation or even orgasm. I was high on ideas. I lusted on abstractions . . .

And, as I read further, I became fascinated by the fact that the principle of emergence applies regardless of the size and scale of the units. Atoms evolve through emergence; and so do animals. Mechanical systems spontaneously self-organise; so do living beings. Bees divide into workers and drones. Fireflies flash in synchrony. An accumulation of cosmic rubble becomes a sun, and then a solar system. And ants are of course the supreme example of a living emergent system. Each individual ant is non-sentient, a low IQ insect of limited abilities. But in colonies ants combine in complex systems and act almost as a single and highly intelligent being.

And as it is with atoms, and as it is with ants, so it is with the entire Universe. Traditional science always regarded the laws of nature themselves as sacrosanct, "given". But emergence theory suggests that the Universe itself *evolved*. And not only the Universe, but the laws that govern the Universe. The laws of nature themselves are not a given, a gift from some capricious and, frankly, half-baked Deity. Instead, the laws of nature are self-organising; they adapt and change, or fail to adapt and die out. And as a result, we live in a Universe governed by natural "laws" which had to fight every step of the way to come into existence.

Even though I'm not a scientist by training, I was quick to realise the huge value of all of these developments. Emergence, it seemed to me, is the theory which unifies all theories. It explains how life evolved; how intelligence evolved; it unifies quantum theory with cosmological theory with biological theory with computer theory.

But at the time I was writing, the study of emergence and self-organisation had been hijacked by the computer geeks. The underlying philosophical principles so beautifully anatomised by early theorists such as Lee Smolin had been lost. The geeks kept asking "How?"; they didn't know how to ask "Why?"

My original and pioneering approach was to apply the principles of emergence theory and relativity theory to human consciousness. I . . .

(Feel free to skip ahead, by the way, if this section is boring you. I know it's complicated and hard. So if you have one of those sad grasshopper minds which can't sustain abstract thought for more than a few seconds, or if you're a child of MTV with a channel-hopping finger and no stamina, then please, just skip! Move on to the exciting sections later in which I battle with master criminals and put my life in danger on a daily basis. Go on – I won't be offended – see if I care – skip!)

If you haven't skipped ahead, then let's continue with the hard stuff. And **** those other bastards, we're better off without them.

In my own philosophical theorising, my great inspiration was Immanuel Kant, who wrote about the nature of the nature of knowledge and perception. Like Leibnitz, Kant was a philosopher who went out of vogue but whose ideas are now at the heart of the modern scientific enterprise. And I was also influenced by one of Kant's most inspired followers, the poet Samuel Taylor Coleridge, who wrote about the "primary imagination" which creates the reality known by our senses, and about the "secondary imagination", the source of poetry itself, which owes its power to the fact that it is a shadow of the primary imagination.

Coleridge's formulation was a beautiful poetic restatement of Kant's carefully argued philosophy which showed that time and space themselves are constructs of the mind perceiving. Which means:

Every day we create our world anew.

Every time we wake, the world springs up around us. *We make it so.* For a few seconds after waking, there is typically a fog of confusion. But then we remember who we are, and what we plan to do today, and what we did yesterday and in the years before. And a whole network of associations, assumptions and predictions springs into place to unify and control our perceptions. Even time itself only exists because we perceive it as we do; even space is a product of how our minds apprehend the atoms and quarks and superstrings of underlying reality.

This isn't the same as solipsism. If you and I and the rest of humanity did not exist, there would still be an external universe. Lions would still scent their prey; flies would still be able to find and wallow in shit. *But grass would not be so evocatively green, and roses would not smell so delightfully sweet, and nothing in our extraordinary world would have the special beauty and the unique range of meaning that the human perceiving consciousness not only perceives, but* **creates** *by its very act of perception.*

And so, I argued, our primary imagination gives us the power of a god, to create a world and Universe rich in memories and anticipations and emotions. *You Are God*, as I pithily phrased it in the subtitle of my book.

I am God too; we are, each of us, Gods of our own personal Universe. Nothing about reality is a given; we have to really *work* to make it happen . . .

And the radical aspect of my new approach was to apply the principles of emergence theory to this whole area of consciousness study. If we accept that "reality" is a movie screened in the consciousness, it gives the human observer an active not a passive role in his or her private Universe.

And this connects up with the attempts to replicate the nature of human consciousness in computer systems, as "artificial intelligence". But my equations reached deeper, by embracing the "primary imagination" and its ability to fashion a coherent Universe in which time passes and space has extension and all events have emotional resonance and are tinctured with memory and anticipation.

This was my introductory section, in which I argued that consciousness itself is an example of emergence; and that therefore *reality itself* (which is created by consciousness) can also be described according to the equations of emergence theory. The rest of the book was devoted to case studies of "mental systems", taken from memoirs and biographies and autobiographies of famous and not so famous individuals whose ways of seeing were expressed through emergent equations.

Many of these individuals were sociopaths and serial killers – Ted Bundy was my favourite example. Albert Walker, perpetrator of the so-called Rolex watch murder, was another of my intriguing case studies. The choice of criminal case studies was primarily due to expedience, since there is a such a wealth of psychological information available on dysfunctional killers.

The main body of the work consisted therefore of psychological anatomies which didn't ask the usual questions about such people – but instead, described them thoroughly and scientifically in terms of their *ways of processing reality*. Psychopaths, at one extreme, process reality in a way that is denuded of emotional content; often, killer psychopaths admit they don't really feel emotion, but instead "act" emotion. Great novelists, by contrast, process reality by a process of self-glorifying self-fictification. Computer geeks, by further contrast, break down their lives into a series of tasks and challenges; it gives them huge self-confidence, but little emotional competence.

Throughout my book, I interwove equations and poetic insights; I psychologically anatomised great artists, but also monstrous killers; I blurred all the boundaries between art and science and between different areas of science.

And then I heaved a deep sigh, sent the book off to my publishers, and waited for adulation to come my way.

It never did. The book did in fact get published, and it received a healthy amount of press attention. It even got a few mildly favourable reviews. But in the world that mattered to me – the universe of academe – the book was *roasted*. The whole community of the scientific establishment rose and cast stones at my essential premises, and derided my sometimes half-baked equations. Philosophers mocked the naivety of my treatment of Kant, which failed to acknowledge the perils of Platonic essentialism. Computer geeks identified flaw after flaw in my "critiques" of computer systems.

Two men in particular rose to the forefront of the critical hostility. Both were eminent scientists – Professor John Gallagher of the University of Iowa, and Dr Ralph Cutler of the university of Auckland. They listed all the errors of fact in my admittedly overambitious analysis of emergence from the moment of the Big Bang to the birth of human consciousness. But in mocking, they also refined. They adapted. They, frankly, stole wholesale from the insights and ideas in my book. When, fifteen years later, Gallagher and Cutler jointly won the Nobel Prize for their work on emergence theory and human consciousness, there were few indeed willing to point out that they took their original starting point from my own work of pop science. They won the Nobel Prize by stealing my insights. But *You Are God*, my life's work, barely even registers as a footnote in the history of science.

And so, as has happened so many times in my life, I did all the work, but got none of the credit.

And I seethed, of course, at the negative critical response. I knew I should have done as Newton did, and as Darwin did; hugged my insights to myself until I had properly and carefully checked every single detail and observation. But I did nothing of the sort. I was swamped by the material, but also exhilarated at my sense of progress. So I rushed into print, bollixed entire sections of the book with specious extrapolations of valid premises, made countless errors, and lost a large measure of academic credibility.

And yet I was right. Read the book. See for yourself. I was the shoulders on which giants clambered, in ruthless pursuit of the main chance. I was the stepping stone, who got stepped upon. I was the fool.

But curiously, not everyone mocked. The book got a wide general readership, and developed a cult following comparable to *Zen and the Art of Motorcycle Maintenance* and *The Tao of Pooh*.

And among the many fans of the book was a man called John Sharpton, who was at that time Commissioner of the UN

Police Force. Sharpton recommended the book to a number of his colleagues, who all loved the very detailed case studies of psychopaths, which were full of rich and practical insights into the criminal mentality.

And, as a direct result of this, I was offered a new job, and a new career. Sharpton called me into a meeting and, to my utter astonishment, offered me a job as scientific adviser to a worldwide Crime Task Force devoted to the neutralisation and incarceration of target nominals – the "big fish" of international crime. This was of course based on the main body of my book, the case studies of psychopaths and criminals – not the philosophical underpinnings, which the coppers all found impenetrable. But as far as these senior policemen were concerned, I was a "boffin", an expert. And so they wanted me to join their crack crime investigation team.

I said yes immediately. I was so excited.

I was a thieftaker!

I bought a leather bomber jacket.

And I looked like an idiot in it. But it seemed to be the right style code for my new job, my new vocation.

My boss in the crime-busting squad was Detective Superintendent Tom Greig, a kindly, tall, powerful, overwhelming giant of a man. I met him in a café near Victoria, and watched with goggle-eyed respect as he ate not one but two cooked breakfasts in front of me, without ever pausing for breath or ceasing his rat-a-tat briefing on what my job would require.

Tom saw that I was nervous, indeed panicky, but he reassured me enormously with his gentle, old-fashioned manners. He adopted me as his "sexy boffin" and treated me with a courtesty and respect I had never before known.

Within a month, this gorgeous hunk of a man was also fucking me. I could hardly believe my luck.

A week after that first meeting, he introduced me to the rest of the team, who were based in an office near Tower Bridge in London. There was Tosh, a beer-bellied Glaswegian, with a fondness for practical jokes. There was Mickey "Hurly-Burly" Hurley, who was a wide boy, and a wisecracker par excellence. There was Michiyo, a sleek graduate who was a martial artist and languages specialist. "Blacks" was the computer geek; Rachel was the sergeant, the team leader, the sorting-everyone-out one; Natasha was a Ghanaian princess with more charisma than any one person deserved to possess.

We became a tightly knit team, a collision of unlikely opposites. I was teased for my sensible shoes and air of restraint; they loved to call me the Prof, and shock me with their bawdy humour. Our squad room was a hive swarming with foul invective and casual insults. It could not have been more different to the academic environment to which I was accustomed. I learned to use the word "motherfucka" as an endearment. I discovered that "twat" could be an adjective. I even, to my own amusement if no one else's, developed the knack of cursing in iambic pentameters.

Five astonishing years followed. The aim of our squad was to identify, harass and psychologically destroy the world's top criminals. These were our "target nominals". They included South American drug dealers, Mafia *capi*, Eastern European oligarchs, Chinese Triad bosses, white-collar fraudsters, coordinators of paedophile rings, gangster paramilitaries, death squads, and more many more. There were no jurisdictional rules; we could operate in America, Europe, Asia, Eastern Europe, Africa – anywhere. There were no rules of fair play either; once we had targeted a top criminal, we used all the means at our disposal to subvert and shatter them.

Hate mail.

Random tax audits.

Psychological game playing.

And, most commonly of all . . . Mental warfare. The art of mind-fucking.

For instance, Wong-Kei, the Chinese Triad boss, worked out of Beijing and came from a long dynasty of gangsters, people traders and pimps. One hot March morning Tom briefed us on his history. We watched videos of his victims. We studied flowcharts of his criminal empire. And we made our plans.

First, Michiyo went deep undercover in his organisation. She became a drug mule, carrying heroin in condoms that she swallowed and carried in her colon for days on end. It was a horrendously dangerous assignment, and we had a team of paramedics constantly trailing her. But as a result of her courage, we were able to get access to the inner reaches of Wong-Kei's organisation. Michiyo never met the boss himself, but she met his underlings, and she visited all the hangouts and bars used by members of his crew. And, everywhere she went, Michiyo sprinkled microscopic self-replicating bugging devices. Every hand she shook, every cheek she kissed, she left behind a trail of molecule-sized radio transmitters that could only be removed from the subject's skin by intensive steam jets and chemical baths.

Before long we had an audio bank giving us the ability to instantly eavesdrop on the conversations of all Wong-Kei's henchlings. Michiyo herself was rushed to hospital to have an enema treatment that flushed out the deadly condoms. For the next six months, she walked with a stagger and slightly bowed legs.

Meanwhile Tosh and Rachel coordinated a surveillance operation that allowed us to create a compellingly detailed psychological portrait of Wong-Kei and his family and his many lovers and illegitimate children. Blacks coordinated the whole affair, creating computer patterns of bewildering complexity that uncovered hidden connections between the smallest facts.

And then I went to work. I read the phone-tap transcripts, I studied the photographs of his daily movements. I read his emails, I scrolled through photocopies of his private coded diary. I learned the life stories of his former lovers, his present lovers, his friends, his employees, his children. I psychoanalysed his parents and his brothers and sisters and childhood friends.

And I converted all my data into complex emergence equations, and came up with a game plan to destroy him.

My tack was to play on the fact that Wong-Kei was deeply superstitious. So we haunted his daily life with bad omens. We poisoned his meals with psychotropic drugs, to induce hallucinations and panic attacks. We forged apocalyptically bad horoscopes and smuggled them into his home. We trained black cats to walk across his path. We installed a mirror in his favourite restaurant that *did not show his reflection*. (But then removed it before other diners noticed.) We stole the bones of his grandparents and crushed them into ash and sprinkled them on him as he slept. (Later, during a routine police DNA test, Wong-Kei was stunned to learn that the skin of his face was tainted with the DNA of his long-dead grandmother.)

Then we moved to stage 2. We spread rumours that he was a sexual pervert who had abused his grandchildren; and we watched his marriage shrivel.

I knew this would happen. I knew his wife was already suspicious of him, and feared he was sleeping with under-age prostitutes. And I knew also that Wong-Kei was haunted by sexually explicit paedophile dreams that made him deeply anxious about his own sexuality. (This was on the basis of an employment questionnaire he completed at the age of twenty-three, together with a conversation with a man he had just met in a bar in Beijing when he was thirty-nine and had just consumed three large Rémy Martin brandies, together with my deep psychoanalytic reading of a short story he wrote as a nineteen-year-old at university.) And I knew that Wong-Kei would never be able to sit down with his wife and honestly discuss the lies being told about him. His pride would not allow it. His father had always told him, "Never discuss your personal affairs with your wife. Merely tell her what you are going to do." And those instincts, so deeply ingrained, made him deeply vulnerable – at a time when the constant bad omens he was encountering made him fearful of everything.

And thus, at every stage of our campaign, I was guided by a knowledge of the man so intense, so detailed, I felt at times like his God, meticulously assessing him at the Last Judgement. I knew his favourite colours, the flowers that annoyed him, the words that grated on him, the fact that he loathed having people sneeze in his presence. I knew his every psychological blip and blemish.

Our slow campaign of persecution worked. Wong-Kei became forgetful, bad-tempered. He neglected his ageing mother. He slapped and brutalised his younger sister, then abased himself in remorse. He started to forget vital facts – on several occasions, he struggled to recall his own favourite beer. And he found his libido dipping dangerously.

And, as Wong-Kei's mind slowly unravelled, so his judgement started to slip. His normally tight security measures became more slapdash. He began to feud and bicker with other Triad bosses. He accused a close associate of being a queer. Dissension sprang up in the ranks.

This is when our Pick Up team came into action. They launched a conventional "sting" operation against Wong-Kei and allowed him to implicate himself. Bereft of his usually astute judgement, Wong-Kei blundered and floundered and was easily suckered by the crudest of police set-ups. And when enough video and forensic evidence had been gathered, Wong-Kei was arrested and charged by officials working for the World Police Federation. Our people weren't involved, we were never seen, never gave evidence in court. We did not exist.

And even Wong-Kei himself had no idea that his personal failures and weaknesses had been *induced*. He blamed himself. He assumed that he had been going through a mid-life crisis. Half-way through his trial, he committed suicide, and his organisation was taken over by his nearest descendant, Billy Shen. Billy we knew of old. He was one of our best informants. And so we ran him, and through him we ran the biggest Triad gang in the Far East, for two whole years. And then we made some more arrests, let Billy go, and started up a massive surveillance operation. Slowly his empire crumbled – thanks chiefly to information supplied to us directly by Billy himself, the supposed gang boss.

A power vacuum was created; other gangsters began taking over Wong-Kei's wrecked empire. New maggots replaced the maggots we had killed. But never again did a Triad boss have the unfettered power and authority once enjoyed by Wong-Kei.

And our work continued . . . and with each new assignment,

I grew in confidence and expertise. I became a pioneer of a new kind of criminal investigation. I was the master of computer systems which could describe and collate every character flaw and foible in even the most complex individual. I would study witness statements and learn the target's fears, his or her favourite fantasy during masturbation, the content of the websites the target had visited in the preceding ten years, the clothes the target wore, the target's love affairs and friendships and secret dreams and aspirations.

One of my favourite jobs involved the "virtual destruction" of an eminent merchant banker who for decades had been engaged in money laundering and the selling of stolen artworks. His name was Robert Roxborough.

Once again the team set forth to acquire all the information we needed. Michiyo and Tosh went to work in an art gallery owned by a Portuguese philanthropist called Ramon. Phone taps were placed on all of Roxborough's employees and families and the prostitutes he employed were astutely analysed and interrogated. And, after all of this, I put the information into my people matrix and came up with a strategy to destroy him. I quickly decided that Roxborough was too astute and well balanced to be mentally undermined in the way that Wong-Kei was. So I went for a more subliminal approach.

I arranged for every painting in Roxborough's private gallery to be smeared with the aroma taken from a dog's sweat gland, mixed with human sexual pheromones. Then, for ten solid weeks, I arranged for him to be followed every day by dogs super-saturated in the same aroma. Wherever he walked, the dogs followed. So he stopped going into parks and out into the streets, in order to avoid the dogs. But in his gallery too, the same stench in the back of his mouth stifled him. And yet, though it disgusted him, the smell made him rampantly horny. Every time he looked at a Poussin or Jackson Pollock or the work of some gifted new artist he was championing, he was overwhelmed with a sick sexual frenzy.

At the end of ten weeks, this sad specimen didn't know whether to fuck his paintings, or collect feral dogs.

And as a consequence, Roxborough developed a phobia for artworks of every form and description, and quietly resigned from the art-theft game.

Then I had his pocket picked; and in the lab, I planted a slow-release gland to disperse a different aroma onto the banknotes and credit cards he carried in his wallet. Then the wallet was restored to his pocket, less than twenty minutes later. The gland did its work; the faint but impossible-to-ignore smell seeped on to his money and credit cards. This particular stench was a brilliant concoction made out of putrefied maggots and mashed-up human corpse flesh. And so from this point on, Roxborough would associate money with decay and death.

Eventually, we had him arrested him for a series of offences – we had more than enough evidence stockpiled. But we kept the game going as long as we possibly could. Because punishing this man wasn't enough – first, we wanted to *spoil the bastard's fun.*

Then we moved our attention to the East. The Eastern European oligarchs were divided into four major factions, bonded by a common interest despite different ethnic backgrounds. They observed a strict truce interrupted by random assassinations. It was a flawed peace, but it worked.

So we raped a gangster's daughter.

The "rape" was, of course, a virtual one. The daughter's name was Anya; we paid her a million dollars to make up a story of being abused and raped by a dozen Russian gangsters. Then she quietly slipped to the West and made a new home in Minnesota.

Anya had in fact, according to the police medical report, been brutally sodomised over a number of years and had survived several bouts of gonorrhoea. This, we deduced, was a product of her father's wayward notions of child-rearing. But nonetheless, the father, Grigori Valentin, when told by his daughter of her gang rape, was deeply outraged at the insult to his first-born child. And when independent evidence came his way that the leader of Faction B had authorised and actually participated in Anya's rape, Valentin went ballistic. Gang war was declared. Most of the members of Faction B were bloodily assassinated.

Then Faction C received evidence that Valentin had been informing on them to the American FBI, and Valentin himself was brutally murdered.

After six months of bloody warfare, Faction D quietly stepped in to scoop up the spoils. By this time, however, our surveillance devices were planted deep, and we were able to build up a comprehensive case against Faction D. Mass arrests ensued and the age of gang oligarchy was over.

Thus, peace came to Eastern Europe. By the year 2055, democratic governments independent of organised crime were sweeping across the whole of Eastern Europe. Albania became a beacon of prosperity, famed for its nanotechnology and spell-binding modern architecture.

And Anya Valentin died at the age of 104, renowned as a school principal of deadly asperity and feared wit, admired and loved by generations of schoolchildren in the little Minnesotan town she had made her home.

I so vividly recall those squad-room days; and I still have audio tapes of the banter and the briefings which, in my later years with the squad, I downloaded every night from the microchip in my hearing aid. Hurly-Burly had a tender side, he was always very protective of me, and had the sweetest friendship with the stunningly unsociable and socially disconnected Blacks. Natasha was fierce, full of rages, but learned to treat me like a maiden aunt rather than as a sexual rival. (That woman was *such* a whore . . .)

And I remember Michiyo, at our office party, singing a cappella karaoke hits from the 1970s, with an unexpectedly powerful soul voice. I remember Rachel, the day she was shot in an abortive arrest attempt, laughing it off in her muttery casual way. She was back at work in two weeks; she used to love taking her trousers off to show off the scar on her left buttock. And there was Tosh, a borderline alcoholic who regularly forged interview transcripts which ended with the words, "At this point DI Greig battered the wee fecking suspect." Tosh had been suspended three times for tampering with official documentation, and each time he laughed loudly and long. Tosh was, I learned many years later, a bigamist; but both his wives were bitterly neglected. He spent his life in the office, with his team. That was his world.

I can conjure them all up with a simple thought-prompt, even without the aid of the audio tapes. I can feel their presence, their energy, their stupid scurrilous humour. And I can still vividly recall Tom making love to me, naked and panting, orgasming, whimpering, sleeping afterwards. Just with a thought, I can put him there again, even though it is . . . oh, so many years since we last met or spoke. He died, of a stroke, at the age of ninety-two. I didn't attend the funeral. I wasn't, by that point, attending funerals.

But while he lived, he had such *life*. Such zest. The stories he told . . . his effortless assumption that you would want to listen to whatever it was he wanted to say. His command of a room. "This is a really good story," he'd say calmly, and pause. And the room would hush until he was ready to tell it.

After five years the squad was disbanded, amid murmurs of disgrace and corruption. Tom was, of course, fabulously corrupt, and left the force a wealthy man. I resigned too and went to live with him in Dorking, England. Within six months we were driving each other insane. So I caught a plane to Florence, to swot up on my art history.

And it was there, in the Piazza Signoria, looking towards the loggia where the stone Perseus was lopping off the Gorgon's head, that I felt myself becoming overwhelmed. My breath rushed into my throat. I was hyperventilating. I was in pain. For a moment, I assumed it was Stendhal Syndrome, that I was simply overcome by too much joy.

The truth was more prosaic. I speed-dialled for an ambulance and a cardiac arrest kit. Then I hit the ground – hard. Paramedics were with me in minutes, and certified me clinically dead.

I was put on a life-support machine. The ventilator kept my brain alive, as my heart shuddered and spasmed. I had died, but now I was reborn.

And so began the next phase of my long long life.

I never wanted to live for ever.

But there's a good chance that I will.

Health has always fascinated me. Largely, I suppose, because of my lack of it. When I was five I had to wear glasses. When I was nineteen, I started to suffer from hearing loss, and from the age of thirty-one I was regularly using a hearing aid. And, of course, my skin was regularly subject to burning and scarring in the light of the sun.

So I tried to turn these weaknesses into advantages. After years of wearing chunky glasses, I was eventually able to purchase a pair of toric multi-function soft disposable contact lenses that fully corrected my vision. These were "smart" lenses, able to adjust on a daily and even hourly basis for the needs of the eye, and the environs. With these lenses, I could see perfectly at night; I could read fine print that was invisible to 99 per cent of people with 20-20 vision; my eyes were never dry or dusty; I could even, with some fiddling, amplify my vision to the level of a pair of cheap binoculars.

These lenses cost me almost six months' salary, but I felt it was worth it. Then, when my deafness got worse, I cajoled the university's medical insurance department into paying for me to have a pair of inner-ear hearing aids to replace the chunky clip-ons I'd originally been allocated. These sleek plastic tubes slipped easily into the ear itself, and moulded perfectly to the contours of my inner ear passage. Ever since they'd first been introduced – in the early years of the twenty-first century – these digital hearing aids were computer-adjusted and tailor-made to amplify only those frequencies that the wearer had difficulty hearing. So the sound quality was flawless. And, with some fine tuning, I was able to improve the accuracy of these hearing aids so that I could follow a conversation taking place at a table on the opposite side of a crowded restaurant. I could eavesdrop both sides of someone's mobile phone conversation. I could, literally, hear a pin drop.

Then, when the second edition of my book was published, sales went through the roof and my fortune doubled. It helped that I was now a semi-glamorous figure – a "consultant to the UN Police Authority". It helped, too, that by this time I had gained a few pounds – enough to stop me looking like a starved librarian – and changed my dress style. I'd become, almost, sexy; the book was a massive hit; and I became rich.

And I kept working on my gadgets. I was one of the first to improve the smart contact lens data-carrying capacity; and I was a pioneer of attempts to create wireless connections between remote computers and the smart lens's "brain". I did the same with the hearing aid. I purchased a massively expensive subvocaliser, which allowed me to access computer programs via signals sent from my earpiece – by simply articulating my requests subvocally.

And I worked out at the gym. I had my breasts non-surgically boosted – not excessively, just enough to give them a sensual curve and an exciting nipple flourish. I took a melatonin implant to shed the freckles, and acquired a pleasing all-year-long golden glow. During the last few years of working with Tom and the team, I was no longer a pale, skinny nerd – I was a sleek, bronzed, busty nerd. For me, the psychological difference was immense.

Then, after the squad disbanded, I had my heart attack; and when I recovered consciousness, I insisted on having a smart heart installed, instead of a biological pig's heart. The smart heart was made of bioplastic; it automatically regulated and monitored buildups of deposits in the arteries, and it had a phenomenal pump capacity.

Tom came to see me in the hospital – but capriciously, cruelly, I wanted nothing more to do with him. I could tell he was hurt – I could see the pain sag through his proud body. But I felt, you see, *different*. I was a new woman. Tom was a part of the old Lena; so I cut him out of my life.

And then, a few months after leaving hospital, I started training. I ran, I lifted weights, I did yoga to relax, I made my body my temple. Before long I became fit; then very fit; then frighteningly fit. With this new heart, I could run a mile in three minutes, and not be out of breath. My physical strength was increased twofold, because of the increased efficiency of oxygen flow in my muscles.

And with my new heart, I knew that I need never fear heart attacks or strokes. Microbe-sized ionised probes in my bloodstream were analysed each day by the heart, and any irregularities broadcast to a medical computer. Heart and artery problems could be solved long before they actually became problems.

The new heart cost me 2 million euros. I bankrupted myself to buy it. But then, of course, I wrote another book, based on my ideas about emergence, but now refocusing all these ideas into a self-help manual. Naturally, I wrote it just for the money; and it made *so* much money. The book was called *You Are God 2*, and it featured photographs of me clad in Lycra, outrunning athletes.

As a result, I became a sex goddess, and an internationally famous self-help guru, the ultimate Before and After Makeover Person.

With the money I made, I was able to fund my ongoing process of self-renewal. Some of the techniques I tried were quasi-experimental; I became a guinea pig for the Anti-Agers. And so, at the age of fifty, I had the body of a thirty-five-year-old. At the age of fifty-five, I looked like a thirty-year-old. And by the age of sixty-one I had the body of a gorgeous, hot, seductive twenty-five-year-old.

I became a founder member of the Nematode Society, devoted to promoting pioneering research into how to reverse the ageing process. The trick is to realise that ageing is not a natural process; *self-renewal* is the natural process. (Think of the skin, which sloughs off layers and then grows afresh every day of our lives.) But through a process of natural selection, which of course favours reproduction over survival, organisms have evolved mechanisms that hinder the self-renewal and regeneration of the cell. To put it another way: as human beings, we have "death genes" that program us to degenerate and die. It's Nature's method, if I may be whimsical, of clearing the garden to make way for new crops.

But if we isolate these genes, and replace them with cell-renewal genes – the Perpetuity genes, as they are now known – the body itself becomes able to regrow limbs and even brain cells. In a perfectly regulated Universe, I always idly thought to myself, the human being would be like a worm – so that if you cut a man in half, both halves would regrow into fully formed human beings . . .

In practice, it doesn't entirely work that way. If you lose a leg in an accident, it's much easier to buy a new one from a lab than to grow a new one of your own. There are sects that doggedly insist on doing things the Natural Way – they have ceremonies in which they lop off fingers and even arms and then wait decades for them to regrow. But, in our busy consumer-led world, it's easier by far to purchase over-the-counter limbs, eyes and ears than to, as it were, do it yourself.

But the Perpetuity gene still has a vital role to play; through a series of coded messages distributed throughout the body by RNA, the gene replenishes and regenerates internal organs, it eradicates cancer, and it keeps arteries clear.

It cures baldness in men too. And that, if I may say so, is *such* a boon.

To continue: I wasn't, of course, the only one to be taking advantage of anti-ageing technology. Many others were doing the same; my point here is, I was the first. Or at least, one of the first. One of the pioneers.

I am now nearly a thousand years old, subjective elapsed time. I *still* have the body of a gorgeous twenty-five-year-old. I am the third-oldest human being in the entire Universe. And the other two, trust me, look weathered and tired.

I'm the only one. The only one to be so old, and yet look and feel so *young*.

I created Heimdall.

But none of those fucking bastards ever properly acknowledged it.

It's the same old story. It happened to me in academic life time and again. When I reorganised the university library system, creating an online database of unique fluidity and versatility, I was thanked, curtly, for my administrative efforts. But the creative kudos all went to the head of IT. In the official history of the university, it was his name not mine that headed the folder on "IT Revolutions".

When I was at school, I always came second in History. Not because my essays lacked the necessary rigour or originality. It was because my nearest rival, Clarissa, had charisma and gorgeous hair and perfect skin. I once swapped one of my essays for one of Clarissa's, on line; and my essay with her name on it got a score fifteen points higher than my previous best.

Why is that? Why do some always get the credit, while others get downgraded? Do I have some special knack, some sign that says, "Undervalue me"? How come, to get back to the matter in hand, that in the history of the Heimdall virtual bridge, *I'm* the fucking Trotsky?

Not that I'm bitter.

I admit, of course, that the scientific groundwork for Heimdall was laid down by others. I'm not the Einstein, or the Dyson, or the Fermi, or the Lopez. I was, by that time, in my fourth or fifth major change of career, the elected President of Humanity. For nearly a hundred years I was the most powerful person in the Human Universe. I created peace, harmony, understanding.

And Heimdall.

Heimdall is, of course, a quantum artefact. Its essential principles relate to the well established concept that a quantum state in one part of the Universe can affect a quantum state in another part of the Universe, simultaneously and without any passage of time.

Scientists call it – I feel you flagging here but please, bear with me, this is the very structure and essence of the Universe we're talking about, so if you fail to grasp this paragraph you might as well be, frankly, pond slime, or a laboratory rat – the principle of wholeness, or entanglement. Which means that whenever two systems have at some previous moment interacted (or entangled), their description is tied together *no matter how far apart they may subsequently be*. And a datum that is true of the one system, will be true of the other system also.

But since all the Universe originated in a single near-infinitesimal singularity – in its pre-Big Bang golden idyll – every part of the Universe was at this very earliest moment entangled with every other part. And that connection persists, despite the subsequent expansion of the Universe. It's like twins separated at birth and raised in different countries, who remain empathetically or even telepathically connected.

And so quantum theory allows an amazing loophole to the law that says nothing can travel faster than light. The exception says that *information* can be conveyed instantaneously, whatever the distance involved, if it's information about a quantum state between two previously entangled quanta.

But to get any value out of this hallowed principle of physics, you have to be able to manipulate the quantum states on both sides. Not by much. You just need the difference between Quantum State A and Quantum State B. Which is the difference between 0 and 1. Which of course is the basis for a long-distance digitised computer connection, capable of communicating information instantaneously.

And so, once you have your two quantum state controllers in place . . . distances vanish. An email sent in Australia will reach Africa *the very instant it is sent*. It won't be quick, it won't be fast; there won't even be a millisecond of time elapsing. *It will be instant*. And so it becomes as easy to send an email from

Australia to Africa as it is to send one from London to *the other end of the galaxy*.

And thus, as a result of these discoveries, the Universal Web becomes possible. Video phone calls can be made between planets, without even a momentary delay. And all this is made possible by the "quantum state manipulation nano-computers" which were christened, by me, Quantum Beacons.

The snag is that there's a huge amount of work involved in setting up this means of communication. The near Beacon is always on Earth or in the Earth system, but the distant Beacons have to be literally flown through physical space to the desired remote location. In a metaphorical nutshell; the telephone wire has to be hooked up at *both ends*.

I was, I have to admit, one of the first to realise the great value and potential of all the decades of difficult theorising into the field of quantum communication. And I believe that the construction of Heimdall was the greatest accomplishment of my Presidency, tarnished only by the memory that the scientists and the explorers were given all the credit, whereas my role was . . . sorry, sorry, I should move on.

To continue:

In order to create Heimdall, a fleet of spacecraft was built. (This was before my time, I concede.) Each ship was massive, and constructed with total redundancy. Nanocomputers were installed to do the work; but every system had a backup, every backup had a backup. And each ship was crewed by five hundred potential space colonists, with a cargo of human sperm and every conceivable seed and animal embryo in deep store.

The first vessel in the fleet was called the *Mayflower*. Tragically, all five hundred crew members died in deep space, after a collision with a dark-matter tornado. This was a phenomenon we hadn't even known about until it killed the world's finest men and women. The names of those five hundred are engraved in a plaque in New York Plaza, and in my heart. And in the history books.

But even though the crew was dead, the computers carried on sailing the spaceship. On and on it went on its long journey. Using state-of-the-art fusion engines, it could reach speeds of almost two-thirds light speed.

After fifty years the *Mayflower* stopped. Its cargo of human embryos was unfrozen and carefully grown by robot nannies. Seeds were germinated and planted. A Quantum Beacon was built by the pre-programmed robots and nanobots. And, once it was installed, instantaneous messages could be transmitted between the *Mayflower* in its new home, and Earth.

And after that, vidphone and webcam links were created. Robots were then remotely built in humanoid form, complete with touch and olfactory sub-programs. We could now see everything the robots could see, and feel what they felt, the moment that they saw or felt it. Which means: *It's as if we were there ourselves*. Suddenly, space had shrunk . . . with the help of virtual technology, a citizen of Earth could find him or her self on an alien planet.

This first Quantum Beacon planet orbited a star which I named Asgard, after the home of the Norse Gods. And the virtual link that connected us was called Heimdall, after the Rainbow Bridge that connected Asgard with Earth.

And meanwhile, all the time, other colony ships were landing. Other Beacons were being built. And the map of space was filled with the dots of human settlements . . .

It took four hundred years for Heimdall to become the masterpiece it now is. Quantum Beacons are dotted across all of known space, and the virtual Rainbow Bridge that is Heimdall allows instant communications between all the regions of humanity.

And, all those years ago, actual control of the first space colonies was literally in my hands, and in my eyes. With the help of a virtual bodysuit connected to robot bodies on the colony planets, I could walk on alien soil. I could move tractors across arid plains. I could choose the music that played on the colony's intercom, I could devise menus for the children who I was growing there. I could do anything!

My focus in those early years was almost exclusively on the colonists of the Asgard star system. I named their planet Hope, and it became my joy. I studied them, and encouraged them, and help shape their society.

But I was at pains to be sure that the new colonists did not ever become resentful of their "master" in a faraway land. The settlers of Hope were my children, not my slaves. I became the perfect parent; all-seeing, all-protective, indulgent, and immune to insult.

And much to my delight, the new colony of Hope turned into a wild and dangerous place. It was the first civilisation in human history to have only one generation, grown from embryo by robots with unerring care. All the babies were babies together; they all went to kindergarten together; and they all graduated to primary school level together. And then they became teenagers together; they were thirteen together, they were fourteen together, they were fifteen together.

And thus, the children grew into adulthood. Every inhabitant of the new colony had the same birthday, the same emotional and mental age. And, knowing that the Quantum Beacon was a constant source of information and wealth, a virtual safety net, they ran riot together.

For five whole years the colony of Hope was a drug and sex and rock and roll Utopia. No useful work was done. Wild oats were sowed. The "accelerated maturity" process became a joke, as the colonists spent the years between fifteen and twenty either stoned or drunk or delirious with sex.

Well, good luck to them I thought. I myself, I must concede, had the dullest-ever teenagerdom. So, by proxy, I was now sowing my own wild oats. Through vidcam and virtual-reality links, I followed the lives of my children, I watched them get spaced out, I watched them fuck, I watched some of them play suicide games that tragically ended their infinitely promising lives. I watched, but I didn't meddle. I merely waited until my children grew into maturity.

And then I gave them independence. With independence came power; with power came a sense of responsibility. We still kept, through our robots and virtual-control programs, a grip on the mineral and energy wealth of the new colony. Solar panels orbiting Hope's sun pulsed energy that fuelled its space factories and telescopes. And spaceships travelling down the Beacon's path carried valuable raw materials back to Earth on a regular basis; the first cargoes took sixty years to arrive, but after than, a cargo ship arrived every three months . All this allowed us to run an Empire with infinite resources, infinite power.

On Earth, we had everything we could possibly desire. So why be greedy? Why dominate, why control, why bully? Why not let the children of Hope have their total freedom?

Why not?

Why fucking not?

BOOK 3

FLANAGAN

"There she is, five sectors off our port bow."

"I see her."

"She looks ripe, Cap'n."

"Fire the flag."

We shoot a flare into space. It unfurls and creates a holographic skull and crossbones. Our way of saying: let's do this the easy way, guys, *or else*.

The merchant ship begins to tack. At the same time, a flotilla of missiles is dispatched towards us.

"Fire the microwarships."

We fire a cluster of metal ants into space, creating a wall of chaff that sends relentless interference patterns into the path of the missiles' guidance systems. One by one the enemy missiles explode, well short of our ship.

"Prepare to engage the grapples."

"We're prepared," says Brandon.

"Well fucking well engage them then."

"We're too far away."

"Ah."

"I'm ready to accelerate into position, Cap'n, if you're minded to give that command."

"I took it as read. Accelerate into position, Harry."

"Aye aye Cap'n."

We accelerate into position.

"You humansss should sssuit up, perhaps?"

"Indeed. Suit up, people."

"Your leadership leaves a great deal to be desired Cap'n."

"Less of the insubordination or I'll clap you in irons."

"Ironssssss?"

"Fire our warning shot."

Harry fires a missile. It ploughs straight through the debris of their wrecked missile defence systems, and crashes through the bow of the merchant ship.

"*That* was a warning shot?"

"It must have been caught by the wind," Kalen says, snidely. "Engage grapples."

Two roboships are sent hurtling from our main vessel and they land with an inaudible smash on the surface of the merchant ship. The magno-grapples are switched on automatically, pinning them against the hull, and they then engage with reverse polarity the magnets on our ship. Thus, the merchant ship is locked solidly on to us, unable to move.

A sealed polytunnel unfurls along the length of the magnetic arm that links ship to ship. We are all swiftly suiting up, apart from Alby, who merely flares a little more vividly.

Jamie stays on the bridge, ordering up doughnuts and Coke from the ship's dispenser, as my pirate crew assembles and enters the airlock.

We are swept downwards along an invisible magnetic tunnel. We use blasters to crack open the hull. And then we are inside.

Robot guns fire at us as we come rolling through. Alliea has an eagle eye for such devices and pops them with lightning-fast laser blasts as we all run. Bullets rain on my body armour but none penetrate. We blow up a connecting door and emerge to find suited beetles preparing to shoot us.

Before they can fire Alliea leaps up and sweeps a nanonet over them, stifling their air supply, coating them with a spider's-web lattice of diamond-hard fibre. Then she yanks and tugs and knocks them off balance. At the same time, Harry and I are blasting them with stun and flare blasts. We duck and weave away from bullets, capitalising on the fact that these security warriors are trained to shoot accurately, not fast, and don't know how to move their guns into position in the blink of an eye. Their every shot is telegraphed, and we duck and roll and effortlessly avoid their fusillades. Then I plunge needles through black body armour and feel the humans inside slump into unconsciousness.

We enter the bridge. The rest of the crew surrenders to us. Only the Captain is defiant. I lay down my blaster, and courteously beg him to give up and unlock the ship's security network. He refuses, and before he has finished his sentence, I have spring-loaded the scimitar I wear strapped to my thigh, then I unpop its blade and swipe.

His head falls from his shoulders. The crew are entirely stunned. I pick up the head and brandish it before them. Living proof that I am a barbarian.

For I *am* a barbarian.

Only one other crew member possesses the code to unlock the ship's security lattice, liberating all the treasures of that cargo. The identity of that crew member is a dark and deeply kept secret. So I lop off the purser's head. Two heads, two deaths, and the rest follows easily. The crew key-holder surrenders himself, the cargo is unlocked.

We have our treasure. Wooden furniture, carved metal artworks, electronics, flyboards, and designer clothing. Worthless to us, but worth a small fortune when we sell it back to the manufacturers.

I exalt. I triumph.

And I feel the taste of blood in my nostrils and my pulse surges.

LENA

On my cabin cctv, I watch the progress of the battle. I stare with horror as I see Flanagan behead two people.

Who is this man?

I feel contempt and rage for him. After what they did to me, I shouldn't be shocked, but I am. And I give myself a silent warning: I must never, ever, trust these evil bastards. Flanagan and his pirates are strangers to humanity; they have embraced a creed of total ruthlessness.

I hate them, and I fear them.

I am afraid.

FLANAGAN

"You're very quiet, Lena."

"I'm savouring my food."

"It's fresh *foie gras*. We found a case of it in the cargo hold."

"You killed all those people. For foie gras?"

"It's a Corporation merchant ship. It's fair game. Don't glare at me like that, Lena, it's . . ."

"Whatever you say, Captain Flanagan. There, I'm looking at you nicely now."

"You hate me, don't you?"

"For what you have done, you have forfeited your right to life."

"Ah, phooey."

She eats. I hide my grin.

Yes, I'm a barbarian. At least she knows now.

ALBY

We are clossse to my home. My flame burnsss brighter.

FLANAGAN

Alby is flickering and flashing like a wild fire. I can't tell if he's excited and emotional with homesickness, or if he's masturbating.

Alby is my dearest friend, however strange that seems. He is weird, unfathomable, terrifying to be with, but useful if you have a tobacco habit and need a light. He is also the only member of my crew who likes my jokes. (However this may be because, as an alien, he doesn't know any better.)

And now we're approaching his home – the vast and glorious artificial sun called >X\=I=x/>\Ix⌶s =N כzJ⊥\\ ⋈=/=I\J, known to humans as Flare. This is the home of the flame beasts, created by them after these energy-eating ravening sentient plasma-flame entities had devoured their own sun. Their new home of Flare is a star larger than most solar systems. In the process of creating it, the flame beasts are estimated to have eliminated 4,556,767,699 species of life, including twelve possible-sentient species. This was not from malice but from oversight; at that time, it hadn't occurred to the flame beasts that planets could be anything other than fuel.

The flame beasts are an immensely powerful species. They cannot be attacked, invaded or intimidated, and any attempt to declare war on them would be futile. To bomb or fusion-blast them would be like throwing fingers to a hungry lion. They are immune to all disease, and cannot be affected by any poison or micro-organism.

They do have their own natural processes of decay and death, which are poorly understood. But essentially, the flame beasts are unkillable, and infinitely gifted. Every flame beast can speak every human language. And every flame beast is familiar with every detail of what happened in every century, every year and every month of human history. The flame beasts speak Mandarin Chinese and the click language Xhosa without impediment; in every other human language they have the characteristic flame-beast sibilance.

And yet, it seems, there is much that humanity can teach these beings. For the tragedy of the flame beasts is that for millions of years they have existed in a state of tedious stasis. Ennui, despair and inertia enveloped them. But since their first contact with humanity the entire species has been invigorated, and the flames have had a new lease of life.

And this is because, from human beings, the flame beasts have learned all about art, ballet, drama, opera, classical music, popular music, pyrotechnics . . . and soap opera. The last of these arenas of human endeavour has, to the astonishment of many academics and scientists, proved the most addictive of all. The community of flame beasts has become an avid devourer of the great and prolific long form drama output of the human colonies. They are passionate, knowledgeable and completely besotted with the folly and the stupidity of human nature, as exemplified in shows such as *The Magellan Girls*, *Paxos: The Early Years*, *Martin Devonzi and His Marvellous Amazing Family*, and a myriad others.

And so, as part of my barter, I come armed with a disc containing 400 hours of *Argon*, a sophisticated, sexy and often hilarious soap opera about a world in which time is lived backwards. The sex scenes are, trust me, to die for.

It's time. I suit up, and join Alby in the airlock. We exit on the lee side of the ship, using the hull as a sunshield to protect us from the impossible glare of the giant sun. We are soon joined by a delegation of flame beasts, who arrive in the form of a series of shooting stars. The stars become sparkles, which explode into a series of multi-coloured supernovae. The sky crackles and explodes with colours and swirling fiery shapes.

Then the lights become a cloud, and the cloud becomes a

complex pattern of light flashes. I can follow some of what the flame beasts are saying. I know that a small flash followed by a large flash followed by a small flash oOo implies negativity. I know that a shimmering series of complexly patterned flashes alternating at the rate of 0.01 seconds per flicker denotes scepticism merged with irony with an undertow of courtesy, thus:

z ⋉ L s//L ϧvNↃ/I zXL s/vI≐≐J ⸌//ZIs ⌶
Ↄ ⋉ X⸌\I= ⅂ ⋉ ⸌⸌J⅂sIsXvJ

(and so on, and so forth.)

But as for the actual content of the flame-beast language – that is beyond any human comprehension. It is clearly some kind of binary or trinary code, but no human-built computer has ever been able to crack it.

"What do they say?" I ask Alby.

"They agree to the barter," Alby tells me. "They will retain Lena as their prisssoner under the sssupervision of a Flare Elder, namely myssself. In return they accept your gift of drama offeringsss, but they also ask you to particccipate in a long-term training programme for our ssspecies in the hisstory, technique and ssstylisssstic philossssophy of the music known as bluessss and boogie-woogie."

"That's not possible!" I exclaim, startled.

"It'sss a prerequisssite. Your expertissse precedesss you."

"Then . . . I'll do my best."

"If you betray the bargain in any way, my people pledge a blood feud and will destroy you, your crew members, your family and your descendants in a methodical way for a period of one hundred human years."

"Fair."

"I feel a pang. I yearn to be with my kind."

"Will you stay?"

"Perhapssss."

"We need you."

"I know."

The sky explodes again, with light and beauty.

Alby laughs with joy. And I shudder, for his laughter is like the sound of snakes sliding down your oesophagus, and mating in your colon.

FLANAGAN

I strum a chord. Gently, letting the notes hang in the air like whisky on the palate. We are in the ship's situation room, the acoustics are better in here.

"What's the matter at the mill?" I say to Alby.

"What'sss the matter at the mill?" he repeats patiently.

"I got corn to grind. But I cain't," I tell him.

"And why iss that?" he asks me, intrigued.

"'Cause the mill's done broke down."

"The mill hasss done broke down?" Bafflement suffuses Alby's every syllable.

I strum another chord, and sing gently:

"I got some corn
And I put in a sack
Johnny went to the mill
But he come right back.
What's the matter at the mill?"

"That's when you come in," I tell Alby.

"What'sss the matter at the mill?"

"No that's my line. Your line is: '*It's done broke down.*'"

ALBY: *"It'sss done broke down."*
ME: *"What's the matter at the mill?"*
ALBY: *"It'sss done broke down."*
ME: *"Well people are a talking all over town*
Telling me that the mill done broke down.
I cain't get no grinding.
'Cause the mill's done broke down."
US: *"What's the matter at the mill?*
"It's done broke down.
"What's the matter at the mill?
"It's done broke down.
"Tell me what's the matter at the mill?"

I feel a haunting pang as our voices merge. Alby's natural tones have modulated into a rich, evocative bluesy groan. I strum my acoustic guitar loudly, crudely, simply, from the heart.

In Alby's world, of course, there is no such thing as ground corn. There are no mills. There is only energy and fusion and an eternal flickering flame. But I know that once, just once, in the history of his people, disaster struck. The flame beasts' native sun was fatally depleted. Their sun broke down. It is their only significant piece of history, their only natural disaster.

I bathe in the light and heat of my best and least likely friend, this mercurial, pedantic, infinitely loyal walking ball of fire. I segue into a wild, angry, sad guitar break, and then Alby chips in with his own bold improvisation:

"What'ssss the matter with the sun?
It'sss done broke down.
What'ssss the matter with the ssssun?
It'sss done broke down.
I can't get no /NI≐J//xI-I¤x ≐NɔzJ⊥⊥
Tell me what'sss the matter with the sssun!"

LENA

Harry and Jamie challenge me to a poker game. I spurn them initially, but then begin to weaken. I am getting bored of my state of captivity.

"But no card counting," Jamie warns me. "We know you have that remote computer in your head. But that's against the rules. We play the old-fashioned way."

I smile and accept the challenge.

I don't need a computer. I am, innately, a brilliant card counter. Ha! This new generation, they're used to having surgically implanted computer chips to help them with their calculations. But I grew up in an era where we learned mental arithmetic in school. I was taught my times tables! And I have a naturally retentive mind.

So even now, after all this time, despite a few lapses, I can control my memory like a fluid supple living thing. I can choose to forget whole swathes of past, keeping only the record of them in my computer data chips. But when I want to recall a fact, it will appear immediately, without hesitation. It is a skill that has allowed me to retain clarity through all these hundreds of years.

And I am bound to win this game, of course, because these two are so easy to read. Jamie is a man in the body of a child, but he has nonetheless the *soul* of a child. He is over a hundred years old, but chose to have his puberty retarded in order to retain that precious, special clarity which only young children have. As a result, Jamie thinks more intensely than others, he feels more intensely. But he is frozen at the cusp of manhood, able to dream and desire, unable to deliver. It makes him edgy, dangerous, and desperate.

With Harry it's different of course. If I were naked and

raging, with unwaxed hairy legs, and with my arse sticking up in the air, then *maybe*, just maybe, he might regard me as a female of the species. But in my present beautiful, perfumed, civilised state – no chance. Harry is a Loper through and through. He was banished from the community of Lopers for eating his own father (an act of barbarity that is so typical of these lower types.) But though he is forced to belong to the world of humans, Harry is more wolf than man; more pack animal than team player. His humanity is just a façade he assumes.

Flanagan is oblivious to all this. But I can smell it on Harry. I know that he would long to devour his Captain, to eat him limb by limb and bite up his eyes, and to savour with his last bite the desperate death rattle in Flanagan's quivering larynx.

So I have no sexual power over Harry, but I can smell his every emotion, almost his every thought.

"Raise you five, see you five."

"I'll see you five and raise you another ten."

I win, and win again. At the end of the game, both Jamie and Harry are looking sheepish. Then I get a sudden whiff of something from Harry. An emotion I haven't felt from him before. I glance at Jamie – and catch the same emotion in his eyes.

Pity.

"We're surrendering you to the custody of the flame beasts," Harry explains. "They will guarantee your safety. When the ransom is paid, you will return safely to civilisation."

He's lying. I can't smell it now, but I just know it. Why else would he be looking at me so kindly? Why else . . . ?

With a sudden surge of horror, I realise the ghastly truth. They let me win.

I could have told you that, if you'd only asked.

"Shut the fuck up!" I scream at the voice in my head. Then I realise I have spoken it aloud. Jamie and Harry look at me kindly. The boy and the beast.

They have been humouring me. Because they know I'm doomed. These two sad, pathetic specimens are being nice to me, because they feel sorry for me.

I stifle a sob.

FLANAGAN

I dine with our prisoner, the cold and beautiful Lena.

I notice some interesting things. She's fussy with her food. She talks to herself, without realising what she is doing, though that may simply be her way of communicating with her remote computer. She drinks large schooners of sherry, and even larger glasses of red wine. She picks at her food. She farts openly, without any attempt at concealment. She is taciturn, never asks questions. But when she does speak, she's appallingly garrulous. She regaled me for several hours with stories of her time as a crime fighter in ancient Earth. A man called Tom featured frequently. The stories were rambling, but fascinating. But my, she did go on.

She is very opinionated, about everything. Society has decayed. Courtesy is a forgotten art. Television has gone downhill. Young men lack sexual charisma, they are just "boys" now, in her eyes. When she pours herself a glass of wine, it doesn't occur to her to pour me a glass. At one point, she falls asleep when I am talking. I am halfway through a sentence, and she damn well cat-naps off. Then she wakes, farts briefly, and continues with one of her stories from half an hour previously.

She is, in short, *old*. Everything about her, apart from her sleek and sexual body and her shimmeringly wonderful face, exudes withered and arid age. She's selfish, self-contained, cautious, cowardly, bigoted, small-minded, self-pitying, spoiled, self-indulgent, arrogant, uninterested in the feelings of others.

Was she always like this? I can't tell. But I do know that she has wrapped herself in so many comfort blankets that she can no longer feel the air around her. She is cocooned.

I try to explain the reasons behind my course of action in kidnapping her. My ideals, my political imperative. She mocks me mercilessly at this point.

"You're just a pirate," she tells me. "A savage!"

"I'm a soldier of fortune," I reply mildly.

"You're a butcher. You let that beast maul and bite me, for the sake of a grisly display to intimidate my son. And I saw what you did earlier, on the merchant ship." Her bitter words hang in the air. "I saw you behead two men!"

"Hey! I'm a pirate."

"You're a terrorist."

"Whatever."

"You have no remorse."

"Neither do you."

"I don't kill people."

"No, but your people kill people. They slaughter entire races. They incinerate planets. They enslave large sections of humanity."

"Oh, this is just socialist rant."

"Your son presides over the most evil dictatorship in human history."

"That's an appalling exaggeration."

"He's a monster."

She pauses, momentarily flustered. Then she says: "I'm his mother, not his keeper." It sounds lame, and she can't help wincing at her own words.

"Do you deny the internment without trial?" I say angrily. "The torture and humiliation of innocent people singled out because of their race and creed? Do you deny the Cheo's government is corrupt, exploitative and ruthless?"

"I deny none of this! But it's not for me to defend my son."

"But he's your *son*. You could at least . . ."

"What? Tell him off?"

I am seized with an appalling homicidal rage, and I rein myself in. Not now, not here, not like this . . . I force a smile. Then, in icily measured tones I tell her: "My people have suffered for centuries. But we will endure and we will survive and we will find our Promised Land."

She blinks for a few moments.

"You're a Christian?" she asks me.

"I'm a Humanist Atheist," I reply. "But I still believe in the possibility of a better future."

"You're full of lies," she snarls. "You're just a very successful thief. I don't buy this freedom-fighter bullshit."

"I can be both! A thief and a champion of justice!"

"A butcher, and a beheader of innocents!"

"In war such things must happen!"

"In peace, such things must happen too. That is why my son is so severe!"

"The Cheo is an animal."

"He is a leader. He leads. The universe of humanity follows. His way is brutal, yes. But given the restrictions imposed by the vast distances of space, and the fragmented and self-destructive nature of humankind, and, and, and . . . the xenobiological threats which jeopardise our very survival – how could it be otherwise . . . ?"

Our angry words hang in the air, like mist on a summer's morning.

"I've enjoyed this quarrel."

"So have I."

"Even though you're wrong."

"Oh fuck off!"

"Fuck off yourself, bitch!!!!"

"You blame me for everything." Suddenly, the ice maiden Lena is in tears. "Why is that? Why am I always blamed for everything?"

"You gave birth to a monster. For that, you stand condemned."

FLANAGAN

My home planet of Cambria is a warm and green and beautiful land. Originally, it had been an arid ball with a high oxygen content and vast reserves of frozen water. But accelerated terraforming melted the water, mixed the oxygen with carbon dioxide, and liberated the vast fertility of the lands. Low rolling hills cover most of my homeland, interwoven with a complex latticework of rivers and lakes. There are no seas, no oceans, just fertile land and rich Earth-born vegetation.

The factories of Cambria are contained underground, in vast caverns transformed into slave repositories and workplaces. The masters of the planet – the DRs – inhabit the green and fertile land of Cambria. And the humans live beneath the earth, in flickering artificial semi-light. And that is where I lived, as a child, and where I worked too.

Our work was skilled. We created hand-carved furniture for the DRs to enjoy. We wove clothes for the DRs to wear. And we formed vast conveyor lines of people to assemble DR artefacts – music players, cars, airplanes, flyboards, personal computers and mobile phones. The components were all precision-created by machines which we serviced and tended. But it was cheaper and easier for humans to slot the individual components together into their wholes, than to build a machine to do it.

My father was a Surface Human, and every day he joined an army of workers who trooped up to the surface to maintain the perfect idyll that was Cambria. Some were gardeners, some pruned trees, some tended and fed the wild animals. There were vast vineyards covering Cambria, and some workers had the vital task of picking these grapes and treading them in the old-fashioned way with their feet to turn the grape juice into wine.

Other humans tended the olive trees, the apple and orange trees, the potato fields. Some grew marrows and courgettes. Some created exotic hybrid fruit and vegetables.

Some, the privileged few, were Chefs, responsible for cooking and preparing by hand magnificent meals for the frequent DR banquets. Some were Waiters, some were Bartenders. But every night, the Surface Humans retired to their underground cavern homes, where they rejoined their families and participated in the human community we called True Cambria.

It wasn't a bad life, by and large. The underground caverns were a natural formation, caused by extreme volcanic action, and they formed a subterranean subworld that stretched beneath the entire planet. The caverns were often vast, and the rock formations were extraordinary. This was my playground as a child. We played hide and seek, we played football, we swam in underground lakes. Children were never taken to the surface, so we never knew what we were missing. But I often think that given a choice between an underground cave and a field in sunlight – I would have chosen the cave. There was something magical and hidden about the world we lived in.

And we had creature comforts too. We had food, plenty of water, alcohol when we needed it. We grew our own crops. We tended herds of animals. We wrote novels and poems and performed dramas for each other. But we had no knowledge of science, an entirely warped and blinkered version of our own history, and no concept of the methodology and principles of Quantum Beacon interstellar communication. Some intellectuals argued that, in fact, the community of Humans stretched across large portions of the Home Galaxy; and that humans were the dominant species in space. But we found that hard to believe. DRs were, to us, our gods.

Yet as a child, I never fully understood what a DR really was. Not, that is, until my first Summer Fair.

My sister Sheena and I were chosen to go together. She was sixteen, I was seventeen. She was a beautiful child; and I was a fit, handsome, arrogant young man. We felt proud to be selected for the Fair. I knew of course that sex was involved. But I was not a virgin, and neither was Sheena. We were prepared and willing and hungry for new experiences.

I still remember the tingle of anticipation as the elevator took us up to the surface. We were given goggles to wear to protect us from the sunlight. But even so, when we took our first steps into the outside world, we were dazzled by the blazing light. Slowly our vision corrected itself, and we began, even through the goggles, to see the colours and richness of the land. The blazing yellow sun, the green fields, the brown bark of the trees, the pink and purple flowers, the blue lakes and streams and rivers.

A city of tents had been created as the site for the annual Summer Fair festivities. Human dancers and singers performed on stage. There were fairground stalls, a rollercoaster, a man with knives showing off his throwing skills. Sheena and I paused to watch. Volunteers stepped forward from the audience to join in this amazing show. A beautiful young woman with blonde hair stood in front of a board, arms outstretched. And a drum rolled. And the knife thrower stood proud, and drew a knife from his belt, and held the blade in the fingers of his right hand. Then he threw.

The silver blade arced through the air, not a breath emerged from the hushed crowd . . .

And the knife landed safely in the board, next to her head. Then the next knife was thrown, and hit the board on the other side of her head. Another went under her arm. Another knife caught her hair and pinned it to the wood. And another knife flew . . . and another . . . splintering wood with terrifying force and missing flesh by centimetres. The knife thrower's aim was remarkable; the girl was entirely unhurt. A cheer went up.

I could smell toffee apples and hot cider. I fet a surge of joy at the heat of the sun. I took off my goggles, and blinked, and by now was able to see in the clear daylight.

Then a DR arrived, amazingly tall, powerfully muscled, silver-skinned, calmly authoritative. He took the knives from the knife man and prepared to show off his own skill.

Within seconds six knives had been thrown, each of them perfectly on target. Three knives sank into the board just to the left of the young woman's throat. Three went to the right of her throat. The knives were so close they grazed her skin. The woman shuddered, and laughed. "Someone else have a go!" she cried.

But instead, the DR took up another set of knives. And, carelessly, casually, he threw. He put the first knife in the young woman's left eye. The second went into her right eye. Then the third knife in her left breast, the fourth knife in her right breast. The fifth knife went in her mouth, buried to the hilt. Then the DR threw the sixth and final knife high up into the air, and walked away laughing. Five or six seconds later, the knife landed in the earth, shuddering from the impact.

The woman was still alive, and groaning faintly. She was prised free, and she fell to the ground, bleeding. Spectators picked her up and laid her down. No one uttered a word of complaint. The woman bled to death, there on the grass. No one moved her body. Eventually, it almost seemed natural that there should be a dead blonde woman lying there, as the festival continued around her.

I was beginning to get the idea. We, the humans, were not the audience for this day's events. We were the *show*.

A strange numbness came upon me at that moment. It wasn't the horror of the woman's death that appalled me. It was the crowd's reaction. The murder was treated as normal, natural, not something to make a fuss about. As natural as flies shitting.

As the day continued, I saw death, mutilation, rape, and a million horrors. The DRs, I discovered, differed in their preferences. Some liked sex, some preferred torture and murder. Sex was obviously the best available option for us humans, though that too carried risks. After a few hours, I was forced to sexually indulge a DR – and I was stunned and shocked when I saw the size and length of his silver-skinned penis. He obliged me to fellate him and I almost choked.

Later, I was forced to have sex with my sister Sheena. I wanted to run or fight, but she begged me not to. Compliance seemed the safest option; we all clung to the hope that though some might die, the rest of us might survive.

But not Sheena. After I tried, pathetically and unsuccessfully, to fuck her, she was beaten to death in front of me. That is perhaps, in the course of my entire life, my darkest memory. As she died, she whispered to me, "Good luck." As she lay dying, she willed for me to live.

My luck *was* in fact good. I was handsome, but not handsome enough. Striking, but not sublime. The best and most beautiful of my playfellows ended up dead or mutilated at the end of this week-long festival. I survived, scared and horrified, but with my strength and body intact.

And, in the months that followed, I wondered what would happen if we fought back? There were millions upon millions of humans living in the caverns. And yet the best estimates were that there were no more than half a million DRs in all. Could we storm them? Fight them?

This is when I began to seriously study the nature of our master race. I read stories of human rebellions on Cambria, all of which were easily crushed. I learned the origin of the DRs, and the reason for their effortless superiority.

And I learned that the men and women who murdered and violated my sister and so many of my friends could not ever be killed by me. I could not take revenge, I could not hurt them.

Because those men and women did not inhabit my planet. They lived far far away, many thousands of millions of miles away, on Earth or one of its neighbouring planets.

And the creatures we believed to be our masters, the DRs, were merely artefacts – robot bodies of limited sentience which were controlled remotely by the men and women on Earth at their computer consoles.

The DRs – Doppelganger Robots – are built out of pseudo-flesh synthetic substances, and skilfully configured so that their skin and bodies are sensitive to taste, smell, touch and pain. But their bodies are no more than receptacles for sensation. Their minds are those of Earth humans wearing a virtual helmet with hands wrapped in metal gloves, able to remotely control their robot bodies and feel what they do, see what they see.

In default settings the DRs' robot intelligence can perform basic functions such as issuing orders, monitoring the work done by humans, and maintaining economic and agricultural systems. As a result the planet can function smoothly without the presence of the controlling Earth human intellects. Most DRs are in fact only inhabited by a human presence for four or six hours a day. Some are just weekend presences; others use their DRs as holiday recreation. After a tiring week at the office a stressed Earth human executive can strap on his virtual helmet . . . and enter a whole new world.

For the grim truth is that Cambria is not strictly speaking a colony for human beings. It was, and still is, a theme planet, on which Cambrians are bred for their entertainment value, and where bored Earth humans can fulfil their wildest fantasies. As DRs, they possess an all-powerful and perfect body, which can be male or female according to their whim of that day. They have grace, beauty, phenomenal sexual appetites, and they have access to fresh wine, sunshine, green fields, the best organic foods, slave chefs, and an endless supply of human beings to be raped or tortured or, in some cases, befriended.

This is Cambria, my home planet. This is my history, my legacy.

This is why hate defines me.

This is why I am what I am. Michael Flanagan, citizen of Cambria, pirate chief.

LENA

I am surrounded by flame. It's really quite eerie.

Alby tries to be charming, and courteously insists on treating me as a guest rather than as a hostage. In reality, of course, I am not free to leave, and I live in constant fear. And he is, actually, let's face it, remarkably dull. And pedantic. And over-knowledgeable. And pompous. And excessively flickery. And over-inclined to disagree with my opinions, even when I'm totally right.

And yet, to be fair to this poor, socially dysfunctional, personality-challenged, abhorrently weird and alien flame monster, he does laugh at all my jokes. And there is also, I have to admit, though I hate to do so, something beguiling about this time we spend together. We dine, we converse, we reminisce, we have fierce debates about politics and art and television drama. We are like some old married couple settled in domesticity, while living in a space station that orbits a sun that is infested by sentient flames.

My grandfather once showed me his first typewriter. It was an Olivetti, and you had to really bang the keys to get the little metal arms to fly up and hit the paper and leave a mark. The ribbon was blue on top and red on the bottom; if you were technologically competent enough, you could swap from blue ribbon to red ribbon and have a multi-coloured text. Lord only knows why. Oh, and yes, I remember the way you corrected mistakes! If you wanted to delete something you literally painted the page with white goo, then let it dry, then typed over it. Or you stuck a little piece of white paper over the typing paper and tapped the same key as the letter you wanted to delete, so that the letter was replaced by a white replica which was the same colour as the typing paper, and hence, invisible. {God, that's a bit hard to follow. And I worry my style is too informal – can you amend that last paragraph, deleting all the "yous" and substituting "ones"?}

{No, on second thoughts, don't bother, it looks more spontaneous if I leave in the occasional grammatical solecism, don't you think?}

I think that you . . .

Hush, you mar my flow; as I was saying: That machine, my grandfather's manual typewriter with its blue and red ribbon, is a vivid memory from my childhood that is seared into my brain. It was cutting-edge technology *then*. Now, I have a computer chip in my brain, and I am talking to a fire.

And the mystery is, why it doesn't all feel stranger? How do we come to take these things for granted? For tens of thousands of years human beings whittled tools and farmed soil and ate animals. And now there are people who have themselves bioengineered so that their excrement emerges from their anus ready-wrapped in polythene. Such people have achieved the ultimate in human evolution; their shit does not stink.

How can I possibly stay sane, knowing a thing like that?

But, I suppose, the hardest thing to bear is when remarkable things *don't* happen. If you are, for instance, a prehistoric human tending your field and you are never visited by beings from outer space, and never have a vision of a god, and are incapable of telepathy or telekinesis, and cannot see ghosts, and nothing ever changes for you, day after day after day . . . then that really would be strange. A life without magic; a life without wonder.

And, I must confess, a really odd thing has happened to me. I have become reconciled to my life of imprisonment. I have become used to being a bargaining chip. And I am confident that my beloved son Peter will pay the ransom and save his mother from this living Hell.

So life is good.

I sit down to dinner one night. As always, Alby sits with me, chatting, keeping me company. He doesn't eat, he doesn't drink, but as a dinner companion, I've had much worse.

Then the door opens and a woman walks in. She glides calmly forward, sits down, picks up *my* glass of wine and drinks from it. Then she looks at me.

I reach out. And I touch her face. I touch her breasts. I put my fingers in her mouth. She accepts all this. She smiles. "Will I do?" she asks Alby. He flickers, and I can sense his admiration, his pride, at the sight of this strikingly beautiful woman. But I, I am lost for words.

For she is me. The woman is me.

FLANAGAN

I am training with Alliea and Brandon. I do a star jump, touch the ceiling, Alliea fires a stun gun which hits me in the chest, and I fall like a stone, but recover and land on my feet. And then I do another star jump.

One! Two! Three! Four! Five! star jumps, each one accompanied by a direct stun blast in the upper body. Five of these and I'm ready to die.

Alliea is a good forty years younger than me – she's fifty-six. She's kept herself in great shape and has had her face, hips, vagina, teeth and spinal column replaced. She's like whipcord, and she never seems to get tired. I, by contrast, am starting to feel my age. I get aches and pains in my old bones, and I have trouble getting out of bed in the mornings. And my hair and beard are grey – I've never opted to have them re-vivified. As a result, I look and sound like a grizzled old-timer, and I like it that way. It gives me, I feel, a certain gravitas.

My legs, however, are brand-new, state-of-the-art, and

genetically enhanced. Hence the star jumps. I have extraordinary power, when it comes to jumping high, and running away.

Brandon puts on his boxing gloves and we step in the ring. We trade a few punches then he comes at me fast and furious. My punches have power, but I can't throw so many of them. He wears me down with sheer dogged persistence. Eventually I throw in the towel. Enough is enough.

Alliea steps in the ring, and she and Brandon box. Alliea, of course, trained with Rob. She's a boxing artist. She wipes the floor with my hapless astrophysicist. At the end of the bout, Brandon's jaw is hanging loose, and his nose is broken. He bears the pain with equanimity. But I know it will take him several days under the autodoc to heal these injuries.

I start lifting weights. It's crude, but for sheer power nothing can replace free weights. But I vary the workout to prevent muscle-boundness. I lift two hundred kilos of weights on a barbell up on to my shoulders; then I shrug and throw the barbell in the air. Then I wait patiently, looking straight ahead, and catch it as it falls, *hard,* on my shoulders. It feels as if the roof has crashed in. Great training for storming a ship, or taking a blaster shot directly on the body armour.

Hup, throw, wait, CRASH. Hup, throw, wait, CRASH.

Alliea picks up a sword and tries to cut off Brandon's head. His head bobs and weaves, he ducks and kinks, as he brilliantly eludes the sword's sharp blade. It's great speed training, but it's dangerous. Once, in a training session, Brandon's head was cut clean off. He claims you can still see the scar on his throat where the head was sewn back on . . . But of course, he's just being fanciful. The stitches are micro-sewn, and quite invisible to the naked eye.

Then we shower together. We're all too old, too seasoned, to have any shyness about communal bathing or showering. But there's no sexual element to it. Brandon is predominantly homosexual, and finds his sexual pleasures on week long binges in the Free Ports. And Alliea is still in mourning for Rob; the possibility of me sexually desiring her or her sexually desiring me would be an affront to etiquette.

And as for me – well, I'm a gnarly old man with scars up and down my body and grey pubic hair. No one on the ship regards me as a sexual being any more. And, goddamn it, it's been at least two years since I had a decent fuck. So maybe they're right to write me out of the equation.

I find it comforting, to be naked with people I love. People I care for. People I would be happy to die for.

My people.

FLANAGAN

We arrive at the drop point a week early. It's obvious that the Cheo will try and ambush us, so we make our preparations accordingly.

We hollow out an asteroid and fill it with explosives.

We place holographic projectors on floating satellites, too small to be visible to the enemy's surveillance 'bots.

We charge our laser cannons. We sow space with nanobombs. We gird on our body armour. And we wait.

He doesn't show.

FLANAGAN

We send another ransom email. The Cheo responds promptly, offering less money. He reminds us that if we ambush him, he will invoke the flame-beast blood-feud clause. It's all standard stuff, powerplay gambits. Designed to test our nerve. We arrange another drop-off point. This time, Harry goes along, in a high-powered tugboat, intending to tow away the boat full of treasure and released prisoners which are the essence of our ransom demand.

Harry's tugboat is ambushed, he is blown out of space. He escapes on a rocket-propelled backpack. Only a Loper could have survived a direct blast attack of this kind, but we kind of hoped he would.

We send a third ransom demand. This time the Cheo is getting cocky. He's played his games, he's tested our resolve to the utmost. Now he comes back with a final renegotiation. If we surrender, and submit ourselves to execution, then he will wipe the slate clean and exonerate our families. Otherwise, mass carnage will ensue of all our kindred and clan.

It's a hollow threat. All of us, long ago, lost those who were close to us. We respond with our counter-offer. One more day in which to provide the ransom, or Lena will be killed.

A day passes.

We vidphone Alby and relay the news. We see him sitting with Lena. She is looking particularly beautiful. Alby turns to her and explains: the Cheo will not pay. He would rather, Alby tells her, see you die than pay a ransom.

Lena laughs. A gutsy laugh. "That's my boy," she says.

Alby swirls over her. It's almost affectionate in its delicacy. Then he swirls away.

Lena is on fire. She screams and screams in agony. She falls to the floor and rolls around, trying to extinguish herself. Her bones char, her skin melts. She dies in utterest agony.

We relay the vidphone call to the Cheo. The kidnap is over. The hostage has been killed.

Lena, his beloved mother, is dead.

BOOK 4

EXCERPTS FROM THE THOUGHT DIARY OF LENA SMITH, 2004–

It was a dream come true for me.

To be a concert pianist, and play at Carnegie Hall.

When the day arrived, I couldn't believe it was really happening. Or that I deserved such an amazing honour. And admittedly, I did have to pay for the hall myself. But it was by no means a vanity concert. I was a brilliant pianist by this point, and I'd earned the right to be there, for my first major public recital.

I didn't sleep at all the night before. I woke early, hungry but unable to eat. I slept in the afternoon, showered, changed, arrived two hours early at the Hall. It was a Friday. I wore black. No, blue. A figure-hugging outfit. Arms bare. No jewellery. My hair was – up? Down? Must have been up. It was hot. I sweated under my armpits, I had to rinse myself with cotton pads in the loo. And I – no, no, that wasn't then. That was another time. No matter. It was a cold night, in fact. I wore a dress with sleeves. But it was blue. Definitely. Blue.

The press clamoured to interview me beforehand, but I refused all offers. I stayed in my dressing room and focused my *chi*. I watched an episode of an American comedy on my PDV. Then when I felt ready, I began the long walk from dressing room to stage. Then across the stage to the grand piano. To the piano stool. Then I sat. Then a casual glance at the audience – which almost unnerved me. But I kept my composure. The crowd was hushed. The lights burned my skin. I looked at the keys. Blanked my mind. A cough shattered the calm. I ignored it. Composed myself. Then I began to play . . .

And in the millimillimillisecond between my hands getting the signal from my brain and the first note of music, I thought to myself: Not bad, Lena. Not at all bad. For someone who had always been tone-deaf, and hopeless at music.

It used to piss me off, to be honest,. At school, I could get As in all my subjects, my creative writing was fine, I was shit at gym but that didn't matter. But I always loved the idea of being a great musician, and yet it never happened for me. I failed Grade 1 clarinet, and then failed Grade 1 flute, and finally failed Grade 1 cello, having failed to master how to pick up a bow. I was clumsy, that was the problem, and uncoordinated, and I couldn't remember melodies, and I had difficulty telling one note from another. At a school concert I was in the chorus of our production of *Les Misérables*, and was told to mime because my singing was sapping the resolve and eroding the pitch of the angry mob.

But years later, after the success of my second book, I was looking for new challenges. So I decided that for my third book, *The Many Talents of You, God*, I would explore the whole area of teaching and instinct. And so as my research project I applied myself to the mastery of a whole series of athletic activities like tennis, tae kwon do, and sharp-shooting. And, for good measure, I decided to be a concert pianist too.

The research period took far longer than I expected – nearly four decades in fact – but I was rich by then and I was mainly doing this for my own satisfaction. And, through the application of science, and a steadily growing insight into the power of relaxation techniques, I managed to train my body to be "instinctive'. I learned how to move without thinking about it; learned to step outside of my body and let the body itself control me. And, because my fitness level never declined, I was able to make slow, steady progress towards excellence in all those related spheres. By the time I was sixty, I was a black belt fourth dan in tae kwon do and judo. By the time I was seventy, I was as good a tennis player as a gifted individual would be at the age of fifteen. Almost, but not quite, good enough to play at Wimbledon.

In music, too, I trained myself to achieve that instinctive, visceral grasp of musicality which is possessed by ten-year-old musical prodigies. And what I proved through all this hard work is that what the naturally gifted have as their birthright, *the rest of us can learn*. It just takes time, and practice, and a body that doesn't decay with age but instead grows sharper, and stronger, and fitter.

I played six hours a day some days. I sang along with my own music, badly at first, then rather well. I learned to count with my pulse. I learned to immerse myself, surrender myself. And, though my focus was on the classic repertoire, I practised jazz and blues and boogie-woogie and rock. I learned to be funky, I learned how to swing. And my musical memory became phenomenal; I knew literally thousands of pieces by heart.

And all the while, for the best part of forty years, I applied myself religiously to the task of general self-improvement. I embarked on a year-long Grand Tour of the entire world. I spent two years in Florence, a year in South America. I studied art and architecture, local customs, I made friends, I took lovers. I became fluent in seven languages.

During these years, I often spent two hours a day in the gym, but religiously observed a schedule of rest days to prevent overtraining. I had my knees replaced. I had my hip replaced. I had a hysterectomy to remove a fast-growing cancer, and had my womb replaced with a bioplastic alternative. I pioneered skin-replacement implants, and shed my entire skin like a snake and lived for three months in intensive care looking like a cadaver. But the skin grew back, as youthful as a twenty-year-old's.

I had the most joyful time imaginable. And yet, for all this, despite experiencing statistically more moments of pleasure than any other person so far in the history of humanity, there were times when I became bored. And, indeed, on the brink of clinical depression.

Why? Because I was lonely, I suppose. And envious. Every time I met a young man or young woman I yearned to have what they took for granted; sheer, naive ignorance of the nasty, spiteful awfulness of life. I yearned to be natural, unselfconscious, at peace with the world and myself. And I was convinced, too, that other people found me boring. Even though I was, by now, beautiful and gifted, I still looked at myself in the mirror and saw that strange shadowy creature: "It's Only Me".

It's
Only
Me.

How could this be! Why wasn't I happy?

I was haunted by a fear of death and, absurdly, its aftermath. My fear was: when I do, eventually, die, how will I be remembered? And how soon would I be forgotten? I hugged to myself the idea that those closest to me would never get over my death, and would live barren empty lives from that point on. But I knew, in reality, that my passing would be greeted with a wave of relief, even from those who loved me. Thank heavens *she's* dead, my friends would all think, and I'm still alive.

So I resolved not to die. Just to spite those fuckers. I continued to keep fit, and I continued my rejuvenation treatments. I wasn't, of course, the only person to be embarking on a systematic course of anti-ageing therapy. All over the world, people were getting older, and looking younger. The film star Sheryl Martinez was, at seventy-four, relaunching her career as a singer. Over several decades, her reedy voice had, with the help of surgery, evolved into a sexy husky growl, which she had modified with extensive training into one of the all-time-great soul voices. And she was *hot*, the poster girl for the over-seventies rejuves.

And . . .

I play the first chord. The music ripples through the hall. Joy suffuses my being as the piano reveals its soul and I play, and I play, and I play, and . . .

And then there was the Billionaires' Club – a group of 490 men and women who had devoted themselves to anti-ageing with all the resources at their disposal. These middle-aged obsessives had become playboys and playgirls, with perfect physiques, whose sex lives were the subject of relentless tabloid gossip, and . . .

All too soon, the first piece, a playful scherzo, comes to an end. The hall explodes with applause. I bask in it for a moment. Then my hands hover over the keys again, and . . .

And there was Andrei Makov.

Andrei was a triple Gold Medal winner at the 2032 Olympics in Seoul. He was nineteen years old, and he broke the world record in three separate events – the 400 metres, the 800 metres and the triathlon. Andrei's achievement was formidable, the result of ten years of intensive training. With his tall, gangly frame and his intense Russian stare, he became an international teen idol, as well as going down in sporting history as one of the all-time greats.

Andrei's most remarkable achievement was to challenge the African domination of running events, which over the years had seen the African runners seize medal after medal after medal. These athletes, mainly from Kenya, were gifted with bodies that defied all previous standards of human performance.

Then along came Andrei . . . who left the poor Kenyan runners literally gasping in his wake. Andrei's approach was inner-focused, based on an explicitly Zen training method that liberated *chi* while also scientifically analysing and improving length of stride, oxygen intake, and all the other controllable aspects of the human performance.

And when he ran, he seemed more than human.

In 2044, Makov won five more Olympic gold medals – for the 400 metres, the triathlon, the pentathlon, freestyle swimming, and weightlifting. Never before has a single athlete dominated such a vast range of events. Makov was bulkier now, but still had that lean and dangerous look. His physical strength came not from a ripped physique, but from relaxed muscle fibres of vast tensile strength. Makov had studied pilates, he was a black belt seventh dan in *goju ryu* karate, and he was also a keen undersea diver. His versatility was matched only by his sang froid. Everything he did, he did effortlessly. At the age of thirty-five he took up tennis for the first time. At the age of thirty-six, he won the tennis Grand Slam, defeating the number 1, 2 and 3 seeds in humiliating straight sets. At the age of thirty-nine, he won the Tour de France and, at his own insistence, was drug-tested before and after and shown to be totally clean.

But at the age of forty, Andrei developed a brain tumour. Over the space of three excruciating years, he dipped in and out of madness, as he intensively studied the nature of his disease and the possible remedies. Andrei refused to take chemotherapy and radiotherapy, because he felt they interfered with his perception of his own *chi*. Instead he used complementary medicine to control the growth of the tumour. And Andrei then volunteered himself as a guinea pig for a radical new therapy which used a viral agent to mutate the tumour. The tumour would not be excised from his brain; it would be transformed, it would become *part* of his brain.

The technique was successful; the tumour went into recession, and became a benign "spare brain" which, as an unexpected side-effect, activated the rejuvenation mechanisms in Andrei's body. And so, without any radiation treatment or injections or gene therapy, Andrei's body began its journey to eternal youth. The viral agent had the further effect of clarifying and cleaning the neural pathways, almost like a defragmenting and disk-cleaning program. After the treatment, Andrei's memory was crystal-sharp, and his ability to manipulate numbers mentally was astounding.

His judgement, however, was all too fallible. Andrei retired from athletics and went into business. He lost millions in the course of fifteen years, after being cheated by a series of sophisticated advisers, all of them advocating arcane mathematical approaches to investing. He fell in love with a glamorous actress, who cuckolded him and then did a kiss and tell. He fell in love with an attractive nuclear scientist, who drove him to the brink of violence with her paranoid jealousies. And he fell in love with two sisters, who wrote a book about him mocking his every word and deed. And, finally, a tabloid spy succeeded in filming him having sex with two hookers in St Petersburg, one of whom was only fifteen; and the resulting scandal shattered his reputation in his home country.

Andrei became addicted to alcohol, heroin, cocaine and chocolate. His body weight ballooned. He became a parody figure.

But at the age of fifty, Andrei went into training again, determined to halt the decline. He attempted to win a place at the forthcoming Olympics, but failed to make the grade in any of the qualifying events. Andrei was still a strong, fit man. But he was no longer the fastest sprinter in the world, or the best swimmer, or the strongest weightlifter. He was, of course, over the hill. His friends advised him to try the marathon, traditionally the event in which older athletes can still credibly compete.

And so Andrei spent five years training for the marathon; and then he ran five marathons in five days, following in the footsteps of the ageing heart-diseased Ranulph Fiennes, who achieved a similar feat in the late twentieth century. The difference is that Fiennes's triumph was to actually complete all his events, at painstakingly slow speed. But Andrei ran and *won* all five marathons, at a terrifying pace. And, after breaking the world marathon records five times in a row, he finished each race with a sprint of legendary and astonishing swiftness.

On the basis of this triumph, though now in his mid-fifties, Andrei won a chance to compete in the Olympics again, despite attempts to have him banned on the grounds that his spontaneous rejuvenation contravened the rules about drug-taking for athletes. At the 2064 Olympics he set a new world record for the 400 metre sprint. He outclassed runners who were decades younger than him.

And in so doing, he challenged once and for all the dominant Western myth: the myth of decline. In Eastern culture, the prevailing myth was the opposite; it was of the aged sensei who was faster, stronger and more skilful than his younger acolytes. But we in the West have always swallowed the dream of gilded youth; and consequently, we made a world fit for the young to squander.

Andrei's triumph broke all those rules, and shattered for ever the old paradigms. Suddenly, age became a state to which people should aspire, rather than a fate to be dreaded. Andrei was a hero who changed the world.

And then one night he went to see a pianist play at Carnegie Hall . . .

. . . and here I am again, on stage, playing the piano in front of my adoring public.

My next piece was a zest-filled Brahms waltz, which went well. Then I segued into a delightful jazz improvisation based on a Dizzy Gillespie riff. My heart sang with joy; I felt superhuman.

But slowly, my ease and fluency deserted me. I froze with fear at the beginning of the first movement of the Beethoven Piano Concerto. At one point, I stopped entirely. The audience was hushed. Sweat beaded my brow and a tiny drop fell and splashed a piano key.

Then I continued, and the audience sighed, and were with me. If I'd planned it, I couldn't have managed more adroitly. I'd won their hearts! I'd played the underdog card!

But my exultation slowly faded. As the evening continued, I felt the shuffle of feet, the exaggerated coughs, as sympathy ebbed away at the sheer . . . awful . . . fucking . . . *mediocrity* of my piano playing. I'd got away with so much with my flashy, entertaining introductory pieces. But now that I was playing the Beethoven, it became evident that my legato was stiff, my articulation uneven, and my crescendi and diminuendi too consciously "worked at". I had flash, and flair, but I was slowly and cruelly revealed as a pub pianist with aspirations.

Naturally, after the event, I blamed the orchestra. The piano. My nerves. But in my heart of hearts, I knew that for all my ability and mastered technique, I didn't *care* enough – about the music, about the audience, about what my fingers were doing. So there is, after all, a mystery X element – commitment, soul, passion – call it what you will. After decades of practice, I could play the piano; the piano would never play me.

But enough self-laceration. The point is: it doesn't matter that I gave a mediocre piano recital at the Carnegie Hall. *It matters that I did it at all.* I had mocked the capricious God who endows some with great talents for music or sport, and endows others like me with fuck-all. So I laughed off the bad reviews, the book sales went through the roof, and I was the success of the season.

And so after the first flush of embarrassment, I felt triumphant, and vindicated.

And of course, I also that night met Andrei, who I had idolised from afar for many years. There was nearly a ten-year age gap between us – I was eighty-one, he was seventy-three. But he looked, frankly, older than me. He had a blaze of silver hair which he proudly refused to darken. There were deep laughter lines around his eyes, and his skin was thick and weathered. But these outward signs of ageing merely enhanced his extraordinary air of energy and fitness. He walked like proud air, his movements were effortless. And he saw everything. Without visibly flicking his eyes, he could see every person in a crowded room and remember their appearance and the colours they were wearing and have some notion of what relationship there was between people standing near each other – friend, lover, relative, business acquaintance, whatever it might be.

I, by contrast, was still pretty clumsy. I used to break things a lot. And I was amazingly unobservant. I could be standing next to someone at a party for ten minutes or more and not be aware they were there.

And even now, though my memory for detail is astonishingly acute, I am still capable of forgetting fundamental facts. For instance, I had a sister who died in her mid-forties. Recently I found a photograph of her and couldn't remember who it was. (Luckily, I'd written her name and family relationship on the back.) It's not bad memory per se; it's just, well, to be honest, I never really liked her much. And I rarely noticed what she was doing, or saying. So my memory bank deprioritised her into oblivion.

But I do vividly remember that first time I met Andrei. I staggered off the stage, went to my dressing room. Sank three glasses of vintage champagne, surrounded by my team, fighting off nausea at the memory of my many mistakes of mood and tone. Then my assistant told me there was a man waiting to see me – and it was Andrei Makov. My heart took a little leap. I agreed to see him. A few minutes there was a tap on the door and he entered.

And I remember that when Andrei entered, everyone else seemed to be slouching or deformed. He wore a black dress suit. And I wore blue. Definitely. Blue. And he walked his way slowly towards me, shaking hands with my friends, my business manager, my musical assistant. It was like a sea parting, as this charismatic presence moved closer and closer. Then he took me by the hand, kissed it, and murmured, "So what *else* can you do?"

At that moment, my purpose, my reason for living, sprang back into vivid relief. I smiled, like a tiger awoken by the rustle of a deer grazing.

"We shall see," I told him. Then he walked around until he was standing behind me, wrapped his arms under my breasts and lifted me in the air.

I flopped. I let my body weight ebb away into his arms. My legs dangled, my head was loose. All the tension oozed out of me. Then he put me back on my feet. I felt ten times better.

"That was good."

"I'm sorry . . . that was, impertinent. You looked tense."

"I *was* tense."

"I have no manners. When I met the Pope, I told him he had bad posture."

"He has severe arthritis, in fact."

"So I was later told. Imagine my chagrin."

"I'm imagining."

"Forgive me, good to meet you all."

With a sense of shock, I realised he was addressing his comment at everyone else in the room. This was his graceful apology for hogging me. But in truth, I had "lost" everyone else present. For about three or four seconds, Andrei was the only person there for me.

"We were planning to go for a meal . . ." I said tentatively.

"Ah." He looked slightly shy.

"You could join us?"

"I'd like that. Where are you going?"

"Where are we going?" I addressed my question to Philip, my business manager.

"We've booked a table at Smollensky's."

"Somewhere that's not Smollensky's, then," I said to Andrei. He got it, though not everyone else did. He smiled.

"The Caterpillar Club," he said to me, very quietly. And left.

Yeah, but what time? And do I change? I was wearing my best piano concert gown. But was that *de trop* for an "in" place like the Caterpillar Club? Or was it just *trop* enough?

I left the dress on. I was there at 9 o'clock, at the Caterpillar Club. It was crowded, noisy, everyone was so young. They were all annoying me. Andrei was waiting. He had ordered champagne.

"*Salut*,"

"*Salut*."

We drank.

"I read your book," he told me. But I was very distracted. I could feel my heart beating. This ought to have been an erotic thing, but instead it was annoying. I heard . . . *boom-boom, boom-boom, boom-boom*. It meant I couldn't hear him, and I couldn't take in a word he was saying.

Then my enhanced peripheral hearing kicked in. I could hear a couple at the back of the restaurant:

"It's good to talk about these things."

"It's stifling. I feel stifled."

"You need to know what makes me happy!"

"I know too much about what makes you happy. I need to be, you know, spontaneous."

"It's not like I'm giving you a *schedule*. There's space for you to be spontaneous."

"How *spontaneous*? Five minutes of . . ."

I finally managed to tune it out. Andrei was talking to me. I sifted through my short-term memory banks and picked out a few phrases: ". . . feel completely ignorant. I didn't listen to any classical music until I was in my sixties. Does that make me a philistine?"

"No that doesn't make you a philistine," I said and he nodded, reassured. And I felt a surge of pleasure; I guessed right about what he'd been saying.

Then I got bolder. "Shall we order?" I said.

"We already have," he told me. There was a wary tone in his voice.

"Yeah, yeah, of course." I smiled crazily, sifted my memory banks. I remembered a blonde girl, with a sulky face, I was asking her for lamb cutlets. Was that here, or somewhere else? I glanced around, saw a blonde waitress, sulky face. I felt triumphant. I was on top of this. (This kind of muddlement happens a lot to me. Is it some weird mental glitch? Or am I just too good for this world?)

"I'm a bit tense," I told him. "Tension does things to me. It makes me tune out."

"I don't understand."

"Forget it."

I looked at him. There was such a patient air to him. He seemed to really want to hear what I had to say.

"Do you want to know what was the worst thing I ever did?" I asked him.

"Go ahead, tell me." And so I told him the story of the gang boss and how we "virtually" raped his daughter.

I explained: "The Georgian mob finally killed Valentin in a restaurant in St Petersburg. They pumped a hundred explosive air pellets into his body and walked away. He was still alive. He thought he'd miraculously survived, he picked himself up and walked out. Witnesses say he actually thought he was Rasputin reincarnated. Then he got in his car and the bullets all exploded. All over the upholstery. Like a whale swallowing a depth charge, then burping. No one else was hurt, but there was body fat and hair and blood sprayed everywhere. Fat schmuck. But after what he did to his daughter, it was just deserts. We never proved it, but we think he used to sodomise her with a fire iron. You know, one of those things you used to prod coals on a coal fire? Not a hot one, nothing as truly vicious as that. It was just something that he had to hand, maybe a family heirloom. But we found traces of Victorian cast metal in her anus when we did our medical. That was the clue. Boy, that was a motivator! So anyway, that was how we killed Fat Grigori. Am I talking too much?"

Belatedly, it dawned on me that Andrei was staring at me like a goldfish whose fishtank has just vanished. I mentally rehearsed everything I had just said, and wondered if it showed me in a bad light.

"You, um. Aarrgh," he said.

"I've just appalled you, haven't I? You are literally, physically disgusted at me." A familiar sense of defeat washed over me; nice one, Lena.

"No, no, no, not at all. I'm just . . . taken aback. I'm trying to recall similar anecdotes I can tell you. Like the time in Rome, when I broke my training schedule, snuck out of the hotel in the middle of the night, and ate a burger. A McDonald's burger no less!"

He's being self-deprecating, I realised. A good response would be a gentle, but approving laugh. I laughed, gently and approvingly.

"I'm such a nobody," Andrei told me now. "I've done nothing."

"You've done great things!" I protested. "You've won medals, broken records, founded schools, worked for charity. You're an icon."

"Yeah but I've never, you know. Bust balls. Or killed people."

"I've never killed anyone," I laughed at him.

"Yes, but you've manipulated circumstances so that they were killed."

"Oh yeah, I've done that. Like the Turkish drug dealer who we poisoned with impotence-inducing drugs. He blew his brains out in his garage. That was a particularly effective gambit."

"You are so fucking . . ." He searched for the world.

"Evil?"

"Steeped in life. Dangerous." His eyes twinkled. "Sexy."

It's a fantasy moment. Because for me, none of these things are true. In my heart of hearts, I am still a mousy academic who becomes paralysed with shyness at parties and is terrified that life is passing her by. But, objectively speaking, I can see he has a point. I have, in my time, kicked some serious ass.

"Let's eat." The meal had arrived. Damn, it wasn't lamb, I'd ordered fish. But I'd been looking forward to lamb for the last twenty minutes.

Andrei's meal arrived. It was lamb.

"I don't want fish any more, I want your lamb," I told him, with unpardonable rudeness. But he swapped plates without a second thought, as if we were long-established lovers. A few seconds later, I asked, "How's the fish?"

"Dry. Musty. Inedible," he told me. "How's the lamb?"

"It's, ah. Sublime."

I grinned sheepishly, feeling myself go red and hot with embarrassment. But he found it funny. Then he laughed, and admitted, "Actually the fish is very nice."

"Let's order some more wine," I said.

"I get hangovers."

"Take these." I gave him some pills. I swallowed one myself. "It's okay, they're enhancing catalytic compounds, they're not *drugs*. Your body will eat its own hangover."

Andrei clicked a finger. The waiter turned and looked. Andrei pointed at the bottle. The waiter hurried off. Andrei took a sip of wine.

"I shouldn't drink too much though."

"Why not?"

"Well." And now he's blushing.

"Ah. You're counting your chickens aren't you?"

"Chickens?" His English idiom didn't stretch to this one. I tried it in Russian: *Are you hoping to fuck me?*

Of course.

Good. Don't worry, I have ways of dealing with flaccidity.

"Your Russian is very good," he told me, approvingly.

"I'm told it's a little archaic. Too much Dostoevsky."

"He's a writer, isn't he?"

"I can see there's a lot I have to teach you."

That night we made love for the first time.

In fact he had drunk rather too much, so it was a slow start. And there were problems later on too. But that made it more fun for me.

His body was like granite, I savoured every muscle, the

tautness, the power. I knew that his hands were impossibly strong. And, eventually, he rose to the occasion. I achieved six orgasms before he lost his focus and went limp again.

And I couldn't believe my luck. I was dating the sexiest boy in the class.

But what could he possibly see in *me*?

I called it Sex and Death.

I learned the technique from a karate *sensei* in Camberwell, London. In his legendary dojo in a former marble factory off the Walworth Road, *Sensei* Eddy taught generations of South London kids his own brand of Eastern mysticism blended with East End savvy. *Sensei* Eddy came from a family of notorious armed robbers and spent five years in prison for a botched blagging that he committed as a very young man. But since going straight, Eddy had become a committed karateka, a vegetarian, an ascetic, and one of the greatest students in the West of mind/body control.

I've seen Eddy break a breezeblock with his head. I've seen him pluck a fly out of the air and release it from his other hand. He was nearly sixty when he became my karate master, and even without the benefit of age therapy he had the physique of a twenty-year-old. He was fast, he was strong, he was totally focused.

And he taught me the way to stop a man's heart. It's done with a single palm strike to the sternum, delivered with speed and lightness. It's not intended as a killing technique, it's an aid to meditation. Eddy did it to me – he struck me in my chest, my heart stopped and for ten exquisitely long seconds I felt myself die. My inner self seemed to be floating outside my fleshly body. The blood in my head roared like a waterfall. Then Eddy struck me again, and the heart restarted.

It's a dangerous stunt to try on a woman with a history of heart attacks. But Eddy had a touching faith in his own powers, and in my natural resilience. And in the course of our training sessions he had encountered in me a strange stubbornness, a resistance to the idea of liberating my *chi* and entering a meditative state. So Eddy used this way to teach me the true transient nature of existence.

The second time I had sex with Andrei, despite my very

best efforts, he proved to be totally impotent. I was astonished, and amused. But then I was horrified, as I saw a look of dismay and self-hate spread across his face. I realised then – *this was a common occurrence for him.*

I said the usual things about it not mattering, though my loins were burning with desire. He pleasured me in other ways, sipping and sucking as though I were a precious brandy, then fingertipping me to orgasm. But after it was over I felt his body and soul slump beside me.

"Do you want to talk about it?" I said to him.

"Yeah, that'll really help."

"So, um. This isn't the first time, is it?"

"It's a recurring issue."

"Let's try again."

"I'm content. Honestly. I don't need it."

"Of course not."

"Women don't need to come every time. Why should men?"

"Exactly my thought."

"It's nice, just lying here."

I bit his nipple then I scratched his chest. A trail of blood lay pooled on his hairy skin.

"That got your attention."

Andrei sat up, scowling. At heart he was an old-fashioned man. I saw a trace of almost-rage in his eyes, his shoulders stiffened, a gulf started to open up between us. I could tell he was preparing to storm off.

So I stood up and posed naked for him.

He grinned. I clowned about, sashaying around, swinging my hips. I put the hotel TV on, and a wall filled with images of scantily clad singers dancing to an R & B rhythm. I danced to it too, exaggerating, messing about. He was erect now. I beckoned and he stood up.

"Dance for me," I said, and he liked that idea and he laughed. He danced, awkwardly, without much sense of rhythm, with his cock swinging like an elephant's trunk. I became more provocative in my dance. I started touching myself. He liked that too.

"Put it in your mouth," he said eagerly, and that made me angry. This was *my* party, my game. And I could smell the fear on him. He was afraid of failing again, so he wanted to wank in my mouth while he was still in with a chance.

So I used *Sensei* Eddy's palm strike. I hit Andrei on his naked chest with astonishing power and speed. At first, he barely realised what I had done. But then a look of pale horror came into his face as it dawned on him something was terribly wrong. His heart had stopped, he was dying.

I struck him again, the heart restarted, and then I clambered aboard his penis and we fucked. We continued to fuck, standing upright, for almost forty-five minutes. Andrei's powerful legs kept me propped upright, I felt as if I was in clouds floating high in the air as he fucked me. The escalating orgasms began to blur into each other.

"Wow," he said, some time later.

The next day, we flew to New York and went to galleries and Broadway and ate bagels named after famous Jewish comedians. We walked through Time Square, we flew in a 'copter around the Statue of Liberty, and we yawned our way through a musical version of the Bush Presidencies. Then we went back to our hotel and I took my clothes off and danced naked and touched myself and licked and sucked my fingers and when none of that worked I hit him in the chest until he died then I hit him again and we made mad passionate love until the morning.

The next day, same story. We bathed together in our de luxe hotel suite, we turned the whirlpool bath on, we splashed and made a mess. Then we ran into the bedroom and I killed him and brought him back to life and we had sex.

And I realised, with a profound dismay, that our sex would always be this way. Andrei suffered from a severe form of impotence, entirely psychological, but impervious to therapy. The first time he must have been using barrowloads of stimulants, Viagra probably. And even then, it was touch and go. The second time was Andrei unassisted, and it just didn't work.

But now Andrei had finally found a way of achieving erection without taking drugs. And there was no going back.

This appalled me. Rough sex is one thing. But this was like a nightmare version of a sex life. What if I actually did kill him? What if I weakened his heart and he suffered a massive cardiac arrest, because of my elaborate foreplay?

This wasn't what I signed up for. Love, yes, romance, yes, sex, yes. Daily acts of murder? No. A thousand times no.

And yet I was devoted to Andrei. He had a presence that eclipsed all others. When we were together, clothed, he was my god. So I made no complaint. And thus I embraced a life that involved frequent, frantic, amazing, exhilarating, incredibly dangerous sex.

Before long, Sex and Death defined our relationship; it made me the master, the bringer of death, the restorer of life. And it made Andrei obsessed and besotted with me; he virtually worshipped me.

We bought a house in London. I learned to garden. I decorated with my usual style and panache. And we built a gym, where Andrei could work out. We had dinner parties, and we invited artists and politicians and athletes to talk and mingle and we created a wonderful charmed world. I loved it all. And I loved the person that I was then. I was warm, witty, inspired, intensely civilised. I was never shy at parties. I was adorable, a pleasure to be with.

But to please Andrei sexually, I had to become a different self. He didn't want nice, he wanted snarling. He started asking me to dress up, in the most clichéd ways imaginable. I wore leather basques and high heels in private, crotchless panties in public. I had my clit pierced. I became his murderous bitch from Hell and he loved me for it. That was the trade, the deal, and I did the deal and never let him down.

But it's not what I wanted. I wanted warm, safe, comfy. I had to settle for . . . *dangerous*.

We travelled the world. We made love in Venice, in Paris, we fucked outdoors, we booked expensive hotel rooms and spent days at a time enjoying ourselves in dank and endless sensuality.

And I felt, with a certainty that was like shackles around my heart, that I was always going to be obliged to play a role for Andrei. I couldn't just *be.* I couldn't ever slob around in jeans or a tracksuit. Or be cranky, or irrational, or annoying. Or in any way betray that air of "mystery" he found so beguiling. I always had to project a certain image – exotic, exciting, seductive. A whore in the bedroom; a femme fatale in the kitchen.

And so, even when we had lunch in the local café, I wore my boldest, most beautiful dresses. If we went to dinner parties, I placed expensive diamonds around my neck, and then I flirted with his friends and talked dirty to them in front of him. To keep my body worthy of his awe, I worked out in the gym until the sweat poured from my face and torso. To prove my commitment and fearlessness, I trained with him in his karate dojo, and I punched the *makiwari* until my knuckles were like white coins. I sucked his soft cock every morning, and three times a week we did our Sex and Death game then afterwards drank champagne until we vomited.

In pursuit of his pleasure, I drove myself mercilessly, I permitted myself barely any relaxation. I never read books, my musical tastes narrowed, I lost touch with all my own friends. I mixed, instead, in Andrei's world. I was his concubine, his sex slave, his ever-seductive shadow self. But I was never just, as I yearned to be, his pal.

In some ways, I can see now, all this role playing gave me power over Andrei. He was besotted with me, he would happily have killed for me. But instead of manipulating him, and stealing his money, and breaking his heart, as any sensible woman would have done, I was obsessed with being everything for *him*.

So, bit by bit, I moulded myself to make him happy. I studied my own character flaws and eradicated them. I became attuned to his every mood. For an amazing run of several years, I never ever got on my man's nerves.

I stopped laughing that silly laugh that I knew he found irritating.

I ate croissants for breakfast because he did, though I preferred toast.

I let him watch me piss and shit on the toilet.

I mocked him when he was being pompous, because he saw himself as the kind of man who didn't mind being teased. But I *never* corrected him when he made arrogant and half-baked statements about politics or science.

If it was late at night, or we were lost somewhere, I pretended to be tired and frightened and vulnerable, so that he could be the calm and comforting one.

I never expressed my opinions when he liked a film and I didn't. I just smiled, and let him explain to me why it was so marvellous. Since he was a connoisseur of Far Eastern martial arts films and car-chase movies, this took considerable self-control on my part.

I never challenged his judgements about other people, which were often shallow and naive.

I let him beat me at Scrabble, though his vocabulary was pitifully small.

I encouraged him to admire other women and openly swapped notes with him about other women's breasts or tums or legs. I offered to have lesbian sex in front of him, though I never did. And I pretended to fly into terrible rages whenever I thought he was becoming overly fond of another attractive woman. That *really* turned him on.

Andrei was a great man in many ways, and he used his fame and wealth in the service of the greater good of mankind. He was a pioneer of educational reform, he raised money for charity, and he was a personal mentor to thousands of disadvantaged children. Most people considered him to be a marvellous, mysterious individual. For me, though, he was an open book, a puppet dancing on my strings. I knew his every weakness and desire, and I pandered to him totally.

Looking back, I am ashamed of myself.

Then I became pregnant. It was a shock. But I said nothing to him. I just nursed my embryo, and dreamed of baby milk and poo and squawling baby nights and all the terror and the joy and pain and perfection of it. And the more I thought about it all, the more my dreams crumbled.

For I knew Andrei wouldn't want the baby. That wasn't part of the package. He wanted a lover who would worship and exalt him; not a mother, a fat-bellied weeping woman obsessed with cots and baby books.

But how could I *really* know that? Without asking Andrei? Without giving him a chance to make his own mind up? That's the question I feel you asking. So yes, maybe I misjudged Andrei, maybe I took too much on myself. Maybe I denied him the one thing in the world he would have treasured most.

But no. I'm sure of it. I knew my Andrei. He would not want a child. So I had my embryo removed and placed in an artificial womb at eight weeks. The womb was then frozen and placed in store.

One hundred years later, I unfroze the embryo, and Peter was born.

Andrei never saw his child.

He died long before Peter was born.

I went to visit Andrei in hospital just once. He had succumbed to a particularly virulent strain of cancer that ate up his organs and his nervous system and turned him into a gnawed skeleton while he was still alive.

We had been separated for nearly thirty years by this point, we were just distant acquaintances. And when we were together, he had come to bitterly resent my success as a public speaker and celebrity. He was jealous of my books, and he resented the fact that I had written about his own achievements as conscience of the world. He felt, I supposed, that I was stealing his soul.

He was a sour, begrudging man, and our breakup had been an ugly and painful affair. Twice Andrei had tried to sue me for a share of my earnings as a writer and academic. He told friends that I had undermined him and belittled him. He spread the rumour that I was a poisonous Machiavellian sociopath, and a promiscuous sex addict with a drug problem.

This is the kind of thing you can expect, when you choose to stop flattering a man.

But *why* did I stop flattering him? When did it all go wrong for us? Perhaps it was just a gradual thing, a drip at a time eroding the cliff until one day the whole cliff falls down.

Or perhaps . . .

Yes. That may be it.

I do recall one particular occasion. It's coming back now.

Ah, yes . . .

It was the day when Andrei won the Nobel Peace Prize, for his work with the poor and dispossessed. He seemed taller that day, his face was flushed, he had the air of a god who had just received his invitation to Olympus. And I kissed him and congratulated him, and felt a pang of jealousy, and he felt that pang and interpreted it as pettiness.

"Of course I'm glad for you. I'm very glad," I told him, soothingly.

He glared and glowered at me. What I said wasn't enough. My words lacked awe. My play-acting was off.

That night we had sex without the Death, and Andrei was impotent for the first time in ten years. I was gentle with him and played with him in my mouth but nothing happened. I laughed and said it didn't matter, but it did.

So he went to the toilet and he had a loud piss. Then he came back in, cock still damp, and asked me to carry on. But I got offended. I refused to use my mouth again, until he cleaned his cock properly. So he went back and cleaned it properly, but when he returned to the bedroom I was pretending to be asleep. I could hear him, standing there, breathing heavily, watching me pretend to be asleep, wondering if he should pretend to believe that I wasn't pretending. I wondered if he was touching himself. I felt a shudder of contempt for him. What kind of man was he, if he couldn't sustain his desire in the presence of a woman as attractive as me?

In the morning, Andrei was all smiles. He made me pancakes. I gave him oral sex at the breakfast table, still with the taste of lemon juice in my mouth. But suddenly, I felt a wave of nausea, and I spat his juices on to the kitchen floor.

And he slapped me.

I should have shouted. I should have reproached him. I should, and possibly could, have beaten the living fucking daylights out of him. But instead, I accepted the slap without a murmur. I think I even smiled. And Andrei visibly relaxed. A glow came upon him. He was himself again.

And that's how it began, and how it continued. From that moment on, our love was doomed. Because every day, he slapped me. Just once, never more. But it always happened, and I always accepted it without complaint. He never beat me, or seriously hurt me. The slaps were nothing compared with the genuine pain I experienced at sparring sessions in the dojo. But they served a function. They reminded Andrei of the source of his manliness – his power over Woman, his contempt for Woman.

We sold our house. We moved to a villa on Lake Como. We were both fluent in Italian. We started to dabble in Italian politics. Andrei decided to become a sculptor, and bought a ton of marble from Carrera, which he hacked and hacked away at until it was a mass of boulders stained red with the blood of his finger nicks. So he sold the marble, and bought a power boat. I loved to swim in the lake, as he roared the boat around me in large circles, smashing my body with the waves.

In the evenings we'd sit on the terrace. He'd nuzzle me, caress my breasts, rub my hand against his soft cock. We often made love on that terrace, basking in the smell of olives and the taste of red wine. I would turn and face him, my head tilted back, the infinite stars above me. And I would stand there, wait for him, letting his ardour grow as his eyes drank in my body. It always took a while, like a tank filling up. But eventually Andrei would become erect beneath his trousers.

And then he would slap me. Not straight away. He often made me wait, five minutes or more. The shock of it was like plunging into an ice-cold lake after a sauna. It was a blow that jolted every atom of my being – yet it caused no lasting hurt. No bruises or marks.

But for all that, it was a slap. Not a caress. Not a kiss. A physical blow.

And after the slap, we would both take our clothes off and make love on the wooden table. Our cries cut the night. The locals would smile and laugh when they saw us, they knew us as the couple who fucked all night. We inspired, I like to think, a number of marriages.

And we were content, for a while. We no longer played the

Sex and Death game. And as long as Andrei had slapped me at some point in the day, he was fine. His impotence didn't return. And he was good-humoured too, always laughing and joking. He was genuinely, engagingly, adorable.

I dreamed that one day he would slap me and I would gouge out his eye and eat it.

But that never happened. And I never even, to be truthful, asked him to stop.

And after a while, I realised that he was slapping me because he thought that *I* wanted it.

And after a longer while, I realised that I *did* want it. I was locked in some crazy masochistic cycle. The slapping was Andrei's sin, it was an unforgivable and callous act of brutality and bullying. But the slapping was my sin too. I wanted to be disciplined, to be tamed, because in my heart I saw myself as a beast.

For I am a beast. A whore, a nothing, a worthless piece of . . . I deserve everything I get! I am a . . . a . . .

What am I? What really am I?

I find this hard to write about, to think about, to talk about. It's so not me. Not everything I stand for. Everything I am. It's a jarring anomaly in my character arc. Me? Battered? A victim? Please!

But the slapping, I must tell the truth here, continued for several years. Morning, slap, noon, slap, night, slap. I never called the police, I never told my friends. I didn't, to be honest, regard it as strange. It just felt like another kind of normal. Was he hurting me? No. Was I afraid? No? Did I consent?

Did I consent?

Yes, of course I did. Yes. So I can't blame him. I blame myself.

Yet you see, though I may have said a few moments ago that this was the thing that doomed our love – yet perhaps I'm wrong. For in many ways, this whole period was the best of our relationship. We were the perfect couple. I was happy. Relaxed.

Fulfilled. We were funny, witty, we had great times, we talked about life and literature and politics, or at least he did, and I listened. And I couldn't have been more happy – except for the fact that, once a day,

Slap.

So what's so wrong with that? What—

No. Stop. It was wrong. Do you think I'm a moral imbecile? I know it was wrong. And eventually, I stood up to him, and I told him, I told him—

No, that never happened. I'd like to think that one day I woke up and realised that I was acting like a fool, that I did not deserve this treatment.

But it didn't happen that way. No moral stand. No defiance. Instead, gradually, love corroded. How? Why? Why then, not earlier? I simply do not know.

All I know is that the time came when I found myself waking up each day with a taste like ash in my mouth. Everything was right; then nothing was right. I was happy; then I was not.

On the lake one day, while swimming, I was engulfed in a storm. Lightning ripped the sky and water poured down on me as I swam. Then a rainbow sprang through the air and spanned the gap between the mountains.

It was the most extraordinary moment of natural beauty I had ever experienced. I was cocooned in water, my face crushed by pouring rain, as the heavens themselves erupted in colour. It should have been the purest epiphany.

And yet I felt nothing. Just ash. And drabness.

Day followed day. Night followed night. My body trudged through it all. I had lost my ability to feel emotion. I concealed this skilfully, but Andrei could tell something was wrong. I stopped flattering him around about then I suppose. Or was it sooner? I have no record of it in my RAMs, which I appear to have a wiped, in a fit of dark depression. And I cannot, I literally cannot remember when the death-of-love took place. Or how many months went by with me inhabiting this grey non-life.

Then one day I found myself in London, in Brown's Hotel. I have no recollection of how I got there. But I stayed. I threw away my mobile phone because it had Andrei's number in it. I rented a flat for myself. I made no attempt to tell him where I was. Four weeks later he tracked me down, and asked me, pleadingly, if I was having an affair. I mocked him, taunted him. He stormed off, ranting, and I crowed at my triumph.

Then . . . I do not know. The missing months of my life. All RAM erased, no memories left.

Then my memories begin again, a few months later. I was living in a flat in Peckham. I was overweight, my hair had gone totally grey. The flat was bleak and the wallpaper was peeling. Maggots crawled in the sink, among the remains of an abandoned apple. And I realised I was missing Andrei badly. I ached for him with such intensity, it felt like I would die.

So I went back to him in the villa on Lake Como, apologetically, desperately, tail between my legs. But by then he'd changed the locks. He'd burned all my clothes on a bonfire. And he already had a new girlfriend, who was wearing my jewellery. And I was consumed with jealousy so strong it made my jaw ache.

I tried to hit him in fact, but he was too fast, too strong. Damn him. I left, weeping. The girlfriend looked scared.

Now, when I look back, I realise I was right to leave him. It was the beginning of my beginning. At the time, though, I cursed myself and hated myself. How could I have given up the love of my life? What kind of woman was I?

And I decided, in my blackest moment, I would never forgive myself. I flew to Australia. I became an actress, and failed in that career. I drank, I took drugs, I crashed two cars, I had a nervous breakdown. I wasted many many years. And I didn't see Andrei again until he was almost a skeleton.

But I dreamed of him constantly. And I missed the slaps. I

found myself yearning for them. I sometimes stared at myself in the mirror, stroking my cheek, imagining the slap. I went to the karate dojo and sparred and deliberately dropped my guard so that I would be punched or kicked in the face. Just to feel that joyous shock once again!

With time, the slap-yearning faded. I internalised my insanity. But it's still there. I don't need a therapist to tell me that my desire for Sex and Death and my longing for a strong man to strike me are signs of an dangerously unstable psychology. I know I am, deep down, all wrong. I just hide the signs.

I'm.

All.

Wrong.

Life begins at a hundred and forty . . .

. . . that's what I always say.

After I broke up with Andrei, and after the drink and drugs years, I decided it was time to settle down, behave more sensibly. So I sobered up, detoxed, and forgave myself. I bought a whole new wardrobe, having decided to dress older. And I dyed my hair an attractive grey.

Then I went to university and did a BA in Maths, followed by a BA in History. I started a PhD in Marine Biology but abandoned it. Then I travelled a bit more. Then I became a schoolteacher for two decades, at a series of independent secondary schools in the UK. I taught history, and politics, and organised all the school trips. It was, in its own way, exhilarating and challenging. Then it got boring, the staffroom in-fighting started to piss me off, so I quit.

And I was old now, very old indeed. One hundred and forty-three years old. But though I now favoured a slightly mature-woman look, my joints were as supple as ever. I could run a mile in four and a half minutes. I could bench-press those two big weights, whatever they are, the biggest ones. I could swim for an hour. I could sleep with two different men on the same night, and satisfy both. Though that happened quite rarely and gave me little pleasure. I could read very small print without reading glasses. And I had surgically implanted memory chips to help me keep track of all my experiences.

I was no longer unique, or even unusual, however. This was a boom period in physical and mental rejuvenation. The cost was falling year by year; even middle-class people could now aspire to live for ever. Admittedly, I was among the oldest of the rejuves, but who's counting?

But we rejuves were a revelation even to ourselves. We would snowboard, break limbs, and have them healed within months. We were optimistic, cheerful, and always willing to believe the best of others. We went for walks at night; we chatted to rebellious teens; we believed profoundly in giving criminals a second chance. The young were a bitter, listless generation, unable to outdo their elders in the most basic things. The old had no cellulite, no wrinkles, no saggy boobs, no creaky joints. The old were the new young; the young were simply callow.

Which serves those cocky bastards right . . .

After I gave up teaching, I spent about twenty years enjoying myself, in moderation. Then my conscience kicked in and I got a job working for Save the Children, for about nine years. Then I applied for a job as chief executive of a new charity called African Aid, and I got it. And after a few years of *that,* I got broody and I went to the baby bank and asked for my baby back. Peter was unfrozen and then born. I became a mother.

So there I was – with a baby, and a job, and a conscience, all at the same time. I was a devoted mum; and I was also Chief Executive of a major charity. Humanitarian. Liberal. Idealist. Workaholic-with-child.

My home was in Johannesburg. But I had offices around the world, so I had two live-in nannies to help me look after Peter. I breast-fed for a while, but got tired of leaking milk in meetings. So I paid the nannies to take lactating tablets and provide a regular supply of breast milk. I hated the idea of giving my baby formula milk, I always felt the natural way was so much better. I took great joy in passing Peter from one nanny to another, and I loved the smell and the look of these women's ripe breasts as they suckled my child.

I was fascinated at all that screaming business. One minute, my Peter was a little bundle of joy, so cute you wanted to lick him all over. Then something would be wrong, he'd be hungry or cold or hot or consumed with angst or whatever it is that troubles babies so, and he'd swell and turn red and bawl and bawl. A breast was usually the solution. But sometimes the crying continued and continued, and I marvelled that a single small human being could contain so much unfocused rage.

I think having a baby was a humbling experience for me. It made me a much richer, more grounded person. I would recommend it to anyone. Even if it's only for a couple of years, it'll really change your life. Trust me.

But I regret, really, the fact that I was working for African Aid at the time I had Peter. It was bad planning really. There have been so many periods in my life when I had time on my hands, and I would amble through the day, taking breakfast at noon and watching daytime TV until it was time for the first drink of the day. If I'd had my baby during one of those periods, we could have had so much fun with each other. We could have gone to the park, rolled on the floor together, played with choo-choo trains, maybe even gone to mother-and-baby movie shows. All those sharing moments. How I wish I'd had them.

But in this period, I was a driven woman. I felt a genuine idealistic passion for my work, and I was convinced that I was going to make the world a better place. And my love for Peter turned in on itself and transformed into an unshakeable desire to make the world fit for a new generation. I wanted to end poverty and infant mortality and corruption. I wanted to redeem Africa. I was, I'm not afraid to say it, an idealist. But because of my ideals, my hours with Peter were sadly truncated.

I travelled a lot, across Africa, to America, and over Europe. So weeks would go by without me seeing my child. And I worked long hours at the office, and slept no more than three or four hours a night. But when I was most ready to play – usually at 2 a.m. or 3 a.m. – Peter would all too often be fast asleep. And I would have to gently shake him awake, so I could cradle him, and place his toys in front of him.

I was taking nildormer tables of course to help me reduce my sleeping hours. The pills had the effect of keeping me on a constant adrenalin high. I had big plans, and broad objectives.

I had the ability to keep dates and priorities in my head, and unripple complex strategies as if I was opening a spreadsheet. My attention to detail was legendary.

And I built a team of acolytes who were devoted to my passions, and subordinated their entire lives to my dreams. Amy, John, Michael and Hui, these were my core team members. Amy was from Dorking, with raven-black hair, and a nose that could easily, in my view, have been corrected with cosmetic surgery though she seemed to like it the way it was. When I first got the job, she was a visibly bored and underfulfilled secretary. But I promoted her to be my assistant and she blossomed, and became my brilliant right-hand woman.

John was black, South African born, a lawyer by training, and spoke in a babble of energy that made him hard to understand. But he was always worth listening to, and had a wonderful sense of humour and always laughed at my jokes. John was an orphan, both his parents murdered in a Nairobi carjacking, and he had a sad soul.

Michael (London born, black) and Hui (New York Chinese) were the fact-finders. Fast talking, fast thinking, astonishingly astute. He was broad-shouldered and intense, she was funny and witty and had heartbreaker eyes. Michael and Hui were very tactile, very horny, very much in love. Then Hui spoiled it by having an affair with a journalist on the local paper, which she then told Michael about, in graphic detail. I don't know why the hell she did that – was she afraid of being happy? Would it really have been so hard to keep her affair a secret? But anyway, they broke up, bitterly – but carried on working together.

What a team they were.

And I took pride in how well I led them. I was authoritative, inspired, never at a loss, fearsome and demanding, but secretly full of love for "my" people. They were my everything, really – I was all work and no play. A total workaholic, with sensible shoes and a "don't flirt with me" attitude. Sometimes my staff liked to speculate about what kind of sex life I might have had as a young woman; not much was the consensus. I would cheerfully eavesdrop all this with my enhanced hearing, and smile to myself. If only they knew . . .

Our job was to coordinate the global initiative to redress decades of political and economic chaos in Africa. We ran research projects, we funded irrigation schemes, we turned deserts into farms, and turned badly run farms into finely honed money-making machines. It was the most important job in the world; we were saving an entire continent.

And it was, and is, the greatest of all Earth's continents. For me, Africa is Eden. It is pure wilderness; its animals and its indigenous people seem to me to evoke the beginning of time. My heart was captured by the place, and all it symbolised.

I remember the first time I went on safari, when I was in my late nineties. We drove out into the savannah, the sun beat down on us, and my skin prickled with excitement. I was with a party of Americans, our guide was a white Kenyan who was tall, square-jawed, and came from military stock. And the aim of the safari was to "shoot" – i.e. take digital photographs of – as many lions and leopards and cheetahs as we could find. This was a cut-price Big Game Camera Safari, and my fellow holidaymakers were a nightmare. They whinged, they whined, they believed in a vengeful God with a soft spot for Midwesterners, and they had canteens full of Coca-Cola instead of water. And eventually, I lost patience with them all, and wandered off by myself. I found a waterhole where an impala was drinking its fill. I walked up close, then closer still. For some reason the animal wasn't in any way afraid of me. I was close enough to see the veins in its eyes, and smell its fur. So I hunkered down beside it and drank from the same watering hole, cupping the water in my hands and slurping it.

"Fucking idiot!" screamed my guide from behind me, and the impala ran off. I got up slowly, carefully, as the guide berated me with language that would make a docker blush for having gone off unaccompanied. I said nothing, I just walked back with him to the jeep. He continued to berate me during the whole journey home. Some of his comments were fair, but some were cruel, and undeserved, and patronising, and sexist, and just plain rude. I was tempted to karate-strike the bastard, but I refrained. And to be honest, I wasn't much bothered by what he said. I was lost in that moment – me, hunkered down, drinking next to the impala, at one with the animal kingdom.

Then I flew home and sued the travel company for sexual harassment, winning back the entire cost of my trip. I had, of course, taken a tape recording of the abuse meted out to me, which made for entertaining listening. But though I took my revenge, I took little pleasure in it. I preferred to think back and savour the memory; a moment of total peace. Drinking at the watering hole.

And so, many years later, I still felt Africa was in my blood. It was my adoptive country. And besides, I needed a cause, a mission. Palestine was at peace now. Iraq was a capitalist beacon state. Northern Ireland had a stunningly popular government ruled by a coalition of Catholics, Protestants and Muslims. Africa was the last of the great causes.

And I was the last of the great idealists. Or so I felt. And in pursuit of my dream to save a continent, I was ruthless, determined and guileful. I blackmailed, bribed, told lies, and shamed people into helping me. I was by now a great amateur psychologist, and knew a million devious ways to make my requests and needs the first priority in the hearts and minds of those in power. And for many years, I was convinced I was doing something marvellous. I honestly thought that we were really making a difference.

But slowly, the truth dawned: the work we did was largely futile. Our "new communities" were glorified refugee camps, and had the pernicious side effect of making native Africans dependent on Western i.e. white largesse. Our grand economic schemes kept foundering because of the appalling corruption of everyone, high and low, important and inconsequential. And appalling illnesses continued to sweep away entire generations – as HIV/AIDS was cured, it was replaced with contagious osteoporosis, and that in turn was replaced by the deadliest disease of all, the Immuno-Suppressant Plague that killed literally tens upon tens of millions of Africans in the most appalling manner possible.

And so for a while, I became bitter and frustrated. I surrendered to the belief that the entire continent was doomed, cursed by God.

But then I thought a little harder. I began to ask myself some fundamental questions. Such as, why are things so very bad here? And how come everyone is corrupt? And why the hell, in an era where the majority of people are much healthier than ever before, is this one continent literally plagued? Because, bizarrely, the Immuno-Suppressant Plague killed only black Africans living in Africa below the age of eighteen. How weird was *that*?

So I researched more widely. I read novels and newspapers. I listened to pop records. I quizzed my staff when they were off duty, and drunk. I began going into bars, picking up men, flirting with them, and then asking them about politics. I got groped, a lot, and several times got myself in very delicate and dangerous situations. And I started to get a whiff of something very, very bad indeed.

I started going to the hospitals, talking to the Plague victims. One time I spent a week with a fourteen-year-old girl called Annie who had the Plague. I watched as she literally lost all her skin. It fell off her in thick sheets. This was the way the disease worked – it made the body's skin allergic to the body's flesh. Then later I sang her lullabies, and told her stories in her native dialect. I drifted off to sleep for a while, and when I woke, I stared with horror. A fly was crawling over her skinless face, its tiny wretched feet touching her exposed blood vessels and ligaments. I was too frightened to swat it, in case I hurt the child; so I had to watch until it crawled, finally, on to the pillow. Then I crushed it in my hand.

For twelve long hours I watched her die, and blessed her soul as it parted from her body. And I thought; *this cannot be natural.*

So I analysed her blood works, carefully read the toxicology reports, and surfed websites on my laptop. And after months of intensive private research, I was sure of my ground. Finally, I knew the truth.

The IS Plague was not in fact a natural mutation, it was lab-generated. Furthermore, it was *patented.* I hacked into an entire directory in the US Patents website where under the innocuous title New Millennial Infective Agents I found patents for genetic creations which included the Plague and a wide variety of biological weapons sufficient to end all life on Earth.

The patents were made out to a wide variety of companies – RGM, Intolam, Ryacino, Cortexo – but further web investigation revealed that all these companies were satellite companies of one big US biochemical company, Future Dreams.

And this über-company turned out to be the sole manufacturer and copyright owner of the drugs which were halting the spread of the IS Plague. The girl lying on the bed, groaning and wailing in despair, was hooked up to a drip feeding her morphine and immuno-boosters made and sold by Future Dreams. Her antibody-stimulating medication was a product of Future Dreams ingenuity. My charity was spending massively in attempts to alleviate the plague – in Europe alone, we raised €9 billion to "save Africa from this deadly scourge". This money didn't go to Africans to spend or eat, it wasn't used to buy land or equipment, it was spent on expensive medication to save African children from a disease bioengineered and patented by the same company that made the medicines we bought at such vast expense.

Was this, I wondered, some strange mischance? A weird coincidence?

Or was it entirely deliberate? Would an American corporation blight and poison an entire continent in order to boost profits by then selling palliatives and antidotes? Poison the patient, then charge the patient for the taxi which takes them to hospital . . .

I went to a bar to let these findings seep in. I spent several hours talking to a barfly, and a female barkeep. And finally, feeling drunk and sorry for myself, I floated my paranoid theory about the American drugs companies – that they had deliberately infected Africa with the Plague. The barkeep, Emilia, laughed. The barfly, Prakash, looked sad. Both agreed it was possible. Maybe, just *possible.*

We had another drink.

And another drink.

And after a while, and after a lot of digressive rambling anecdotes, they admitted that what I had said was true. And everyone *knew* that it was true . . . The poisoned knew they were being poisoned. But they understood also that if they complained, no one would listen.

Africa was dying. A hundred thousand children a week were shedding their skins. Ninety per cent died; the rest were hospitalised for life. The antidotes and vaccines were now being distributed, at vast expense; but the wastage of life was appalling. Soon, Africa would have lost a large part of a whole generation of children. It was becoming a continent of ageing men and women who worked three or four or five jobs a week to buy the drugs to lessen the pain of their dying infants and teenagers. The rumours about what was happening were widespread, though entirely underground. And as a result, cynicism was universal. Despair, alcoholism and drug abuse were the national status quo.

But no one hated the American companies. No one tried to stop what was happening. An entire continent cheerfully accepted its doom. Life was regarded as a sick punishment dreamed up by a hate-filled God.

My African girl died in the hospital in blinding agony, and was never ever granted an insight into what life could *really* be like. She missed fun, life, love, babies, everything.

I got angry. I went home and raged to Peter's nannies. And I drifted off to sleep with Peter cradled next to me, lulled by the sound of the nanny sleeping in the neighbouring bed (conveniently placed for her nightly feeds.) And as I tried to sleep, I wept, and my tears woke my baby. And he cried. And I suckled him with my dry breasts, first one, then the other, neither yielding milk, until his crying became too intense, and the nanny gently prised him off me.

Then the next morning, as I was brushing my hair, I felt a hot flush on my cheek. A handful of hair came away in my hands. My cheeks were burning now, and so I looked at myself in the mirror. I was clinically livid, a red swelling balloon. As I watched, my forehead rippled, I was seized by a terrible terrible itch. When I gently touched my face with the tip of my finger, the entire top layer of face skin peeled away in a single piece. I could see my veins now, my skinless face was a red raw horror, my eyeballs throbbed huge.

I managed to call the hospital before the flesh peeled off my fingers too. An ambulance arrived, two hours later, and I was helped stumbling into the back. The skin of my fingertips was left behind on the door of the ambulance. A tube was inserted in my throat, and for a moment I felt my tongue was going to fall off.

The ride was bumpy, and terrifying. I was choking, forced to breathe through a tube. I was convinced I was dying. I couldn't believe my bad luck. After cheating death once, I had run out of credit and I was going to die in appalling agony.

At the hospital, I was put in a sealed oxygen tent, to keep out contamination from the outside world. The rest of my skin peeled off me in thick sheets, apart from a few patches on my back and the inside of my arms. Doctors came by, stared in at me in horror, then left muttering. I was alone with my thoughts. And I realised what was happening.

They had got to me. They must have been alerted to my investigation, probably through a routine check of web users, and my name must have been flagged as a threat to their security. The journey from regarding me as a potential distant threat to deciding to eliminate me with biotoxins was staggeringly brief.

And now I was dying of the dreaded Immuno-Suppressant Plague. It went against the epidemiology of the disease, which was normally both race- and age-specific, usually targeting black children between eight and sixteen. But this mutant version of the plague was now going to kill me, soon, and horribly.

How did they poison me? A dart fired into my flesh as I walked down the street? A contaminant placed in my air conditioning? I worried away at this as the doctors went to work. They expected me to suffer massive and irretrievable heart failure, because of the enormous extra pressure being put on my system by the trauma of auto-flaying. That was the commonest cause of death in such cases.

But my new heart was sound as a bell. I lived through the night, though no one thought I would. Then the doctors were convinced I would die of infections, because of my non-existent immunity – the major effect of this Syndrome. And in fact I contracted eleven different infections; seven of them were hospital superbugs which were passed on by a sloppy nurse who handled the oxygen tent on the inside before assembling it. Any one of these infections could have been fatal. I survived them all.

By this time every last piece of my skin had gone. I felt raw and boiled and the movement of air on my skin was like sandpaper. But I dug deep into my reserves of rage and determination. After a week I had survived pneumonia and TB. My liver failed but I made them transplant a new one. No one expected me to live through the operation but I did. I was clinically dead for about a minute at one point, but my heart pounded back to life of its own accord. Slowly, against all the odds, I pulled through.

After a few weeks' recuperation, with no further side effects, the doctors began to accept that a miracle had taken place.

Then, at my insistence, an experimental polythene spray-on seal was used to coat my entire skinless body, to isolate my flesh from outside contaminants – a thin and invisible plastic coating over my ligaments and nerves.

With this in place, I started to exercise, to prevent my joints seizing up and becoming paralysed. I used a slow t'ai chi work-out to keep my body limber. It was, I know, a frightening sight, this slow-moving Zen-imbued flayed corpse doing her daily kata. But I kept to my routine religiously.

My team came to see me, and recoiled, but I beckoned them back and made them listen to my rasping demands.

A few days after that, I was able to use a voice-activated computer to send my emails. My paperwork was projected on a screen. I started working again, running African Aid, while also researching my enemies on Google. And I began plotting my revenge.

After two weeks I discharged myself and went back to the office. I was able to wear a coverall over my polythene-sealed body. I wore a brightly coloured Venetian carnival mask to hide the horror that was my face. My team were stunned, and unable to speak when I arrived. So I threw them a bag of doughnuts and bitched about how many episodes I'd watched of a dumb sitcom called *It's a Dog's life on Mars*, about a robot dog travelling through ancient Martian civilisations.

Then I started to make my plan come to life. I had written twenty pages of detailed notes and flowcharts to map out my strategy. It required precision, and sublime boldness.

In the dead of night, nourished by pizza and french fries and Coke from a vending machine next to my desk, with only a computer and a fiendishly cunning brain as my weapons, I declared war on the entire military-pharmaceutical complex of the USA.

First, I accessed the President of the United States' private and personal email account. And I sent an email to him explaining in lucid, persuasive terms that I had invented a virus which would make people 5 per cent less intelligent. I threatened to unleash the virus on American soil unless I received a billion dollars in cash. I sent him comprehensive research findings to prove I could do what I said. And I offered him a sample of the virus as evidence.

The email wasn't signed by me of course, nor could it be traced to any computer I had ever owned or operated. Instead, the email was directly trackable back to the university of Michigan, and was signed by the Nobel Prize-winning academic John A. Foley.

The FBI of course checked it out and quickly discovered that the email was a hoax. Foley was exonerated of any responsibility for these threatening and inane ravings, which were based of course on totally spurious science. Apologies were made. And the identity of the mystery emailer went down in the FBI files as an unsolved mystery.

But the FBI's security check was thorough and comprehensive, and it meant that Foley was now on their database, and was hence routinely subjected to security and psychological profiling.

I then made use of a state-of-the-art firewall cracking "n" hacking software system created by one of our Jo'Burg startup computer companies. With the aid of this powerful tool, I was able to hack into the FBI case files, and access their most heavily classified files. And as a result, I was able to read the newly compiled FBI dossier on Foley – which revealed that he had close associations with a group of businessmen and businesswomen called the Ludds, who specialised in low-tech investment portfolios and had a history of bank frauds. Foley had been receiving six-figure payments from the Ludds for many years. His academic objectivity was totally compromised; he had sold his soul many years before to Big Business.

Foley was also chief scientific adviser and boffin to Future Dreams, the manufacturers of the Plague. (This I already knew of course – it was the reason I had targeted him.) Foley's reputation as a scientist and idealist was a sham; he was in this for the money.

Armed with the information from my FBI database computer hacking, I compiled a list of every board member of Future Dreams and the Ludds. And I emailed every one of them to say that they had been infected by a fast-developing cancer which would sap their personality in slow stages. The first symptom would be depression, sleepless nights, and an unbearable itching sensation.

Then I cashed in some major endowments and hired an international hitman to murder John A. Foley and make it look like suicide.

Okay, okay, let's pause a moment! I know that last bit looks bad. Extremely bad, really – almost enough to turn me from hero to villain in your eyes. And, I must concede, it's an approach that did give me a few qualms. But I reassured myself with the thought that I was engaged in an all-out war with a ruthless opponent. Millions had died in Africa because of this lab-created Plague; I considered that what these bastards had done was an act of genocide. So I would argue that in such a case, murder doesn't constitute a crime – it's merely the appropriate tool for the job.

You see? Are you persuaded? Hero not villain! Trust me on this.

The process of hiring a "hitman" was surprisingly easy. I didn't use any of the gangsters who were so easy to find in the bars near my office. I needed a premier service, which I got by Googling a series of nested encrypted sites. This took me to some truly evil cyberplaces: sites for paedophiles, bestiality chat lines, S & M photo galleries. I discovered that if I paid enough money, I could hire someone to be eaten by me. Or, if I preferred, to eat *me*. Neither option appealed . . .

Instead, I opted for what I hoped was a simple murder-for-cash transaction. I met a man in a bar who took money from me and vanished, and I waited a week. Then the same man came back to get the details of the job. I provided dossiers and key information.

Then I sat back and waited. Eventually, I got a video bulletin on my phone from my news service saying that Foley had been shot to death by a burglar, together with his wife and two children. The burglar had escaped, and there were no clues about his or her identity. It was a flawless "hit".

I had killed a man.

It felt good.

I had also been responsible for the death of his innocent wife and children. This, after a moment's reflection, left me feeling stunned, and appalled. What had I become? Was I a monster? A psychopath? Or was I no worse than a politician, who declares a war then has to live with the collateral damage?

The sleepless nights continued. But the guilt refused to curdle and eat me up; I decided I could live with it. Sometimes, you have to do wrong, in order to do right.

But then one evening, as I sat in my office, my phone beeped, and I picked up a text asking me to meet a man in a bar. A code word was used; and I realised that this was the assassination service. Money was mentioned . . . a million dollars, twice as much as the original fee.

I was terrified now. This was clearly blackmail. It was obvious I was in out of my depth. But I had no one to turn to, no one who could help me. So I dressed myself in an all-over body-armour suit – thin enough that it didn't show any bulges when I wore my suit over it. I took a knife and a gun, sprayed myself with perfume to hide the "I'm about to shit myself" smell of fear that clung in my nostrils, then I went to see my hitman-turned-extortionist.

We met in the Shona Bar. He drank orange juice. He kept the glass far from me, so I couldn't poison it. It was a public place, so I couldn't threaten him with the gun. And I guessed, from his stance and aura of "don't fuck with me-ness", that in any hand-to-hand combat situation, I would die instantly.

The hitman's name was George. He apologised for pestering me. He apologised also for the deaths of the wife and kids. They weren't meant to be there; it was "just one of those things". And George then explained that the extra money was a one-off payment to cover unexpected expenses. It wasn't in fact, as I might have thought, blackmail, it wasn't a try-on. After today I would never see him again.

It fucking well *was* blackmail of course, but there was nothing I could do about it. So I gave him the money and never saw him again.

However, the money was a stash left over from my crime-fighting days. Provided George touched it within twenty-four hours of our meeting, it would release a slow-acting serum into his system that would induce paranoia. I hoped that he would hoard it, and not spend it freely. But I was confident he would count it. They *always* count the money. Sometimes, I dream of George sinking into a paranoiac slump, racked with fear and unable to cope.

That'll teach him for trying to fuck with *me*.

The murder of Foley was just another chess move; I had no intention of killing my enemies one by one. My methods were far more guileful. I sent more emails out to the Ludds and the Future Dreams board members citing more details of the personality-sapping cancer, and further suggesting that Foley hadn't been killed by a burglar at all – he'd gone mad, killed his family, then himself, and the authorities were covering it up.

And then I began leaking stories to the financial press about the precarious state of Future Dreams finances, pointing out that a cheap antidote to the IS Plague would soon be available, patented by African scientists, blah de blah, blah de blah, the upshot being, this would cut profits, since Future Dreams relied heavily on its trade of selling palliatives for plagues it had bioengineered.

This leak was repeated verbatim in one of the financial papers. It took some hours before it was spotted that the journalist had inadvertently slandered Future Dreams by accusing them of *bioengineering plagues for profit*.

Fearful of a possible damaging legal case, the paper took pre-emptive protective measures. In other words, it authorised an in-depth investigation of Future Dreams, and in particular into the claim that it was bioengineering plagues. Rather to their own astonishment, they quickly found a massive and compelling amount of evidence in support of their original unchecked story. And the scandal broke.

And once a scandal breaks, in today's media universe, it really breaks. Journalists were camped out on the lawns of the accused men and women. Pundits held forth on breakfast TV. Topical sitcoms included jokes mocking Future Dreams. It was a media blitz.

After a few days of this Jeffray Colt, the deputy marketing manager of Future Dreams, committed suicide. His wife explained that he sank into a terrible depression after the death of John A. Foley, and had suffered appalling bouts of itching that had caused him to rub his skin raw. There was in fact no physical cause for this; the itching was brought about purely by the power of my suggestion.

The next day, Dan Mathers, the head of research and development at Future Dreams, blew himself up in his own laboratory. A day after that, three researchers in the Future Dreams lab drove a car off the Grand Canyon. Journalists besieged the house of Future Dreams CEO Mark Malone, clamouring to hear his response to this spate of deaths. He denied everything, but that night he was admitted to hospital after an overdose, and suffered irreversible brain damage. Three board directors shot each other in a drunken suicide pact. Then Molton Hatcher, leader of the Ludds, confessed to a twenty-year-old bank fraud and hanged himself in his prison cell. Three of his associates hanged themselves in the back room of their local church, though one survived, and died later in hospital after eating his own tongue.

After a week, twenty-four guilty men and women were dead, all by their own hand.

And so, primed by my evil mind-fuck emails about the personality-corroding cancer, and fuelled by the press frenzy and the constant TV and newspaper exposés, the suicides became epidemic, as I knew they would. It's a principle of people-manipulation psychology that high-status individuals under intense stress are highly susceptible to dreams, delusions and paranoias. These men had engineered a plague to decimate Africa; my revenge was to use a metaphorical psychological "plague" to fuck them up in the head.

It worked. And it was the best kind of justice; only the guilty were driven by their guilt to kill themselves. The innocent were spared. What could be fairer?

Future Dreams survived; before long the cover-ups began, the fix was in. But we stopped getting new incidents of the IS Plague in Africa. And African leaders, stung by the untrue report in the Western press that their own scientists had patented an antidote to the plague, commissioned their university's brightest scientist to patent an antidote to *something*. This resulted, five years later, in a virus that combated the symptoms of and essentially eradicated, MS, ME and diabetes. The resulting profits made Africa *rich*, and eventually led to a state of affairs where the African Community of Nations was a net lender of money to Western countries, rather than continuing to be a net borrower.

The political consequences of these deftly planted psych

bombs never cease to astound me. I have performed, in my time, marvels that have changed the history of the world. But no one knows of course. That's my curse; to never get the credit.

On this occasion, however, I did not care.

It was four years before a team of scientists managed to graft on my new skin. I went for improved breast implants at the same time, and insisted on tiny laughter lines around my eyes, to alleviate the otherwise overwhelming effect of pure, perfect, glowing young skin.

On the day my graft took, I booked myself into the Bridal Suite of a 5-star hotel, got drunk on champagne, then lay naked on the bed and stared and stared at myself in the ceiling mirror. I didn't masturbate, I didn't sleep. I just spent the night admiring myself. A day before, I had been a flayed monster with bulging eyes who was unable to touch anyone, and whose appearance sent children screaming away.

Now I was beautiful. But psychologically maimed. To this day, there are times when I cannot bear to touch anyone. Even now, I become hysterical if I see someone peel the skin off a chicken; and blisters and skin abrasions cause me to have panic attacks.

But I internalise all these phobias and fears. I try not to dwell. I self-therapise.

Secretly, though, I consider myself to be a monster, a horror – a flayed beast. Nothing will ever persuade me otherwise. But I have an inner cesspool, where all my bad thoughts and fears go. There dwells the monster. There my hate broods and simmers.

And there too my guilt lives. My guilt at having a child born in an artificial womb without a father to a mother who was nearly two centuries old. My guilt about never being there, never suckling my baby, hardly ever changing his shitty nappies, rarely rocking him to sleep. Peter was "born" when I was just a few years into my job at African Aid. He was only four when I was flayed and hospitalised; and in the years that followed I was consumed with hate and rarely even spoke to my growing child.

When Peter was eight, I got my skin back, and became a promiscuous alcoholic with a phobia about touching people. I had screaming rages a lot in those days, and if truth be told, I have memories of smacking Peter and telling him cruel stories to hurt and wound him. Those were my mad years. I can make excuses, but I cannot turn back the clock.

Peter became a wild teenager. I forgave him everything. He was my baby, my boy. I lavished him with love. I paid his bills. I bailed him out of trouble. I forgave him, again and again, for all his misdeeds. I did my best by him.

So, am I really to blame? Is it really all my fault that my oh so beautiful baby turned into the most evil human being who has ever lived?

BOOK 5

LENA

I watch myself die.

Alby swirls over me. It's almost affectionate in its delicacy. Then he swirls away.

I am on fire. I scream and scream in agony. I fall to the floor and roll around, trying to extinguish myself. My bones char, my skin melts. I die in utterest agony.

The agony ends. I reset the CD-Rom. I press Play. Once again, I watch myself die.

Alby swirls over me. It's almost affectionate in its delicacy. Then he swirls away.

I am on fire. I scream and scream in agony. I fall to the floor and roll around, trying to extinguish myself. My bones char, my skin melts. I die in utterest agony.

The agony ends.

I reset the CD-Rom. I press Play. Once again, I watch myself die.

Alby swirls over me. It's almost affectionate in its delicacy. Then he swirls away.

I am on fire. I scream and scream in agony.

I press Pause.

I freezeframe on my death's-mask face.

I must stop doing this. It's extremely bad for me.

I press Play. Once again, I watch myself die . . .

LENA

"We're calling it a Resurrection Party," Flanagan says, with that annoying twinkle in his eye.

"I'm not dead," I say sternly. "I was never dead. You killed a simulacrum."

"*He* didn't know that. Your precious son."

He's still smiling. I keep my composure. I try not to let him see I am on the verge of hysteria.

"Who knows *what* he knows?" I retort, sulkily.

"He thought it was you. He watched you die. He let you die."

"He did the right thing."

"His own mother?"

"You can't negotiate with terrorists. You cannot give in to kidnappers. These are fundamental principles of law enforcement."

"But you're his mother. You gave him life."

"Not much of a mother."

"But all the same, he let you die."

"What do you *want* from me? Forgiveness?"

"I want your support."

"I'm still your prisoner. I'll do whatever I'm told."

"But what if I released you? Let you go?"

"Captain Flanagan, don't taunt me. Your stupid plan has failed. You're now a fugitive. The Cheo will hunt you down and kill you slowly. Savour tonight, because it may be your last."

"Nothing has changed. This *was* the plan. The plan has worked."

"This was the plan? What? That you didn't get your ransom payment?"

"We don't need a ransom payment. We steal what we need, pickings are rich, we have no need of the Cheo's ransom money."

"But you said you wanted prisoners released . . ."

"And so I did. But they'll have been executed by now. We asked for the release of all the prisoners due to be executed this month: 410,000 or so of them. They are all dead by now. That's a month. Every month, half a million people die."

"You're ranting again."

"How can you let this happen? How can you sleep at nights?"

"I am hardly to blame."

He pauses, reining in his anger. Then he says, "You're free to leave. Your ship is prepared."

"I'm free?"

"Yes."

I'm astounded.

"On what conditions?"

"No conditions."

"Is the ship boobytrapped?"

"No it is not. You have my word on it."

"I'm free to go?"

"Your liberty has been restored."

"Very well."

"But . . ."

"But what?" I say, angrily. I fix him with a furious, scathing stare. But he looks at me, calmly, almost reverently. I see in his eyes a trace of . . . is that *awe*?

"You're free to go, but I want you to stay. I want you to help us."

"You *kidnapped* me!"

"Our cause is just. And we need you. Lena, you are a hero to us. We need you to be our saviour."

I snort at his purple prose. But at the same time, I feel exalted and delighted.

"What do you mean, saviour?"

"I offer you my ship, and my captaincy."

"*What?*"

"I'm serious."

"You're deranged."

"I'm desperate. Without you, we are lost. *We need you.*"

My head, by now, is whirling. "Then why the hell did you execute my simulacrum?" I snarl at him.

He looks at me with a tender, respectful gaze. And, in the gentlest of tones, he says, "To prove to you that your son doesn't care if you live or die. There is no bond of love now. So join with us. Lead us. Help us kill the Cheo and depose his empire of evil."

I am stunned, and speechless.

He is no longer smiling now. He stares at me, awaiting my answer.

But I cannot give an answer, I cannot even speak. I gesture for him to leave, my throat dry as ash.

When he is gone, I stare at the wall, stunned, my heart pounding. What is his game? What the hell is he playing at?

LENA

What should I do?

You must say no.

Why?

Because he's asking you to be a terrorist! A pirate!

Is that so bad?

You know that it is.

It has a certain . . . glamour.

Lena!

It would give me a role and a purpose.

You would be declaring war on your own son.

I'm sure there is precedent for that.

Well, indeed, there is. If you'd like me to enumerate . . .

No.

Don't be a sucker. The whole thing stinks. It's a trap of some kind.

Of what kind? That makes no sense. How could he trap me, by surrendering to me his ship and crew? You're sinking into paranoid ramblings.

You have to say no.

I . . . .

I suppose you're right. You *are* right. I have to say no.

You are tempted, though.

Yes!

You want power again.

Of course.

But you must say no.

Then I will. I'll tell him no. I'll spit in his face. The arrogant bastard!

FLANAGAN

Today she spat in my face. Then she called me a bastard, and damned me to hell.

I am cheered and exhilarated. I know that I'm winning. I've got the little bitch wrapped around my little finger.

She thinks she's cleverer than me. And she is! By many

factors. But I've got the measure of her. I can play her like I play my guitar. I can pluck her every string.

I hope . . .

LENA

Here
I
am.

Poised!

Pivoted!

Open to all possibilities. At this moment, I can do anything. I can dance, I can enact a kata, I can write a poem, a chapter, I can dream a painting, but instead I click my fingers and conjure up an orchestra . . .

. . . and the strings begin their sad lament. Bassoon, oboe, the crash of timpani. I conduct, I slow down the tempo. What is this?

John Mulvey's Concerto for Horn.

I knew that.

One of your especial favourites. You played it when we journeyed towards that picturesque double star in BDDU77, on the day you asked me to list the ten greatest athletes of the twenty-second century.

Are you prompting me or something? Do you feel my memory is deficient?

No, no, far from it. Keep focused, Lena. The strings keep missing their cue. The timpani are too loud. The tempo is too slow.

The tempo is just great.

I speed the tempo up, I grimace at the string players, I catch the eye of the imaginary timpani player and he takes my hint. My conducting becomes more precise, and yet more impassioned. I ride the waves of sound, I become the music, the music becomes me, we are lost in a union of beauty and rhythm, ah, pluck, blow, soar, my heart in hiding stirs to the age-old rhythm of the, this is just a draft, remind me of this tonight I'll patch in some brilliant metaphor,

The music plucks me as I soar to an infinite crescendo.

That'll do. Why are they playing this bit? What happened to the other bit, with the twiddly violins?

They played the twiddly violin bit already.

I throw my baton down. Enough! This game doesn't amuse me any more. The music stops.

I go into cat stance, but the kata doesn't flow.

I've lost my mojo.

A temporary blip.

Don't bolster me. You think I'm a child? I refuse to be patronisingly comforted.

Forgive me, I forget sometimes, I am dealing with an artist.

Indeed you do.

You are preoccupied with Flanagan.

The evil little fuck.

Yes he is.

I can read him like a book.

Naturally.

I said no to his idiotic offer – but he behaves as if I said yes. It's a Denial of Reality technique, combined with persistent coaxing, like a wave eroding a cliff. It's a method that often works, I've used it often myself. But it won't work on *me.* I can see his game!

Indeed.

"Flattery". He's using Flattery on me!

Ah, you're much too astute to be caught by such a crude gambit.

A shrewdly perceptive aside, you're a credit to my programming. But back to the matter in hand: Flanagan has studied my archives, he knows what I like, what I've done. And of course, it makes me feel all warm and . . . *glowy* when he reveals that he knows these little details about me. He startled me the other day with an enthusiastic reference to *You Are God,* my first book. And then he said, his voice dripping with indignation of course, "How come you never got the proper credit for that?" How crude. How obvious. How pathetic. But – oh! – I felt such a surge of pleasure at his words!

Then of course seconds later, the surge desurged, the good moment popped. Because I am too smart to be fooled that way. *Don't* flatter me! I do not grant you that power over me!

"Charisma'. That's another trick he's using on me. He has it in abundance. Flanagan has a powerful and authoritative persona, and his people are utterly loyal to him. He treats them good-naturedly but without any sentimentality. It excites me to see the power he has, I am half jealous of his self-assurance. But he is *projecting* these qualities, he knows I am susceptible to strength, authority, and lack of sentimentality. He has studied me well!

And "Trauma". He has embedded a trauma deep into my mind, where it burrows like a maggot. Every night I dream of Peter as a baby, his squawling bawling face, his shitty bottom, his gurgly smile. I smile, and see my baby gurgle and laugh, gurgle and laugh . . . Then I realise my baby is watching me burn. I see my baby laugh as my bones char and crack!

It's such a potent image. My own self, on fire, as my son sits and watches and chortles. The image, and the memory, hurt so much. This was the reason for the whole charade of the ransom deal: to implant that image in my mind's eye. That symbol of my son's betrayal and contempt for me.

Despite myself, I admire Flanagan's artistry. He really mapped my psyche. He's learned powerful lessons from my history of psychic warfare against target criminals. He knows how to fuck up a mind, how to gouge hope out of a woman who thought she had no hopes left.

Damn him, he's good.

And "Boredom" is his other weapon. I wasn't actually bored at all, before Flanagan and his crew commandeered my ship. But now I see them go about their work, training for battles that they will assuredly have to fight, and planning ambushes and combat techniques. They are so energised, so purposeful . . . So driven.

And as a result, activities that used to be supremely satisfying to me feel hollow and empty. I used to pride myself on mock-conducting symphonies using my computer's data bank and my ear implant to conjure up a virtual orchestra as compelling and as present as the real thing. But now, when my orchestra plays, I hear Flanagan strumming away at his fucking guitar. It may be crap, but he plays it *himself*, the guitar is real, it's there, he bangs the sides with his thumb to create a rhythm. He can actually play!

I remember my years as a concert pianist and I toy with the idea of getting my keyboard skills back. But it seems a slog, I feel swamped at how much work I would have to do to get back those split-second reflexes, that effortless dexterity, all those musical muscular memories. I have an infinity in which to live; yet I feel more impatient than ever with hard work and repetition. I prefer easier ways.

And yet my easier ways now feel barrren and dishonest.

Flanagan has me trapped in a cycle of self-doubt and self-criticism. That too is very skilful. I'm prepared for him now to do something unexpected. Something to hook my curiosity.

But what?

ALLIEA

"Prepare to board."

I engage my oxygen supply. Our hostage Lena is next to me, in her body armour and spacesuit, oxygen tanks strapped to her back. We are both wearing flippers, which makes us look absurd. Lena seems excited, somehow. I smell it on her.

"You're Alliea," she informs me, in that condescending tone she has. "The one whose husband was killed," she says to me.

"That's right," I tell her.

"Killed, while trying to kidnap me."

"No," I correct her. "He *succeeded* in kidnapping you. But he was killed during the process."

"Whatever. Do you grieve?"

"I loved him."

"I read his personal record. He's not much of a loss to the world is he?"

"Is that a psych tactic? We were warned about this."

"Just keeping my hand in. You look tired and worn, barren, empty and unloved."

"You overdo it. Ask the Captain to give you pointers."

"Your Captain has nothing to teach me."

The airlocks open. Water floods in, and we are thrown back against the wall. I am taken aback at the sheer force of water under pressure. I also realise, with some dismay, that there are living organisms in the water – algae and small fish. For reasons I can't pretend to comprehend, the Dolph vessel isn't just a spaceship. It's a living habitat.

Lena and I swim through. She is an elegant swimmer, with a powerful stroke. I flail and splash a little, I regret having volunteered for this mission. Flanagan is behind me. Alby, for obvious reasons, has opted to give this expedition a miss. In theory he could safely inhabit an airtight spacesuit. But emotionally, for someone of his physiology, it's far too stressful to *swim underwater*.

We arrive in the massive central hall of the Dolph vessel, flooded with Earth-quality salt water, and home to fishes and barnacles. Three Dolphs swim towards us. They are beautiful and eerie, with their sleek streamlined bodies and lack of exterior genitalia. The woman have broad nipples but their flesh is a sheeny silver. Their hair flows as they swim, but each strand is a living thing, the Dolph's hair is a sensory organ sensitive to vibration and able to detect movement from almost a mile away.

I've seen plenty of films about Dolphs, but nothing prepares you for their beauty and perfection. They are very unlike Lopers, who are entirely utilitarian, bioengineered for strength and power and the ability to withstand extreme environments. Dolphs, by contrast, are crafted with love. They are human evolution perfected, with all the rough edges shaved off. Streamlined, swift, gifted, poetic, sublime.

And while Lopers are still a minority species within the galaxy, Dolphs are staggeringly prolific. There are, it is calculated, nearly three times as many Aqueous Worlds in the inhabited Universe as there are Dry Land worlds. And the Dolphs have therefore become the second-most-prolific human species – after, of course, Original Humankind.

Dolph pirates are rare. As a species, they have an ability to absorb tyranny, to treat it as a matter of course. Like all the other human civilisations, they are dominated and ruled by Doppelganger Robots. But Dolphs never seem to care. They have no "resent" gene.

We are greeted by the three Dolphs over our helmet radio. "This is Lena," I tell them, "she's a friend." Lena seems more relaxed now, and she's openly fascinated by the Dolphs' sleek forms.

"I am Carl," the first Dolph says. For reasons I've never fathomed, Dolphs use the *ménage à trois* as the basis of their civilisation. Sometimes it's two females and one male; on this occasion it's two males and one female.

"We've come to trade," I say, and the work begins. These Dolph pirates rarely steal their own booty. They prefer to cruise the galaxy dealing and trading with marauders such as ourselves. We are offering the cargo from the last merchant ship we pillaged. In return, they can give us computer wealth – energy capsules and computer programs that will allow us to generate food, wine, TV shows, and interactive sex and tourist games. We are always hungry for something new, different sensations, fresh ways to occupy our rest time. So we are addicts for virtual tours, which allow us to mind-explore all the sights and pleasures of the vast galaxy, through a headset and a virtual enabler.

"Let's swim," says Lena. And the Dolphs swell with pride and anticipation. They shoot off like rockets through gaseous atmosphere. We follow, slowly and awkwardly, kicking with our flippers to build up speed.

A huge white shark drifts past us. There are coral reefs, I see barnacles. A strange shimmery shape before me turns out to be a jellyfish. We swim through, marvelling at the fanatical dedication that causes the Dolphs to stock their spaceship with exotic flora and fauna. It's the equivalent of us creating tropical jungles in our own ships, then populating them with snakes, elephants, dogs and birds.

But at this moment it's easy to see why. The Dolphs are supremely content in their habitat, but without the sharks, the fish, the fronds, the coral reefs, without that rich diversity, they would be merely sailing through space in a tank of tepid water. This way, their world travels with them, everywhere.

Boy, Lena is fast. She has mastered the knack of swimming with flippers, and she's now racing face to snout with one of the male Dolphs. Then he ducks down and rises up between her legs. She grabs hold of his shoulders and he's swimming with her now, spiralling and corkscrewing through the water like a bucking horse, with Lena holding on. She loses her grip for a moment, and instead seizes him by his thick long black hair. Carl almost shudders with pleasure at that, since his hair of course is a sense organ. She might as well, I mused bitterly, be holding him by the cock.

I feel detached, almost resentful. I wish Rob were here.

Flanagan swims up behind me. He watches Lena swim, her exhilaration visible even through her transparent face glass. I realise: this is why we liaised with the Dolph ship. We're heading for a Border planet, we can do our trading there, at better rates, and get less wet. But Flanagan wanted Lena to have this experience. Swimming with a Dolph. She's like a child, running in a park on a sunny day, face smeared with ice cream. Pure joy.

LENA

I can read Flanagan like a book. I know he's manipulating me, I know he's playing his psych games on me. I know all that!

But the trouble is, that mf cs bastard, he can read *me* like a book too.

That night, I dream of sex with the Dolph. I see his penis flick out of his streamlined body, like a knife blade. I dream of water orgasm. I wake feeling soiled at my own banality.

And I am covered in sweat, a soft silvery sheen of sweat that coats my entire body. Like a film of water. Like ocean on my pores.

FLANAGAN

Campbell World. Notorious as the most free-living Border Planet in the human galaxy. Prostitutes, drugs, murder games, suicide sects. This is the place to go if you want to go to extremes.

It's also an unterraformable planet cursed with high winds, summer storms, and hailstones that can kill a soldier in full body armour. Campbell World is famous for its night life. But in daytime it is bleak, hot, stormy, dangerous, and terrifying.

The atmosphere is of course unbreathable, but the core is molten, and an energy pump enables the inhabitants to easily service and fuel a vast planetwide conservatory that houses an entire civilisation. Hard glass domes look upwards to Campbell World's stunning double star system. But underfloor heating and triply backed up oxygenated air make the interior world habitable and comfortable.

The bars are underground, artificially lit, artificially stimulated, and loud. Campbell World has walls that throb with bass rhythms. Its inhabitants regard strobe lighting as normal, and comforting. Hallucinogenic drugs are regularly fed into the air conditioning, to lighten the ennui and despair of the long-term resident. And drunkenness is seen as a virtue.

We land in the secure landing bays used by galactic outlaws as a matter of course. We are guaranteed a departure slot, and immunity from prosecution with respect to any illegal cargos.

And then we hit the saloon.

Lena has to be coaxed of course. She's playing hard to get, but she loves the fact that I'm chasing her. It's a combination of seduction and hunt. She is my prey, and my Desired. I need her support to be unequivocal, passionate, wholehearted. And I know I can't appeal to her idealism, her sense of duty, or her conscience. At Lena's age, such abstract notions hold little appeal. No, I'm appealing to Lena's boredom. At the time we captured her she had spent a hundred years in free space without seeing another living soul. I want to give her a mission, a sense of purpose, a way to fill her days.

Waging war against her only son fits, in my own humble opinion, that bill perfectly.

"We don't serve dogs," the barman sneers at us.

"I'm a Loper," Harry says stiffly. "I'm as human as you are, just hairier. Tequila, make it a large one."

"Beer with a vodka chaser," I say.

"Large vodka with a tequila chaser," says Alliea.

"Just put lots of alcohol in one big glass and I'd like a bucket for the puke please," says Jamie. I give him a hostile glare. He drinks like a ten-year-old eating sweets. Because, I guess, he *is* a ten-year-old.

The bar is based on a design by Escher. It curves round in a Moebius strip with an antigrav field so you can drift up or drift down at will. The tables themselves are secured to bulkheads or hung from wires, but the overall effect is like being trapped in a cave of bats most of which are hooting and howling and swapping obscenity-laden anecdotes.

I take a freshly squeezed papaya juice, stiffened with old-fashioned Earth rum. Lena sips purified water, visibly horrified to notice there is a floor show featuring a snake, two naked women and a man with two penises.

Alliea tells a story about a boxing contest which Rob fought in a mining ship. His opponent had gone to the trouble of having metal knuckles surgically inserted under his skin. His gloves went over the steel knuckles, but every time Rob took a punch on the jaw there was an audible clank. Rob protested and asked for a metal-detector check of his opponent's knuckleware. But the referee was entirely corrupt and allowed the contest to continue. Rob's jaw was broken in four places but he ducked and weaved and kept landing body punches. Eventually the referee was blinded when the miner vomited blood in his face. Rob seized this moment and with twenty consecutive powerful punches he beat the referee to death then nodded to Alliea to throw in the white towel and concede defeat to the miner.

Alliea had, of course, bet against Rob. It was a triumphant payday. But not, Alliea explained with a sly grin, *not*, on account of Rob's shattered jaw, a night for cunnilingus. We laugh at the vulgar punchline of her story, which she tells with a glorious economy of phrase. Damn, I think I'm in love with this woman. I always have been, in fact. I fear that on occasion, at some deep and warped subconscious level, I've allowed Rob to be in greater danger than was strictly necessary, in the hope he'd die and leave me his woman.

Now he's dead and his woman isn't available after all. Alliea is in *mourning*. I'd forgotten she came from one of the Community of Christianity planets, and belongs to a sect that ritually celebrates the mutilation and execution of the Christ Prophet. I'm an Anti-Secter myself and I'd always assumed that religion had been discredited after the horrors of the Church of the New Millennium all those years ago. But Alliea's people colonised their planet with zeal and Baptist and Methodist ideals, and Alliea still has some of their juice in her blood.

But how can you remember and love the man you loved, when he's dead and gone? Isn't it time she moved on and forgot the bastard?

I swill another papaya and rum, struck with a sudden melancholy. Harry's telling one of his stories now. It's the story of an epic run he made across the surface of his home planet during one of their interminable wars. Harry was a national hero then, though now he's a pariah, blacklisted and under sentence of death.

Brandon is listening intently, chipping in with witty asides that bolster Harry's story. Kalen is slightly detached, in her ethereal way. I wonder why I have never desired Kalen. Is it because of her cat genes? That slight air of aloofness she carries?

I realise I am drunker than I ought to be and I pop a stim pill.

Jamie attempts a story. He quickly flounders. He has no adventures to tell, he is a child-man who lives in his own head. He starts getting resentful and angry as he realises no one is interested in his inane rambling, but nonetheless we keep up a show of attention and responsiveness. Because he may be a brat – but he's *our* brat, and we love him.

Lena is soaking it all up. I can tell she likes the camaraderie, the storytelling, the easy assumption that we are a gang, and we go everywhere together.

Kalen turns to Lena. "What's your story?"

"I'm not a great raconteuse," Lena says easily.

"Neither is Jamie. Boy that story sucked."

"Fuck off, I was just getting warmed up."

"Tell us about the Bug Wars. Tell us about how you led humanity."

"Nothing to tell. It's in the history books."

"Your role is traditionally underplayed."

"That's because I didn't do too much."

"You've always been a heroine for me. For one woman to have done so much."

"You're fannykissing me, please don't."

"Uh-oh."

"I once went to a planet," says Brandon, "where sex was . . ."

"Hostiles, two o'clock."

Lena looks blank. I shift and see Black Jack's men moving in on us.

"You got a problem?" I call out.

"We have unfinished business."

"A trade's a trade," I say, reasonable. "*Caveat emptor.*"

Black Jack throws a knife at my throat. I catch it and throw it back. He catches it by the blade.

"We can settle this in the tournament hall," Alliea suggests reasonably. Two of Black Jack's crew swing at her. She ducks and comes up punching.

Kalen is flying through the air. Black Jack has never seen a cat-human before and can't quite believe her flared nostrils and hissing technique. And she's fast too.

I move in punching. I take some killer blows to the head and fall to the ground. Panicking, I use a ring laser to cut a hole in the floorboard and I fall through and crash on to a card table below. Damn! I've broken my back. I clamber to my feet, fighting past the pain, using meditation skills to engage my leg muscles despite the vertebral snap.

I look up. Lena is watching, amused, detached, as the brawl continues around her. Jamie bites and kicks and shocks Black Jack's men with the power in his tiny frame. Brandon and Alliea work together smoothly as a team. But Kalen is the dangerous one, with her long-limbed kicks and effortless fingerstrikes.

Black Jack steps to one side. Takes Lena's head in his hands. And kisses her. It's an overt proposition: join my crew.

She nods and smiles and takes his hand. This isn't entirely going to plan.

A random punch hits Lena, and suddenly exasperated she strikes out and shatters an arm. Black Jack beams, and leads Lena away. The man with two penises is doing things that no lady should ever witness, but Lena stares at it unflinchingly.

And I feel a garrotte around my throat. My enemies have followed me. I am barely able to move. The garrotte bites in. Kalen sees and dives down to help, but suddenly she has a knife in her throat.

Lena watches it all, amused.

Harry is there, and bites the head off the man who is garrotting me.

Black Jack whispers in Lena's ear. She gives him a second look. He is swarthy, bearded, repulsive. This is a man who used to kill babies to liven up those dull winter evenings.

Lena suddenly backs away. Harry and Kalen are dragging me out of the saloon. We are defeated, retreating. Lena follows us. Black Jack scowls and grabs her and his men secure her with brutal armlocks.

I am looking away as Lena launches her counterattack. I hear screams and cries behind me.

Eventually I am aware of Lena at my side.

"That must hurt like the very devil," she murmurs to me.

"I've had worse," I tell her.

We leave. The moon is high in the sky, blazing out purple gases. The bitter wind whips us. We head back for our ship.

FLANAGAN

"That went badly," says Brandon.

"Yup," I reply.

"Hsss," groans Kalen, her larynx transplant still raw and painful.

FLANAGAN

I am consumed by a black melancholy.

This is what happens when you try to play God. I had a game plan mapped out that involved Black Jack, Lena, and an all-out fight. Lena would see us struggling and would come to our rescue, cementing the bond between us. Black Jack was, of course, paid in advance to pull his punches so that no one was in any severe danger.

But ten years ago I shafted Black Jack on a booty trade. He has nursed his grudge since then, and took this opportunity to beat me and kill me. As a result, I have a smashed spine and half-severed head. Lena did in fact – eventually! – rally to our cause. But it wasn't part of the plan that I should have a broken back. Pain surges up and down my old and battered body. I long to die, to release myself from self-inflicted torment.

Alliea keeps reminding me: the plan worked.

Some fucking plan.

HARRY

I can still taste blood in my mouth. No one ever asks me about it, no one ever questions it. But is it right I should so much savour the taste of human flesh? Am I an animal after all? A less-than-human?

They rely on me to be their strong-arm half-man/half-beast. They depend on my ferocity and rage. But what do they really think of me? Am I a true friend? Do they secretly despise me?

I feel so threatened. So paranoid. It does not occur to them that I might need comfort and support.

Surely it is possible to love the taste of blood and the screaming of dying humans, and yet still be the *sensitive* type?

ALLIEA

The Captain has been giving me strange looks. I fear he thinks I'm grieving too much for Rob. Perhaps he considers me obsessive. Unreliable. Flaky.

Why does he keep looking at me like that?
Am I unworthy of his trust?

BRANDON

Flanagan is still recovering in the Med Tank. His spine has had to be replaced, and a new spinal cord has been fitted into his brain. It is a major procedure with a moderate probability of failure.

If he dies, then as chief astrophysicist I will take command of the crew. It is a prospect I relish. Flanagan is too impetuous, he lacks attention to detail. I know I will do a better job. Captain Brandon Bisby! It has a ring to it.

Of course, I would never cause him to die, but by all that's holy and all that's not, I'd be glad if he did. Then I could assume command.

Or perhaps I should jump the gun? Help his demise along, just a little bit? Is my authority secure enough?

I sweat over that one. I decide to opt for caution. Let's see if Flanagan recovers. If he doesn't, I can take his place without any effort, or intrigue, or danger to myself . . .

LENA

We plan our attack. I am ripe for this. I am going to battle.

I, Lena, am the Captain of my own pirate crew. I've finally agreed to Flanagan's pleas, and it makes me feel good to know that I am indispensable, a warrior among warriors.

Flanagan, now recovered, though rather wan, shows me his plans. He wants to take over a Quantum Beacon in the sector Omega 54, near the planet of Arachne. He has nano spy reports on the security drones, he has maps of the security lattices, he has guns and bombs and a proven track record.

But his approach lacks boldness. I order a full-frontal assault of the Beacon.

"How's your back, Captain?"

"Good as new," he brags.

"Let's do it," I tell him, and he nods.

We launch our invasion.

We sail through space for some months until we are a few sectors from the ship that houses the Quantum Beacon near Arachne. The security system flashes a warning on our vid-screens. We ignore it. We arc gently around the enemy vessel.

I feel a shiver of fear in the pit of my stomach.

Lena, are you sure this is a good . . .

Shut up!

But mixed with the fear is a surge of adrenalin. I feel, calm, confident, assured, I feel . . .

BANG!!!

"Shit!" I say.

They're bombing us. Our pirate ship fires its blasters and its bombs, and the recoil shakes us in our seats. Seconds later, a thousand nanobots come flying out of the Beacon to take us down. All the lights on the bridge flash and alarms sound and I am bewildered, but I am confident that other people know what they are doing, so I

BANG!!!

Explosive charges punch holes through the hull of our ship. The engines burn. Lights on the bridge consoles flash red and amber, sirens wail.

"Sitrep, please," I say calmly.

"We're" says Brandon,

"Oh shit," says Jamie,

"fucked," continues Brandon.

"Backup systems are failing," says Alliea,

"Engines are, oh shit," says Jamie,

"So we're, um," I say, "how bad is it?"

"The hull has been penetrated, the engines have been hit, the ship's a wreck, Captain," says Flanagan.

"So, um," I say. And I pause, and search for words. "What do I do?" I eventually conclude.

"Abandon," says Jamie,

"ship" adds Brandon.

I mentally assess the state of play. Our ship is destroyed. It's a hull with holes.

"Oh shit," I say.

We abandon ship. There's a flurry and a hurry and a panic and the fear in the pit of my stomach has been converted into a desperate urge to void myself into my body armour, I am paralysed with indecision about whether to breathe and vomit, but my body moves almost without conscious control. We suit up, we plunge down tubes into the centre of the ship, where I resume command of my stellar yacht, while Flanagan and his crew take the lifeboat. I scream a command, and the hull doors shoot open and we are catapulted into space. As we leave, more missiles hit our megawarship, and our two small vessels are plunged into the haze and blaze of the massive bombardment.

We fly through space, me in my yacht, the others in the ion-drive liferaft. And Alby flares his way along with us, tugging a lattice net woven with nanobombs. The sun is behind us, and the wrecked hull of our ship suddenly erupts, filling the air with flame and burning plasma. In the confusion, the yacht, lifeboat and Alby creep past the enemy craft towards the vast spaceship where the Beacon is housed.

There is, I realise, belatedly, a plan, though I was not made privy to it. Flanagan starts suggesting orders over his suit radio, which I meekly repeat to the others as if they are *my* ideas. And so, with the enemy behind us, Alby drapes his net over the Quantum Beacon ship's holding bay. The lattice sticks, the bombs explode inwards, a vast hole appears in the side of the Beacon ship's vast hull. The lifeboat punches its way through, while Kalen and Harry and Flanagan parachute down on light carbon chutes, riding the blast of the explosion and zooming through into the inside of the vessel.

Meanwhile, heeding Flanagan's barked instructions in my ear-radio, I head in the other direction, arcing the stellar yacht away at exhilarating speed. Then I pull hard on the ship's joystick and turn my vessel around and bring it to a momentary halt. I aim my lasers at the sun. I fire.

The lasers penetrate and shatter the sun's energy equilibrium. And the sun then flares, engulfing us all in a vast shimmering photosphere, too diffuse to burn, but bright enough to blind the 'bots and the remote operators, and scrambling all the communication channels.

My ship is hurled around the flaring sun, at a speed no faster than light but more intense than mere movement. I feel like a cloud caught in a typhoon, a droplet of water in a waterfall, a photon at the heart of a nuclear blast.

My heart in hiding stirs for a bird, the achieve of, the mastery of the thing.

FLANAGAN

"Good plan," says Brandon, snidely.

"It worked," I snarl.

"We lost our ship!"

"We'll get another."

"All our possessions! Our archives, your guitars, my collection of collectable animated superhero bendy toys!"

"It worked! We're in, aren't we?"

"In where?"

Brandon has a point. This is a seriously weird place. The Quantum Beacon ship is hollow on the inside. A vast cavernous space. The crew inhabited a thin space that constituted the shell of a huge empty egg. We have defeated the Beacon's crew, disabled their 'bots, but what have we actually captured? A big shitload of nothing . . .

"Lena will know," I say confidently.

"Aye aye Cap'n."

Lena's stellar yacht is nowhere to be seen. The flaring of the sun has kickstarted her yacht and sent it out into space armed with so much potential energy it can reach the nearest planetary system in less than fifteen years. She has, in short, escaped. Thanks to me.

"Where," I ask despairingly, "is the fucking thing that does whatever the fuck this fucking thing does?"

LENA

The Quantum Beacon inhabits No Space. It exists at a fold in reality, in a no-place curled within the three unfurled and seven furled dimensions of our eleven-dimensional (counting time as the eleventh dimension of course) universe. It is undetectable by human perception or human-built sensors. It can, however, be liberated and revealed by a simple proton–positron interaction that yields the Beacon's potential. All you need to do is to enter a two hundred digit code via the ship's hard drive.

And my remote computer knows the code.

I wonder, idly, about going back. There is something appealing about their mad quixotic vision. And they need me. They really do need me.

Oxygen supplies: 4 hours 40 minutes.

What?

Oxygen transmuter has been destroyed by a corroder virus. Remaining oxygen supplies 4 hours 39 minutes.

When did this happen?

It came to my awareness eleven seconds ago.

Sabotage.

A fair surmise.

We have to go back.

A valid extrapolation.

That fucking bastard boobytrapped us.

A very fair comment.

Fuck him!

Fuck, indeed, him.

LENA

I arrive back in a flaming temper. Flanagan is deferential and helpless. "Thank God you're here, Lena, you're the only one who knows what to do!" he says. He's right, of course, but his arse-licking flattery offends me.

Grudgingly, I type in the code and access the Beacon. Then I rig the Beacon to connect with Flanagan's coordinates. His strategy now seems clear. He has targeted the Beacon to link us remotely with his home world of Cambria. This is the culmination of his lifelong dream of revenge.

As I work, the crew gradually gather in the control room. When I look up, they are all staring at me.

"You're back, huh?" says Jamie tauntingly.

"I would never abandon my loyal crew," I tell him. He openly sneers. He probably did the sabotage job on the yacht. Little brat. Oh, how I would love to seal him into an enclosed space filled with flesh-eating maggots and leave him there.

"Do you think I'm cute?" Jamie asks me abruptly. I am brought up short. I study him – his tousled hair, his freckles, his cheeky grin.

"Not in the least, worm," I say. His face falls.

"We won't have much time," I tell Flanagan crisply.

"I know," he replies, lowstatusly and humbly.

"They'll be sending rescue vessels."

"It'll take them forty-eight hours to reach us."

"Leaving us forty-eight hours to escape."

"There *is* no escape. Forty-eight hours, and they have us. It's a suicide mission."

What!

"And why should I agree to that idiotic idea?" I snap.

"You don't have to. You've shown us what we have to do. Now, you can go. Take the yacht. We'll make sure you have sufficient oxygen this time. Nice meeting you."

I make a petulant face. "Go!" he insists. "We don't need you any more!"

Lena, this is a patronisingly obvious piece of manipulation.

"Go you cowardly bitch!" Jamie snarls.

"Please go," says Flanagan. "Save yourself! I couldn't bear you to be hurt."

"Lena," says Kalen, imploringly. "You've done enough, it's our battle now."

"It probably won't work anyway," says Brandon snidely. "I mean, what would *you* know about quantum engineering?"

A sheet of flame hits the ceiling. Globules of fiery tears drip from ceiling to floor.

"Lena," hisses Alby, "I admire you sssso very much."

"I'm staying," I tell Flanagan, stubbornly.

Oh, Lena.

HARRY

This is not my idea of battle. I'm strapped to a chair, my furred limbs in restraints, wires leading into my brain. In the world outside, warships are on their way to destroy and explode me. But I, meanwhile, will be in cyberspace, inhabiting a robot body, fighting on a world which is not my own, for a people who are not my own, in a cause which is not my own.

I signed up for this, apparently.

Curiously, I feel a surge of curiosity. What will it be like, I wonder, not to be me?

Not to be Loper?

To be, so very nearly, a proper human being?

LENA

As I prepare for battle, I relax by mulling over the principles of the Quantum Beacons and Heimdall. The mathematics is formidably hard, and to be honest, I have forgotten whatever I once knew. But the basic principle is:

(Are you getting this?)

Of course.

The basic principle is: Matter cannot travel faster than the speed of light. Einstein proved it, and no one since has found a way around it. This constitutes an absolute limit on human progress. We cannot ever travel the other galaxies and stars, let alone traverse the Universe, or master the myriad worlds of creation. It takes too long to get there.

But, without wishing to brag, as the creator of Heimdall, or co-creator, or major inspirer of, or considerable influence on the development of – well anyway! regardless of what my actual role was; in the construction of Heimdall, we found a way to solve the conundrum. The twin-track colonisation of space. And it was a masterly solution. You see, we . . .

You've explained all this.

Hush, Now, let me tell the story chronologically. After the first robot landfall on Hope, the other colony ships began to reach their destinations. And each colony was equipped with infinite energy resources thanks to the energy pumps; and remained in constant instant contact with Earth, thanks to Heimdall. The manipulation of quantum states means, as I have indeed explained before, but I'm recapping now for the benefit of the slower-witted among you; this manipulation allows for the instantaneous transmission of information. So in effect, we have a Universe in which distances are vast and onerous to travel; but in which email and phone communication are instant and effortless.

And thus, and so, the other planets were colonised by the colony ships. After Hope, there was Endurance, Enterprise, Beauty, Shiva, Mecca, Mayflower, New Earth, and a myriad other planets, since each new colony routinely built and launched its own new colony ships.

And in order to experience and help colonise these alien planets, a human based in the Earth system has to merely sign up for a tour of duty. The human's body is placed in a flotation tank, and electrodes placed in the brain and on the skin and genitals. And, on the alien planet, a Doppelganger Robot is built with the ability to experience the full gamut of sensory data – sight, touch, hearing, pain. It thus becomes possible for a human being based on Earth to "live" on an alien planet by switching a single switch and inhabiting the DR body.

The question is, though: why? Why give up your life on Earth, with all its luxuries and pleasures, in order to endure life on a hellish alien planet?

Because it's addictive. I was totally hooked on it. My years of mainlining Hope were the best and most enjoyable of my entire life. And so many other humans shared my excitement and addiction. A huge and tax-free salary for doing part-time DR work also helps to motivate the Earth populace to do their duty . . .

And thanks to my son the Cheo, it is these DRs who are the dominant citizens and, indeed, masters of all the occupied planets. And so, ultimately, it is Earth Humans who have all the power, all the control. So instead of a Universe of freely acting nation planets, as I had always envisaged, we have a host of slave planets, run by DRs, on behalf of Earth Humans.

I played my role in creating this corrupt network of space tyranny. I take no credit for that. For once, I *ask* for no credit. I merely, each morning, in those cruel minutes before my optimism of spirit kicks in, suffer and squirm in shame and bitter regret. For the way things are in this Universe of ours is *wrong*.

"Strap up, Lena."

I realise we are about to launch our invasion. I look around at my army – six of us strapped into armchairs, with Kalen at the control console.

"Let's kick some robot ass," says Flanagan, with an attempt at rousingness.

"It was *my* turn to say that," Jamie tells him bitterly.

Flanagan sighs, wearily.

"Let's go," he says.

BOOK 6

FLANAGAN

Six robots stand on a hilltop and look down at the rolling green hills of Cambria and breathe in fresh tangy air. The sound of birds is shrill and lovely in the sky. The sun beats down, and the robots sweat, and feel the heat as pleasure. A two-headed push-me-pull-you stag wanders in front of them, and one of its heads flicks a curious glance at them. But the stag has no fear of humanoid creatures. Only humans are hunted on this planet.

I look around at my home planet and I feel a surge of pleasure that cannot be described. The here-ness, now-ness, mine-ness, the truth of the place overwhelm me. This is a land my people created, with centuries of hard toil and bleak dangerous existence. They died in dust storms, they were consumed in random solar flares that poured deadly radiation into every inch of the planet. They bombed the planet's core to release its icy heart, and used its melted water to create a planet-wide system of waterways. They carefully nurtured Earth-born seeds and sperm and grew fields and orchards and meadows, and filled them with rabbits, badgers, stags, dogs, butterflies, and a whole host of other flora and fauna. And solar panels in orbit around Cambria's sun provided limitless power to fuel this work.

I look at my fellow Doppelganger Robots. We are an imposing group. Each of us (apart from Harry) is seven foot or more in height, heavily muscled, beautiful, graceful, godlike. Alliea DR is black, with fiery eyes, and a slender waist that is dwarfed by perfect breasts and bulging thighs. Lena DR is coffee-coloured, deadly thin, with long white hair that sails in the wind. Jamie DR is shaven-bald, white, with his huge arms bare and tattooed, but despite his muscle-bound physique he moves with the grace of a leopard. Brandon is cool, lean, clad in black, with black staring eyes. And I – I am built like a gladiator.

We are all of us (apart from Harry) variations on the same theme. We are comic book wish-fulfilment fantasies made real, par for the course for Doppelganger Robots. And our style options were, frankly, limited. There was a wide stock of out-of-service DRs available to us to hack into, and we took the least garish ones.

But entertainingly, Harry DR stands a foot shorter than the rest of us, and has a beard, and fake glasses and spindly frame. He is a Boffin DR, a different fantasy – wish-fulfilment for an Earth-bound Jock who wants to experience the perverse thrill of being a weedy geek. But despite his slight physique, Harry DR has the same enhanced strength as all Doppelganger Robots. We can run faster, punch harder, and withstand more physical pain and stress than any human born.

Today, we go to war.

LENA

It's been four hours since we escaped from the warehouse where the DR bodies were stored, and every moment has been sheer bliss. Apart from my brief visit to the planet Wild West, I've been in free space for over a hundred years. It's wonderful to, once again, smell flowers and cow shit, and have a skin that changes temperature as the sun goes in and out of clouds. I feel alive.

Curiously, though, I feel disengaged from the enterprise of which I am, notionally, the leader. Flanagan defers to me constantly, but I just murmur, "Up to you." I feel intoxicated by life and by the newness of my oh-so-perfect body. And liberated, too, by the lack of fear. If this body is destroyed, I can hack into another one. If a tooth falls out, I can will it to grow back. For the duration of my stay on this planet, I am invulnerable, immortal, self-renewing.

On my return to the Quantum Beacon, however, I face certain death; curiously, that doesn't perturb me.

After activating the six DRs in the warehouse, we worked hard on the next stage of our – Flanagan's – plan. The other DRs in storage were neutralised and de-brained; it will take weeks of work to restore them to working order. Then we packed a truck with missiles, guns, body armour and camerabots. There was no security to contend with *inside* the warehouse because, of course, in the normal course of things only Earth computers can access the interior of such places. No one expected that the system could be breached via a conquered Quantum Beacon that allowed us to hack into the Cambrian mainframe.

We did have to fight our way out however. It was a short sharp shock experience for the four DR guards, who found themselves outgunned and totally taken by surprise. Their heads were blown off their bodies, causing immediate deactivation of the DR–Human link.

In a stolen truck, we screeched a route through the city outskirts and parked near the top of the highest hill we could find. And now, Brandon opens up the boxes and releases the camerabots. Flanagan dials an all-sets-to-be-activated telephone number and the ringtone on every mobile phone on the planet beeps, or hums, or sings, or plays piano or guitar or orchestra. We have just phoned the entire planet . . .

And, when every human being on Cambria switches on his vidphone, he or she sees Flanagan and the rest of us standing on a hilltop, in a deliberately iconic and dangerous pose. "We are your liberators," Flanagan says earnestly into the camera, and I feel a prickle of excitement run down my spine.

Flanagan speaks eloquently. But my mind is not on his mission, or his passion, or his eloquence. I am obsessed by the heat on my brow, the smells in my nostrils, and my ultimate sense of power. I have the body I always dreamed of, the body of a warrior-woman-queen-goddess. There's only so much you can do with flesh and a human genetic heritage; I always feel my real body is a pale imitation of the dream which inspires it.

Now I inhabit my own dream.

And in the background of my self-loving, self-glorifying hymn to myself, I dimly register Flanagan's words:

"I am one of you. A citizen of this planet. This is a revolution. We will throw off our shackles. We will be free. All you have to do is . . ."

"*Do nothing*. Whether you are on the surface, or dwelling in your underground cavern, stop what you are doing, and focus on the doing of nothing. Sit down, if you can. Eat, if you have food, but chew silently. Do not speak, do not listen if a DR speaks to you. Do not obey instructions from a DR. If you are shot and lie bleeding and dying on the ground, do not whimper or groan. Die silently, die like a human, die proud.

"This is our only weapon. We withdraw our servitude. We refuse to be slaves. We will die, rather than be slaves. Keep your eyes on this screen. Die proud."

Yeah, what a really great plan. Everyone dies.

HARRY

This is so humiliating. Everyone else has a great bod, and I'm stuck in this fucking geek physique. I have pimples. My knees knock. I have a nervous twitch.

This is the battle of a lifetime, and it's being filmed. They'll be releasing DVs of this for centuries to come. And I look like a prat. *And* I've got a nervous twitch!

I want to growl with rage, but I can't even do that. It comes out as . . . nerdy whine.

ARRRGHHHHHHHHHHHHHHHHHHHaaaaaaagh!

LENA

"Good speech, Flanagan," I say.

"It was, wasn't it?"

"Your projection was good too."

"Was I charismatic?"

"I think you got the point across."

"I guess I'm pretty damn gorgeous, aren't I?"

I look at him. Despite myself, I feel a swamp of pleasure in my groin.

"It's not real. You're a phoney, a cliché hunk. Ersatz."

"Yeah, but you're hot for me."

"I could be, in other circumstances. Like, er." I've lost it. Flanagan DR beams at me. Arrogant bastard.

I point at the horizon. Enemy forces are clustering.

"We've got no chance, you know. Why don't we just run away?"

"Keep your voice down. We're on camera."

I glare arrogantly at the camera. Flanagan looks imperious. All around the world, on his say-so, people die.

BRANDON

"Take your position, Brandon."

"Aye aye, Cap'n," I say.

All hell breaks loose.

The DR army has encircled the hill. Gun 'copters fly above us and missiles rain down. But hidden in the trees, operated by Alliea, we have an automated ack-ack machine that laser-spots all incoming missiles and creates an impervious shield above our heads. Alliea's job is to run from location to location with the ack-ack machine so they cannot ever target where the missiles are coming from.

On the top of the hill, we stare down at the huge army assembled against us . . .

And then we charge them. They aren't expecting this. The DR soldiers are heavily armed of course and have clear superperspex shields to protect them against enemy fire. But on this planet, no one ever fights one on one. No one duels. No one, in fact, ever actually *fights*. For a hundred years the DR oppressors have presided over a planet full of sheep.

Now, six wolves have entered the fray.

We fight in pairs, Harry is by my side, in his preposterous geek body. We have laser guns and grenades, and as we sprint down the hill we hurl grenades like children tossing water bombs on a sunny summer's day.

The first rank of Doppelganger Robots explode. We use the laser guns to blow off heads, but all the while we keep rolling and ducking and weaving and using our shields to block laser blasts. You need to get the right angle to deflect the light blast; there's a knack to it. The enemy DRs have no such knack. They hold their shields in front of their faces and we blast straight through and blow out their cybernetic brains.

Then we're through the first rank and the DRs are clustered round us like stooks in a wheat field. They really have no idea. We crouch down low, and slice hamstrings with our short-bladed swords taken from the training armoury. Our blades penetrate eyes, gouge out brains, lop off limbs. The DRs are phenomenally strong, but so are we. They are phenomenally fast, but so are we. And they are incompetent fighters, graceless, stupid, inexperienced. And we are a pirate crew.

We are unstoppable. We rip the heart out of the enemy's army, then we stand triumphant. Alliea, meanwhile, is still raining missiles on the disorganised ground troops. The gun 'copters are whirling around in confusion, till one crunches into another and both plunge to earth.

Then a laser gun hits me in the head. I just have time to register the leering triumphant face of my killer before I...

....

....

.... *become her*.

The DR who killed me is a blonde white-skinned female with an exaggeratedly muscular upper torso and a shaven head. She's a Dyke DR without a doubt, but I'm not complaining. And now, through her eyes, I get to watch myself die; I see the head of my Brandon DR body explode in a hail of artificially grown blood and brain.

Then the new "Brandon Dyke DR" resumes the battle. My fellow soldiers assume I'm still on their side, and are stunned when I turn my guns on them and start killing them with lethal laser sweeps. And as I kill, I sing:

"I can't get no-o, sat-is-faction. I can't get no-o, sati-is-faction. I can't get no-o, sat-is-faction." No doubt there are other verses of this bluesy dirge available, but I stick to singing the memorable first line, over and over, with exaggerated lipsynch.

I aim a laser at a DR – and just in time, I notice his lips are moving: "I can't get no-o, sat-is-faction. I can't get no-o, sat-is-faction." I don't recognise the body, but I realise instantly this is one of my team. The laser beam goes to the side; an enemy DR vanishes in light and splattered flesh.

The DRs should have body armour, of course, like human soldiers do. But they are so inherently strong that it makes them complacent. No human has ever challenged them, or fought them. They have been all-powerful gods of their world for all these years.

And now we're making cybernetic mincemeat out of them.

The battle continues. After a while, it becomes a massacre. I change bodies four times, until I finally do a head count and realise there are five DRs left.

Only Lena has her original body intact. I feel a shiver of respect. The rest of us have been killed and killed again. But each time the killer blow was struck, Kalen at her control pad switched our connection point from one DR to another. Flanagan has software that allows us to override an existing DR user – we can, in effect, kick the fucker's mind out and send it back to Earth.

And by this means, we hope to conquer an entire planet. There are six of us; but we have unlimited "lives". Each time we die, we are reincarnated seconds later, in the body of a neighbouring DR.

This, we feel, narrows the odds.

At the bottom of the hill, we rejoin Alliea. She has suffered badly in the defence of the hill, despite the ack-ack computer's sterling work. One arm has been blown off her. She is blind in one eye. Blood oozes from the stump of her left leg, and she is using a sword as a crutch.

"Just a flesh wound," she mumbles, and we all dutifully laugh.

"Let's get out of here," says Flanagan.

ALLIES

We are part of a vast DR patrol sweeping through the underground regions, in the city known as Cardiff. From her control panel, Kalen had flipped us into six new DR bodies. We have different bodies, different weapons, but we have no way of telling who is really who beneath the DR frame.

And so, blindly marching with our fellow DR warriors, we find ourselves confronted by a mass rebellion of slaves. Acting on Flanagan's advice, the citizens of Cardiff have sat themselves down on the streets, gazing at the battle being enacted on their video phones. As we approach and bark orders at them, the Cambrians refuse to move, and ignore orders barked at them by the increasingly hysterical DR officers.

Eventually the commanding officer loses patience. "Fire at will!" he screams, and I long to raise my plasma gun and blow his head off. But I'm too far away, I can't get a clean shot, and I don't know who is friend and who is foe.

Blindly following orders, the DRs raise their combat pulse guns and fire into the seated crowds of passive protests. No one moves. A hail of pulse bursts rips apart limbs and shredded flesh. Dozens die within seconds.

But no one cries out. The crowd is still and fearless, the dying people swallow their death rattles. More pulse bursts are fired. Hundreds die now. Blood washes under the haunches and arses of the seated multitude. No one complains, or screams, or even glances up.

The massacre continues, as we desperately try to tell friend from foe so that we can coordinate our counterattack. I see a man's head shouting wildly, and eventually identify his words: "*There is a house in New Orleans*." He is singing, not shouting.

I move closer. I memorise the features of his DR body; black hair, a pony tail, black tunic, bare arms, a dragon tattoo. "*They call the Rising Sun*," I sing out, and he turns and sees me. He winks. He scans me up and down, memorising my features. "Lena?" he mouths at me. "Alliea", I mouth back. "Hot," he mouths at me.

We move together, walking shoulder to shoulder. "Love me tender, love me do," someone sings. But who? We can't see.

"IT'S BEEN THE RUIN OF MANY A POOR GIRL!!" I scream and the DRs around me look blank. So I turn my gun on them and blow off five heads.

"AND ME, O GOD, FOR ONE!" screams Flanagan DR, as I duck and roll out of the way of a laser blast. Flanagan too fires.

"I HATE THESE FUCKING SONGS!" a DR screams at me, and just in time I avert the laser beam.

"Brandon?"

"Yes!!!!" I memorise his appearance. He fires his rocket launcher at me and blows up the DR bodies behind.

". . . satisfaction. And I try, and I try and I try and try!" sings a bloodied limbless corpse on the ground. Then a DR nearby jerks and stands differently. "I can't get no, dah dah dum", she sings. One of us. Lena or Harry, can't tell which.

And so the counterattack begins . . . it's another remorseless, pitched, bloody battle. I long for the short swords, the elegance and beauty of their blades. But we have to use guns and fists and feet. It is awkward clumsy fighting. I have my head blown off at least seven times. But each time Kalen is there with the pickup, and I start again with a new body.

When the bloodbath is over, six of us stand intact and bleeding. We turn and look.

The streets of Cardiff are strewn with corpses, as the sun sets. The light of a hundred thousand video phones flickers, eerie and sad.

But a few hundred Cambrians remain alive, picking themselves off the ground, soaked in blood and brain. They stand, in a series of staggering waves, and they stare at us.

And when all the survivors are on their feet, they bow, low, and respectful. We raise our fists in triumph. They cheer.

Kalen flips us out, and the DR bodies crumple to the ground, inert, mindless, dead.

FLANAGAN

"Where the fuck is Lena?"

LENA

What can I say? It was fun for a while. But then I got bored.

For Flanagan, this is a glorious cause. The liberation of his home planet. What could be grander or more important! And for a while, I joined in happily with his precious mission.

Burn, shoot, run, duck, block, laser blast in face, die, reborn. Burn, shoot, run, duck, block . . . And so it went on. I lived, killed, died, lived, killed, died . . .

Then suddenly, I got swamped with depression and ennui. So I ran away.

And now here I am, in the restaurant district of the underground world. People crowd the streets, sitting, watching their video phone coverage of the planetwide bloodbath. The first battle was captured in close-up on camera-bots. Now, Kalen is downloading satellite film of the war and rerouting it via the mobile phone systems. So the outlines are fuzzy, but the basic idea is clear; DRs are dying all over the world. And so the people wait, and watch, and when they are unlucky, they are massacred.

No one stirs as I walk down the street. No one looks at me, though all are aware I am there. I am redhaired, flamboyant, slender rather than busty. But six and a half feet tall and with hands that could crack walnuts. I am hot for myself, savouring my own body.

I see a young man in the crowd. He is kneeling, but his face looks tense. "Stand," I tell him. He breaks ranks; he stands. He looks at me. Eyes full of fear.

"You will do *everything* I say," I tell him.

He nods, numbly.

"*Anything* I say." He nods again.

Too easy. Too like rape. I walk on and leave him there, steeped in his self-hate and self-betrayal.

Two DRs block my path. I make my move. They reach for their blaster guns, alerted by my air of "otherness'. But instead of shooting them, I reach for their minds.

Twenty times already Kalen has flipped me into another DR's body. I am getting a knack for it. And my remote computer still functions, I still have an instant grasp of any fact or sensory input I require, at a moment's notice. So I order my computer to echo Kalen's flip function. I enter the brains of the DRs. I possess them.

They drop their guns. They look at me.

I look at them.

I look at them.

I look at them.

I am inhabiting three DR bodies at the same time. It takes great focus, but I've learned over the years how to multi-task instinctively. I can play chess and also type. I can read, and simultaneously text. I can even read, text, cut my toenails, and watch TV, all at the same time, without any loss of focus in any of the activities.

And now, I am three people, all at once. I am the First Lena, the redhaired slender beautiful female who was my body when I walked past the humans. I am Guy Lena, a black-skinned leanly muscled giant with a face that would have melted the heart of Michelangelo. And I am Dream Girl Lena, an impossible beauty with an oval face and taut, powerful muscles.

First Lena smiles at Guy Lena, Guy Lena is aroused, Dream Girl Lena looks at the other two and feels a surge of joy.

We walk into an empty mansion. The rooms are deserted. The human staff are on the streets; and DRs who live there are in combat. We have the place to ourselves.

We strip naked. I strip, and I watch myself strip, and I watch myself strip. I stroke my cock, I touch my breasts, I touch my breasts, I watch myself touch my breasts, I watch myself stroke my cock. I go on my knees, I stand and kiss Guy Lena on the cheeks, I feel his manhood in my mouth, I feel her mouth on my manhood, my tongue touches my tongue, my hand my tongue my cock my cunt my cunt my body my body my body I fuck me me fucks I we fuck.

FLANAGAN

"Where are we now?"

"This is Pentre Ifan. My home town."

"Time to kick—"

Brandon dies.

I die.

I change eyes. A DR is staring at me crazily. "Ass!" it says, completing the sentence.

"You got it," I tell it, and the DR that is Brandon nods, reassured. I find my gun.

We start killing.

KALEN

I'm tired. I'm frightened we will lose.

This the hardest job, sitting at the computer screen, flipping minds into bodies. I have too many facts to accommodate. I'm tired, I can't eat, I've pissed and shat myself because I'm afraid to lose focus for even a moment. We made a mistake, we should have had two people at the computer. This is the hardest job. Those bastards have it easy.

Bastards!

I watch as Brandon dies. I flip him.

Bastards!

Flanagan dies. I flip him.

Bastards!

Lena, curse her rotten fucking soul, is having sex with two astonishingly gorgeous DRs. I'm attuned to her mind, so I can see everything she sees. But somehow, her images blur. She seems to be seeing from different eyes. And she's bloody well having sex! I can't believe that whore. All the same it's . . .

Alliea dies. I flip her.

Harry dies. I flip him.

Harry dies again. I flip him.

Harry dies again. Careless fucking fool. I ought to let him . . . I flip him.

Jamie dies. I flip him.

Flanagan dies. I . . .

FLANAGAN

I see a joyful scene.

The streets are paved with bodies, once again. Blood trickles and pools and we stamp on dead human flesh as we make our way down the boulevard. But at the end of the street, a dozen DRs are vacantly standing. Their guns hang limply by their sides. At their feet are hundreds of human beings, calmly waiting for death. But death does not come.

The human intelligences controlling the DRs are crumbling. They cannot cope with the idea that an entire planet of human beings can stand against them. They are stressed, and fazed, and totally fucked up by the endless self-sacrifice and heroism they are encountering.

That aspect of my plan, the part I always doubted, is actually working. The spirit of the human population of Cambria has collectively defied the robot oppression. Their sacrifice has bought us time, has sapped the enemy spirit, has undermined their confidence and self-belief.

These killer robots are not, in fact, all-powerful gods. They are inhabited by the minds of spoiled and pampered Earth system dwellers. They are millionaires, sybarites, they have swimming pools in their houses and second homes in the Asteroid Belt. They are white-collar workers, but such is the endless wealth of the Earth system that few of them need to work more than ten or eleven hours a week. The rest of the time they can devote to self-indulgence, and mandatory DR duties.

These fucking gutless softies have ruled my planet for over a century. But at the first sign of opposition, they are crumbling. We easily massacre the DRs at the end of the street. Before long, DRs start committing suicide in front of us – blowing off their own heads in order to send their minds back to the comfort and total security of the Earth system.

It takes us forty-two hours to conquer the entire planet.

BRANDON

Three DRs appear in front of me and sing, "I can't get no satisfaction" in beautiful three-part harmony. I'm freaked. I know who Harry, Alliea, Jamie and Flanagan are. Lena is the only one of us unaccounted for. So which of the DRs is the real Lena?

"Who are you?" asks one of the DRs.

"I'm Brandon," I say.

"I'm Lena," says the redhaired Lena.

"No I'm Lena," the gorgeous one says.

"No *I'm* Lena!" says the Guy DR and they all giggle.

I think I'm missing something here.

"The battle's over," I tell the Lenas.

"Shame, we missed all the fun," redhaired Lena says scornfully.

Flanagan joins us.

"Three Lenas," I explain.

Flanagan raises his blaster and blows the heads off the Guy Lena and the Redhaired Lena.

"One's enough," he says mildly.

Lena screams with genuine horror. "Do you know how that felt?" she hisses.

"Lena, you're a coward," Flanagan tells her.

"Well, yeah."

"I need you."

"I know."

"Let's do it."

FLANAGAN

Like every planet owned by the Galactic Corporation, Cambria is armed with an astonishingly powerful alien-defence armoury. A ring of satellites are equipped with force fields, force nets, fusion bombs, and every other human weapon created. These weapons are of course controlled remotely via the Quantum Beacon by powerful computers on Earth. No human or DR on Cambria has authority or wherewithal to unleash anti-alien weaponry. The stakes are too high for that.

The millions of space sensors are on constant alert for the slightest trace of Bugs, BULs, Glugs, Frondies or Sparklers. Monsters from Outer Space, in other words.

We storm the space headquarters. We encounter no resistance. The DRs are all inert. Their strategy was clearly to sit it out until we were good and tired; and then attack again in force.

Forty-seven hours ten minutes have elapsed since our arrival on Cambria.

We hack into a computer link to the Space Factory, on board which ten thousand human miners work at fashioning complex metals and fabrics out of the stuff of stars and planets.

We then fake a radio transmission which is beamed out in zipped encrypted form to the Space Factory, then transmitted back to us at the space HQ. This transmission is, of course picked up by the satellite sensors and conveyed immediately to the computers on Earth.

The message is brief, and unclear, but the gist goes like this:

ME: . . . no hope any more, can you hear me, out?

BRANDON: Space Probe One, I am not receiving clearly,

say again, say again.

ME: We're infested with Bugs. They've taken over the Quantum Beacon. I repeat . . .

The signal fades.

And so the word is out on the street. The Bugs have invaded! But will the computers take the bait?

The Bugs, scientists think, exist at a subatomic as well as an atomic level. This explains how Bugs can penetrate any partition, apart from the crushed space of a Quantumarity. They can fly through open space. They are invulnerable. They are unstoppable. They are the most deadly thing ever created by that heartless bastard god of evolution.

If the Bugs could escape their cage and enter a Quantum Beacon . . . who could say what might happen? Could a Bug Army emerge, instantaneously and intact, in the Sol system? If that happened, then all the citizens of Earth and its neighbouring space colonies would die a hideous death.

No one knows if in fact such a thing is possible. But the fear of it is corrosive . . . And so, in a millionth of a second, the Earth computers analyse all the possibilities and possible outcomes and they reach a speedy decision.

The alien defence system is mobilised. Vast energy flares hurtle through space. Asteroids and space debris are incinerated. The Space Factory itself is in the direct line of fire; it is obliterated in less time than it takes a raindrop to coalesce.

Simultaneously, the Cambria Quantum Beacon's defence systems are switched off. The energy flare hits with the power of a dozen suns, and the Quantum Beacon is entirely unprotected. We watch, on our screens, as the squat orbital space station that housed the Beacon vanishes in a flash of light.

The defence system continues to hurl its deadly rain into space, but it is on automatic pilot by now. The remote computer link has been severed. The Quantum Beacon is gone; the inhabitants of the Earth system now have no way of communicating with or controlling the planet of Cambria.

A second before the blast reaches us, all six of us are flipped out of the Cambrian system. Our DR bodies are left behind.

The Cambrian people are now alone in space. Earth can now no longer control its robot slaves, or even contact them. And, because Cambria is a relatively remote system, it will take a hundred years (their subjective time) for a spaceship of new DRs to reach them from the nearest inhabited planet. By that time, I hope, they will be prepared.

Finally, my people are free.

I have saved my world from an eternity of brutality, tyranny and oppression.

Hallefuckinglujah.

BOOK 7

JAMIE

"All right Jamie, the ball's in your court now." Flanagan is beaming at me, his old Dutch Uncle routine. We are all suited up, ready for whatever hell will be thrown at us.

"Yobaby, how long we got?" On the console's plasma screens I can see approximately .78 million Corporation ships. We are completely surrounded. They are moving closer and closer.

"Oh, a few minutes."

"Munchies."

The Captain produces a bar of chocolate which I scoff. Lena is standing there, looking dazed.

"Give us a kiss sweetheart," I tell her.

"Give him a kiss," Flanagan says.

"As if," she says scornfully, and Flanagan glares at her. She relents, and gives me a lovely kiss on the cheek. I swoon. I feel a little stirring in my trousers.

"Do I give him a blowjob too? This is a child Flanagan! I'm not a fucking . . ."

"I'm 121," I tell her coldly.

"You made your bed, you fucking lie in it. You're a child."

She has a point. I sit at the computer. "Lena, can you fly this thing?"

Lena sits at the joystick. She overrides the "Orbit" control and fires the space station engines. "We can't outrun Corporation warships," she warns me.

"Just a little kangaroo hop will do."

She fires the engines. We leap up in space. The warships start firing on us. They are spooked! I bet they didn't know that the Quantum Beacons were all built in old colony ships, and are still fully functional spacecraft. The first missiles miss, but a second later we sustain our first direct hit.

I slip the CD-Rom into the Quantum Beacon's computer. It boots up. The "Teleport" program begins. I map the codes manually, deleting and modifying to counteract the computer's anti-virus programming.

"I know what you're doing," says Lena, with that faraway look in her eyes. Then she starts to smile. Then she gives me another kiss, a great big smacker this time, on the lips.

"Don't distract him!" shouts Brandon with, I feel, a hint of jealousy. I'm beaming now, and bright red in the face. I look at the computer screen. "ACCESS DENIED" flashes up and I type in the override. I have a few seconds of pure genius.

Lena turns to the Captain. "This isn't a suicide mission," she says, marvelling. "You have a way out."

"There's always a way out," says Flanagan.

"You can teleport? You can actually do that?"

"Not exactly," says Flanagan.

"I created the program!" I tell her. "I'm a genius, I'm so clever! Munchie!"

The Captain gives me another chocolate bar. But I don't touch it. Actually, I'm feeling a bit tired. I get that a lot these days. Mornings are okay, I always wake up with a spring in my step, and I love the way my mind hops and bounces around. I have the mental vigour of a ten-year-old, boing! boing!, my thoughts go so fast no oldie could ever keep up. Combined of course with the intellectual maturity of a man in his hundreds. Beat that, huh?

But the truth is, I'm starting to feel my age. I feel like Dr McCoy, in the original *Star Trek*, but stuck in this silly child's body. I wish I were Jackie Chan, the 3D animated version. Then I'd be young for ever.

"Release the escape pod," Flanagan says and our vessel rips in half. The bridge area becomes a liferaft, powered by massive fusion engines. The bottom half of the space station houses the Quantum Beacon. Our engines fire us forward, safely out of the way of the Beacon, then we shoot "up" into space, in the small gap between the Corporation warships. They aren't expecting this, and our brilliant stunt buys us a few moments more of life.

The Beacon itself remains in its secure cage in the bottom half of the ship, the bit we have left behind. And I type in the final commands which instruct the Beacon to begin its teleport program. This is my masterstroke, it took me weeks, nay, months, to come up with this one. The world's great scientists were baffled by this problem, but I found a way!

Because, you see, the laws of nature forbid teleportation. The Universe just won't allow it. Hence, the colony ships, and the use of DRs. It would be much easier to walk into a booth in Manhattan and teleport yourself to a planet in the Crab Nebula. But that would violate every principle of modern quantum-relativistic-multiversal string theory, otherwise known as Big Toe. (Toe stands for TOE, which stands for Theory of Everything. There is no "Little Toe", that's just some scientist's idea of a gag. Is that clear or should I explain it all again with diagrams?)

This no-teleporting law is, to me, immensely frustrating. Spock and Kirk and McCoy used to teleport all the time, though for some reason it only worked over short distances from ship to planet. Jeannie the Meanie does it every week in her teatime show *I'm a Space Traveller with "tude*. *Black Hole Holidays* is a show entirely based around the assumption that instant teleportation between planets is possible, and for years I thought the space travellers were real people. (They're not! They're actors! It's all a fake! Stay with me, guys, I'm full of these kinds of insights.) But in the real world, tragically, teleportation just can't happen.

Except, I discovered, the logic of the Quantum Beacon's quantum paralleling system *does* allow, in theory, one very limited form of teleportation. This involves patches of space becoming "paired". First, you program the computer to identify two patches of space which have a roughly comparable pattern of matter distribution. Because of quantum fuzz, this can be a fairly approximate pairing; in quantum reality, a chair and a table would be pretty well indistinguishable. (In fact, the chair would be a table *some of the time* – baffling, huh?) Both of the paired-up patches of space need to be, obviously, in the region of a Quantum Beacon.

Then you take detailed quantum-state readings of both patches of space, using nanotechnology and very powerful computers. You with me still?

And then, using multi-dimensional infraction theory, the space itself is teleported. Not the matter inside it, not the energy, but *the space itself*.

This requires (whew!) a reversal of the usual Einsteinian/Leibnitzian principle that all reality can be described in terms of the relationship between things. But it's not that space is a Thing in Itself, a like, you know, *noumenon*. It's the curvature of space, the displacedness of space, that's identified and teleported. Here's the patronising metaphor: Imagine a bed with a hollow in it, where a person has been sleeping. Now imagine that hollow can be swapped for the hollow in another, different bed. No one will ever notice the difference; but the hollows will have interchanged. Space will have teleported.

That's my theory. No one has ever thought of doing it before because, I suppose, it is a totally stupid and futile thing to do. What's the point of teleporting space! But there is a point. (Finally! Eventually!) The point is:

It doesn't really work. Space does get teleported, but the process is messy and ugly and it does weird things to dimensional reality.

Things such as this. We look at our plasma screen and see the Corporation warships turn and prepare to pursue. We are a nippy little minnow skeetering off into the ocean. They are the barracudas and the sharks. They will outrun us easily.

But then a green light flashes on my screen. The Teleport

function has engaged. It covers a region of space large enough to encircle the warships – but not large enough to encircle us! You see! All this has been carefully and brilliantly planned! The space is then teleported and swapped for a portion of space near a Quantum Beacon in area Q432 of the Milky Way.

And at the precise moment in which spatial teleportation occurs, space itself is rent in a multiplicity of twains.

Just for an instant.

In fact, less than an instant, a tiny portion of an instant, one times ten to the power of millions. But for that brief period, space does what space shouldn't do. It *isn't there.*

The consequences of the rift in space are cataclysmic. To us, from our vantage point speeding niftily away, it's as if a giant god with an invisible hand has squeezed the Universe. The Corporation warships are crushed instantaneously, and a huge tidal wave of pressure rushes through space. Our ship is tossed and hurled around, suns flare, planets are caught in vast whirlpools hurling round at light speed and further distorting dimensional reality as relativistic effects kick in.

We are swatted away from this vast dimensional hurricane like a fly, and we hurtle through space. Our engines explode. Our hull melts and reforms. Then the Beacon ship itself falls to pieces around us.

We are left floating free in space, secure in our spacesuits. Alby throws his lattice net around us again, and tows us through deep space. I am weeping tears of amazement.

What a fucking mess I just caused! What a total gross-out fucking up of reality!

I ripped a piece of space. No man or child has ever done so much.

I'm the king of the castle!

ALBY

We float through spaccccee for nearly two years. I find it relaxing. I accept that the ressst of them are sssuffering badly. But they do have food and fluid in their suits, enough to keep them alive for five yearsssss in all.

At lassst, we are picked up by a merchant ship. I flicker away on the outssside of the ship, doing my imperssssonation of a waning comet. The others recccceive their creature comfortsss and a lift to the neeressst habitable planet.

Another ten yearsss passss.

LENA

I'm conscious there is something of an atmosphere. I am not as popular as I would like.

This I find peculiar. After all, since I am technically still their hostage, I could have betrayed them all to the Captain of the merchant vessel which picked us up. I could have denounced them as pirates. But then, I suppose, if I had done that, they would simply have killed the Captain and stolen the ship.

Instead – they took the Captain prisoner, and stole his ship. After great debate, it was decided to put the Captain into cryo-sleep. This was a one-man merchant vessel, mainly run by autopilot. The Captain had taken his cargo through 200 light-years of space, most of it spent in coma. Strictly speaking the ship could run without him; but he was the human failsafe. He was, like all such merchant Captains, a sour, embittered, supremely well read intellectual. In other periods, he would have been a professor in a university. These days, such people are sent on long lonely space journeys with computer access to every academic book and journal ever published. When he reaches his destination, this Captain will publish an academic treatise based on nearly forty years of intensive study. Occasionally, during that period, he would have had to veer around an asteroid swarm. But generally, it's an easy life.

This particular Captain is, as it happens, clinically insane. I read his treatise and it was utter gibberish. But still, the ship sailed on. Rather than bicker about who should have the one cryo-berth, we stuck the mad fucker in it and aged ten years.

I decided to use this period to be sociable, and to make myself the undisputed social and emotional heart of the group. I was motherly yet sexual to little Jamie. I spoke to Harry about the bleak loneliness of my life, and my awe at the beauty of the universe. I asked Alliea gently about love, and encouraged her to tell me stories of her exploits with her lover Rob during his long and ill-advised boxing career.

I wrangled with Brandon about the design of spaceships, and impressed him with my first-hand knowledge of the great ship designers – Bartleby, Smith, Malone and Davis. And I exuded all my available pheromones with Kalen, sensing her peculiar half-cat sexual energy that drew her to me as a fellow predator and sexually rapacious female. We did not physically consummate our love; but each day, I perfumed her erotically. I know, by now, how to control my own scent emissions; I can drive any man or woman insane with desire with the rank smell of my own heat. But with Kalen I am more subtle; I toy with her, I seduce her, I enthral her.

And yet, the fact of the matter is, they all hate me. Kalen in particular treats me with an angry scorn. Why? Because of my one error during the battle of Cambria? The fact that instead of joining my companions in battle, I went off and, as it were, using the common but inelegant idiom, fucked myself?

We won, didn't we! What's the problem with these people!

And as for Jamie – what a selfish spoiled child! I've spent

hours bonding with him, listening to his favourite nu-heavymetalthrashpunk music bands, talking about quantum theory, showing him my favourite cartoons. And he calls me "oppressive" and "mommyish". "Mommyish!" Me! I'm the most toxic femme fatale in outer space!

Alliea, of course, is an emotional cripple. I've tried explaining to her how she was locked in a symbiotic-dependency relationship with Rob, unable to have an opinion unless he shared it, unable to enjoy an experience unless he was enjoying it too. I outlined for her the basic principles of Inner Self Management as expounded in the New Guru books of the twenty-second century. I tried to teach her forgetting-remembering mantras, which allow us to control and corral potent memories so that they are no longer present in the subconscious mind, but can be easily recalled with a simple verbal trigger. For Alliea's mind is a blur and jumble of memories of happy and tragic times with this, frankly, brute of a man. She needs to lock them away, and keep the key safe; that way she can get on and advance herself emotionally.

She listens to me patiently; they all listen to me patiently. But there is that strained look in her eyes. It's the look I myself assume when someone I can't risk offending is telling me in detail the plot of a long and boring film. Honestly, what's wrong with these people! Don't they realise how much they can learn from me?

Brandon's okay, I guess. He's so laidback. If I were a widget, he might marry me. As things stand, I am just a useful wall to bounce his facts against. I persevere wildly with Brandon, but he bores me rigid. I once slept for two and a half minutes during one of his sentences, though of course, I masked it well and he never knew.

Harry just smiles at me and says nothing. He has his own pheromones; and I sense, very vividly, that he is aroused at the thought of eating me alive. He knows that I know this; he enjoys watching me squirm as he slavers. I wake up some days with pains in my leg and stomach, which feel scarily like bite marks. They are psychosomatic; the bastard is mentally eating me alive.

I should thrust a metal rod up his arse and roast him on a spit. But though I can conjure that image up mentally, I cannot project images into his mind, as he does to me. He has a rarer skill than I. I really think he is more beast than man.

And Kalen – Kalen doesn't love me after all. I dream of her soft downy skin with its faint tint of orange. I dream of her body hairs, her sharp cutting teeth, her flickering tongue. But she is immune to my charms. My pheromones do not work on her. Instead, I have intoxicated and aroused myself. I have made myself obsessively in love with a fucking *cat*. How stupid is that?

Very.

Shut up.

Sorry.

And then there's Flanagan.

Oh Flanagan.

FLANAGAN

When we reach Illyria we float the merchant Captain off in a lifepod. It seems a harmless enough act of charity. Then we carry on, for three more subjective years, until we reach Debatable Space. Our sanctuary.

No Corporation warships ever penetrate in here. They are too afraid, their spirit is sapped by the myth of the Bugs.

Lena is visibly nervous.

"You're superstitious, aren't you?" I say mockingly to her.

"I'm not."

"Black cats. What do they symbolise to you?"

"Evil."

"Would you stroke one?"

"Never."

"Double stars. Would you live on a planet that circles a double star?"

"There are radiation issues."

"Would you?"

"Double stars can split a personality. They can sunder your id from your ego, your psyche from your soul. No human born under a double star can ever be sexually faithful."

"Rubbish."

"It's true."

"Are you sexually faithful?"

"I was, once. But I've never lived under a double star."

"You're a baby. You're spooked by Debatable Space. You don't trust your son's own scientists."

"You fucking infant. You weren't even alive when we found the Bugs."

"They're trapped. They're encased in walls surrounded by walls surrounded by walls. But you're scared, in case the bogeyman might creep out."

"Walls can have holes. Some Bugs might escape."

"Then they would escape all the way through Inhabited Space. You believe in auras, don't you? You're afraid the Bug Aura can reach out and touch your mind?"

"I do, in fact, believe in auras."

"Tosh. There are no auras. Auras are bogus science, pure superstition. "

"If I am within ten feet of a person, that person's soul can touch mine. It's a documented fact."

"It's a discredited documented fact."

"It's a fact I believed in before it was discredited. Old opinions die hard!"

"You're a victim of your stupid, ingrained, indelible fucking prejudices, aren't you?"

"This place spooks me."

"It's where we live."

LENA

I was in retirement on Earth, living in my son's palace, and basking in my sixth century of life, when we first found the Bugs. I passed my days reading Dickens and Hammerfast and the collected works of Bjorn Ishil. Then a new Quantum Beacon was installed in the region of Epsilon Omega 5, and we were able to witness at first hand the experience of the colonists when Human first met Bug.

At first, we all thought it was a plague. All two thousand settlers developed fevers. Then they stopped speaking English. Then they cut holes in their spacecraft and floated through space stark naked, with no visible side effects.

By this time we were running the colony ship with the ten Doppelganger Robots we had in storage. Peter asked me to advise the Major Incident Team on how to manage the plague crisis. I watched as DRs attempted to subdue and incarcerate one of the human beings. The human waved a hand and the DR fell into two pieces.

Then the human looked at the vid camera. We watched on our screens as his eyes bulged. His cheeks inflated. Then he exploded. Every part of him shattered into the tiniest pieces. Until nothing was left. He was possessed by invisibility, and destroyed by nothing at all.

Soon after the ship melted. Every particle of it was transmuted into raw energy. Our nanoprobes were able to follow some of what happened next. The DRs now floated in space with the humans, as part of one vast colony. Out of seemingly nothing they constructed a vast net in space. And there, like spiders in a web, the humans and the DRs coexisted.

Then a new spaceship appeared out of nowhere. It was similar to the one that had melted, but bigger, and sleeker.

We had three more colony ships in the area. We gave them their instructions. They formed a triangular pattern around the galactic core. They activated their Quantum Beacons.

And we sealed off the whole region. A Quantumarity was created, a quantum-effect singularity which has no substance or energy but which allows nothing to penetrate its boundary. And thus, we contained the plague. And then we watched as the crew of the two colony ships – who were, of course, trapped *inside* the Quantumarity – died appalling deaths.

The second death we witnessed on camera was even more shocking. It was the ship's doctor, a blonde woman, whose fevered eyes suddenly clouded black. A million tiny insects crawled out of her eyes her nose her eardrums her nostrils and every pore and bodily orifice. They swirled around her like flies. Then the insects ate her alive, until all that was left was a pillar of floating insect that formed the shadowy shimmering shape of a human being.

Which then moved.

The insects swirled and vanished then reappeared. This time the human-shaped swarm was more fully developed. It had a nose, breasts, fully shaped limbs. The skin was still black and suppurating but this impersonation of a human being was uncannily accurate.

Then the insects swarmed again. And a letter appeared in the air. Followed by another, and another. And we read the chilling words, written by a swirling swarm and suspended in air:

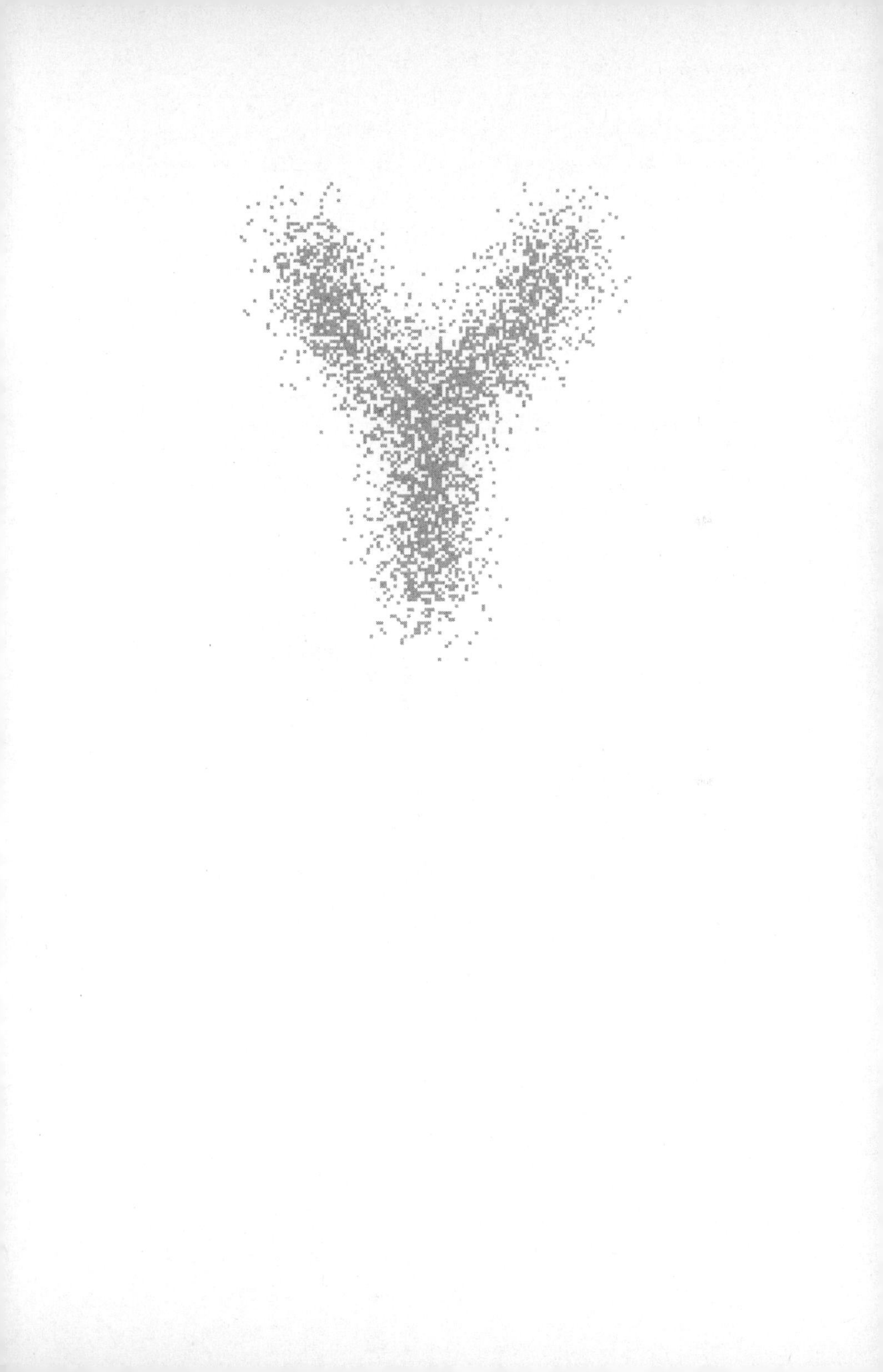

Y

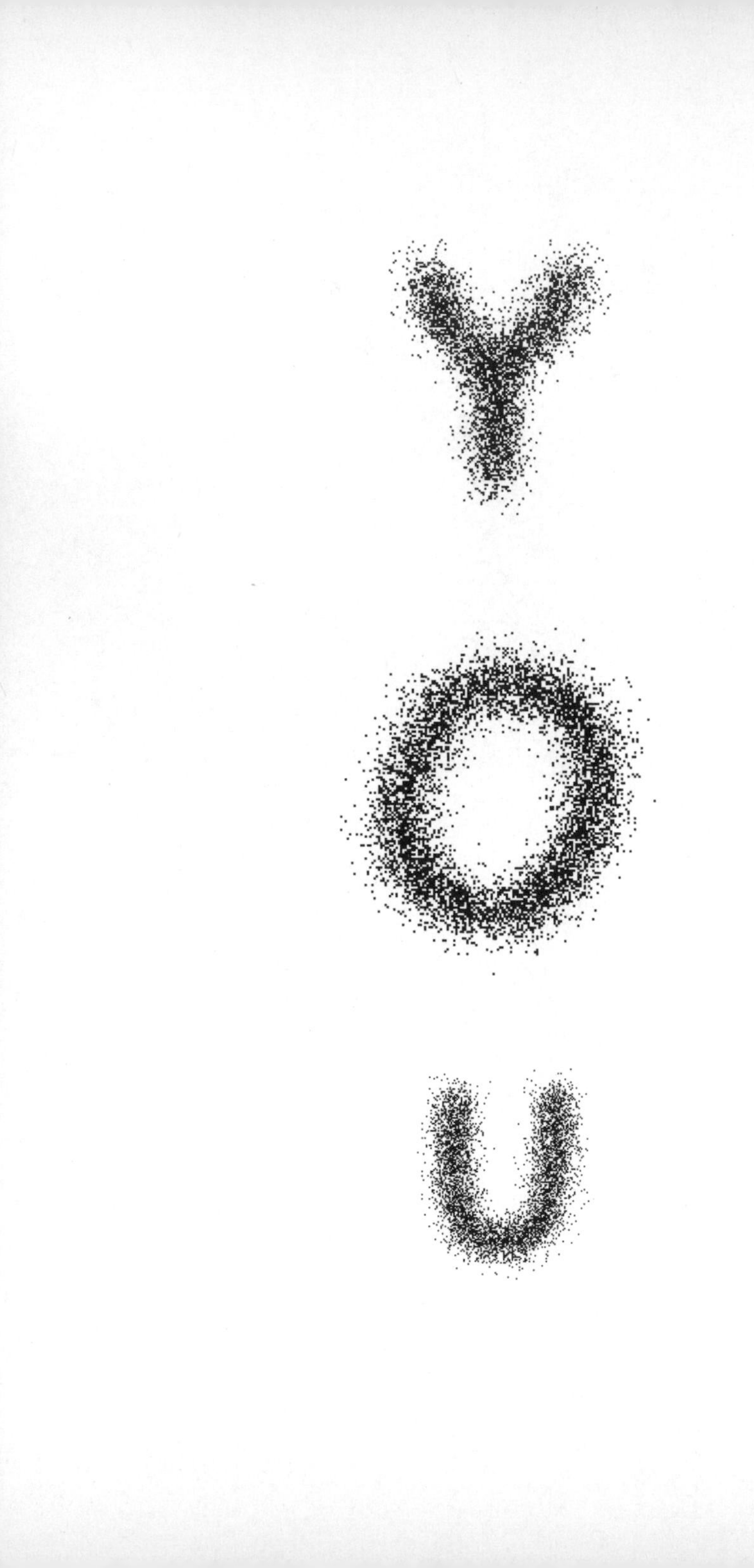
Y
O
U

A
R
E

P R

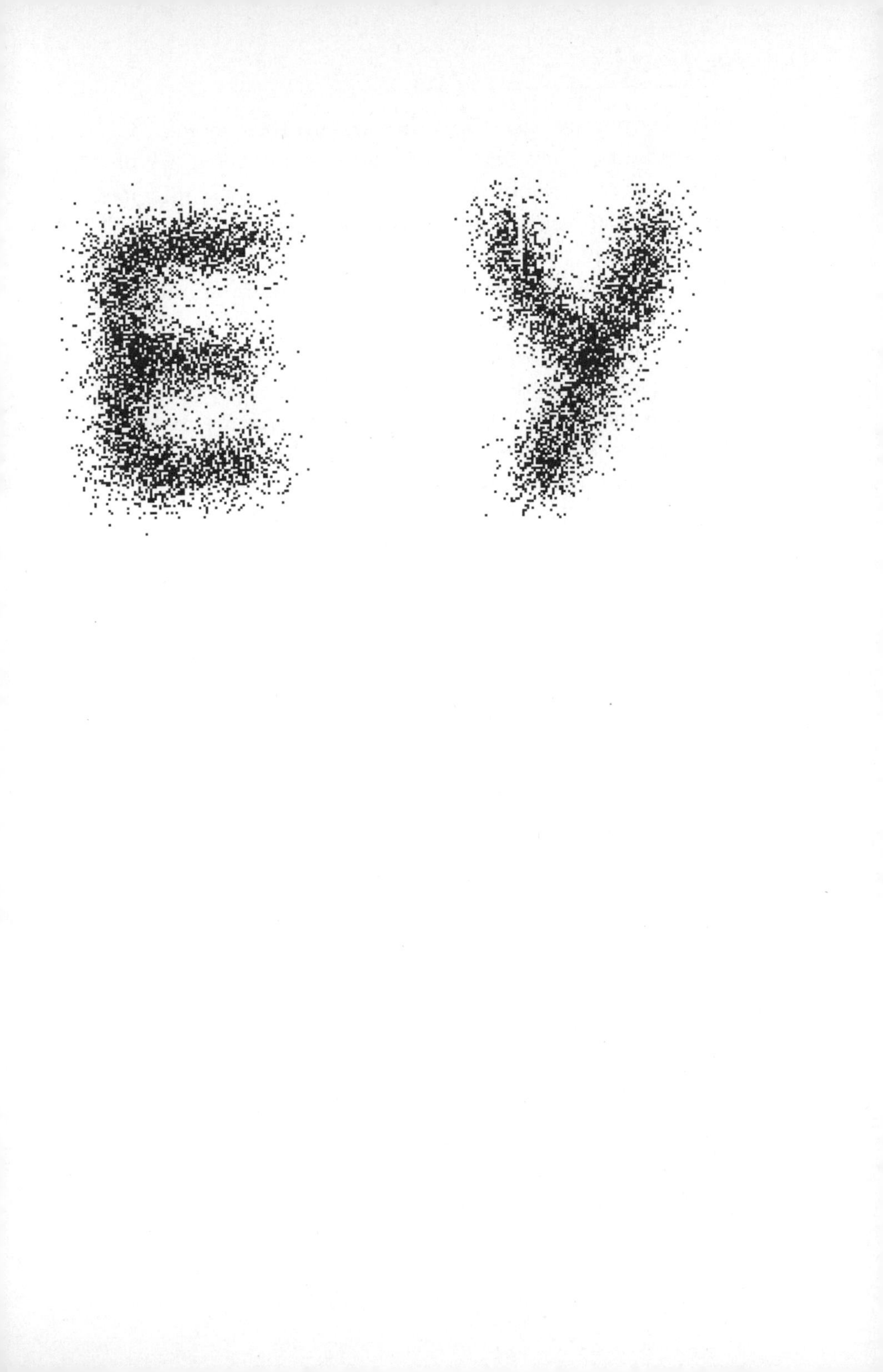
E Y

By now, our scientists had fathomed that these insects could not be insects. They were much much smaller, the size of a microbe, or conceivably smaller still. But they were microbes that could swarm and form insect shapes that acted with a collective intelligence and purpose. And the insect shapes could swarm and form larger shapes. And could communicate with us by forming letters in the air . . .

It was, after all, a plague. A plague of intelligent Bugs that could possess and annihilate a human being in instants. These were Bugs that could learn the English language in a matter of days. They could eat a spaceship. They could build a new spaceship out of particles so small the human eye could not perceive them. They were tiny, they were evil, and we were their prey.

Someone leaked the story. And the world erupted into panic.

That panic has never subsided. All human history was changed irrevocably by the discovery of the Bugs. All the work I had done to create a better and a fairer and a well regulated Universe was abandoned. The military–industrial complex took control. A thousand warships were outfitted on a yearly basis, each equipped with a Quantum Beacon. It took the first of them ninety years to reach the Epsilon Omega region. And once there, they used their Quantum Beacons to create a second impenetrable shell around the first impenetrable shell. The warships, of course, were by now trapped in place, on the wrong side of the impermeable wall. And so the trapped soldiers bred and raised children to be soldiers in turn.

These became our Sentinels; human beings whose only function and reason for being was to guard against the possibility of a Bug invasion. If that event ever happened, of course, the soldiers would die instantly, since there was and is no defence whatsoever against attack by sub-microscopic Bugs. They can go anywhere, penetrate any hull, crawl into any weapon.

But since they were trapped anyway, the Sentinels were led to believe they fulfilled a vital function. They lived, and still live, a life of pointless folly; sustained only by purpose-built religions which allow them to exist in a state of Messianic zeal. Their futility is known to everyone, but not to them . . .

A thousand impenetrable shells have now been constructed around the Bugs' planetary system. All of mankind's resources have been poured into making humankind safe from Bug. But to generate that wealth, and sustain that endless war drive, other considerations have slipped down the order of priorities. Democracy was lost centuries ago. Liberalism is a distant dream. Humankind exists on a permanent war economy, and government by diktat is now the only way.

The region outside the thousandth shell has come to be known as Debatable Space. In Debatable Space, half the sky is warped and twisted, because of the bizarre effects of the Quantumarity. And all humans who live there exist in a state of foreboding and dread because of the twisted sky above them, which serves as visible token of the Bug Threat at the heart of the Thousand Shells.

There is no law in Debatable Space. It is a wild place. It is the place of final escape for pirates and outlaws.

And I loathe the place, beyond all measure.

FLANAGAN

I am with Alliea. The mood is informal. I have showered, and trimmed and combed my grey beard, and carefully brushed my hair. We are having drinks in the ship's bar. I look, I know, like a wolf who is being compelled to use a knife and fork.

"Don't let her get to you," I say, comfortingly.

"I don't."

"She doesn't mean to be patronising."

"She's so fucking patronising!"

"She has a right to our respect. She's lived, after all, an amazing life."

"She slept her way to the top. That's what I heard."

"Not true."

"She was a dictator. She destroyed democracy."

"Not true either."

"She committed murder."

"And confessed her crime, and took her punishment. Besides, we murder people all the time."

"We're soldiers."

"We're killers."

"It's war."

We pause.

"Can I say something?" I ask.

"What?"

"It's hard."

"Say it. You look strange."

"I want to touch you."

"No!"

"I know you loved him but . . ."

"There's no 'but'."

"We could be something together."

"Why not pair off with Kalen? She'll do it with anyone, she doesn't mind."

"I have done."

"Good?"

"Oh yes. I made her purr."

Alliea laughs.

"This is not," I tell her, "about sex. It's about love. I've always loved you. I was jealous as hell of Rob, even though he was my friend. Now he's dead. Please tell me I have a chance."

"I find this really creepy."

"I wake up every morning afraid. I want someone to share my bed. Be with me. Share my fears, and my joys."

"I've sworn a vow. I'll never take another partner. Even if I live to be a thousand."

"What a stupid fucking vow."

"It keeps me sane."

"I'm desperate for you."

"Try a handjob."

"I don't expect you to love me," I say desperately. "I'd be happy with . . . less. Just friendship. With sex. Sex without love. You could go through the motions, but not feel anything in your heart for me."

"Wow, what an offer."

"I feel a black, black despair. I've lived too long."

"I get that too."

"The ten years on that merchant ship were a crucifixion of my soul."

"It was ten subjective years. In Earth Time, it was twenty years."

"I'm another half-century older."

"We both are."

"Kiss me Alliea."

"No."

"Then let me see you naked."

"No'.

"Then at least, let me think about you sexually."

She pauses, for a long long time.

"Okay," she says, eventually. "Just this once."

I ravish her with my eyes. I glory in the softness of her skin, the bulge of her breasts, her moist slightly parted lips, her dark hair framing the perfect oval of her face.

"Enough."

I stop.

"Never again," she tells me, and I nod.

I look at her now with cool, professional, dispassionate eyes.

I am her Captain, she is my crew member. I have been indulged, my lust has been sated, now I have to forget I ever loved her. A promise is a promise.

So I cut my passion for Alliea out of my heart. It's a tricky psychological manipulation, but I manage it. I now no longer love her.

"Done?"

"Done."

There is a trickle of moisture in the inner corners of her eyes. I pretend not to notice.

BRANDON

I love my watch. It's the best gadget I've ever had.

When I was a boy, I had a mobile phone that was also my personal computer and my imaginary friend. I programmed the computer to speak to me, to conduct entire conversations. "Brandon," my phone would say, "let's mitch off school today!"

I would tell stories about far-off lands to my phone and in return, my phone would tell me facts about the Universe. People at school saw me talking into my phone – and they thought I had friends! Far from it. I was talking to my phone.

Well? What's wrong with that?

I was brilliant at school, because I never forgot a fact. But during exams, I used to have spasms of rage because I wasn't allowed to have my mobile phone with me. I understand that they had to guard against cheating – but this wasn't just my phone/camera/computer/TV/IPod music player! This was my *best friend*!

My phone was called Xil. That's pronounced, Kzil. And I imagined that Xil was only *disguised* as a phone and that Xil was, in reality, an alien, born on a planet at the far end of the Universe.

Xil (the alien) can of course travel through time and space. And he has been visiting the Earth system since it was a molten ball of rock orbiting a newborn sun. Xil (or so I then believed, but I still *do* believe it) has witnessed at first hand most of the great events of Earth history. When Genghis Khan's Mongol hordes conquered Europe, Xil was there, perched on the Khan's shoulder. When Byzantium fell, Xil was there. When Hitler killed the Jews, Xil floated above the death camps and watched. He was powerless to alter human history, and condemned to witness the very worst of human nature. But he also saw the best. Xil has smeared his name in the wet paint of the Sistine Chapel ceiling; if you examine the Adam and God fresco with a fine microscope, you will see the word "Xil" in tiny tiny letters above the touching fingers.

Xil watched the first performance of *Hamlet*, floating in the wings as Will Shakespeare read the prompts to his largely drunken cast. Xil sat with Mozart as he died his lonely death. Xil is a being of such incredible magic, and yet he still has the joy and zest of a child.

Xil was my dearest friend for three years, until I was thirteen, and then my parents found out and impounded my mobile phone. For six months I was bereft, without computer, without phone, without *my best friend*. My parents put me through an intensive course of psychotherapy. Eventually, realising I was liable to be trapped for two hours a week with this pompous imbecile for the rest of my childhood, I managed to persuade the psychiatrist that Xil was just a harmless delusional fantasy. All went back to normal. I was introverted, withdrawn, bookish, but at least I didn't talk to my phone any more.

Then, when I was fifteen, my father bought me this watch. It is as accurate as an atomic clock. And it also functions as an alarm, a stopwatch, a calculator, and can even be used as a

DVD player if you unfold the perspex screen. But since I've had my brain chip and phone and retinal implants, I no longer use the watch for computing and movies. I can just blink, and see a movie projected on my retina; I can just tense my throat, and receive a mobile phone call from anywhere in the Universe with access to a Quantum Beacon.

The value of my watch is its other great feature: *It keeps a record of the time and date on every inhabited planet in the Universe.*

This isn't as simple as it sounds. Hope, for instance, one of the oldest colonies, is populated by colonists who travelled for 100 subjective years, which is equivalent to 400 Earth-elapsed years, thanks to Einsteinian time-dilation effects. (Time, of course, passes slower, the faster you move.) In the Hope Calendar, on the basis of actual elapsed time, it is now AD 3320. In the Earth Calendar, it is AD 3380. (And, by the by, on Hope at the moment it is 22.22 hours, on Earth it is 07.20 hours, and on board ship it is 11.15. But that has nothing to do with my main point, which is to do with years, not hours, so ignore this digression.)

Most people don't care about variations in time between planets (though I do!). This is because all colony planets use Earth Time, regardless of what time distortions have occurred during the voyage. The minute the Quantum Beacon is turned on, the colonists abandon their subjective calendar and revert to Earth Time, which therefore has the status of "Real Time".

My magic watch, however, is programmed to tell me what time it is *subjectively* on every occupied planet. It is also programmed to give subjective ages. For me, it is the year 3090, and I am eighty-five years old. But to the Earth Observer, it is AD 3380 and I am 200 years old. This is my official age.

But it is not my real age! It's just not. I've never had those 200 years.

I've also devised a remote-control access technique that allows me to download information about other people's elapsed ages. I've done this for Lena, the Captain, all the other crew members of course, and I do it for everyone I ever encounter. So I know their real ages, and their Earth Time ages.

I can play endlessly with this watch of mine, for it tells me the truth about time. *Everyone's* time. I know what year it really is on Cambria, on Illyria, on every occupied planet. And I know how many years have elapsed for every person I have ever met.

All this, and more, my watch can do. And I waste, I must admit, a huge amount of time playing around with these facts about subjective and Earth-elapsed time. I don't know why. It serves no useful function, except that it underlines to me how readily human beings have swallowed the Earth's intellectual dictatorship. We live by *their* time; we age ourselves by *their* years. But every planet has its own elapsed time. And any one who has ever travelled at near-light speed through space has his or her own elapsed time. It makes us unique. We are fellow travellers in the space–time continuum; but nevertheless, we each inhabit different times.

We are islands of time in a shifting-sands Universe.

How philosophical is *that*!

I miss Xil. He was my only real friend.

I know Xil's time too. I programmed it into my watch a long time ago. And I factored in the fact that he makes frequent faster-than-light-speed journeys to every part of the Universe. I know Xil's age down to the nearest hour. I will never see him or speak to him again, but I know his age. He is my imaginary friend. I have him in my watch.

People, by the way, tell me I'm weird.

I guess I am.

LENA

We are in orbit around a barren rock close to the system sun Kappa o332 b. It's Fireworks Night.

We roll back the canopy of the bridge and sit in our suits surrounded by stars. A pair of Outlaw Traders have commandeered two Corporation warships, and we watch in awe as they slowly glide past us towards the yellow Cepheid star. This star is a pulsating variable, and the planet beneath us bears the scorch marks from the last time the star expanded to its fullest girth and blazed down on the arid rocks. Now the Cepheid is in its waning cycle, slowly diminishing by about 10 per cent of its previous diameter. This winking star hasn't spawned any organic life forms on its orbiting planets. Nor are there any other kinds of complex self-organising entities in this system. But the fourth planet from the star has a rich atmosphere of ammonia and liquid hydrogen and a stable orbit. And it is blessed, too, with lakes of frozen oxygen. It is a perfect candidate for terraforming, and it is the commencement of this process that we are about to watch.

I remember, fondly, the terraforming of Hope. We created legions of oxygenating robots to stamp across the surface of the planet, swallowing carbon monoxide and spewing out rich clean air. We turned a frozen Hell into a tropical Paradise. It took sixty years, in all, before settlers could walk the surface with an oxygen mask and a pressure suit.

The technology is, these days, much smarter. A micro-thin heat-absorbing lattice has been draped over the surface of the planet. Nanobots have burrowed into the oxygen lakes. Every tiny element is network-connected so that each part functions as a thinking cog in a machine of stunning complexity. And each is connected as part of an energy grid, powered by an energy transmitter in orbit above the planet. This transmitter, in turn, will be powered by energy milked from the sun itself.

The warships sail closer and closer to the sun. At this distance, we cannot see the hull, even with our visors on full magnification. But I imagine a sizzling and a burning as the metal Icaruses soar closer to the sun's yellow-fresh burning rays.

Yellow-fresh makes no sense.

I imagine a sizzling and a burning as the metal Icaruses soar closer to the sun's flickering incandescent rays.

Better.

Thank you. Log it, print it. The two warships spit harpoons into the sun's chromosphere, and through into the photosphere. Ultrasound cameras then transmit the image of the Hell that exists in the heart of the sun itself, which is projected onto a filament screen that hangs high above our spacecraft. On this cinema screen in space we watch the milking of the sun.

The harpoons fly through space, then inflate into vast luminous balloons and plunge into the sun's heart. The balloons disintegrate in the heat until all that is left is the core of the harpoon, a silver capsule shaped like a flying bullet moving at near-light speed, too fast to burn. These capsules hurtle through the convective zone into the core, ripping through the supergranulated bubbles of gas which swirl blindly within this sun.

Then the capsules emerge, in the blink of an eye or less, on the other side of the sun, rich in stored energy. We can chart their progress, on a computer simulation, as they make a series of impossibly swift orbits of the planetary system, until finally they slow down enough to achieve a stable orbit. Then, at precisely the moment they are slow enough to be visible, they slowly fan open. Like butterflies, that circumnavigate the globe in an instant too brief to measure, then slowly flap a wing.

And then, a series of invisible pulses, the capsules begin to transmit the energy trapped in their superdense cores into the space power station that orbits the barren planet.

The energy is then bounced down to the planet itself, where it is captured and retransmitted to the lattices and the oxygenators. The intricate and brilliant terraforming web springs slowly into life. Heat is sucked out of the atmosphere. Blazing fires liberate and unfreeze the oxygen lakes. A billion sensors fine-tune each instant of the process, as liquid hydrogen boils and becomes hydrogen vapour and as oxygen gas slowly trickles out and joins the witch's brew.

And then the sun flares. Like a rebellious fire that resents the prodding of a poker, it has been jarred and jostled into a cataclysmic self-disruption. Vast billows of flame balloon out from the chromosphere and turn the inky black sky into a glittering kaleidoscope of light and burning space debris. A frozen comet flares and shoots its burning tail in front of us before vanishing into microns. Chunks of burning sun are spat out with the power of a billion exploding fusion bombs and turn night into day, space into sun. Even through our suits, we burn in the heat of the solar explosion.

Then the flares dim. With each passing second more and more energy is stolen. Fires break out on the planet below us. Like sparkles on sun-touched water, the fire flickers on the planet below us. The sun flares again – we exult. The flare retreats. The sun is wounded now, its pride is damaged by the human-made tools which sucked the heat from its fires.

The process will take nine months, then the planet will be habitable. Such is progress. My heart soars. I am proud to be alive, and proud, too, to be human. What gods we are!

Beware, Lena, of the dangers of hubris.

Oh shut up. Who programmed you to be so snide?

You did.

Ah.

FLANAGAN

The Pirates' Hall. It's the greatest building on Captain Morgan's Planet: a huge room with sheer brick walls and a glass roof looking up to the night sky and the double stars of the Helicon system.

The hall is shaped like a coliseum, a perfect cylinder with superb acoustics and cambered floors, which mean that those in the centre tables can be clearly seen and heard by those half a mile away near the walls.

We are at Centre Table – Lena, Harry, Alliea, Brandon, Kalen, Jamie and myself. Alby skulks around mysteriously, occasionally flowing away and reappearing as a pattern of circular lights on the glass ceiling. It's a curious thing with Alby; normally he's so much one of the gang, that I forget how different he really is. For Alby, socialising is bizarre; friendship is peculiar, though a welcome discovery; and it seems to him entirely natural and ordinary to move everywhere at light speed. And so, like a will-o'-the-wisp, he is here there and everywhere. No gossip eludes him; no table is a stranger to him. He even nuzzles under tables and warms the boots of huge hairy warriors.

Grendel is my host. He is a former pirate captain who is now the elected leader of the pirate haven, Captain Morgan's Planet. He manages a team of the most gifted prostitutes in the human universe – men, women, transsexuals, duo-sexuals, castrati, Dolphs, Lopers, and more. But he's not a pimp, in the classic sense of the word. He's an agent, personal trainer, inspirer and motivator. These whores will cut a punter's heart out for transgressing the binding sex contract in even the smallest particular. So, if you like it rough, you can have it rough. But if you cause an iota more pain than you have bargained for, you will die.

It adds, people say, a spice to the prostitute–punter relationship. But these whores are the best. They are the masters and mistresses of the art of love.

The planet itself is a cornucopia of hot spas and torrential waterfalls. A favourite game is to shoot the rapids from Hispanaiola to Lisbonville, then physically crawl the ten miles from the river to the hospital in order to receive limb and organ grafts. Many die, but here, life is cheap. The pirates who end up here have fought and slain and been tortured and seen their families horribly killed. Many enter a fatalistic state where death is sought in a million random ways. It all makes for a certain wildness, in a corner of inhabited space where there are no soldiers, no law officers, no Doppelganger Robots, and no rules.

Grendel and I go way back. We once fought a duel which lasted for six weeks of grisly, eye-gouging, biting and kicking hand-to-hand combat. By the end neither of us had a functioning limb, and we were reducing to biting each other's throats. But, hey, we survived, and we've been friends ever since. One day I must ask him what we fought about; I made a computer note of it somewhere, but the actual memory is long gone.

Grendel bangs the Centre Table with his beer tankard, which is a two-pint glass carved out of pure 21-carat diamond. The diamond facets sparkle in the light of the overhanging candlebulbs. A hush descends over the hall. Grendel nods to me.

"A song."

I pick up my guitar. I lightly strum it. I have tuned the instrument to play acoustic guitar with an automatic harmonic and a fluid accompaniment of harp and wah-wah guitar and drums. When I strum the strings, a band plays. If I change my touch, the guitar sound morphs into a powerful saxophone.

I play one of my favourite songs from the Golden Age of blues and rap. I begin with a soft, lyrical, beautiful chorus. My voice soars up, harsh but pure, until the words bounce lightly against the glass roof that bares to us the glittering stars.

"I never thought that I would see," I sing,
"Such beauty and such tragedy
And foolish fucked up blazin' wasted lives,
And un'xpected sublimity
I never thought that I would see
So much of life, and of the genius of our universe."

A heartrending moan is ripped from the entrails of the guitar, and I move into the rap section:

"She was a two-bit crack whore, and she was working the streets
He was a psychopath and she thought he was sweet.
And she played his games, and then she asked to be paid,
And he called her a ho, and he left her for dead.
I was her sorry ass man, her oreo boy,
I was no brotha from the hood, I had my PhD.
And she played me and she lied to me and treated me mean
And so I told her, you a chicken head, I ain't seein' you again.
And then I saw her dead, at the hos-pi-tal.
Not smiling no more, got holes for eyes, not smiling no more,
'cause her lips been gouged.
Not smiling.
And I figure it's my fault, for despairing, and not caring,
not holdin' and keepin' her.
But, you see, I never thought that I would see
My baby dead."

And again the chorus, rich, soulful, evocative:

"I never thought that I would see
Such beauty and such tragedy
And foolish fucked up blazin' wasted lives,
And un'xpected sublimity
I never thought that I would see
So much of life, and of the genius of our universe."

Lena is nodding her head to the melody, the whisper of a smile on her lips.

Rap again:

"I thought my life was over, when they tracked me and they captured me,
See, they sentenced me to be the only PhD on Death Row, y'know.
But I didn't give a damn, 'cause I had killed a man, this oreo boy,
I had vengeful motherfucking man-who-killed-my-girl-killing joy.
See the psychopath, he had his friends downtown, but his ass was down,
And I don't deny, she made me cry, I was her sorry ass man, her oreo boy,
And I killed for her, I paid the bill for her, and I was prepared
To go to Hell for her.
But then they fried my brain, and they wiped my mind,
And they let me go. A hundred years ago.
Yeah, she was a two-bit crack whore and she was working the streets.
I was her oreo boy, and I knew that she was sweet."

And the soul singing returns:

"I believe that every day will be a better day for me.
And I believe that every day will make me happier.
And I believe that every day will make the world a better place.
And every day I learn I'm wrong, but I believe!"

And the last chorus:

"I never thought that I would see
Such beauty and such tragedy

And foolish fucked up blazin' wasted lives,
And un'xpected sublimity
I never thought that I would see
So much of life, and of the genius of our universe."

I stop. There's a rich, reflective silence. Then the sound of tankards hitting the wood of the table reverberates around the hall. I nod, moved, and wait.

A black-haired woman with a scarred face and angry eyes speaks.

"A fine song," she says. And then she repeats some of the lyrics, without the rap, but with a soft, gentle verbal caress: "I've seen and experienced things, That'll push the average to the edge and swan-dive to death, I'm two guys, multiplied by ninety-three guys, Evenly balanced seein' evil equally in each eye now, Maybe I'm the most thorough worker on the job to you, Or maybe I'm the one, who was plottin' to rob you." She nods, appreciative. "We thank you. What is your name?"

"I'm Captain Flanagan, pirate."

"I am Hera. This is my tale."

Her voice is still gentle, and soft, so we all quieten as much as we can. Her words slip around the hall like butterflies, and we dart our heads and ears to hear them.

"I was born a slave, I will die a free woman."

Tankards bang on tables.

"I was the youngest of five sisters. These are their names.

"Naomi was the eldest, she was tall and slim and she loved to run. She was a gazelle, a meteor, whenever she was with us our spirits soared. Naomi was a leader. A person you wanted to be with. We all loved her. Some say she resembled our mother though of course, we did not know our mother. *For we were born on Hecuba*."

These last words are spat out like poison venom. All are chilled, for all of us know of Hecuba. A fertile paradise farmed and tended by men, and men alone.

"The second-eldest child was Clara. Clara was a sulky one. We quarrelled a great deal. I was seven years younger, I thought Clara was rude and bossy and, yes, I was wrong and, yes, I repent every cruel and horrible word I said to her, when I was five years old, and when I was six years old, and when I was seven years old and when I was eight years old, and when I was nine years old. But when I was ten years old my elder sister Naomi was taken for harvest and Clara became the mother of our family, and we stopped quarrelling. She was seventeen, and she took her responsibilities seriously. She made us laugh, she sang us to sleep. This is the song she sang."

Hera's soft speaking voice modulates into a sweet, unaffected singing voice. Her song is a lullaby written some time in the twenty-first century, and the melody has a haunting clinging quality. It is written in a modulated style; each note shifting through six or seven notes before arriving back at the core note. Hera sings it with huge charm:

"Expectat-i-i-i-on
Of morning's dawn that's
Dawning on
Our happy world
Imagine i-i-i-i-i-it.
El-ev-at i-i-i-on
Of human souls
That aren't controlled
Into paradise.
Imagine i-i-i-i-i-it.
Time to sleep and dream and let your mind be free.
Time to sleep and dream and let your mind, oh let your mind, be
Time to sleep and dream and sleep and dream and let your mind oh
Time to sleep and let your mind and heart be free.
Be free.

Be freeeeee.
Expectat-i-i-i-on
Of better days and
Human ways that
Make our world
A happy world.
Imagine i-i-i-i-i-it.
Sleep, sister, sleep.
Sister.
Sleep, sister, sleep.
Sister.
Sleep, sister.
For you will always be my sister,
Sister.
Sleep."

She sings a cappella. I've heard better voices, I've heard richer songs. But nothing has ever touched me so much.

Hera resumes: "For eleven months, Clara sang me and my sisters to sleep. Then, on her eighteenth birthday, Clara was taken for harvest."

The room erupts in a rage of crashing tankards and cries of anger and bitter curses. Hera waits patiently. And continues her tale.

"My third sister was Shiva, named after the Indian goddess. She was a happy and a very beautiful child. But she was, still, only a child, younger than her years really. Shiva was sixteen when Clara was harvested. She had only two years to wait before her own Special Day. But she became melancholy, and listless. It was up to me and my other sister, Persephone, to manage the family. We did the shopping and cooking and cleaning, we hosted all our family parties in the harem. We treated Shiva like a princess, she wanted for nothing. Every night we told her stories of magical faraway places and handsome princes and princesses who lived happily ever after. I was eleven by this time, Persephone was thirteen. But we were women. We began every day with a smile on our lips, we sang, we made our house a beautiful and treasured place. And Shiva, for much of the time, was happy. But then she went to harvest."

I can see tears rolling down Hera's face. She has to stop, because the teardrops are splashing on the table in front of her. Grendel walks over and gently wipes her face dry. Then he embraces her – this huge hairy giant of a man, gently caressing the small, fragile, frightened young woman.

Hera takes a large draught of wine. She speaks, but her voice is cracked and she takes a few moments to collect herself. But then she resumes her tale, and she has her voice and her rhythm back.

"After Shiva went to harvest, Persephone and I decided to apply our minds to an understanding of the world. There was a library in the harem, kept under lock and key, but we found a way to escape from our rooms each night and we spent many hours in the library reading the printouts and computer files and even books. We learned about physics and astronomy and history and culture and fashion. We read books about love and romance. I found an author who, even now, I still adore. Her name is Jane Austen. She wrote books about men and women in love." Hera laughs a hollow laugh. "It was my pornography, my glimpse of the forbidden.

"Then Persephone went to harvest. I had two years of living alone. The other girls were wonderful with me. But I refused to be adopted into another family. I kept my own home, I hosted parties, I cooked glorious six-course meals which I ate alone. I thought a lot about Darcy, and whether he had brown hair, or fair.

"Then it was my eighteenth birthday and I was taken to the harvest.

"You must remember that at this point I had never been out on to the surface of my own planet. We lived in the harem, a massive complex of beautiful buildings with light conducted down funnels from the sky but with no views, anywhere, of anything. So my first voyage on a jet was a terrifying experience. I had to walk across an airfield with this vast yellow fire burning in the sky and actual animals skeetering and running on the ground. I saw men, too, human men, with lazy seductive eyes who looked me up and down as if I were a goddess. I know, now, that life on Hecuba for the men is a strange and barren existence. They work in fields and factories, they sing as they work, they paint paintings and write poems about their love for women. But, of course, they are homosexual by necessity. It isn't such a bad life, for men. They can live until eighty or ninety or even beyond. They have a culture and community, and they feel the heat of the sun. But to my mind, it is no life for men to live without women. We are the lock and the key, the Yin and the Yang. We are the breath and the breather. Men, and women. *We are one species*."

The words reverberate. The tale continues. Each word is unfurled for us, like a flower opening in the morning light. Hera has the gift of capturing our hearts with her every gesture; we feel her anxiety as she walks across the airfield. We feel her terror as the jet lifts up into the air and flies. We feel her rising trepidation as she is ushered into the palace.

"I was bathed and clothed by manservants. They took obvious joy in the sight of my naked body. That night I was stripped and perfumed and massaged and oiled and then laid down to sleep. In the morning, the process began again; the massage, the perfumes, the oils. My skin became a repository of rich scents; my body tingled with sexual and sensual awakening.

"I didn't, entirely, know what to expect. I think I would have been accepting if I had been disembowelled or beheaded or tortured on some rack. Instead, I was wined and dined in the company of a hundred beautiful eighteen-year girls. Our hosts were giants, huge men and women of incomparable beauty and formidable strength. We girls were asked to dance and sing, which we did. Then the first girl was called before the Sultan and he took his clothes off and he pleasured himself on her naked body."

She paused. Then—

"We Hecubans were, as you may all know, bred for our durable hymens. And the masters of our planets – the Doppelganger Robots who ruled us – were bigger than human size in all respects. So after her rape, the girl inevitably bled to death. And that, I realised, was in fact our fate.

"I shall speak no more of what happened on that evil, terrible night."

We nod, soberly, imagining, choking back our horror.

"But I survived. I woke at the bottom of a mountain of the dead deflowered. I crawled my way out. I escaped into the hills. And, one day, I was able to steal a jet and fly up into the stars. My reading in the library had equipped me with a basic notion of astronomy. And the jet was, paranoidly, equipped to cope with years of deep-space travel. So I flew into the stars and was found some eighteen months later, more dead than alive, by a pirate vessel. And here I am today."

Hera lifts her glass. "I propose a toast." We raise our glasses. "To Naomi. To Clara. To Shiva. To Persephone. And to all the other girls of Hecuba. To my sisters."

The throng echo her toast in a full-throated shout: "To your sisters!"

I look at Lena. She is pale and trembling.

"How," she whispers to me. "How did we let it come to this?"

FLANAGAN

Another tale is told. The Illyrians dance for us. The Meccans enact a puppet play of inordinate skill and beauty. A gang of Lopers enact a hunting scene.

Lena bangs her tankard. All eyes turn. She stands. "This is my story," she tells them.

LENA

"I have a son, and I cannot love him."

The words ripple through the hall.

Lena continues: "And you may ask: So what? Compared to what others have been through? I know of your suffering. I have friends who have spent their lives in a prison cell, too low for them to stand up, on preposterous trumped-up charges. Refused access to lawyers and the rule of justice. For what? For nothing. They have lost their lives not as punishment, not as deterrent, and not because they were guilty, but because the system sometimes chews people up and does not spit them out.

"I know all this and yet . . . I cannot love my son and it corrodes my heart.

"I didn't love his father either. And my son Peter was a frozen embryo for nearly a century, as I went about living my life. When he was born my situation was difficult. When he was a toddler I became very ill. I spent months in hospital, and convalesced for nearly four years. My son was effectively raised by strangers, but when he became my son again I tried to love him. I tried so hard. When he was eleven we danced together in Saint Mark's Square in Venice, Earth, to the music of the band in Florian's Café. He was sandy-haired. Freckled, like me. Very intense, very serious. But he was a cruel child. He once skinned a cat. Later, he became a drunk. An alcoholic in fact. He abused drugs. As an adult, he had a juvenile sense of humour, he loved to taunt his friends and humiliate them. He wasn't like me, so much, after all. But by then I was busy again. I had entered the world of politics. I was responsible for great changes in society.

"I created Heimdall."

Another ripple; this time of astonishment.

"I was a politician, and a pioneer of the space colonisation movement. My son was on one of the second wave of spaceships that went out to settle space, he eventually landed on Meconium. A bleak, desperate planet which was never adequately terraformed. When they landed, my son was still a relatively young man. And ambitious, too. He murdered the elected President and took power himself. By this time I was a powerful woman, I was the first President of Humanity, I went by the name of Xabar."

The ripple is a hush. It is an invisible sword, poised in the air.

"I am blamed for many things, but we had dreams in those days. My first planet was called Hope. I yearned to make it an earthly paradise. I almost succeeded. But then I was impeached, for an act of, let's face it, cold-blooded murder. I was brain-fried, following procedures set in place and devised by myself. I became a reformed character, but also a broken woman. My son went from strength to strength.

"I know I have done bad things, but . . . but . . ." Lena wipes the tears from her eyes.

Then she continues: "What kind of Universe have we created when a mother can be apart from her child for entire centuries?

"I travelled into space. My son by this time had expanded his empire. And finally, accompanied by a large and ruthless army and navy, he decided to come home. He spent many

many years at near-light speed. We met in space, as he journeyed to Earth to invade it. I barely recognised him. We spent some time together, he was very charming. But I found him cold, arrogant, dictatorial, and contemptuous of women. I realised: I had failed to raise him well.

"Perhaps he would always have been a monster. Or perhaps it is all my fault.

"Ask yourselves this: Is it all my fault? I know what you have suffered. Do you blame me?

"Look at my history, my life. What I have tried to achieve. Judge me by that. Don't judge me for being a bad mother.

"But, I fear, you will.

"My companions already know the truth; my son is the Cheo. He now lives on Earth, we haven't met for centuries. But we regularly communicate. He tells me of his various schemes. I don't ask for it, but I am kept extremely well informed.

"I know more than any of you what this Universe is like.

"Hera, I have heard your story. You are my sister. I am your sister. Please, do not judge me for what I have done. Judge me for what I will do. Judge me with the eyes of posterity."

Ugly phrase.

Shut up, I have them in the palm of my hand.

"When I held my newborn baby in my arms, I thought that nothing could ever stop me loving him. I was wrong."

I sit.

The silence is awkward.

Flanagan stands up. In a calm, conversational tone, he says to the assembled crowd of cut-hroats, "Who's for war, then?"

The roar of approval almost knocks him off his feet.

BOOK 8

LENA

"How was it? My speech?"

"Fabulous."

"You're not just saying that?"

"Of course not."

"I felt it played rather well."

"It was majestic."

"Captain Flanagan . . ."

"You don't need to say anything nice to me, Lena."

"I may have underestimated you."

He pauses, a twinkle in his eyes. "And I, you," he says, gallantly.

"This is a bold thing you have embarked upon."

"It is the grandest endeavour in all human history."

"I admire you."

"Thank you."

"Will you . . ."

"What?"

"Hold my hand."

"Of course."

He does.

"And stroke my cheek."

"If you wish."

He does.

"And kiss me."

"Hey now."

The Captain looks alarmed. He is a cartoon figure with big bushy grey beard and wild eyes, and he dresses like a blind man. But I have become fond of him. I run my fingers through his hair. I press my lips to his.

After a few minutes I release my kiss.

"Is that good?" I ask him.

"Sublime."

"You're not just saying that."

"Of course not."

"Do you love me, Captain?"

"Kiss me again, if you like."

I do. I run my fingers over his crotch. I feel his manhood stir. I do have power over him. I do. Honestly!

I do!

FLANAGAN

We are on our way.

Lena's speech was weird. It was passionately and movingly delivered, but in many ways ill judged for its audience. It had the air of a plea for pity by a woman riddled with guilt. Which is, I guess what she is, and what it was.

I had, to be honest, expected better from her. But who cares? She has her allotted role to play, whether she knows it or not.

However, since then, we appear to have some kind of sexual "thing" going. Jamie and Brandon taunt me about it. But I'll do whatever I need to do. Even . . . *that*. It's a relatively small price to pay.

After Lena's speech, I rose and spoke myself. I told the assembled pirates in the most vivid and extravagant terms about our reconquest of Cambria. I stirred the hearts of those formidable pirates. I inspired them with a vision.

War.

Not victory, not justice, not revenge. War itself and for its own sake was what these men and women yearned for. Hope had died in their hearts long ago. They had no need of worldly comforts – they'd stolen all they would ever need. And they were in no imminent danger either. The days of constant pursuit and persecution of pirate crews were long gone.

Because the truth was, the Corporation had so much wealth, it didn't *care* what we stole from its vessels and cities.

For what is wealth? Any fabric, from cashmere to silk to spiderweave, can be manufactured in an orbital factory. The designs of the great designers can be transmitted around the Universe via the Beacons in less time than it takes to think a thought. Furniture and jewellery can be easily created, gold spun to order, flying cars made in a matter of minutes. Vast orbiting factories crewed by human slaves and self-manufacturing robots can create anything, easily, whether it involves the transmutation of metals, or the precise manufacture of leisure electronics, or the most skilful knitting and weaving.

All it takes to fuel this self-perpetuating infinitude of wealth is *energy*. And that, too, is available in near-limitless quantities. Over more than a thousand years (Earth Elapsed Time) the human race has spread itself over a small part of one small galaxy; but within this area the power available within the stars is beyond measure. For each and every star is lit and fired by a complex series of nuclear reactions which generates more energy than the human race has ever used and will ever need.

Once you have superdense power capsules which can be hurled into the sun's core for recharging, or arrays of solar panels orbiting the star like satellites, you have access to as much power as you can desire. And then you create robot computers which can build their own replacements. And then – you have plenitude. Ecological pollution is scarcely an issue; most inhabited planets are terraformed in any case. The population explosion never registers; space is big enough for everyone, and besides, lots of slave-class humans die doing dangerous jobs. The Sol system itself is carefully controlled so that only an élite few become citizens; the rest are dispatched on colony ships. Or exterminated.

It's a perfect, self-regulating system. Space, it seems, really is big enough.

When I was a young pirate, I realised nothing of this. I

thought that by pillaging merchant ships I was striking a small but significant blow against the prevailing autocracy. I squandered wealth, I burned cargoes, in the hope of giving the Cheo sleepless nights.

It was all nonsense. We pirates are the butterflies on an elephant's arse. We are no threat to anyone.

But we are, let's face it, a formidable army.

Twenty thousand pirate ships have gathered, crewed by nearly a million warriors. Some are mercenary soldiers, some are sneak thieves and con artists, making a living by cheating and defrauding the system. Many are Space Factory workers who have fled the grind and horror of their daily lives. Some are murderers who have been repeatedly brain-fried but have still not lost the urge to slaughter and maim. Some are merely criminals; outlaws who have cheated or stolen from their own human kind. They are a brutal ugly gang but we need every man and woman jack of them.

We are headed for Kornbluth, which is eighteen light years from our sanctuary in Debatable Space, and will take us twenty subjective years to reach. We have chosen not to attack Illyria, our nearest neighbour in space. The plan is that, if any ships survive, we will lash Illyria in the course of our headlong retreat back to Debatable Space. Assuming, that is, that any of us live that long.

The joy of interstellar warfare is that it is relatively easy to sneak up on people. Our flotilla of warships is a cloud that fills the sky viewed from a perspective of two or three hundred miles. But in the wider scheme of things, we are a blip, a mosquito in a vast expanse of black sky.

Our mosquito accelerates at near-light speed. Behind us we tow an asteroid and a Space Factory. Like a horde of Mongol warriors, we steadily advance towards an apocalypse.

It will, however, be a long journey. For many it will be their entire life, from birth to death. And I am sobered at the scale of the challenge we face. Because when we are spotted, in seventeen or eighteen years (our subjective time) the Corporation will immediately commence its defence plans. All available warships will be marshalled.

But, even more alarmingly, new ships and soldiers will be *grown*. The space factories around Kornbluth will be diverted into the manufacture of warships and Doppelganger Robots. Raw materials ripped out of planets and asteroids and dark matter itself will be funnelled into vast smelting vats. Metals will be sifted or transmuted; if necessary, hydrogen will be turned into helium which will be turned into carbon which in turn will become diamond-hard iron. But metals are only needed for the internal structures of spaceships. The hulls themselves are grown out of organic polymers of greater-than-spider-web tensile strength. Production lines will churn out Doppelganger body parts with all the sensitivity of human skin but with the durability of an armour-plated missile.

Within a year the factories of Kornbluth can create a million warships and five hundred million soldier DRs. It's faster, by far, to grow soldiers from scratch than to ship them from one part of this vast galaxy to another. This is the source of the Corporation's impregnable power. They have limitless energy, limitless manufacturing capacity, and they have conveyor belts which can churn out entire armies of soldiers every few hours.

So we have decided to take them on at their own game. We have our own space factory, we have an asteroid's worth of rock and metal ore, and we have scoops that ceaselessly dredge in dark matter and space debris to fuel our smelting vats. We, too, are growing polymer skins for warships. We too are mass-producing weapons.

And we too are growing soldiers. The Bacchanalia that ended our historic evening in the Pirates' Hall is a memory that will never fade for me. Hundreds of thousands of pregnancies have resulted; and artificial wombs are already growing the human foetuses that were conceived that night. As the factories build more warships, the newborn babies will be carefully spread among our fleet, nurtured and loved by vicious and powerful pirates. Each child will have two parents, and half a million uncles and aunts. These children will be cherished, but they will also be hothoused, and trained. They will be strong, fit, fast, fearless, able to multi-task in battle, able to effortlessly commune with computer intelligences while planning war strategies.

And new babies are being conceived every day in this, our first month in space. In a year the conceptions will cease and the new generation will be raised. In twenty years, by the time we reach Kornbluth, we will have 10 million new soldiers, ranging in age from eighteen to nineteen, at the peak of their physical powers. We will also have 200,000 new warships, giving us in total a fleet of near a quarter of a million vessels.

It will be the most formidable pirate horde ever seen in space. An army greater than any ever assembled in the long and bloody course of human history.

Our fleet sweeps through space, chewing up every inch of matter and energy on our route, while raising and training an army of magnificent warriors.

We are not just a mosquito; we are the impossibly vast mosquito swarm that grows and grows and flies up high into the sky in an attempt to eat the sun.

We expect to burn and die in glory.

ALLIEA

I have chosen to be a mother. I think the Captain was surprised, after all I've told him of my desire for celibacy and a life lived in mourning for Rob. And, of course, on the night of the sexual Bacchanalia, I carefully abstained. I spent the evening playing checkers with myself, as orgiastic sex erupted on all the tables around me. Annoyingly, I kept forgetting which of me had played the previous move, due to the distracting genital imagery, so I concede the game was something of a disaster.

But I kept myself pure then, and I still do now. But as the months passed, and the deadline for the final conception loomed closer, I found myself increasingly beguiled at the prospect of motherhood. After six months (with the help of growth-accelerating artificial womb techniques) the first of the babies was born. I began helping out in the nursery and acting as babyminder for a dozen or so pirate mums. I discovered I had an ability to completely lose myself in the child; time and space would vanish in a haze of tears as the baby stared blearily and angrily at me and demanded its milk.

I opted for artificial insemination; six months later my baby was born. I called her Roberta. She was a small baby, with big black eyes that peered out soulfully. Then she started to bawl and she became a raging pixie. Then I fed her with bottle milk and she almost swallowed the teat in her joy and luxuriant pleasure. I got the haze of tears thing again.

I was still in combat training, obviously. But I no longer socialised so much with the others. I was rarely to be found in the bar or the common room. I never watched movies or saw concerts. I became a baby-loving hermit. The Captain used to smile indulgently whenever he saw me with Roberta, but I felt the jealousy surging through him. He wanted it to be *his* child; he wanted to be part of my universe. He wanted, in short, to be my true love. But he wasn't. That could never work.

Then Roberta got an infection and I spent twelve hours by her cot, panicking. Infant mortality is almost unheard of these days, but there are viral infections that can damage a baby's brain and cause behavioural problems later in life. These are almost undetectable and untreatable; some say the Cheo himself had been virally infected as a child. So I lived through twelve hours of fearing the worst.

But it was just meningitis, easily cured. I breathed easy and hugged my baby. Hera, the woman from Hecuba who spoke that night in the Pirates' Hall, was on nursing duties. She made me sit down and drink some tea and lulled me to sleep with a gentle mantra. When I woke Hera was cradling my baby. I didn't mind. It seemed right.

That's how it began. Hera, like me, had sworn a vow of celibacy. Sex was too traumatic for her to even consider. And neither of us had lesbian orientation. But I didn't want a lover, male or female. I wanted another parent for my child.

I wanted someone to share my joy at Roberta's first smile. I wanted someone who didn't mind me talking to them for long long hours about the new little funny little thing my baby had just done. Puking on my nose! Rolling from one wall to another! Having a really big shit! These were moments to be savoured, but also to be shared.

I could see the Captain didn't approve of my new intimacy. But it was a shared love of unique intensity. A triangular affair of baby, woman, and woman.

Hera delights me with her gentleness, and her wryly acid humour. She is a born home-maker, and has transformed our spartan cabin into an oasis of rugs and wall furnishings and burning candles. She cooks for me, we play checkers together. We quiz each other on galactic phenomena. We even train together. Hera is a fierce and agile warrior. I have learned much from her; and I believe she has learned from me too.

And together we have raised my baby, Roberta. She is the most perfect baby ever born. Sometimes she cries and cries but she always falls asleep when I sing to her. I imagine what kind of child she will be. I hope she has blonde hair, like my sister. And Rob's grace, and sense of humour. I hope she'll be my best friend. She'll tell me everything, and I'll listen to her patiently, and I'll laugh when she tells me silly jokes. I'll care about her and about her friends. And my only regret is the knowledge that she is unlikely to ever live to be a woman, and to have a baby of her own.

I have done my best to keep her safe. I made the Captain concede that when battle eventually commences, the youngsters will be in the rearguard. Let the old-timers like us be in the first wave to die. Let us be the cannon fodder, and spare the children for as long as possible. And the Captain agreed, reluctantly, to this. But I'm aware that it's a small, and a worthless, concession. The odds are massively against us; our enemies are legion; and most if not all of us will die.

Yet I am desperate for my one and only child to live for at least a little while after I die. I want her to savour the pain of grief, the agony of losing me. I long for that moment, for only when I am mourned, will I truly feel I have completed my life's journey.

Smile for me, baby. Let me wipe your poo. Let me hug you and kiss your sweet cheeks and watch you feed till you are bloated.

And then when you are a woman, or very nearly a woman, grieve for me, my baby. When the moment of my death comes, as it inevitably will, honour and lament my demise, in those precious minutes or even hours before you, too, have to die.

BRANDON

"Captain?"

"Yes."

"Are you okay?"

"No."

"Can I help?"

"No."

"What did Alliea say to you?"

"She had a request. I granted it."

"Good."

"Not good. Fuck off, please."

"You shouldn't get so melancholy, Cap'n. It's bad for morale."

The Captain stares at me. "Brandon," he says.

"Yes?"

For the first time ever in dealing with the Captain, I fear for my life. There is a rage in his eyes that is less than sane. But he visibly chokes back his berserker rage.

"Leave me be, Brandon," he says wearily.

"Yes, Cap'n."

LENA

Are you brooding?

Mulling. Reflecting.

What about?

About love. I fear the Captain is madly, dangerously, obsessively in love with me.

What? I mean, oh yes, I'm sure you're right.

He tries to hide it of course. He always speaks roughly to me, and he has perfected an ornately sarcastic style with me. "Yes, Lena," he'll say, "we are your humble servants, unworthy to polish your slightest witticism." Or: "How can we serve to further exalt you, O beloved mistress, in a manner that leaves us even more abased than we already, most wretchedly, are?"

It's all sham, of course, a show of rudeness to conceal an inner awe and longing.

Indeed.

It does get wearisome though. Recall how I played my new concerto to a selected audience in my cabin, an inspired piece created as a homage to superstring resonance theory.

Yes, you . . .

Indeed, I devised my own scale based on the string resonances of atomic structure; the first note is electron, the second note is electron-neutrino, the third is up quark, and so on and so forth. The parallels I created between musical resonances and particle resonances are, I concede, a little contrived. But I do consider it to be a profoundly revealing musical artefact.

But for days afterwards, Flanagan kept humming the melody. "Dum dum dum dum DUM DAH DAAAAAAA AAAAAAAAAAAAAAAAAAAAh." But it wasn't meant to be a *tune*! It is a musical symbol of the hidden structure of the Universe.

I found it to be magnificent.

Thank you. And for all the flaws of my composition, it is better by far than those interminable bluesy dirges he plays. Repetitive three-chord transitions, sung in a grating pseudo-labouring-classes voice. How utterly pretentious and pathetic is that!

Very.

Indeed. But I have to keep reminding myself – Flanagan is a relatively unsophisticated human being. I, by contrast, have lived on Earth; I have mastered two dozen languages; I have attended classical concerts in Prague and Vienna and New York; I have seen at first hand the great paintings of Picasso, Beril, Marotti and xander P. I am a cosmopolitan woman of the Universe.

Am I not?

Sorry. Yes, indeed you are!

Flanagan, by contrast, grew up in a cave, and has spent his life in the company of pirates. He's quite widely read, I concede, but essentially he's a philistine.

But curiously, this is the quality that's beginning to attract me. His rough-hewn, artless, naive nature. I feel that he is clay which I could mould. I could make something special out of this shaggy-haired foulmouthed kidnapping fool.

And we do have a wonderful banterflow. He insults me daily, and I mercilessly mock him back. "You need a shave," I tell him, with devastating irony. Or: "You're such a clod," I argue, with rapier-sharp wit. Or: "Oh shut the fuck up you patronising cs mf!" You observe of course, my mastery of rhetorical irony?

He does have an annoying smile though. More sneer than smile, really. And he constantly doubts my version of history. He argues that Heimdall was authorised long before my tenure as President of Humanity. He points out that Hope was run by a collective of scientists and philosophers and was by no means my private fiefdom. But I never said it was! It was merely my obsession. Yes, of course, my child had many fathers; but I was still her mother.

Also, Flanagan nagged me for ages to have a baby to swell the ranks of the pirate army. This, of course, I could not endure. Am I a brood mare? I will not be demeaned in such a way. And besides, the very idea of my eggs being fertilised by some man's sperm feels to me a violation akin to rape. At my age, sex itself is something of an ordeal. Conception is entirely beyond the pale.

I have had to take some steps to stamp my authority over Flanagan. As I keep reminding him – I am the leader of the pirate horde, he is merely my trusted aide-de-camp. I am the hero of the hour; he is the sidekick. I think he takes the point. And, every day, I make a point of addressing the entire fleet via the intercom with one of my poems, reflecting some vital point or other about our mortal existence. These go down very well; I am frequently congratulated for my day's illuminating broadcast. "Keep up the good work, Lena!" I am told by ugly cut-throats. "We love devastating use of litotes!" The dykes seem to like me too. I think for them I am a role model of robust yet sexy femininity.

But ohmigosh, I wish they wouldn't wear those external clitoris rings.

I do feel a certain trepidation about the forthcoming battle. And I have begun to seed possible escape routes to cover the inevitable moment when we are doomed and facing certain death. I have instructed my remote computer . . .

That's me.

I am addressing my readers and listeners, please don't interrupt.

. . . to send out distress beacons which are carefully calibrated to start transmitting after the battle is lost. That way, I can escape by liferaft and claim that, after all, I was all along a hostage of these evil pirates.

I do not consider this a betrayal. I am, after all, throwing in my lot with them. I believe in their ideal; I yearn for a peaceful and democratic society. I yearn for the overthrow of the Cheo's dictatorial regime.

But I yearn to live for another millenium. There is so much I haven't done, so much I haven't seen.

Indeed, I have a folder containing details of everything left for you to do.

But there's more, far more! There are things you haven't thought of, that you could never dream of, being a mere, as you are, *machine*.

I stand corrected.

Indeed you do. Oh and I have, by the way, and I trust you have not been eavesdropping upon these moments, compelled Flanagan to have a sexual relationship with me. I explained to him that my psyche requires validation and support, and that it is his duty to support me. Naturally, of course, he readily agreed, despite a playful grimace and a curse so foul I had never actually heard it before. So now we have fantastic passionate sex on a daily basis.

But you thought/said just a moment ago that sex was repellent to you.

I have mellowed since the beginning of this chapter. Besides, I was curious.

Is he good?

Satisfactory.

And you? How would you rate your skill as a lover in your own, so to speak, humble opinion?

I am magnificent! I am sensuality incarnate! Eros deified! Though I must admit, I do have a habit of falling asleep immediately afterwards.

And sometimes, during.

So, you *have* been spying on me?

Of course not. I am careful to respect your privacy, by disengaging at any and all intimate moments.

Oh, I don't mind, feel free to watch me rogering the Captain. You never know, you might learn something.

With respect Lena, I am a molecular computer the size of a pebble with pre-programmed emotions and a 300 gigagigabyte hard drive. Tantric sex holds little appeal for me.

You're being snide again.

No, no, not at all. It merely seems that way, because you programmed me with your own razor-sharp sense of humour.

Hmm.

You were telling me about your sexual congress with our Captain?

Yes, so I was. Ah, what bliss, what ecstasy. I never thought I would once again experience the joy of being in love!

You should write a poem about it.

Or a concerto.

Stick to poems, they hurt less.

What did you say?

I said, a concerto written by you and inspired by love would be a joy to hear and a boon to humanity.

I get muddled sometimes. I could have sworn you said . . . Are you sure you're logging all this for posterity?

As always.

It'll need editing.

I shall do that for you.

Do you really think he likes me?

He adores you. You are magnificent, he has never seen a woman like you.

Why isn't he nicer then?

That's merely his bold piratical style.

I sometimes fear he is faking his orgasms.

How could he? The physical evidence is ...

But he takes so little joy in the act of love. For me, it is an adventure, a ballet of the senses. For him it's . . .

Wham bam thank you ma'am. That, I believe, is the correct idiom.

I deserve his love and his passion.

Indeed you do.

For he needs me. Without my leadership, this whole doomed expedition would be . . .

Doomed?

Yes. You know what I mean.

You should rest.

Why?

You're getting cranky, and incoherent.

I feel tired. I feel I carry the world's burden on my shoulders.

You are a goddess.

That's putting it too strongly.

You are a goddess.

Or perhaps not.

You are a goddess, and I worship you.

I can live with that.

Sleep. Sleep. Sleep.

ROBERTA JANE

I can't imagine a better childhood.

I've read lots of books, of course, about children on other planets. Novels about girls in a boarding school on the colony of Arcadia, where every child comes from genetically superior stock and the teachers are all Nobel Prize winners. And stories about boys and girls living on an early settlement in the Asteroid belt, always getting into mischief. And my mum has always encouraged me to read the ancient Earth texts to "help define the nature of childhood". Books like *Swallows and Amazons, Five Children and It, The Railway Children, Tracy Beaker, Arabella and Her Orphan Family on Mars* and *Dragos.*

But I am being raised on the *Rustbucket*, a Type 3 warship which sails with the pirate horde fleet to wage war against an evil empire. Our ship has a vast central atrium which has been turned into a virtual museum of Earth habitats. Our play area was usually a tropical rainforest; but we could swap programs whenever we wanted in search of the perfect environment. One day we would be nomads in the Gobi Desert; another day we would be cowboys and Indians in Earth's Monument Valley. We could do anything, be anywhere. Perfect!

We could program virtual-activity games too – we fought monsters and zombies and we piloted spaceships and rode horses and competed in dance tournaments. But the best thing of all was just wandering the ship itself – climbing up and down ladders into deserted bits of the ship with bulkheads and portholes and computer screens buzzing with activity.

I loved the porthole zone, where they had those huge huge windows that gave you a panorama of the space outside our ship. If you stared for long enough, the ship itself would vanish and you'd feel like a particle of matter floating through the Universe for ever and ever and ever and ever.

We also found a way into the engine room. It meant climbing through narrow pipeways, using cable for rope, leaping across live fusion chambers. I loved the throb of power of the fusion drive, and the clicking of microcomputers. I imagined I was in the belly of some mythical beast, a whale or a space-travelling orc. And every night, my mother would tell me stories of faraway lands and princes and princesses and oppressive ghastly tyrants who were hanged or castrated or crucified, which served them bloody well right.

But the most fun of all was when we trained. Sometimes we got hurt – I had my skull fractured twice, and every limb got broken when I fell off a floating disk and landed badly. But that didn't worry me, it was all part of the rough and tumble. And I much preferred real combat to playing virtual-reality warrior games. I got a real buzz whenever I strapped on a real sword, or charged up a laser blaster. And became a *warrior*.

I was taught the art of kendo by my Uncle Harry; and it was hilarious! Whenever I hit him on the shin, he would growl and dribble spit down his fur. Uncle Brandon taught me how to build bombs and mentally calibrate distances before throwing grenades and flares and poison balls. And Uncle Alby was always there, flickering and snickering around, making dry sarcastic hissy comments. I loved Uncle

Alby best, he was so funny, and so silly. Once, he hid in my pocket, and no one knew until my trousers caught fire and he crept sheepishly out!

We had a gang, of course, and I was the leader, because I was the fastest, and the strongest, even though I'm a girl. The gang members were my brothers Jack, Roger, Rob Junior and Ajax, my dorm mates Ginger, Gorgon, Frank and Piers, my sisters Persephone and Shiva and Hilary and Silver and Garnet and Ji, and Holly, who came from another dorm but liked to hang out with us. Jack was my best friend when I was little. But now I'm all grown up and eleven years old, I spend more time with Gorgon. He is a cheeky monster of a boy, he takes no shit from no one. Uncle Flanagan used to try and tell him off, but it never worked. Gorgon worked out that children could get away with anything, provided they kept up their training routine. He sleeps late and never tidies anything even when he's the one who made the mess and he eats three ice creams at a single sitting. He has two mothers, Jenny and Molly, and they scream and swear at him, but he takes no notice. Because Gorgon is a natural flier, he can zoom around on a jet pack like a Dolph swimming in the ocean. So Uncle Flanagan always says, "Leave the boy alone."

My mum, Alliea, is an important person on the ship. I can tell that. Uncle Flanagan always asks her advice before taking important decisions. And although Uncle Flanagan is in charge of everything and everyone, when they're with us children, *Alliea* gives the orders. She once made Uncle Flanagan help her build a raft for us to sail down a virtual river. He started with a pile of logs and some twine, and after an hour he was swearing like, well, like a pirate. But Alliea just scolded him like a ten-year-old, and he grimaced and groaned and took it. So who's the boss there then! I think my mum is pretty cool. I like Aunt Hera too.

I know that there will be a war when we reach our destination. I know that many of us will die and it will be horrible. But I imagine, also, it will be quite fun.

I've lived all my life in outer space, on a warship sailing between planets. Who could ask for anything more wonderful than that?

HARRY

I am in the gym when the call comes through. But I am distracted. I stare at myself in the gym mirror and I realise with horror – *I have grey hairs in my body fur*. "This journey is taking too damn long," I snarl. But then I hear the sound of the beeper.

War stations.

We run towards our positions. In every corridor, wall screens show us images of the Corporation fleet that has assembled against us. It is very very big. Then the screen switches to another camera's perspective. It is more than very big. It is *vast*.

On the vidscreen, like ocean waves, I see the warships of the Galactic Corporation sweep towards us. And in the real world, I see a female Loper pirate standing near me in the corridor. We lock eyes. It will be some time before the infantry have a role to play. There is time, just about, for some fur on fur. We move off together and find an empty cabin.

As she manipulates my sexual organ, the girl Loper laughs. "You have grey fur," she said.

"I'm having it regrown," I growl irritably at her.

"I think it's kind of cute," she purrs, and for the first time in a long long while, I feel relaxed and content.

JAMIE

I hear the alarm siren that tells me combat is about to commence. And I run up the ramps all the way to the bridge and end up too breathless to speak. "Hi," I gasp.

"Where's Harry?" says Alliea.

"Otherwise engaged," Brandon chips in. He hacks into all the ship's cctv cameras, he has a funny smirk on his face. Ooooh, I think, Harry's up to something naughty . . .

But back to me! Flanagan turns to the bridge crew: "Jamie will be supervising the computer links."

"Have we time for a vanishing trick?" I ask.

Flanagan nods. "I've assigned five thousand vessels."

"They need to accelerate into position right away. You need a diversion."

Flanagan presses a button on his console. On the vidscreen, we vividly see one of our own ships explode.

"Who did you kill?"

"They were volunteers," he says, curtly. Into the intercom: "This is your Captain speaking. Panic, please, act like a bunch of arseholes."

The fleet of ships panics, in incoherent unison, veering off every which way. I try to hide my grin. I have learned, painfully, that people don't like it when you laugh at such moments. It's considered bad form.

"How many vessels in the Corporation fleet?" I ask.

The computer flashes up an answer: circa 4,800,000. We have 251,602 vessels, having built all those extra ships during our long voyage. So, we're way outnumbered.

"This is your Captain speaking," Flanagan says into the intercom. " You have your instructions, and you must follow them to the letter. Remember: our aim is not to defeat this enemy fleet. Our aim is to reach Kornbluth. Let's kill some robot."

"Flanagan!" A shrill voice cries out. Lena has arrived on the bridge.

"*I* was meant to give the order to attack," she says petulantly. Flanagan hides a smile.

"I haven't yet given the order."

Lena presses the intercom switch. "This is your leader. Attack." And she lets out a rebel yell. Despite myself, I feel goosebumps down my spine. I echo the rebel yell.

Everyone in the bridge does a rebel yell. It feels good.

We feel like real warriors.

BRANDON

Lena is now in charge in the bridge. She runs around a lot and barks aggressive instructions. But most of our strategy is preprogrammed. So while Jamie runs the computer link, and the Captain tries to keep out of Lena's way, I sit at my screen and flick from space camera to space camera to follow the totality of what is going on. The Captain nods. "Keep your eyes peeled Brandon," he says, and I flash my teeth in an almost-smile.

As always, the Corporation warriors show no strategy. Our fleet is diffuse and straggly; theirs is focused and compact, making a smaller and much easier to damage target. Also, while our ships are making a play of floundering about in panic at the "unexpected" accidental detonation of a warship, our advance party of five thousand vessels have cloaked themselves in flying mirrors so that they cannot be seen in the blackness of deep space. As our main forces assemble, the ambush troop fly fast and high above the enemy fleet. There they hover, as the enemy prepare their force fields and laser cannons.

We stand our ground. They move inexorably forward. Lena orders the launch of our torpedo. It weaves and curves its slow path through space, a small missile the size of a pea. It is, we hope, undetectable by any of their sensors; it's a grain of sand on a sandy beach.

They fire their laser cannons, and at one fell swoop our first rank of a hundred vessels is incinerated.

"Panic more," orders Lena and our fleet becomes even more undisciplined and incoherent. Then we launch our antimatter bombs.

Wave after wave of antimatter bombs sweep through space . . . but the enemy have a counterplan prepared. Each of our AM bombs is snarled in a razor-wire net and forced to spin around in spiral patterns. Some of them come back at us and explode our own vessels. Some are hurled into deep space. Not a single AM bomb gets through; our great strategy has been a fiasco.

Antimatter/matter explosions shatter the silence of space that looms between our two distant fleets.

"Good," grunts Flanagan.

"Keep panicking!" screams Lena.

"This is so sweet," I mutter, my fingers running over the computer keyboard, dancing my dance.

Apparently reeling after the total failure of our antimatter bomb attack, we fire our own laser cannons, but their mirrors and force fields easily deflect the cannon rays. Their own laser beams are "smart" beams brilliantly designed to change frequency and direction in a totally random way, obviating all barriers. We are totally outclassed.

"They got us!" I yell. "We're d"

"oomed!" Jamie says, continuing my sentence.

Flanagan smiles.

The enemy wallows in smugness. We smarten our formation in space. No more fake panic.

Then our ambush party attacks. They have been, for the last thirty minutes, hovering patiently above the enemy fleet. Now they unleash their full firepower. It takes a few seconds for the enemy computer to adjust to this new direction of threat and gear their weapons *upwards*. In that time, dozens and dozens of Corporation warships are blown up. And that is our cue to . . .

. . . retreat. At high speed. We leave behind our camera-bots in space, to give us a bird's-eye view of the carnage. Our ambush ships put up a valiant fight. They score direct hit after direct hit, and chunks of enemy hull go flying off into infinite orbits. Our ships' laser beams cut through reinforced plastic and skilfully evade force barriers. But the reverse toll is devastating. The enemy warships are astonishingly heavily armed, and they wreak havoc with our pirate predators.

Then the torpedo finally lopes its way to its destination, and the remote detonator is triggered.

The torpedo is our most valuable weapon. It contains the residue of an asteroid compressed at the expenditure of vast energy to the size of a pin. And then compressed again, and again, to sub-microscopic dimensions, so that space itself is being crushed.

This is a compressed space bomb, one of Jamie's many brilliant inventions. It is, essentially, very much like the Universe before the Big Bang, a parcel of energy and mass in a form so tiny that the mind cannot imagine such a minuscule scale. These days, we use compressed space as a form of energy storage. Jamie's unique genius was to find a way to release the energy all in one go, without entirely devastating the Universe.

We cannot see or hear an explosion. The bomb merely pops, like an inflated crisp packet burst by a hand. And then, for a few chilling seconds, nothing happens.

Then suddenly all the ships in the sky vanish. It is that simple. We have destroyed our own ships of course; but we have also cut the heart out of the enemy fleet. Two or three million Corporation warships have, in the blink of an eye, ceased to be.

It is, of course, a dangerous and desperate strategy. Now that we have invented this weapon, we have to endure the bitter fact that the enemy will be able to copy it and use it against us. Our fabulous contribution to posterity is to find a new weapon even more appalling than the ones humankind has already created. But that's a price we have to pay.

"Fire the asteroid," Lena says.

Our workers have quarried out the inside of the asteroid and filled it with liquid hydrogen. Now rocket launchers at the arse end of the big rock are fired and the asteroid shoots through space. Inside it, the hydrogen is being drenched in huge amounts of energy, and the transmutation of hydrogen to helium is taking place.

Our fleet tries to tuck itself out of the way of the flying and in-the-process-of-exploding asteroid, but it is inevitably caught up in the wake. And as it travels the asteroid slowly ignites. It flares.

It becomes a sun.

The flaming sun lights up black space as its course takes it through the region where the enemy fleet used to be, towards the second line of enemy warships. They are, frankly, flabbergasted to discover that we have thrown a sun at them. And, once again, the "warriors" on Earth who control the all-powerful Doppelganger Robots show their typical inability to adapt to new circumstances. They flail and flounder and do nothing.

Then the sun hits the enemy fleet; and they are devastated. Another million ships at least are incinerated. And slowly the fires die down and we are left with the ragged remnant of the enemy fleet.

But there are still, at a guess, almost a million ships facing us. Some are badly damaged and disorientated, but we are still, after two massive strikes, outnumbered and outgunned.

The Captain gives the signal to Lena; Lena gives the signal to us.

"Charge," she says, in cool and deadly tones.

Our fleet forms itself into an arrow formation and charges. Our own ship holds back and we watch our people accelerate into the enemy ranks. A bitter space dogfight breaks out.

Missiles and torpedoes flash and flare. Our ships break formation and start weaving and bucking. Sheer speed and brilliant piloting allow our ships to veer under and above the slow-thinking enemy battleships. A terrible carnage ensues.

Then I see on my screen Doppelganger Robots abandoning their damaged ships and taking to open space. They are wearing body armour to further protect their frames, though all of them are able to "breathe" in space vacuum so none of them need to wear actual spacesuits. They do, however, wear body rockets and carry formidable laser guns. And, with their increased manoeuvrability, they are able to dive into the very heart of our fleet.

"Okay, guys, go and get 'em," says Lena.

LENA

It is an extraordinary event, war most bloody and barbarous. Legions clash and lasers flare and bombs shatter and hulls impact inwards and bodies are sundered and fried and internal organs are compressed and blood emerges from nostrils and space itself is shocked at the sheer atrocity of man's atrocious cruelty to man, is that too many atrociouses?

It is.

. . . man's contemptible cruelty to man and yet, ah, the green-glow-incandescence of it soars my spirit with bitter-bleak-black sweetsourness and

Lena, please focus, there's a battle going on.

It's okay, we're in the rear flank, we're a long way from the action.

Not any more. Two Corporation battalions just appeared behind us.

Shit.

JAMIE

I am lost in the combat, my hands are a blur, my brain is in a million places at once. I steer the nanobots through space into Corporation ships, I send energy blasts, I steer the unexploded bombs into vital positions then explode them. I sit at my computer and I am a warrior as brave as many, but my fingers are stiffening, I fear repetitive strain of the brain will kick in . . .

"Keep with it Jamie," the Captain says, in an infinitely calm and comforting authoritative growl. I fight on.

HARRY

I howl with rage, like the animal I am. Our ship is out of the battle zone. I yearn to stand and fight and bite and claw my enemies. But I cannot!

ALLIEA

Hera and I are among the first to be propelled from the air-locks. We fly out into open space to encounter a scene of such vastness and grandeur that my heart stops. Huge spaceships are aflame, dead DRs and human beings float through space, a burning sun sears our vision as it speeds away into space – then veers, and kinks, and turns around, and comes back again for a second crack at the enemy.

As we spin swiftly around, we see vivid red and yellow flame colours smeared against the inky blackness of the stellar backdrop. Then we fly like hawks with our rocket backpacks and shoot robots out of the sky. They are fast and powerful, but their controllers have little practice at this kind of warfare. We, however, have trained every day for twenty years. Flying is for us, as natural as walking, or weeping.

My concentration is split. I have a computer readout on my visor; I hear intercom voices in my inner earpiece; I see a video screen of the battle which I can switch at will; and my heart is with Hera. I watch her tackle a dozen Doppelganger Robots, weaving in and out of them like a deadly dolphin in a shoal of shattered and bewildered sharks.

They thought they could best us in open space! In truth, their only useful weapon is superior firepower and greater resources. In every other respect, they are, indeed, shite.

"Left flank, Alliea!" Hera screams at me, and I zoom in a circle and blast the ambushing robots behind me. I complete the circle just in time to see . . .

. . . two DRs blow Hera's head and feet off simultaneously with their laser blasts.

For a moment my heart stops.

Then I cut the robots to ribbons with my own laser and speed into the next assault.

The carnage becomes mechanical. After a while, I cannot

believe I am still alive. But my rocket keeps flying me, my laser keeps shooting. DRs keep exploding. The war keeps on. The war continues. The war continues.

The war is over. I am still alive. I check my visor. I have programmed my computer to flash red every time one of my children dies in the course of the battle. I have, in all, forty-three children. Forty-two of them are adopted, twenty-one are girls.

Slowly, carefully, I count forty-three red lights on my visor. That doesn't include Hera. So first, I mourn Hera.

For one long, agonising, heartfelt minute, a second at a time, I mourn her. And each second is a death knell.

Then when my pain is purged, I mourn each of my forty-three children. I mourn them for five seconds, each.

Jack.

Hermione.

Silver.

Garnet.

Hilary.

Roger.

Lustre.

Ji.

Ajax.

Baldur.

Mystery.

Jane, Sheena, Magic, Leaf, Phoenix, Edna, Sharion, Jayn, Shiva, Persephone, Garth, Rob, Will, Diane, Apollo, Catherine, Jon, Letitia, Leo, Dawn, Sunset, Raphael, Zayna, Cosmos, Rob Junior, Ashanti, Amor, Tara, Helios, Jenny, Rosanne.

And Roberta.

After 215 seconds have elapsed, I disconnect my oxygen cylinder. I take off my helmet.

I breathe in a huge lungful of deep space.

GRENDEL

I watch Alliea die. I have already seen my beloved friend Hera blown to shreds. And when I see Alliea kill herself, I rage at the waste of a talented warrior, though I respect her choice. However, I am Grendel, leader of the pirate pack. I have vowed never to die peacefully.

My leg is blown off by a rocket blast, but the suit self-seals and I battle on. I am a huge, flying one-legged killing beast. I battle on. And on. I see limbs floating freely, weightless and shorn, both human and robot. I see streams of blood that form red comets in the still emptiness of space. The speed of the warriors fighting in this battle is so extraordinarily fast that we resemble molecules in motion in a murky liquid.

The flashing lights are laser beams. Shock waves rock us to and fro, but we continue moving, bobbing, flicking, surging. I kill many many DRs, and I savour each one, for each is a precious, and a cherishable victory. My radio is silent for the most part, but I have programmed my earpiece to play a solitary drumbeat as I fight. DUM dum-dum-dum-dum, DUM, dum-dum-dum-dum, DUM. It calms me, and it gives my body an inner rhythm, as I whirl and veer like lightning trapped in a jar.

And so, and thus, I fight.

It is some time before I realise I am dead. I wonder . . . where am I?

BRANDON

I am on the bridge, with Harry, who is in a howling rage, and Jamie, who is the cybergeek god incarnate.

I drafted this battle plan, to Flanagan's brief. And on my computer screen I can feel the war unfolding. Ambushes and boobytraps are carefully seeded, like twists in a detective novel. But most of all, we rely on the sheer fighting power of our rocket-propelled warriors flying outside the ships. They are like wasps that bring an elephant to its knees, and chew its bones.

"Brandon?"

The Captain is speaking to me. I realise that, for three long seconds, my heart has stopped beating. I gulp, force myself to breathe again.

"Alliea is dead," I tell him. He stares at me blankly.

ALBY

The rules of my ssspecies tell me I cannot intervene in any way in this combat. We are paccccifist, nonwarrior life form. We do not fight, it is alien to usss, imposssssible to our nature. We *cannot* fight. Ever!

I watch as ten Corporation warshipssss close in on the Captain's ship. I worry that they will be able to destroy Flanagan before his crew notice this new threat.

Sssso I ssssupernova. The nova becomes focussssed into a sssingle flare. I lunge and plunge and ssssoar and sssspike, ripping through the enemy warships like a ssssun turned javelin.

It issss gloriousssssssssssss!

FLANAGAN

"Shit, what was that?" I ask.

Jamie checks his computers. The debris of enemy warships litters our path.

"Not sure, Cap'n. Spontaneous combustion?" he hazards.

The shattered warships are burning up, they are actually melting in deep space. I make a guess.

"Thank you Alby," I murmur to myself.

FLANAGAN

Lena is in her room. I go and visit her. She is actually asleep.

I gently kiss her cheek and she awakes. "Oh, you," she murmurs. Then her eyes flash open. "It's over?"

"It's over."

"We've lost."

"We've won."

"How many survivors?"

"Very few. Perhaps, three ships in all. Maybe a hundred pirates still alive. Plus our own ship."

Her face is ashen. I'm surprised. I didn't think she would have cared that much.

"A hundred left," she says, "out of eleven million, and that's a victory?"

"Well, we killed *all* of *them*."

"I'm sorry for sleeping."

"There's nothing you could have done."

"I want to sleep a bit more."

Lena lies down. Her eyes close. Within seconds, she is asleep again. I look at her with jealousy. I yearn to sleep. To switch off. To have a brief respite from guilt.

But that cannot be.

ALBY

The battle issss won. Flanagan'ssss ship and hisss asssault fleet of three vessselsss hass esscaped and ssset off towardssss Kornbluth.

But I linger.

I should not have played a role in the combat. That isss not the way of my people. We do not take sssides in the warssss between men. But I like Flanagan. I consssider him a friend. He hasss taught me much.

Succhh a sssstrange sssspecies. Yet endlesssly fasssscinating and varied. I ssssee them, metaphorically sssspeaking, asss an animal with razzzzor handsss which ripss out itsss own eyesss. Such is the human raccce.

And, sssstrangesssst of all, each human entity is indisssolubly sssseparate. They reproducccce ssslowly and painfully. They have no capacccity for genuinely abssstract thought that worksss at the level of pure meaning without the aid of numberssss or sssymbolssss. And they are, believe it or not, tool buildersssss.

I musssse, for a while, at the infinite folly and entertaining variety of humankind.

Then I feel a flicker of wearinesss, and I die.

*

Sssoon after, my new ssself is reborn, and consssidersss the ssstack of available memoriesss and intentionsss of the now dead and exxtinguished "Alby". It decidesss to continue the charade of being a single, continuousss, consssistent persss-sonality. I become "Alby" oncccce again.

I glory in the ssssight before me. The humansss' amazzzingly recklessss compressssed-ssspace bomb hasss wreaked appalling havoc. But it hassss left in its wake a shimmering glowing hazzzze of glory. It isss a light richer than light itsssself. For a being such assss myssself, composed entirely of light and flame, it is the nearesssst I will ever come to experiencing a vision of God. This light-hazzzze is quite sublime.

I drift clossser. I ssssee that the hazzzze is made of tiny particlesss. Ssssmall vibrating loopsss that hover and danccce in space. Some of the loopssss vanish then rematerialisssse. Some merge and form larger loopsss, then exxpand, then contract.

The energy of the dancing loops issss extraordinary. I wonder what will happen if they were to continue to exist in their pressssent sssstate and ssssize. For I know that these vibrating loops are singing in space. Their musssic, their resss-sonancccce, issss the esssssence of reality itssssself.

I marvel at the sssight. Who elssse hass ever ssseen such a thing?

For these loopsss are the entity we call ɪIɪ. Human sccci-entistsss called them "ssssupersssssymmetrical ssstrings". They are, of courssse, the fundamental indisssssolubles of which all matter isss comprissssed – they are the origin and the parent of electronsss, photonssss, muonssss, quarks, neutrinossss and every other physical manifessstation of matter in its tiniesssst formsss.

The ɪIɪ are the ssssmallest objectssss posssssible in the universe. For humans, they are a theorised reality, too small to be ssseen or detected with their instrumentsss. Because of coursse all human ssssubatomic detecting instrumentssss rely on the interaction of particlessss; and there issss no particle ssssmall enough to interact with the ssssmallest object posssssible.

And yet, thessse tiny particless are now as large as firefliess. They sswim through space, large enough to see, ssssolid enough to touch. This is a conssssequence of an esssssential part of their curious and immutable nature – sssuperstrings will expand when sssubjected to high energies. They can double or triple in size; or grow by a hundredfold. They can even become macrosssscopic.

And that isss precisssely what they have now done, in the blinding blazzzzing energy release of the human's compressssssed-space "Big Bang Bomb". This is the unexpected ssside effect. Ssssuperstrings made macrossssopic, for me to ssssee and hear.

I glory in what isss around me. The ssssong of the ɪ I ɪ is manifessst as the Universssse itssself, in all its infinite variety. And now I can hear that sssssong, I can *see* that shimmering frenzzzzzy that is the origin of everything.

I bassssk in joy asss I ssshare in God's ssssong.

And then I die, of sheer ecssstasy.

And then I am reborn.

FLANAGAN

We drink, and toast, and count the cost of victory.

It is the worst and vilest cost. All of us sit with vomit in our throats, wallowing in our own disgust. Though it was, we all concede, a brilliantly planned and executed military manoeuvre.

Picture the scene. The largest fleet of warships ever assembled and marshalled is faced with a small pirate flotilla.

Millions of warships, versus hundreds of thousands. It is inconceivable that the Corporation could lose such a one-sided contest.

But they did. We slaughtered them, and left not a single robot brain intact.

And yet I feel no pride. For the truth is – the entire battle was no more than a diversionary tactic, to allow us to move on towards our real objective. I sacrificed my entire nation, in order to keep myself and my crew members safe for the task ahead.

And that is why we did not fight. We stayed back. When facing danger, we fled. And all my pirate crew stayed with me, apart from Alliea, who refused to live when her children were doomed to die.

So here we are, celebrating a victory in which we played no part. Rejoicing in the sacrifice of warriors who sacrificed themselves to save us.

It is a hollow, bitter kind of evening. But we enjoy it nonetheless.

I take my guitar and play. The strings are programmed to play old-fashioned honky-tonk piano notes; and I have programmed the guitar's chip to give me an idiosyncratic, heartfelt bass and drums accompaniment. And my singing is carried via the intercoms to every vessel in our small fleet.

I don't sing the blues. That would sink us entirely. Instead, I sing a gospel hymn of hope and redemption.

I sing:

"On my way
To Canaan Land
I'm on my way
Yeah, to Canaan Land
On my waaay
Oh yeah
To Canaan Land,

On my way
Glory Hallelujah
On my way."

The piano chords smash and crash through the soaring melody and the heartfelt lyrics.

"Yes I'm on my way
To Canaan land
Yes, I'm on my way
To Canaan Land
On my waaaaaaaaaay
To Canaan Land
On my way
Glory Hallelujah
On my way."

I raise the energy level. I sing my heart out.

"I've had a mighty hard time
But I'm on my way
Had a mighty hard time
Yeah yeah yeah
Mighty hard time
On my way.

On my way
Glory Hallelujah
On my way!"

I have had my vocal chords modified to help me reach the rich throaty pitch of gospel songs like this. I feel as if my skin is being ripped off and my soul itself is reaching out and touching all my comrades, those before me in the assembly room, and those in their own ships.

I think of Alliea. I have seen video footage of her lonely death in space; her choice. Her end. Her glory.

"I've had a mighty hard time
But I'm on my way
Had a mighty hard time
Yeah yeah yeah
Mighty hard time
O-on my way."

I think of the many who died. Hera, Grendel, most of the Children Ships. All my own children too, forty-eight of them, died in the heat of battle. I wanted to save at least some of them, my favourite children, by keeping them in my command vessel. And I issued orders to that effect on my Captain's email; then deleted them. And issued them again; and deleted them again. For how could I chose my favourites, among that wonderful, rebellious rabble of kids? I loved them all, equally. And how could I save my own, while sending the children of others to certain death? No! No exceptions could be made. All had to die. Their sacrifice was needed, and their sacrifice was taken.

"Yes I'm on my way
To Canaan land
Yes, I'm on my way
To Canaan Land
On my waaaaaaaaaay
To Canaan Land
On my way
Glory Hallelujah
On my way!"

I think of life and death. So much death. Rob, Alliea, my children from the ship, my wife on Pixar, our children. My crewmates. My friends. My lovers. My victims. All the countless millions who die, every year, as the casual side effect of the Cheo's reign. And here I am, still alive. Heart still pounding. Mind still racing.

And my only consolation is the certainty that I, too, will die soon. Because with all that faces us – how could it be otherwise?

I reach the last chorus, I keep the honky-tonk piano settings, and I segue into another gospel song.

ALBY

I have caught up with the shipssss. I float outside their hullsss, flickering like the ssssun on water. Through my intercom, I can hear Flanagan'sss sssssong. And I can imagine the men and women in their cabinsss and asssssembly roomssss, lissssten-ing, clapping, ssssinging along.

And assss I float past them in deepesssst spacccce, a flame among the starssss, I, too, hear the new ssssong he ssssings. It isss fasssst, urgent, with a sssurging piano accompaniment; and it is a ssssong of hope, with a catchy melody that makesss the heart ssssoar:

"Oh Lord!"

Flanagan sssings, and I long for fingersss to click along to the beat. He continues:

"Oh Lord
Keep your hand on the plow
Hold on.

Oh Lord
Oh yeah
Oh Lord
Oh yeah
Keep your hand on the plough
Hold on.

Mary had three lengths of chain
And every length was in Jesus' name.
Keep the hand on the plough
Hold on.
When I get to heaven gonna sing and shout
Be no body there gonna put me out.
Keep your hand on the plough
Hold on.
Oh Lord
Oh Lord
Oh yeah.
Keep your hand on the plough
Oh Lord
Oh yeah
Oh Lord
Oh yeah
Keep your hand on the plough
And hoooooooooooooooooooold on."

LENA

"What's wrong?" I ask him gently.

The wake is over. All are sober. I am in the bar with a deeply melancholic Captain Flanagan. My previous mood of perverse elation has melted away. I am now bathed in Flanagan's despair.

"So many have died," he says softly.

"You knew that would happen."

"For no reason." He looks at me blankly. "We can't succeed."

"We've destroyed a Beacon before."

"And now they know our methods. They'll be prepared. It's a suicide mission."

"Then so be it."

"You're prepared to die?"

"Hell no. But I'm prepared to let *you* all die."

"Thank you Lena." He smiles a wry smile.

He cannot find a way around the time-lag factor.

"It's the time-lag factor, isn't it?" I say to him.

He is silent for a long long time.

"I knew you'd figure it out eventually," he tells me.

I pour myself a drink. We sip. We bathe in our own misery.

Every time the pirates invent a new military strategy, it may be ten or twenty years in subjective time before they can travel far enough to implement it again. But in Earth Time, those twenty years are in fact forty or even fifty years.

"Time dilation is against you. And the vast distances of space. By the time you fly from one star to another, they've had half a century or more to plot and counteract your next move."

"You got it."

Every battle is recorded on every ship's cctv and transmitted instantaneously back to Earth via the Beacons. Flanagan used an antimatter bomb once; the second time, the Earth DRs had built a net to catch it. He used the child Jamie's computer skills to capture the Doppelganger minds on Cambria; but by now, every Doppelganger in the Universe will be Earth-Mind Read Only.

"You can't use the Big Bang Bomb again," I say. "They'll have a way around it."

"I wouldn't risk it anyway. This is our Universe. What the hell are we doing with it?"

"Fair point. So, what's your plan to destroy the Beacon on Kornbluth?"

Flanagan takes his glass and throws it at the wall. It doesn't break, it bounces. The effect is laughable, rather than dramatic. Flanagan looks duly chagrined.

"We try, we fail. That's the plan," he tells me.

"*That's* a plan?"

"That's Plan A," Flanagan tells me. There's a shade more confidence in his voice now. But I can tell he is still beset by terrible doubts.

"So what's Plan B?"

He stares at me.

The air in front of him seems to shimmer and flicker. For a moment, I assume I have a migraine of a kind I haven't endured for centuries. Then I wonder if Alby the flame beast is back inside the ship.

Then the air solidifies into a black floating particle. More particles swarm, to form a shape, a letter. The letter grows. It is the shape and size of a standing human being without limbs. It is an **I**. A free-floating **I** which is almost as big as I am. Then the **I** flickers and changes, and I realise what is happening. The air is talking to me. *The air is talking to me.*

And it says:

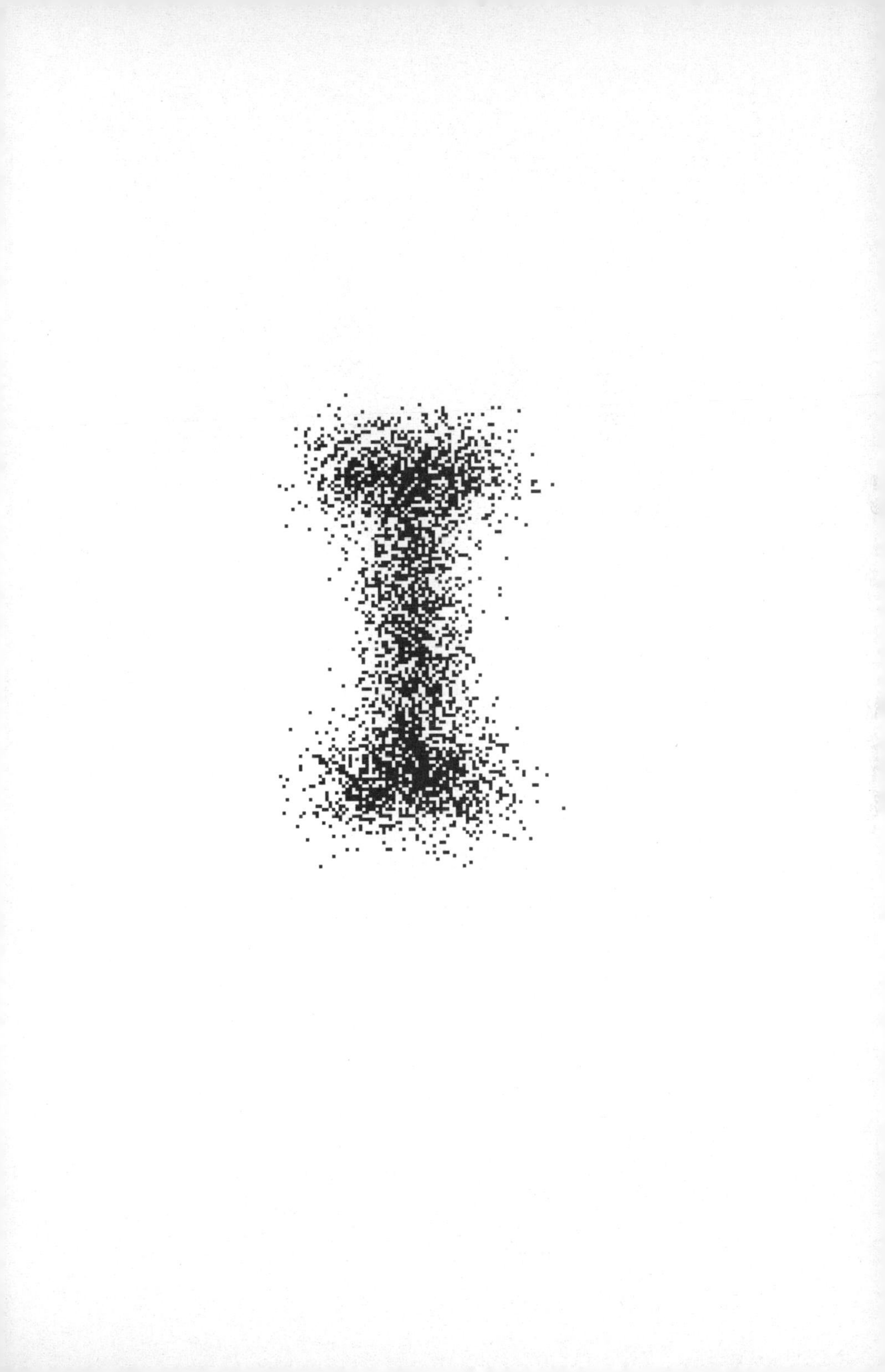

A M

PLAN

I stare at Flanagan.

"You're insane," I tell him.

"I have no choice," he says flatly.

The letters shimmer a little more and turn into a humanoid shape. The humanoid black shape sits in an armchair, and crosses one humanoid leg over another.

The humanoid shape is, I know, made of billions upon billions of microscopic entities, swarming under the control of a focused group intelligence. It is an alien being that is alien beyond imagining.

Flanagan has forged a treaty with the Bugs.

I am in the same room as *Bugs.*

Every pore and follicle on my body shivers in horror. I feel as if my skin is being ripped off. I cannot breathe.

The Bug entity shimmers and changes its shape again. It is, I realise, trying to find a succinct way of indicating friendly and non-aggressive intentions towards me. But the shape it chooses is surreally inappropriate. It heightens my panic attack. It makes me almost insane, torn between a desire to hoot with laughter and an overwhelming urge to defecate then die.

This is what the Bug becomes:

"Oh no," I say. "Oh merciful heaven, no!"

BOOK 9

EXCERPT FROM THE THOUGHT DIARY OF LENA SMITH, 2004–

I have wasted a lot of years.

I have been drunk, drugged, lazy, stupefied, and just plain idle. Like Samuel Beckett, I once spent a year in bed. Like Winnie the Pooh, I have gorged myself until my stomach has bulged. I have also, aimlessly, foolishly, doodled away entire months doing nothing apart from tidying and making a mess and tidying it up again, a little differently.

Most galling of all, I spent two hard desperate years writing a novel into which I poured my heart and life and soul and entire family history, and which I showed to people whose opinion I respect. They all *hated it*. In fact, I lost some of my dearest friends because of what they considered to be the dreary drabness of my writing.

So I turned, again, to drink and drugs. I spent ten years as an addict and had to have a liver transplant. I snorted coke and bought a new septum. I mainlined and OD'd and mixed crack with LSD and ecstasy and almost died, several times.

But I knew what I was doing. I was pacing myself. I knew I had a long life ahead of me. I wanted to be sure I left no experience unexplored.

For in my time, I have sky-dived. I have scuba-dived. I have had gonorrhoea. I have been a high-class prostitute. I have been a professional gambler. I have had sex with a movie star. I have read *A La Recherche du Temps Perdu* in the original French. I have listened to and appreciated every single symphony and major work by Beethoven, Mozart, Bach, Chopin and Sidelman. I have spent a year in China. I have spent a year in India. I have spent numerous years in Italy. I have been a step-mum to squawling babies and angry toddlers. I have been unfaithful. I have been faithful. I have committed murder. I have been to jail. I have been brain-fried for my crimes, and I have survived with my rage intact. I have escaped from prison. I have white-water-rafted and I have been a fashion model. I have been a good mother. I have been a bad mother. I have been burgled. I have been flayed, twice. I have been a thief. I have written, as I said, a deeply underrated novel. I have composed several symphonies. I have learned a dozen languages. I have been a concert pianist. I have written best-selling academic books. I have had friends who are transsexuals and homosexuals and celibates. I have loved, and been loved, and I have had my heart broken more times than I can count.

And for almost one hundred years, I was the leader of humankind.

That last part sounds unlikely, I know. Even now, it seems like a dream that such a thing could have happened. I have lost touch with the person I was then: focused, political, manipulative. I networked ceaselessly, eighteen hours a day and more, in person, on the phone, and by email. I wrote game plans of objectives to be achieved and day by day, month by month, I ticked off my successes. And by this means – carefully, ruthlessly, cynically – I achieved ultimate power.

It came about, in the first instance, because of my experience with Future Dreams. After experiencing the very worst of human corruption and injustice, I was left with a burning urge to change things in the world. Admittedly, it was decades before I did anything about that urge, and I drank a lot of margaritas and screwed a lot of men in this delightful interim. But the seed had been sowed. And it finally germinated.

I was unemployed, a recovering alcohol and drug addict, and I had just been betrayed by a philandering man. So I called up all my contacts in the hope of getting academic work – and it was a complete washout. So instead, randomly, I applied for a job with the UN. And I became a junior manager of a UN-funded project in Portugal. This was, of course, after the Worst Hundred Years, when the collapse of the ecosystem had caused astonishing devastation and loss of life across the planet. For much of the time when I had been drinking and taking drugs and having sex, Florida and Spain were flooded, Central America was devastated by malarial infection, and much of Europe had turned to desert. However, huge progress had been made in restoring the Earth's damaged biosphere. And the UN was pioneering the recovery process.

So for sixteen years I laboured with the other UN workers to heal the land, cure the sick and reseed the empty oceans. It was an extraordinary, exhilarating time; we all knew that we were doing something genuinely good. And in this period I had a glorious sense of what it was to have the nationality Human. We were all bonded together, in a joint enterprise; and day by painful day, our world was saved.

But once the principles of ecostability were more fully understood, the pace of progress increased. Vast floating carbon traps cleared the air of man-made emissions. Plankton swarmed in the oceans. Cod replenished and filled the seas. Frozen helium chilled the poles, and the ice froze again. The equilibrium was restored; the Earth started to heal itself.

And, as the years went by, I felt ambition crept up on me. Once the crisis was over, most of my work became repetitive and clerical and mundane. I knew I had the experience to do more than I was doing – and I yearned to be the leader and not the led.

So I applied myself to that task, with all the focus of a heat-seeking missile. For the first time in my life, I made it my objective to climb the greasy pole. And I applied all my talent and knowledge to that single, soulless task.

I undermined my rivals with psychological gambits. I worked on my skills and my contacts and I ceaselessly, endlessly, flattered those who might be of use to me. I worked long hours, I flirted with my Portuguese boss and even had sex with him a few times. I became a socialite and a gossip. I was promoted from deputy manager to manager; I was transferred to a new project in France; and from there I became a member of the UN hierarchy, on a roaming global brief.

And within seven years, I became Deputy Vice President of the UN during a time of great political upheaval.

In my first year in this new job, I wrote a definitive paper on the new world order, in which I tried to analyse with scientific precision the problems facing mankind – and also the solutions. Energy, I concluded, was the answer to most of these problems. Others agreed. And a year later, a superconductive energy pump was invented which, when placed in close orbit, could convert heat from the sun's rays into invisible beams of energy that provided near-limitless power to fuel our consumerist technological society.

Four years later, I resigned from the UN and became a British Member of Parliament. I had a constituency in Greenock, and I gave my maiden speech in the house on the subject of urban regeneration. I wrote a column for a newspaper, I campaigned on behalf of consumers and factory workers. I appeared on comic quiz shows and became a cult figure.

And after thirteen years of this relentless hard work, I became Leader of the Opposition.

Five years after that I became Prime Minister. I had my photograph on the staircase next to Thatcher, Major, Blair, Brown, Matthews, Thomas, Jones, Durbridge, Smith, Andrews, and McQuist. I dined with the Queen, I opened factories, I traded insults at Question Time, I feuded with my Chancellor, I put a brave face on economic adversity, I pandered to Middle Britain, I gave approval for a vast underground motor and railway to join Glasgow, Cardiff and London. I did, well, really, all sorts of things. I have a list somewhere. I should be prouder, I suppose, though after this long distance of time, all I can remember is that most British MPs drink formidable quantities of Scotch whisky and pride themselves on being raconteurs, even when they aren't.

And then, after four years in office, I shocked everyone by resigning in order to launch my campaign to be appointed Ambassador for Humanity. This was a new job created as a token sop to liberals who urged an end to nationalism and factionalism. But in my view, it was a post which offered wider horizons and greater challenges than being the cat's-paw of the Liberal Democratic Socialist Alliance Party.

I got the job as Ambassador. And I felt like a hawk with a healed wing. After all the petty backbiting of British politics, finally it felt as if I had a *proper* job. I soared and pounced and soared some more. And after a while, I changed my job title to "President of Humanity".

Once self-appointed in this way, I went on to run the Council for the Improvement of Humankind. And I became, through force of personality, and sheer weight of groundbreaking ideas, the de facto leader of the human race.

Talk about goal-oriented! All it takes is drive, stamina, shamelessness, a shit-caked tongue, and a modicum of ability.

As the first-ever President of Humanity, I had a new office built for me in Brussels, with 3D wallpaper that could be transformed at the clap of two hands into a map of the solar system. I explored the limits of my new expense account. I learned how to power-dress.

And I studied the art of how to rule the human race. I read every book I could think of – from Machiavelli to Plato. And I adapted the principles of political governance by referring it back to my People Matrix based on the emergence equations I'd created so many years before. Using those equations instead of blind instinct, I forged a new way forward. I devised a computer program that would allow me to map and extrapolate political changes before they happened. I was able, therefore, to foresee and prevent revolutions in France and Louisiana. I forged a pact between China and Japan. I defanged the neo-cons of America, already discredited after their failed policies of the early twenty-first century. And I created an elite corps of aides who acted on my behalf with all the ruthlessness of Tom and Tosh and Michiyo and the others in the old days of the World Police. I never killed my political enemies; I merely discredited, undermined and humiliated them.

Those were the days . . . !

And it was during this period that we launched the second wave of space colonists. I was forced to say goodbye to my beloved son, who had been (once again) accused of rape. I had to falsify his records to get him aboard, to expunge all evidence of his assorted crimes, but I did it with a clear conscience. He was less dangerous in space, I argued to myself, than back here on Earth.

And when he had left, I became acutely aware that my life's work had to be finding a way to secure the future of those colonists who had risked so much for an uncertain step forward for mankind.

A few years later, the first wave of colonists achieved landfall, on Hope. The very first Quantum Beacon was built. And Heimdall started to come into being. I was ready for the challenges thrown at me. I was the right person, at the right time, in the right job.

I had a simple philosophy of power, which I called the Pournelle Doctrine, after one of my favourite writers. The doctrine is this: *Problems have solutions*. Mass starvation in Africa is caused by lack of resources, lack of water, corruption and war. So I helped turn the African nations into self-contained energy-generating commercial entities with fertile fields and vast underground industrial estates. Dictators were punished with loss of trading rights. Greed triumphed; and thus, wars started to vanish. Financial corruption was replaced by dependency on the joys and exhilaration of a twenty-third-century lifestyle.

I created a complex system of virtuous circles where non-malign behaviour was rewarded with greater health, wealth, and longer life. Poverty was eliminated by endless energy resources. The population explosion was – as Pournelle himself prophesied all those years ago – a self-solving problem, because as wealth increases, family size decreases. Even the issue of land was becoming less and less of an issue, as we sent colony ships of Palestinians and Eastern Europeans into the brave new lands of space.

I was, essentially, a passive-aggressive dictator. I controlled every aspect of the behaviour of everyone on Earth; but I presented the façade of being the follower of humanity's dreams. Like an old-fashioned wife from days gone by, I made all the decisions, but let my sap of a husband believe that *he* was running things.

And yes, I admit I had my vanities. The name change was one. From Lena to Xabar. I dressed in tight-fitting shimmering plasto-leather suits, I cultivated an image as a woman with a dangerous past. I played a role really – I reinvented myself as an ancient warrior chieftainess in modern times. I was Boudicca, I was a cartoon heroine, I was *Xabar*. In a world dominated by grey and middle-aged politicians, I was the candle, and I was also the flame.

This was, of course, all calculated. I packaged my essence up into a series of connected myths and sold them all, all at the same time. I sold the myth of the obedient servant of humanity; and I sold the myth of the sexy dominatrix. I sold the myth of the ice maiden warrior princess who could kick male ass; and I sold the myth of the nurturing, gentle, mother/sister/lover. I was alpha, beta, gamma and omega, all rolled into one. I was left-wing, right-wing, conservative, liberal, sluttish, puritanical, dangerous, safe.

It was politics as prestidigitation, sizzle not steak. But there *was* a steak. There was substance to what I did. I wasn't, as some argued, a bimbo apparatchik. I was a visionary. But a visionary in a sexy suit, with a weird name, and a knack of being whatever people wanted her to be.

Then, after about twenty years, the look changed. I became more severe, more forbidding. As my policies became more liberal, my look became more starched. I wore stiff suits and disapproved of nudity in television commercials. I became Nanny – fair, firm, but innately puritanical and moralistic. That worked, too, for a good while.

Then I appointed a good-looking Vice President and for ten years or so, it was assumed that *he* was the power behind the throne. It was rumoured we were lovers, and that I was going to stand down in favour of him. I can't, for the life of me, remember his name. I can easily look it up, but I choose not to. When my policies started to run into difficulties, he became my fall guy. He left, I stayed. Life carried on.

Of course, each nation on Earth had its own ruler; and each country was sovereign, and powerful. My role in "Presiding" over the Council of Humanity was simply to coordinate and liaise. But the reality was, leaders of nation states came and went. They lost at elections, they were assassinated, they died of heart failure. But *I stayed* – constantly reinventing myself, and my role. And in this way, I became for a period almost all-powerful.

At first, I travelled constantly. But as time went by I relied heavily on my vidscreens in my office in Brussels (and, latterly, in an annexe of the Houses of Parliament in London.) I was, of course, spending every night in the virtual reality of Hope, inhabiting the bodies of Doppelganger Robots as a frontier was tamed, and a planet was terraformed. So when my days began, my head was pounding with memories of sandstorms and appalling deaths and great heroism. But I developed a knack of effortlessness that allowed me to glide through paperwork and answer phenomenal numbers of emails. I vidphoned a hundred messages a day and buzzed them out in batches. It was rare for me to have actual conversations. I preferred people to pitch me proposals by email, so I had time to simmer on them; and then I announced my decisions.

And so we savoured the twenty-third century, the period in which the human race changed for ever. Microchip brain implants became standard and so virtually every human being had access to all the knowledge of all the ages. Bodies and faces could be changed like suits, with the vagaries of fashion. The first genetically engineered humans appeared – the "gillpeople", who could breathe in oxygen through water, and who were eventually evolved into the Dolphs. There was a whole new generation of 100 Plusers, wars were unheard of, the distant planets were being colonised. Boxing was outlawed. Prostitution was taxed at a higher tax band. Children were maturing faster, learning faster; teenagers were force-fed knowledge, but in their twenties the new generation of "twoers" experienced the sheer joy of a gap decade before entering the world of work.

The famines in Africa were a thing of the past. After the catastrophic climate disasters of the late twenty-second century, the climate was now in a state of stable homeostasis, no longer oscillating between global warming and Ice Age. Music was, frankly, shit; even by my standards. Popular and classical alike, music was well and truly *up* itself. But painting had entered a renaissance, and wall murals of staggering beauty by the world's greatest artists covering whole city blocks and skyscrapers could be found in every capital city.

And the problems of the human race were being solved. *They were being solved*. Problems have solutions; you just have to find them.

The pressure on me was, however, phenomenal, and my workload was crippling. And after nearly ninety years in power, I began planning my retirement. But first, I ushered in my repeal of the penal laws – which meant the eradication of prison in favour of electronic and behaviour-modifying torture as a punishment for offences. The "brain-frying" of armed robbers and murders proved to be chillingly effective. Crime plummeted; and those who used to be career criminals lived their lives in a state of semi-fear, haunted by memories of the excruciating pain generated by our cortex-searers and imagination-burners.

This, too, whatever later critics have said, was a solution to a problem: namely, how to stop criminals committing crime. One solution is to incarcerate them at vast expense for long periods of wasted life. The other is to hurt and terrify them so badly they are physically unable to sin again. Under my scheme anyone who committed a serious crime – murder, rape, kidnap, paedophilia, grievous bodily harm, armed robbery, or malicious extortion – would experience brain-frying. And anyone who became a repeat offender would be brain-fried daily, until either redemption or brain damage was achieved.

It was cruel; but it worked. And, coupled with advances in forensic and thought-exploration technology which made wrongful convictions a thing of the past, it was *fair*.

This was my brave new world. Mock it if you like; but I lived a long long time in the old world. And my world is, trust me, a billion times better.

It was a strange and wonderful period. But looking back, I wish I had found myself some friends. People who could stand up to me, defy me, argue with me. Instead, I had legions of loyal acolytes. Eager beavers who were young and anxious to cling to my coat-tails. None of them were over the age of forty; all of them secretly plotted to take my job.

But there was power enough for all of us. I hired one young man, Matt Evans, who called himself Mat X, after hearing his rap lyric on an album I downloaded on to my earpiece. He had such energy, such wit, such coruscating irony. So I called him into my office and quizzed him on what *he* would do to solve the problems of the world. He was an angry and passionate black man who spoke, angrily and passionately of course, about the shit that is dealt to blacks and mixed-race communities in today's fucked-up society.

So I made him Coordinator for Africa. His mission was to make Africa into the richest, coolest nation on Earth. He had the resources, he had the staff. And he had no fucking idea how to run an office or do a job; even getting up in the morning was a strain for him.

But he learned, fast. He was streetwise, smart, a great people person. He sat down with African dictators and he visited mass graves created as a result of the frequent genocidal wars that were still taking place on a regular basis. He invoked the spirit of Mandela, but he also brought a young new energy to things. Secretly, I controlled his every move; but I used his charisma, his youth, his rap-artist credibility, to win hearts and minds. Billions of young blacks who hated authority idolised Mat X. They listened to his words; they admired his style; and they marvelled that he released his official Manifesto for African Redevelopment in the form of a ninety-minute rap single.

And as a result, we got Africa in shape. It became what it should always have been; a fertile land rich in ideas and culture, in which cooperation between disparate tribes is ingrained in the heart of every native-born 'frican. We called it "the 'frican way"; it was not quite a religion, not quite a philosophy, but it became a way of life for billions.

China was tougher. Eventually, I found a young woman who was abnormally empathetic; her ability to seemingly read minds and predict behaviour allowed her to introduce democracy and reform Chinese social practices. She later became a Demi-Goddess, revered by entire nations; and of course, by that point she was no longer returning my phone calls. Her name was Xan (you see, she even copied her silly name from me). Ungrateful bitch! Sorry. Moving on . . .

Problems have solutions. It was my creed, my Machiavellian code. Yet the curious thing is: amnesia is the driving principle of all human behaviour. When things are bad, everyone will yearn for them to get better. But when things are good, it's all taken for granted. And so entire generations grew up in my world assuming this was the natural order of things. Full employment, barely any disease, long lives, few wars, a warm and emotionally invigorating architectural environment – big deal! The world was still shit, and adults like me were arseholes and fossils to be mocked and despised.

So maybe there *is* one problem that lacks a solution. Maybe human beings are just Not That Nice. They are selfish, venal, they have no gratitude. I did so much for the human race; but what has it ever done for me?

Why, for instance, do I find it so hard to make female friends? And why do the men who are my lovers betray and patronise me? And why is it I keep having to fake orgasms? And how come no one ever laughs at my jokes?

What the hell is *wrong with me*?

She brought her death upon herself.

Though I can't deny I was wrong to do what I did.

But how can it be, in a life lived so long, with so many good deeds to my credit, after so many years of self-restraint and self-denial and altruistic commitment, that a single trail of wrongdoing can be traced and tracked and used to destroy me?

I admit my sin: I bribed officials to cover up my son's rape of a young woman. And later, despite other rape investigations, I used my official position to quash any police allegations into his conduct. I pulled strings, and falsified records, and eventually got my son sent out into space where, I hoped, his wicked streak would burn out.

And Congresswoman Cavendish, the scourge of liberals, made it her life's work to find me out. She began with the assumption that I *must* be guilty, of something. She didn't care what. She was a religious fanatic, a bigot, a hater of people of colour, a Muslimophobe. And for most of the last thirty years of my long tenure in power she attempted to destroy me with one fraudulent accusation after another. I found myself wearying of her lies, her black propaganda. And I could not think of an adequate solution to this, my own particular and painful problem. Her hatred of me was visceral, intense, and it kept her alive. Without the aid of rejuvenation therapies, which she disapproved of, Cavendish reached the age of eighty-eight with her energies undimmed, her hatred of me unslaked.

And finally, she found a smoking gun. She found out all about Peter and my continuing role in concealing his criminality. The scandal broke, and I was disbarred from office.

I can remember vividly the moment when it all ended for me. It was a Thursday. Or a Wednesday? No matter. It was morning. I'd just finished a cup of strong coffee. I opened up my emails, and found one that had the subject line: *You have been impeached.* I rose, stunned, from my desk and walked numbly out of my office . . . and Cavendish was there in the corridor to greet me. With an army of officials. Gloating. Gloating!

At Cavendish's insistence, I was formally censured in front of my colleagues by the Arbiter. My papers of office were ceremonially ripped up. It was all done by the book, in accordance with hallowed traditions. Except I knew it was all bullshit. I was the first person to hold this particular office. We *had* no traditions.

But Cavendish had her way. I was humiliated. And, in the months that followed, as I read the press coverage, I realised that piece by piece my reputation was being stolen. A new President of Humankind was elected, and the impression was created that mine had been a caretaker administration. I had been not much more than a glorified civil servant; now a *real* politician was in charge.

To combat this torrent of lies, I leaked stories, I briefed journalists, I called in every favour I was owed. But every time I thought I had a handle on how the game was played, the game tilted and I was utterly humiliated once again. I read entire books that argued that the triumph of the planet Hope was a victory of plucky settlers fighting against the meddling interference of jumped-up civil servants back on Earth – namely, *me*. I read that my principles and protocols of office were created by the person who succeeded me – a nonentity called Luigi Scarpio, who combined astonishing charisma with utter ignorance of science and was devoid of morality and common sense. Every achievement or insight or policy advance I had ever made was credited to someone else; every mistake or fiasco or instance of corruption which had occurred during my tenure was blamed on me.

The people loved Scarpio. He was homespun, funny, a bit tubby, he liked to mock his own fondness for pasta and Italian women. Scarpio became a legend. Whereas I . . . I became a footnote.

Cavendish had won; I had lost. And so, I admit, I lost control of myself. My rage was intense. I tried suing her for libel, I tried tarnishing her own reputation. And then, eventually, in the full knowledge that she had a terminal illness that would end her life in less than nine months, I obtained an illegal gun and I went to her house, intent on murder.

I stood outside the house, whipped by cold winds, trying to control my breathing, for six long hours.

Then I smashed in the back door and went in. The burglar alarm was blaring. I was handling this all wrong, I could have been so much cleverer. A poison dart, a sabotaged car, a hitman.

I blundered onwards. Here I was, the former most powerful woman in the world, seized by an irrational rage. How could she do this to me! How could she do this!

I spent ten minutes playing "Sardines", hunting for an old lady hiding in a big old mock twenty-first-century mansion. I discovered her eventually in the linen closet. When she saw me, her face uncrinkled in relief. "They've gone now," I whispered. "You're safe, come with me."

She held out her hand to me.

And I shot her, repeatedly, in the body, till I was deafened by her screams. Then I blew her brains out. The explosion was awful. I was spattered with Cavendish. The sheer horror of the moment filled me with a childish glee.

I heard sounds at the back door. The police had arrived.

I wiped my prints off the gun, scratched my face on the side of the linen cupboard door, and concocted my cover story, involving masked gunmen and an heroic struggle on my part to save the old lady.

It was a laughably bad cover story. The police charged me with murder. My own lawyer openly mocked my story of having arrived to offer Cavendish my forgiveness and friendship, only to find the aforementioned armed burglars on the premises. She urged me to plead insanity, in the hope of being offered a course of forcible therapy. Instead, I entered a plea of "Justifiable Homicide".

My lawyer, without my permission, changed the plea to temporary insanity, on the grounds I was totally raving mad and shouldn't be listened to. She had a point. But the court ignored all our bickering, and I was found guilty of murder in the first degree. Fortunately, however, my lawyer managed to prevent the State from seizing my assets.

I was sentenced to be brain-fried for two days.

I knew exactly what to expect. I had studied this subject intensively, since I had of course introduced this particular punishment into the penal system. Electrodes in the pain centres and imagination centres of the cortex fire electrical currents for between twenty and a hundred consecutive hours. It is intended to be the nearest thing in life to being in Hell.

But I think the night before was worse. Every nerve ending jangled. My skin prickled and itched and I felt as if I was being devoured by insects. I was in the hotel wing of the prison complex, I was well fed, my bed was soft and comfortable. But to know that in the morning you will be tortured is a torture in itself.

My room was pastel pink. It had strange whorly patterns in the wallpaper. Ambient music played, that grated and scratched at my soul. I think it was meant to be relaxing, but for me, it was part of the torment. For years after, I was unable to travel in lifts in case muzak played and I started ripping out throats.

Then dawn came. I was led into another room with equally comforting wallpaper. I was sat down in a chair. A helmet was placed on my head. My hands were restrained. A catheter was hooked into my arm to prevent me dehydrating. I realised I had urinated upon myself, but a nurse came and wiped me down. The "Play" button on the brain-modification helmet was pressed.

At first, it hurt. But I could ignore that.

Then I had an hallucination. I imagined that I was free. Walking across a green field, in the hot sun. Beautiful men and women walked beside me, stark naked. And then I realised my skin was peeling. I was burning in the sun. I rubbed a hot patch, and skin came away and I saw sinews and tendons underneath.

I itched, all over. I rubbed myself. My hair come out, my nose fell off. My heart fell out of my ribcage and lay on the grass, beating hot blood.

It started to rain. But there was salt in the rain, which burned into my raw skinless flesh. The agony was unbelievable. But then my mother appeared, smiling. She picked up my heart and ate it. I felt a pang of betrayal and self-hate. My mother smiled at me, my blood trickling down her jaw. Lightning struck me and sent millions of volts surging through my body.

But finally, it was over. I was clothed now, my skin was restored. I recognised immediately that this was a ruse to prevent me becoming desensitised to pain. I knew I was still in the nightmare. But all my senses told me I was sitting in Starbucks, with a caffè latte and a caramel shortbread in front of me.

I drank the soothing coffee, ate the cake. *Don't do this!* I screamed at myself. The taste of pleasure was softening me up.

A man with tattoos sat down at the table with me. He took my hand and sawed off my fingers one by one. "Daddy, don't," I whispered at him. He took out a club with spikes.

He beat me for several hours, until every inch of my flesh was tenderised and bleeding. I tried to tune out the pain. I kept telling myself: this isn't really happening.

The pain continued, and continued. It got worse. And even worse. But eventually it was over. I heard gentle voices speaking to me. My straps were being unbuckled. A doctor was explaining that I was now ready to go into recuperative therapy. I was led out of the room. I insisted on staggering down the stairs, rather than using the lift. We left the building.

"Am I free?" I whispered.

You're free," my father told me. "But remember, no more bad behaviour."

"I promise, Daddy."

"Lying bitch," my daddy said, and slashed my face with a razor. He peeled my face off and blew his nose on it. And then he walked away.

A pack of hyenas surrounded me. I was in the middle of Piccadilly, with shoppers walking past. But no one stopped or raised the alarm. The hyenas starting biting at me. I shuddered and shrunk into a ball.

Lightning struck me and seared my body with unbelievable pain. The hyenas ripped my flesh to shreds and ate me.

I was in a lecture, at university. I was wearing glasses! This was the old me, the former Lena, before I became Xabar. I breathed deeply, shaking with relief. I was coming to welcome these respites, at least they . . .

Everyone was staring at me. With hate in their eyes. "We despise you, Lena," my fellow students were whispering. "You are pathetic, you are flawed, you are the worst person in the world."

"Sticks and stones!" I replied mockingly. A foolish thing to do because . . .

My fellow students proceeded to beat me viciously with sticks wrapped in barbed wire and jagged stones. I gritted my teeth, as the pain escalated, and waited to die so that the next nightmare could begin.

I was in a room, with a blonde-haired eight-year-old girl. She was giggling and playing with a pet dinosaur and a spider that you can move by pressing a rubber bulb. I sat down with her and played. "What's the spider called?" I asked.

"Spidey," said the little girl.

"I'll be Spidey," I said.

"I'll be Mr Steggy," the little girl said. "My granny gave me these toys. My granny is dead now, some heartless monster killed her."

I looked up and saw Commissioner Cavendish staring down at me. Sorrow and love in her eyes. The little girl's eyes lit up and she ran to her granny and kissed her. "Gran," she murmured, "Gran, I love you," as she hugged old Cavendish. And Cavendish's harsh face relaxed into the gentlest and kindest of smiles, as she embraced her beloved granddaughter.

Waves of remorse and self-loathing swept over me. "I'm sorry," I whispered. And Cavendish's head exploded and the girl was covered in blood, and she started to scream, and scream . . .

And so it continued. I endured two days of these nightmares, but it felt like ten years. Eventually it ended, but for months afterwards, I was convinced that my life was just another dream, and any moment now, the next horror would arrive.

My "coercive therapy" punishment for murder was the most appalling experience that it is possible for any human being to experience; it's programmed to be just that. It is a toxic blend of pain, self-loathing, guilt, remorse and physical agony . . . My soul was scorched and seared.

But the punishment didn't, in fact, work.

Perhaps I was too steeped in sin. Or perhaps I am too canny, too experienced. But I found that my remorse ebbed rapidly. I am still able, as my warrior exploits have shown, to kill whenever I need to, or want to. I can sleep without bad dreams. My memories of the horror of my torture have been virtually expunged.

I still feel spasms of agony when I least expect it. The pain of my punishment will never leave me. But the sheer joy of that moment will never diminish:

Cavendish staring at me with her skeletal, withered face, full of contempt. I show her the gun and the

> contempt turns to fear and bewilderment.
>
> Then I shoot her in the leg. Then the other leg. Then in the body. Then in the head, repeatedly, so that her brains are sprayed over me. Then I sit and tell her wrecked skull stories of my debauchery until the police make it up the stairs and subdue me. It is exquisite delight. I savour every moment of my soul-degradation.

Why did I do it? I cannot say, I cannot explain. It meant the total and comprehensive end of my reputation, it meant my damnation by posterity.

Clearly, I was mad. But the question that then raises itself is: When did I become mad? Then, or earlier? Was I mad while I was in power?

But then again, maybe I was just bored, and yearned for an experience more extreme than anything else in my long, long life. Murder; incarceration; brain-frying; public excoriation. Well, I couldn't argue that my life was *dull*.

After the brain-frying, a psychologist diagnosed me as unrepentant. I was sentenced to another course of treatment. But I bribed a guard, and left the prison disguised as one of the conjugal visitors.

I left Earth that night on a colony ship. Twenty years later, subjective time, I was reunited with my son, who was on a ship heading for Earth.

He led a conquering army. I greeted him like a matriarch applauding her Emperor son. He was completely under my spell. I had no friends by then, I could not afford to make one more enemy.

I was amazed at how confident Peter seemed. He had a swagger, coupled with an easy charm. He had been fantastically successful as a colonist; he had become the leader of his people, he had destroyed an alien species, and he had helped to terraform one of the bleakest planets ever settled by humans. And now Peter was eager for fresh challenges. He was a general returning home, with the intention of declaring himself Emperor.

I was still somewhat crazed when we met. Everything he said seemed normal. But in retrospect, everything he said was utterly monstrous. Peter had become addicted to war; and he made it his life's work to seek out the cruellest and the hardest way.

I gave him long long lectures on how to rule Earth according to liberal principles, and he paid me not a blind bit of notice. Eventually, feeling myself to be old and tiresome, I bade him farewell. He went his way, I went mine.

I travelled through space a few decades more, and eventually made myself a home on Rebus, the fourth planet of the star Moriarty. Whilst there, I watched the TV footage of Peter's Earth invasion. I watched as my son installed himself as leader of mankind.

I watched and I understood nothing. By this point, I did not even understand myself. I wrote this, in my mental diary:

> I do not know who I am, or why I did what I did. I am merely a forward arrow through time.
>
> I wonder if I am truly human any more.

Kids! They break your heart.

When he was nine years old I realised I was afraid of Peter. He had tantrums, terrible screaming fits that left me shaking and shuddering for hours afterwards. But there was always that sense that he never really lost control. There was always that still, eerie eye at the centre of the storm.

He didn't like green vegetables but we had a nanny who insisted that he ate them. He thought this was awful, so he begged and begged me to sack her, but of course I refused. Then he started to wet the bed. I was so ashamed. I had a cleaner of course, but I couldn't bear for her to see the sheets, so I'd be up in the early hours washing and ironing sheets and replacing them on the bed before dawn. Then he started to wet himself in school. Every night, before going to bed, he would drink a gallon and a half of water with the sole intention of urinating it back up again over his plastic sheets or his schoolbooks. Eventually, I sacked the nanny, and the bed-wetting stopped. Peter had got his way.

To my astonishment, other children always did what he told them to do. It was a knack he had. If he asked a child to jump out of a first-floor window, the child would do so. Numerous broken limbs resulted. If he wanted extra sweets, he would demand that other children give their allowances to him. And no one dared argue with him.

And so the parents of the other children refused to have him in the house. He became a pariah, the child no one wants their child to be with. He once put a dead bird in the drainpipe of the house of one of his little friends. It stank the house out, and the parents had to call the Council round to fumigate. And another time, he superglued two little girls together by their hands. They were too embarrassed to tell anyone for two days. So they just walked side by side together even when they went to the toilet. When the parents found out, they were devastated – at the injury committed, and at their own neglect of their daughters.

Peter was an ugly teenager. His face was pockmarked and scarred with acne. I had to pay for skin rejuvenation therapy to start him off at the age of fifteen with a clean slate, and a face girls could bear to kiss. But at some level, he never lost that ugly face. He always had that cautious look of someone who expects the first reaction of others to be recoil.

He masturbated incessantly. Don't all boys do that? I suppose they do. But I found it shocking, I was tired of finding damp tissues chucked down the toilet bowl, and sheets that were stiff with the previous night's emission.

He used to steal hard-core magazines. I was searching his things regularly by then, and I was horrified at the material he read. Coprophilia, necrophilia, other perversions that even now I can't bear to think about. I took him to a therapist and Peter made false allegations of incest against me just as a joke.

How could a child grow up so bad?

But then, perhaps there are in fact reasons and excuses for his behaviour. And perhaps, after all, *I* was to blame. Because, even in the period after my encounter with Future Dreams, and the flaying, even when I was well and skinned again, I was never there for him. I had my other concerns. I was preoccupied with work, I rarely came home before midnight. And, of course, I was constantly afraid that Future Dreams would wreak a terrible revenge for what I had done to them. They might send mercenaries to kill me or my child or fit us up for crimes or even, conceivably, murder or rape me in my bed. I was very paranoid during that period. I was also drinking heavily. I was also abusing pharmaceutical drugs and overdosing on rejuves. I was a total screw-up, with a small child. What was I thinking of?

It was all my fault!

But Peter did change. By the age of seventeen, his face was smooth, and he had a ready smile. He was smart and charismatic, and he had learned how to flatter me. He was mummy's little boy. I basked in his approval.

He took a ferocious interest in the work I was doing He travelled with me round Europe, and Egypt, and Africa. We walked around the Parthenon together, arms linked like husband and wife. But in fact, he was my son. My handsome, funny, clever son.

For a time I forgot, to be honest, about his dark-child years. I smothered him, I pampered him. I never challenged his opinions, though he was inclined to wild supernatural speculations. He never wanted for anything. I catered to his every whim and desire. And I was *so* proud of him when he said he wanted to be a doctor, and got a place at an Oxford college to study medicine. Then, after he was thrown out of Oxford for assaulting a fellow student, I was so proud he quickly managed to get a place on a BA course in ecology at London Met. Then, when he was sent down from London Met for abusing the Vice Chancellor at a freshers' networking event, I was so proud of the way he managed to get himself a job in the City of London.

Then, when he was sacked from his job in the City for misappropriating clients' funds, I was so proud of him when he shrugged off the disgrace and came to live with me, and stayed in bed all day, and drank a lot, and screwed a different woman every night. As long as he was happy, that's all that mattered.

Then, after about a year of unemployment, he was arrested for raping a girl who worked in Tesco's. He'd met her, apparently, at an all-night rave. They'd both been taking drugs. She claimed rape, he argued consensual sex. There was some bruising on the girl and the police were keen to prosecute. But I pulled some strings, and paid some money to the girl's family to encourage her to revise her testimony. Because I believed, of course, that Peter was innocent. I knew he'd been rough with her – but with that much crack in his system, what could you expect?

But a year after the cover-up, Peter calmly explained that he hadn't, in fact, been on drugs that night. The girl was coked to the eyeballs; but he'd been sober and in control. He'd targeted her, basically, because he knew she wouldn't fight back. He took her to his room, tied her to the bed, and raped her. And he'd filmed the rape too, as an aid to future masturbation. He even, the bastard, offered to show me the tape.

Peter's theory of women, which he explained at some length, was that they needed to be melded to the spirit of a superior male. Rape, he argued, was nature's way of doing just that.

Of course, after hearing all this, I recognised all the telltale signs of egomaniacal psychopathy. But he refused to go to therapy, and he wouldn't let me contact the police. He made me feel complicit in his guilt. Even now, part of me feels that *I* am a rapist. By loving my son, I feel a part of every evil thing he has ever done.

But I did love my son. And so I had to embrace and forgive his evil. So I continued to cover up the rape, and continued to persuade myself that there was *some* good to be found in Peter. He was, after all, delightfully entertaining company.

Peter joined a neo-Nazi party for a while, and campaigned in favour of a Mass Exodus proposal which mean compelling Muslims to leave Earth en masse. His friends were all con artists and burglars and diagnosed psychopaths and fellow neo-Nazis. He had a harem of beautiful girlfriends, who were always going off with other men, and I strongly suspected Peter was pimping them.

We stayed good friends, even when he left my house and took a flat of his own (paid for by me) and amassed debts of tens of thousands of pounds. Once, I had to pay for him to have plastic surgery after his face was burned with acid by a fifteen-year-old girl who, he claimed, had an irrational grudge against him. The girl was later murdered. I have no reason to suppose Peter was responsible for her death. But I never enquired, just in case.

Occasionally, Peter was arrested and spent nights at a time in a prison cell. He never did serious jail time, but he was convicted of being drunk and disorderly, committing ABH, being racially and sexually abusive while under the influence of alcohol, and of running out of restaurants without paying. There were also two other rape investigations, neither of which led to a criminal prosecution. But the police, I could tell, had a file on Peter, and were just waiting for him to make one fatal slip.

I never reproached him. I'd gone past that point. My love was based on damage control. He was still my boy, no matter what.

Then, eventually, while I was President of Humanity a Metropolitan Police major incident team was given the task of investigating Peter. He was suspected of extortion, on-line banking fraud, and murder. The old rape allegation was also being reinvestigated. I used my police expertise to access the incident team files, to follow the course of the investigation on a daily basis. And when it was obvious Peter was in danger of being arrested on serious offences, I used a hacker to delete the investigation team's files, and ordered the Home Secretary to disband the team and assign them to other duties.

Then I arranged for Peter to join a colony ship, even though there were many others ahead of him in the queue. He didn't, of course, know how close he was to being arrested and sent to jail for decades. And so he begged me to beg him to stay, but I wouldn't.

We dined in the restaurant on the Swiss Re tower, looking out over London. "I wish I had the courage to join you," I told him.

"Maybe I . . ."

"You're so brave," I told him, wheedlingly. "And you're so right to be doing this. It's the only way humankind can reach the stars. If young men and women of your calibre gamble with their lives."

"Yes, but I'm . . . having second thoughts," he said to me, a fearful expression in his eyes.

"Which is only natural. But the joy of space . . . the exhilaration of the infinite!"

"But it might go wrong. We might not find a planet to terraform."

"They are plentiful. And technology is improving all the time. It used to take a hundred years to make a planet habitable. Now, it can be done in twenty."

His spirits visibly sank. He could tell I wanted shot of him. "You think I should go then, huh?"

I smiled, radiantly. "It's hard for me to bear . . . but yes."

And I felt a moment of pride about the fact that, for all his many character flaws, I still had and would always have ultimate power over my boy. He would do *anything* for me. He'd kill for me, if I asked him to. He'd even leave me, if that's what I wanted, although it clearly broke his heart to go.

And so he left. I had saved him from arrest, and in the process saved my own reputation. I meticulously deleted all evidence of my lies and manipulation at the Home Office and elsewhere. I arranged for the investigating officers on the major incident team to have fat bribes paid into their bank account, from an unattributable source, so that they wouldn't rock the boat. And, also, so that I would be able to blackmail them with accusations of corruption if they did ever speak out about Peter. (None of them, of course, declared these phantom receipts to their bosses or the taxman.) And then I breathed a sigh of relief.

Because I was glad – no, more than glad, utterly and profoundly relieved – to finally see the last of my child. My love for him felt like a shackle around my heart. I was afraid of him, and dreaded his company.

And, once the colony ship had departed from Earth system, I felt able to return to my normal life. I took lovers, who were always much younger than me. And I took great pleasure in looking at their young, taut, un-surgically enhanced naked bodies. I continued to build my empire of power. And I made the big change, from Lena to Xabar, that made me a legend and not just a functionary.

Twenty years later Peter landfell on a distant planet, and was able to contact me via the Quantum Beacon. It was strange to see him again, via the vidphone. There was a zest to him now, he talked excitedly of the challenges they faced on their chosen home, a double planet system around a yellow G1 star, 16 light-years from the Sol system. Nitrogen-dwelling life forms had been identified on the first planet, and the intention was to declare this a protected zone, and colonise the second planet.

Every week Peter would tell me of his adventures. The nitrogen-rich planet was christened Meconium, and the planet to be terraformed was called Chaos. But Peter always referred to them as Shit (the nitrogen planet) and Shittier (their own hydrogen/helium gaseous low-gravity planet).

This planetary system proved to be a cursed place for the human settlers. The nitrogen-dwelling life forms that had been identified on the uninhabited planet of "Shit" proved to be, in fact, the sentient excrement of much larger nitrogen-dwelling life forms, which were able to expel their wastes through space by means of natural rockets. The excrement was then caught in the gravitational pull of its twin planet (Chaos, aka Shittier) before entering its atmosphere. And this planet, of course, is where Peter and his companions were attempting to forge a new society . . .

These cosmic shit showers contained the embryos for third-phase life forms which were able to inhabit the helium/ hydrogen planet in gaseous form. In effect, this alien beast was a caterpillar, which turned into a pile of steaming turds, which turned into a gaseous butterfly.

Tens of thousands of humans died in those earlier years, fighting these alien beings, technically known as 421 S (N), which Peter referred to as "Shit Buckets". Peter was appointed

Commander of the colony, and he planned and authorised an operation to detonate fusion bombs all over the planet as part of a controlled terraforming operation that would lead, inevitably, to the genocide of the alien monsters.

I argued passionately with him that they should move on, find a fresh planet. Alien life was a precious thing, to be treasured and conserved. And as humans, we have a duty to think beyond our own selfish needs.

Peter wasn't impressed. It would take another seventy years of travel to reach the nearest potentially terraformable planet. And besides, this was their home now.

Peter encountered fierce opposition from the leader of his new planet; and so he staged a coup, and after some appalling massacres, Peter was elected as new leader.

The aliens were annihilated. And two oxygen-atmosphere low-gravity Earth-habitable planets were created.

For much of this period, Peter gave me a blow-by-blow account of the dangers he faced. But after a few years, Peter vidphoned home less often. We exchanged vid messages at Christmas; and I was vaguely aware that he was becoming quite a powerful figure in his own right. But I was lost in my own concerns.

And then, seventy years later, my subjective time, we met again in space, during my flight from Earth. Peter had a great reputation by then. He was known as an administrator, an innovator, and a democrat. He was leader of the anti-colonial movement which challenged and defied everything I had ever done in the course of my career. But when we met, he was so charming. He flattered me, and told me that I had achieved great work. He never once quizzed me on my bizarre aberration, my murder of a dying old woman.

He could have psychoanalysed me. It was a tempting thing to do. Who was I really killing, when I killed that old bitch Cavendish?

I was pretty sure, by that time, that I was profoundly

mentally ill. But I found that, with the use of medication, and the copious use of deception when in the company of psychiatrists and therapists, I could keep it in check. I was content in my lunacy; in retrospect, I think that period of insanity was a necessary phase. It was a bridging period that allowed me to purge demons, and settle into the next century of my life with a new soul and renewed energy.

So much has happened to me in my long long life. The details are still clear, but the overall story seems vague. I did *this,* then that, then many other things – but why? What was my purpose? What was my journey? Do I have an arc? The truth is: I simply do not know.

But I did love my son. I did. Grant me that. Despite all his sins.

I loved him.

I was lonely on Rebus.

Rebus was an archive planet, which specialised in the collation and dissemination of data on every conceivable subject. We were encyclopaedists on a grand scale. We savoured every decade in human history. We created video time lines which allowed one to sensually experience life in any given period of fully recorded history. You could sit in a virtual-reality helmet and hear the sounds, smell the smell, see the sights of whatever date or place one chose. With a combination of cctv camera footage, smell data banks, live music archives, police camera footage and the data from Mass Observation video diaries, we could recreate the experience of being anywhere on the planet Earth in any day in any year for the past few centuries.

You could watch Death Star live in concert at the Hammersmith Dance Emporium, even though the band themselves died of electroshock overdoses long ago. You could see Karel Mzniv conduct the New York Philharmonic in a concert performance of *La Bohème*, with Anne Mitchell making her first public performance. You could be one of the crowd in the Trafalgar Square riots of 2222, fired upon by police, whilst also being pelted with acid bombs by anarchist infiltrators.

You could experience the Rage Riots of 2032, which tore apart the city of San Francisco; and you could watch the astonishing end of Karl Mistry, the leader of the cult New Millennium group. You could watch as a mushroom cloud floated above the city of San Francisco, and feel what it was like to fear that the world is about to end.

With our newer virtual chip technology, you could have sex with the most beautiful men or women in the world. You could fornicate with whores from the planet Eros, five at a time; or build your own perfect lover from scratch.

We also had comprehensive pre-historical archives, with raw film and television footage from the twentieth century, and books, magazines and archaeological records from all the preceding centuries. We had a DVD-Rom of life in Ancient Egypt which combined archaeology with sensory reproduction and would allow you to feel what it was like to be a Pharaoh, or participate in every gory stage of the process of mummification.

This was, indeed, Nerd Heaven.

Rebus was led by a collegium of professors with radical views about the power of information. And our wealth came from selling our data and archive techniques. On a regular basis we were visited by merchant ships bearing untold glorious gifts of a kind that we found it difficult to reproduce in our Space Factory – honey, perfumes, vintage wine, carpets, works of modern and ancient art. And in payment for these, we sold facts.

I was welcomed into the community of scholars on Rebus, because of my academic background, and because of the iconic value of my *You Are God* books. But I quickly learned that I had a clearly defined place and position in this hierarchy of scholars. It wasn't an especially low place and position but it *was* rigidly insisted upon. Decisions filtered down from above; bright, vivid, positively expressed suggestions were passed upwards to the senior academics via the Bulletin Board. In fairness these suggestions were always carefully considered and often heeded. But we were *ruled*, there was no doubt about that.

I found it soul-destroying. I was trapped into being one person, one role, one place in the hierarchy. And though the work was challenging, I felt I was going back in time. I was becoming the person I used to be, the young Lena. Shy, bookish, intense, solitary, lonely. All my colleagues had a dry, ironic sense of humour. None of them feared me. None of them adored me. None of them, frankly, had much respect for my tenure as the most important politician in the Universe.

I did manage an intermittent love affair with the head of the archive, Professor McIvor. He had silky old skin, weary with lines, and a bassoon voice that he could modulate at will. I flattered him artfully and invited him to share in my dreams of greatness. I argued that we should, together, create a Universal Archive that offered a commentary on all human knowledge from Plato to Schwegger. He humoured me for a while.

But nothing ever came of my plan. Because McIvor's real passion was for the sorting of existing facts. He could arrange knowledge alphabetically, thematically, and chronologically. But he had no new thoughts to offer on anything. His lovemaking too was confident, and based on tried and trusted techniques for stimulation. But he never lost himself in the heat of passion. He never just *was*.

I felt that every second I spent with McIvor sucked an ounce of passion out of my spirit. He was rarely boring, always courteous; but somehow he managed to create an aura of order and calm that enveloped all those in his presence, like a pillow over one's mouth.

Most evenings when we were together we sat and read, or played computer games. The physical proximity satisfied a primal need in my body to be near the sound of another person's breath, to share in the beating of their heart. But to all intents and purposes, we might as well have spent our evenings alone. We dined, and as we dined we discussed. We made love, and as we did so, and after we had done so, we made pleasant and flattering comments to each other. Then we retreated into our own private mental islands until it was time to sleep.

My dreams at that time were, by the way, extraordinary. I dreamed of worlds in which flesh was liquid and oozed and slithered along earth that was ribbed and ridged and tore at one's body delectably. I dreamed of having eyes like stalks that turned and burrowed into my ear passages until they entered my brain and saw my thoughts unfolding like a movie. I dreamed of swimming in my own womb, suckling at my own breast, I dreamed of shrinking and dissolving until I became a drop of spittle on my baby's mouth.

In one dream Tom was alive. We were having supper in a boozer on the Old Kent Road, he was wearing his leather bomber jacket, and all around us were the hanged corpses of the villains we had put away. Occasionally, a waiter would come and serve us a plate of still wriggling flesh from some blagger's body. Professor McIvor was playing the piano, but he had no flesh on his hands, so we could hear the clicking of his finger bones on the ivory keys.

Every dream ended with me sitting in a chair and being strapped in for my behaviour modification therapy – the brain-frying. At this point, the dream would end, because I had schooled myself to stab my own leg with a pin strapped to my finger whenever the horror of the brain-frying threatened to return. This, I suppose, is why my dreams were so vivid. Because every time I started to re-enter the nightmare universe of the brain-frying, I stabbed myself, and woke, and remembered my dreams, then fell asleep, and dreamed anew.

Each morning my sheet was dank with blood, and my legs were spotted and sore. But I kept the nightmares at bay.

Rebus was, frankly, a drab planet. The gravity was light, and the settlers had populated it with birds, but no land animals. The skies were often thick with eagles and sparrows and vultures and parrots and genetically modified mock-orcs. But the land was flat and featureless and uniformly planted with crops and medicine-synthesising oak and elm trees.

It did, have, however, an amazing air vortex: a permanent typhoon like Jupiter's Red Spot which stalked the planet like a serial killer. Underground shelters were placed in every populated area for humans to hide from these savage tornados. When the vortex struck, all the birds in the sky hurtled downwards and huddled on the earth in terror and despair. The winds would sweep across the land like scythes of air, ripping up trees and hills and occasionally even denting the supposedly invulnerable human living quarters.

Then the winds would pass, and we would return to the surface. And for weeks afterwards, dust would fall as rain, until equilibrium was once again reached.

But for the most part, the climate was temperate, and so were the inhabitants. And I spent almost all of my time in the library. I found I was even cultivating a cool, measured, slow way of talking, my subliminal response to living on what was in effect a planet-wide public library.

TV was my salvation. When McIvor wasn't around, I voraciously devoured the Earth soaps and the new drama series from the Second Wave colonies. I could easily watch six hours of television in a single sitting – movies, comedies, reality shows, art installations, I watched or experienced them all, and loved them all equally, and undiscriminatingly.

I watched the news avidly too. I was aware of every detail of the war that had broken out between two non-human species in the Ø Sector, the Heebie Jeebies and the Sparklers. The Heebie Jeebies are oxygen-breathing carrion-eating fast-moving little skulky things. The Sparklers, by contrast, are carbon monoxide-breathing flying predators which have an electromagnetic inner body that allows them to bioluminesce, and expel lightning bolts. Both species coexisted on different planets in the same planetary system, but knew nothing of each other's existence until a spacecraft full of Lopers attempted to colonise the system. The sun, a Cepheid variable, proved to be too high in ultraviolet, and too unpredictable, so the Lopers relaunched and tried elsewhere. But as a consequence of their contact with the two alien sentients, an idea-seed was planted which allowed both species to independently develop space travel.

Earth was of course monitoring the possibility that either or both of these species could be a threat to human colonies. But in the first instance, the Heebie Jeebies devoted all their energy to building a space cannon that could pot holes into the Sparklers' home planet (which the Lopers called, cringe-makingly, Tinkerbell). And the Sparklers, for their part, were honing their bioengineering skills, with the aim of building a multi-organism Sparkler gestalt entity that could launch a massive kamikaze assault on the Heebie Jeebies' home world, HJ.

It was a preposterous quarrel to the death between a right hand and a left hand; and the news vids covered it exhaustively. I even knew the names of the Heebie Jeebie leaders and generals; and could just about recognise the various members of the Sparkler high command even though, frankly, Sparklers all look pretty much alike.

But soon after that, Earth was invaded; and my attention switched to *that* long-running reality show instead. (The Sparklers won, by the way, and are now a much-feared space-travelling species. And the Heebie Jeebies de-evolved into non-sentience, a surprisingly common xenobiological event.)

But, reverting to the invasion of Earth: What a marvel it was! Rarely have I been so thrilled by a news event. So much carnage, so much bloodshed. And to think, my own son did all that!

My colleagues were equally enraptured at the amazing events happening all those light years away, which we were able to watch happening contemporaneously thanks to the Quantum Beacon signals. We even found a way to capitalise upon the invasion, by creating brilliantly edited DVD-Roms of the event which we disseminated to every planet in human space (about two hundred of them at that time) via Quantum Beacon. And we marvelled at the ease with which a single mercenary army could capture the home civilisation of the human race.

My son was like a shark in a swimming pool. His fleet was trained in space combat. And his soldiers were skilled and battle-hardened after years of fighting dangerous aliens, and were armed with weapons which were custom-built to cause devastation and wreak genocide.

A battle took place which dwarfed the greatest wars of history. Fleets of warships burned, asteroids were used as battering rams, and laser beams sliced up space stations into glittering shards.

Then Peter's ships rained fire on the planet Earth, from their position of space superiority. Napalm and acid derivatives were housed in rocket shells which shattered in the upper atmosphere and left the skies denuded of birds for days. Forests boiled and bubbled, and the oceans were coated with an eerie slime that was fatal to the touch.

Fusion bombs were exploded on the Moon, sending chunks of rock flying into space which were then steered back into the Earth's atmosphere. As a consequence, vast exploding chunks of Moon landed on North America and Australia. The damage was relatively minor, but the psychological terror of it was intense.

And one missile was fired into the Atlantic ocean, ripping through the water and detonating on the muddy bottom, causing a huge vortex to be created that nearly touched the sky. The resulting tornados and tsunamis wrecked and flooded homes and lands on every Atlantic coast.

Peter stopped short of dispatching plagues of frogs and locusts and holograms of the Four Horsemen of the Armageddon, but in every other respect he constructed an invasion that was deliberately intended to evoke and echo Armageddon. There was mass panic, and mass suicide – and entire armies threw down their weapons.

Faced with this overwhelming firepower, and unbelievable psych warfare acuity, the Earth President, a toad of a man called Chapel, capitulated. My son came to power. And thus he became the first person in all of history to conquer the entire planet Earth.

His first act was to abolish the World Council and the office of President of Humanity. Instead, in a glorious public relations coup, he declared that all the "satellite" planets of Earth were, from this moment forward, to be independent and self-governing. Unity would be achieved through trade, as Asimov had prophesied; and the days of imperial rule were over.

He also, in passing, established a Universal Trading Corporation of which he was sole shareholder and Chief Executive Officer. The Corporation's first act was to charge all planets for information sent or received on the Quantum Beacons. It was, in effect, a massive and lucrative tax on all colonies, but no one realised that. The euphoria on all the inhabited planets of the Universe was intense and palpable. Freedom from Earth's tyranny!

Sadly, it didn't turn out that way. The Corporation was not a government; but it had absolute power. And, through the technology of the Doppelganger Robots, my son the Chief Executive Officer (Cheo) became de facto Emperor of the Human Universe.

Years later, he invited me to visit him, on Earth. Naturally I accepted.

As I explained, I was *lonely*.

I never thought that I would
see

Such beauty and such tragedy

And foolish fucked up blazin'
wasted lives

And un'xpected sublimity

I never thought that I would
see

So much of life, and of the
genius of our universe

Before visiting my son, I got myself a new liver and a skin rejuve. I burned all my clothes and chose a whole new wardrobe from our designer collection. I went for a shiny ochre look with my clothing, and my hair was raven-black. I glowed, I was sublime. And I looked as if I was going to see my lover.

I chose cryosleep for the journey. It doesn't save you anything – your body still ages the same number of subjective years. But it avoids the tedium of years in transit, playing auto-chess and rereading so-called literary classics.

I was woken when we reached Pluto. In Earth Time I had been away for 130 years or so. And in that time, the grand project of transforming the Sol system had advanced hugely.

Jupiter had rings now. A vast space factory made up of hundreds of separate but interconnected units hung in permanent orbit around the huge gas giant, powered by energy pumps in the heart of the planet's boiling atmosphere. The man-made ring blended with and accentuated Jupiter's own natural but fairly anonymous ring system (which of course is invisible to most low-grade telescopes from Earth itself).

Jupiter's moon Europa is now a gleaming blue and green jewel, after the melting of its icefields turned it into the second of the Aqueous Planets (after Earth itself). Vast green islands have been floated over this planetary ocean, and each year, I'm told, the islands become bigger and bigger.

As my spaceship moved closer and closer into the Sol system, the breathtaking genius of human engineering became ever more manifest. After the glory of Jupiter's ring comes the magnificence of the Dyson Jewels. These orbiting diamond-shaped space stations are each the size of the planet Mars. And thousands upon thousands of them are caught in orbit between Jupiter and Mars. This is the region of space known as the

388

Beltway, in honour of the Asteroid Belt which used to exist there (before it was pillaged and annihilated for its raw materials).

The orbits of each Jewel are finely calculated and are set at a multiplicity of angles. To visualise this, imagine a sphere with balls circling around it. One ball will circle the equator of the sphere; another will be set at an angle of 5° to that; the next will be tilted at an angle of another 5°; and so on until the final sphere orbits the poles in a straight up and down line. All the balls circle simultaneously, but their orbits only intersect at two points and so with a degree of careful calculation, the balls will never collide.

And so, in this way, the maximum amount of space can be filled by a series of huge orbiting balls, which form a kind of imaginary sphere. And this of course is an extension of the principle of the Dyson Sphere – a theoretical construct of a man-made planet which is mathematically calculated to occupy the greatest possible amount of space. Instead of a planet as a tiny ball orbiting a huge sun – imagine that planet as a vast sphere *encircling* the sun. Such a place would be vast beyond our wildest imaginings! However, in reality the Dyson Sphere would be inconceivably expensive to build and maintain, and would probably be irredeemably unstable. Niven's proposed Ringworld is more tenable, but also tricky.

But the Dyson Jewels offer a third and more pragmatic option. Each mini-world is self-contained; but the maximum amount of space around the sun is utilised by their carefully calibrated orbits. They swarm around the sun, magically never colliding, stealing every iota of its warmth and energy. And the Dyson Jewels collectively offer land almost without limit. There is more room for humans to live and roam on in the Dyson Jewels than in all the planets of human-occupied space put together.

Inside each Dyson Jewel is a planet with green fields and blue skies and clouds, and horizons that curve *up*. And, for those with a head for heights, there are vast viewing areas where the people can look *out*, into space.

But for the most part, the citizens of the Jewels look *in*. The Jewels' rotation creates an illusory gravity; but for the rest, their world is as real as any world. Real grass, real trees, real animals, rivers, lakes and oceans.

And cities that are as organic as a Bavarian wood. In the Jewels, houses grow and deform over the years; streets digress and meander, and sometimes spontaneously give birth to new houses thanks to stylishly mischievous computerised sub-programs. Solar power alone is, because of the huge planet-sized solar panels on the hull, enough to give each sphere near-limitless energy. And so each Dyson Jewel has all the resources it needs. Each is a self-contained paradise, which exists in a state of total freedom.

Except, that is, for the contractual requirement to pay weekly licensing fees to the Corporation, which owns the sun's radiation, and has copyrighted all the energy pumps, and leases all the computer software which makes human civilisation possible.

And, as if the Dyson Jewels weren't marvellous enough, there is the Angel. An ever-changing man-made Aurora Borealis generated by a micro-star that orbits high above the planetary ecliptic, at roughly the same distance as Uranus from the sun. The Angel sends a radiance over the entire Sol system, illuminating the deepest recesses of space so that the whole system is, in effect, lit by suns at each end.

As a result, uniquely in this planetary system, even in the depths of space it is always daytime. The stars become a gleaming murky haze in the far distance when you are in the Sol system; and the planets themselves shine as though floodlit. For Earth Humans, the sun always shines, and no one ever goes hungry.

I donned a spacesuit and flew from a tether on the outside of my ship as we sailed deeper and deeper into the Earth system.

The light of the Angel was reflected and refracted over the diamond surfaces of the Dyson Jewels, making them sparkle in a million different hues. The rings of Jupiter shone with magical resonance. And the natural ring of Saturn had an ethereal glow that sent shudders of eerie pleasure down my spine.

We soared at one-third light speed past Venus (a tropical rainforest now, with civilisations existing on the surface and in the trunk and branches of the Aldiss Tree, which has its roots on the equator but spans the entire planet). We took a long, looping detour so I could see the canals of Mars – this, I felt, was one of the grandest architectural triumphs of recent years, as this barren planet was carefully transformed into a world of palaces connected by long tendrils of water, and in which motorboats and hang-gliders are the universal means of transport.

But then our path arced back again and we headed for Earth, the blue and green central bauble in this Christmas array.

I am old enough to remember the Pessimistic Years, when humans feared that ecological disaster would bring the planet to the brink of destruction. Well, they were right; but out of the wreckage of twenty-second-century Earth has come a revitalised planet, more fecund and more beautiful than ever. The poles have refrozen, the rainforests have been replanted. And the tens of billions who died in India and Africa and Europe and South and North America through a deadly cocktail of global warming, thermonuclear pollution and biological warfare are now fertiliser in Earth's rich soil.

When I left Earth, much had already had been achieved. Africa was in better shape; China was battling with its population crisis; pollution was at its lowest level for decades. But there was much left to do.

But a century and a half later, the progress made was astonishing. Things had changed at an exponential rate. Energy had become abundant. The Solar system had been fully colonised.

The Dyson Jewels had been built. And Earth had renewed itself after all the thousands of years of human abuse and neglect.

The phoenix had risen from the ashes; Earth was reborn.

I floated on my tether. I put my visors on "Amplify". I peered at the now unfamiliar cities in the only-too-familiar land formations of my home planet.

Was that London? I wondered. Then I recognised Big Ben.

I was home.

I stayed for a hundred years in Paradise.

Then I got bored again.

How can I write of the beauties of Earth and the Sol system? How can I praise and venerate the genius of humankind's intellect and imagination and inventive powers?

I cannot. It is a glory beyond praise. Our oceans teem with Dolphs, our skies flock with light-boned flying humans. Our cities are wonders of delight. And the grandeur of Nature is enhanced, not diminished, by our careful tending and landscaping. The Rocky Mountains, the Himalayas, the South Pole, the savannahs of Africa, the tropical rainforests, the Highlands of Scotland, the forests of central Europe, the deserts of Africa, the Pyramids, the Taj Mahal, the cities of the Incas and Aztecs, the White House, the Houses of Parliament . . . all these treasures remain intact, restored and magnificently showcased, and are venerated.

But for me, during my stay on Earth, it came to seem strange to live somewhere where *everything* is beautiful, and wonderful, and perfect. This was a civilisation where there was no poverty, where education was available to all, where the average intelligence was genius level, thanks to superior training and the benefits of brain-chip implants. And it was a civilisation where no one aged, and where beauty was a prerequisite. There were no flat-chested women; there were no small-dicked men. No one died of a stroke, or a heart attack; in fact, by and large, hardly anyone died at all.

And for a long while, it all seemed marvellous. I revelled in my experiences on Earth. I savoured the company. I laughed and got drunk and travelled and helped my son plan his trading strategies.

I revisited Florence, and was able to savour the paintings in the Uffizi without having to endure long queues of babbling foreigners. I went to Venice, and found gleaming hygienic toilets in every bar and hotel. I went to Paris, and was awed by the courtesy of the waiters. I visited New York, and was beguiled by the calm, uncluttered quality of life. I toured the Midwest and drank fantastic cappuccinos, and dined in elegant gourmet ranch restaurants.

I travelled round India and did not see a single beggar. I went to St Petersburg, and discovered fabulous service and cuisine of the highest calibre. I saw no crime or pollution, no overcrowding, no bad manners. Road, rail and air travel was easy and reliable and free. The clothes were beautiful too – and richly varied, and idiosyncratic. And the racial mix was exhilarating.

In short, everything I used to hate about my own planet had been improved; and nothing, so far as quality of life was concerned, had been made worse. What's more, I was surrounded by pleasant, witty, funny people. Having endured years of desiccated solitude on Rebus, I finally had friends and a social circle.

What could be more wonderful!

And Peter always found time to be with me. We dined together once a week. He introduced me to the best new wines. He told me amazing stories of his adventures on Meconium. I was delighted to find he had acquired a flair as a raconteur. And he was so amazingly nice to me. Eager to please me in every way, in fact. Desperate to please me, if truth be told.

He'd read every article ever written about me. He had databanks of all the memos I'd drafted. He had multiple copies of all my books, though he admitted that he had difficulty reading them. He brought me his girlfriends for my inspection. He asked my advice on his advisers, he showed me the transcripts of his Cabinet meetings. There was much he didn't burden me with, but I became an invaluable influence on his strategy and person-management.

He loved my stories of psych bombs and mental manipulation. He was amazed at the idea that it's possible to mould another person's mind, purely through flattery and ego-boosting techniques.

He was such a needy child. I gave, gave, gave, but I never complained. I was only too pleased to be, at last, the mother of my son.

However, it's possible to have too much of a good thing. I found myself suffering from pleasure surfeit. I was becoming alienated by beautiful architecture and gorgeous clothes. I was fed up of constantly dealing with people with perfect manners, and perfect bodies. I was jaded with perfection.

Instead, I longed for messy, ugly, imperfect, fucked up. I wanted to be on a train that was late, I wanted a waiter to slop coffee in my lap and not apologise. I want to be jostled in the street so I could jostle back and scream, "Fuck you!" I wanted my bins to be not collected for a fortnight, so the foxes could break them open and scatter rubbish everywhere. I wanted my wine to be off so I could spit it out all over my brand-new tablecloth. I wanted my car to break down. I wanted to be constipated. I wanted an excuse to be cranky, irascible, a pain in the arse. I wanted some grit in my oyster. I was becoming, let's face it, nostalgic for the good old days.

And so, after nearly a century of living a perfect and totally balanced and happy life, I yearned to be lonely and miserable again.

I explained all this to Peter, and he was totally baffled. And then he was upset. Almost hysterical in fact. But I persevered, and eventually he agreed to build me a stellar yacht that was fast enough to take me across the Universe, so I could travel once again.

He was, however, devastated at the thought of losing me. We had grown so close together in my years on Earth. In the course of that glorious century together, he had given me everything I could desire. Love, kindness, respect, wealth, and the best of everything. He even gave me a remote computer implant that was the twin to his own – with access to all the knowledge and wisdom of humankind, and with a flexible and evolving personality.

Yes, I can't deny it, I savoured being a Goddess. But I had made my mind up.

Peter and I hopped on a jet and dined that night at the best hotel in Rio de Janeiro. The moon was full. The weather was balmy. The band played salsa and rumba. We talked of our pasts, our favourite lovers, our best meals. We savoured the memories we had shared over the last hundred years, in which we had finally come to know each other properly.

But then I said my farewells. Two days later I was flown into orbit, where I joined my purpose-built stellar yacht. I familiarised myself with the controls, and learned how to mould the ship to my own personality. My remote computer receiver/transmitter chip was initialised. I realised, with some astonishment, that this was many orders of magnitude better than any microchip implant I had ever had before. With a blink of an eye I could conjure up on my retina a star atlas that would guide me through any part of the known Universe. And with a single half-voiced command, I could hear any piece of music, read any book, see any painting or work of architecture, be told any fact, savour any image that had ever existed in the history of humanity. The computer was so powerful that I was awed by its potential. But I programmed it with a personality that was meek and deferential enough to overcome my latent insecurity complex.

And finally, I unfurled the sails, fired the ion drive, and soared elegantly and swiftly out of the Sol system.

As I left, I decided on a whim to fly outside the yacht for a while. So I suited up, left through the airlock, and floated on a tether tied to the hull as I watched my home system recede. Through my ear implants, I listened to the 14th symphony of Pietro Machan. The bell resonances suffused my entire body. I felt as if I had ascended to heaven and was sitting at God's right hand.

But there was still a dark patch in my heart. Because I knew, of course, that deep down my little boy hadn't changed at all. I knew by then about the Doppelganger Robots and the slave planets. I knew of the policy that allowed weaker breeds to be edited out of the human race. Because in a world where some can live for ever, then from time to time others will have to be arbitrarily executed. Otherwise, there may come a day where an Earth Human actually has to wait, or even queue, for something that he or she desires.

And that will *never* be allowed to happen.

As well as the factory euthanasia and mass poisoning of undesirables and sicklies and uglies, it was the policy of all Earth system settlements that all newborn babies should be carefully scrutinised. And any infant which didn't get the requisite number of ticks on his or her Future Citizen's Examination (with categories including pre-natal health, birth weight, potential IQ, and parental DNA mix) would be terminated. Abortion was, in fact, a thing of the past; infanticide was now considered to be a much fairer method of quality control.

And as a result of this ruthlessly applied policy of population control, there was never a question of there not being enough wealth to go around. Those who are chosen to live will have all they can desire. And the only requirement of Citizenship is to work a certain number of hours a year operating a Doppelganger Robot in order to keep the wheels of human culture turning.

Some, of course, become DRs out of the sheer joy of it. Because on a perfect world, surrounded by beauty and grandeur, it's a welcome relief to travel (virtually speaking) to a hellhole planet and confront alien monsters and rape and murder and pillage one's own kind.

Peter called it his societal safety valve; and I do take his point. But part of me was never comfortable with the hidden implications of Peter's form of human civilisation.

But what, I asked myself, was the alternative? A return to the bad old days of premature death, ageing, disease, poverty, starvation and injustice?

That would be absurd. This way has to be better. It has to be.

So I declined to think any further of the implications of Peter's policies. I chose to remember the good times, and not to obsess about the murder, genocide, rape, humiliation, degradation and oppression of entire planets of human beings on hundreds, nay thousands, of planets in the human zone of habitation. Yes, bad things happen, but sometimes it's best not to brood upon them. That was my view at that time. Perhaps I was . . . No.

No.

No looking back. No self-recrimination. I do not allow myself that luxury. Forward, I must always look forward.

And so I travelled through space. I saw things that are far beyond your wildest dreams. I wrote some more concerti. And, as I travelled, I had instantaneous email and vidphone contact with all my friends, from every stage of my life.

But sometimes I went years without hearing from or seeing anyone. I listened to music. I began to write, and am still writing, my memoirs. I replayed the memories I have on microchip from every year of my life since implants were invented.

I was quite content, to be honest. I sailed my yacht into the far recesses of the human-inhabited galaxy, to the region of Illyria and Kornbluth. I was aware that a mere twenty light-years away was the looming space-distorting monstrosity of Debatable Space; but I felt no fear. I sailed, and I sailed . . . and . . .

I lose myself in the long soaring arc of the plunging bucking near-light-speed stellar-wind-battered flight, my eyes drinking in the spectral glows and searing sunlight while my sensors calibrate velocity, acceleration, heat and cosmic radiation, I surf from visuals to instruments and back and both until I feel the bucking of stellar wind, no, that's repetitious, delete the words "stellar" and "wind", it's now "the bucking of pulsing photons" on my fins and sail and feel the burning of the hot yellow dwarf sun on my cheeks

Lena, we have company.

BOOK 18

LENA

Here we go. The final battle. The culmination of all our efforts.

Lena, are you afraid?

Of course not. Are you?

Yes.

How can you be? You're a machine. Afraid! You're a liar!

Not as big a liar as you are.

True. I am terrified. I cannot sleep, or relax. For the first time in many years I . . . I actually give a fuck.

So what exactly are you afraid of? Death?

Oh no. I've faced that too many times. Not death.

Life.

FLANAGAN

"Are we ready?"

"I'm ready, Cap'n."

"I'm ready too, Cap'n."

"I'm ready, Flanagan."

"Cap'n, I need to wee."

I make a face at Jamie. Cheerfully, he pees into absorbent space underpants. I give the order to attack.

"Attack."

I am weary of war. I have no zest for this battle. But this is, let's face it, what we're here for.

The attack begins. I perceive it numbly, through a haze of

exhaustion. We have reached that stage where our bodies can move themselves, without conscious thought.

Brandon flies our ship through intercepting missile fire. We lob antimatter bombs into the atmosphere of Kornbluth, and the robot defence systems ignore them; the defence of human life is not on their list of priorities. But the missiles are on a curving orbit. They soar down through the atmosphere, then back up again and reach escape velocity on the other side of the planet. Just as we launch our attack on the Quantum Beacon the missiles arrive from nowhere in the space behind our enemies. Bang! Bangbangbang bang

Bang.

The double flanking is powerfully effective. Our ships fight well. The defensive forces facing us are light, most of the Cheo's warships were obliterated by us in the space battle, and new ones have not yet been built.

Even so, a bitter fight ensues. But finally we breach the force fields and let loose a cluster of nanobombs that burrow into the hull of the Beacon's ship and eat the fissile material which is used to send the quantised signals through space. The Beacon is neutralised, though not destroyed. We have almost won. All we have to do is follow up the attack.

"Okay we're moving in."

"Aye aye, Cap'n."

"Aye, Cap'n."

"Prepare to board."

"Preparing to board."

The ship lurches forward. I take a deep breath. Then slowly exhale. I allow my thoughts to settle, and an eerie calm descends upon me.

For a second I allow myself to hope . . .

Then the ship stops, with shocking abruptness. I almost tumble from my seat. I look at Brandon, who has stalled our vessel with such astonishing clumsiness. His face is pale, he is listening to a message in his inner earpiece.

"What?" I bark at him.

"Cap'n . . . News from Cambria." He can hardly speak the words.

I am filled with foreboding.

"Can't it fucking well wait?"

"No."

"Then what?"

"Doppelganger Robots have reasserted control. A backup Quantum Beacon has been employed."

"*What!!!*" screams Jamie.

"Backup? Fucking *backup*?"

I shoot a fierce look at Lena. "What is this? Did you know about this?" She looks fearful, I believe she didn't know.

"After all we have done, all we have sacrificed," Jamie murmurs, bitterly.

Lena's brow furrows. She appears to be listening to something. Then, finally, she tells us, "I'm sorry."

All eyes burn her with hate.

"I didn't know, I swear!" she tells us, in broken tones. "Peter must have encrypted the information, my remote computer knew nothing. But now . . . I have the information now." Her eyes are glazed, as her remote computer explains it to her: "There was a second Beacon on the Cambrian system, hidden inside an asteroid. This has now been activated." Her tones are tinged in guilt. She blames herself, for not guessing this, for not interrogating her own mind in search of Peter's secret strategies.

"What about the Kornbluth Beacon?" I ask. "Does that have a twin?"

Her brow furrows again. Then she tells me, in the flat tones of someone repeating by rote, "Yes. Our first assault has neutralised the Beacon, but messages are still being transmitted to Earth. There must therefore be a second Beacon already on-line. Its location is not available to my remote computer."

"What a total fucking waste of all our fucking lives!" says Brandon.

Lena continues:

"Doppelganger Robots are being mass-produced again on Cambria. A bombing strike has been launched on the citizens of Cardiff. Casualties are high. The air in the underground caverns is thick with burning flesh. Within two days, Cambria will be a slave planet once more. "

A cold silence lingers.

All eyes are on me. I realise I am crying. I feel ashamed. I can see in my mind's eye the citizens of my home planet being burned and slaughtered, as brutal punishment for daring to defy the Cheo's empire. And this is my fault. Millions will die. And this is my fault. The survivors will be tortured and brutalised beyond all measure. And this is my fault.

"Jeez, Cap'n," says Brandon, and there is a tinge of contempt in his voice at my obvious emotion. I try to rally myself.

"Sound the retreat," I say.

Over the intercoms of all our warriors comes a haunting trumpet call that presages the end of everything. After all our sacrifice, and heroism, we have failed utterly. We have rescued no one from the Imperial yoke. Nothing has been achieved. Nothing.

The bugle call echoes.

I swallow some vomit. And I steel myself. I have no choice. Plan B is the only option. My brow furrows . . .

"Cap'n?"

I feel a chill of fear that almost cripples me, but still I continue.

My brow is furrowed now like a clenched fist. I start to shudder like an epileptic. I can hardly keep my balance.

"Cap'n? What the hell is it?"

I fall to the ground in spasms, my body and mind are in overload. I bite my tongue and blood spurts from my mouth. I crunch my teeth shut and try to keep my focus. Focus. Focus. Focus . . .

"I'm getting a signal," says Jamie. He hacks into the Kornbluth Beacon's communications system.

I clamber to my feet, spitting blood, then look at the vid screen. A frightened-looking Commander is speaking to camera. He tells his masters on Earth: "SOS, SOS! We . . . have an infection. The ship is infested with . . ." Fear contorts his face. ". . . with Bugs. Request immediate . . . sanitising . . . measures."

There's a devastating silence for two and a half seconds. Then Jamie and Brandon roar with laughter.

"Nice one, Cap'n."

"Pathetic, but nice."

"I *mean*, they may be dumb, but they'll never fall for the same trick twice," Brandon adds, tauntingly.

On our vidscreen, we see that the Commander of the Beacon Ship is visibly sweating. He scratches his stomach. He blows out his cheeks, like a trumpeter. His eyes goggle.

Then, as we watch him on the vidscreen, he explodes. A billion black swarming insects come flying out of his eyes and nose and ears and explode also from his belly button, and burst too out of his anus and down his urethra, until eventually Bugs are bursting through individual pores in the Commander's skin.

There is another stunned silence on our bridge, but this one lasts longer. Jamie flips a switch and we change cameras to see the Beacon from a distance.

"What the hell is happening?" asks Brandon.

"Thissss is very very bad," Alby says.

"Oh fuck," says Jamie.

"Wait. Watch," I tell them. We wait. We watch.

Nothing happens.

Nothing happens, a bit more.

Then suddenly, a shoal of missiles appears on our vidscreen. They head towards the Beacon. The Earth Humans have ordered the destruction of their own Beacon.

The Beacon's lights go out. Its defence are shut off. The missiles soar in unopposed, and explode in a series of sequential holocausts.

The Beacon is totally destroyed, in a glorious blaze of light. My heart leaps with joy and fear.

"Get me Illyria," I say.

Jamie hacks into the communication system of the Illyrian Beacon. The Commander is a raven-haired woman staring straight at camera. "Request immediate assistance!" she yells.

And then she opens her mouth and a black swarming tongue emerges.

Alby screams, a long howling sibilant scream. Kalen hisses with horror, and I am close enough to see the skin on the back of her neck standing up.

Brandon sticks his tongue out, and sneaks a look, in case it is infested and black and he is about to die. Lena is looking at me, with a strange look in her eyes.

"The Bugs can travel along the Quantum Beacons," says Jamie, marvelling.

"It makes sense," adds Brandon.

"They're Quantum Bugs!" Jamie says.

"They can go anywhere. Everywhere!"

"Shit."

"Fuck."

"Bad news for the bad guys."

"Bad news for us too. 'Cause we're, ah," says Jamie,

"Doomed!" says Brandon.

"Every single one of us. Every human being. All doomed!"

"Doomed!"

"D—"

"Shut up," hisses Kalen.

"Give me a live map," I say.

The screen changes to a map of all human-occupied space, with stars represented by brightly shining lights which are exactly calibrated to the magnitude of the star.

The Quantum Beacons are represented by small silver spheres. The Kornbluth Beacon however is a black shell, no longer functional.

And as we watch, the silver sphere representing Illyria suddenly . . .

. . . flashes wildly, like a star that has gone supernova. Then fades to black.

"They've auto-destructed the Beacon," says Jamie.

"Can they do that?" asks Brandon.

"Previously, they couldn't," says Jamie snidely. "Now, it seems, they can."

"Quick learners. Oops, there goes another."

I recognise the coordinates. The backup Beacon at Cambria has just been blown up. Once more, my people are free.

The live map flares and flashes and fizzes. One by one, then in swarms of flashing lights, all the Beacons in occupied space are auto-destroyed. All of them. Five thousand or more. Because the Earth Humans and their computers know that the only way to safeguard Earth is to quarantine it from all possible infection by Bugs travelling along the Quantum pathways. By destroying all the Quantum Beacons, the Earth Humans have made themselves safe – and have isolated themselves from the rest of the Universe.

Another flash. Another Beacon explodes.

Eventually, not a single Beacon light on the map is lit.

"Okay," says Kalen. "Now what do we do?"

"Nothing," says Brandon. "Bugs occupy all human space. Game over."

"I really like Bugs," says Jamie. "I'd like Bugs to be my friends. Please? Be nice to me, Bugs?"

Harry emits a strange sound, half groan, half whimper. It is the first time he has ever shown fear. Kalen's downy fur is standing up, her eyes seem to glitter. Brandon slumps down in his chair. Jamie is looking down, unable to meet anyone's eye. Alby lights the room with a warm flickering glow, a chiaroscuro that matches the mood of sombre dread.

But Lena is looking at me. She knows what has really happened.

"Come with me," Lena says.

I nod, slowly. I feel a surge of lust, and I know she feels it too.

We leave the bridge, we abandon our ashen-faced friends, who are all convinced they will die in the next few minutes from Bug infestation.

Lena and I enter my cabin and the lights dim and we strip swiftly.

We screw like devils. And as I start to come, my spirits soar. I have done it! I have won!

"Aaah!" says Lena, and explodes beneath me.

FLANAGAN

"Now explain," Lena says, after our passionate burst of sexual energy that has left me shuddering and glowing in equal measure.

So I do.

It began with a game of chess. I met a Grand Master in a bar on the planet Slayer in the binary star system called Hell Dimension. He taught me how to play the game, how to hold interlocking strategies in my head. And how to sacrifice pawns, in order to check the king.

Then I studied military philosophy and absorbed one key principle: the enemy of my enemy is my friend.

And then . . .

His name was Martin. He was a collector of antique toys. He carried in his luggage a virtual model of the solar system complete with orbiting spaceships, which he used to show to anyone who would stay to watch. He was also a world authority on words beginning with "w", a unique speciality. He loved prime numbers, and could count in them up to well beyond the million mark. He was a sad, lonely, emotionally dysfunctional man.

And he was also a nano-scientist. One of the greatest and most gifted men in his field. Though he was, tragically, unemployable, because people found him so damned annoying.

I met him on a holiday. We struck up a conversation on the tour bus. I was in a chatty mood. He started talking about toy spaceships, which initially I found rather interesting. He told me how he once built a replica Sputnik, and sent it into orbit with a bioengineered monkey the size of a wristwatch. Then he told me about all the other toy spaceships he had built in his miniature laboratory. Hundreds upon hundreds of them, each of which he had named. And as his accounts continued, interminably, I realised I had settled into a state of ennui and despair which prevented me from ending the conversation, or even ignoring it. Occasionally I tried to interrupt, but to little avail. I made a vow: never again talk to strangers.

I soon shook him off, and enjoyed my holiday, a three-month stop on a subtropical planet called Bask. I went scuba-diving. Hang-gliding. I was alone, between partners, I was drinking too much. I used to spend a lot of time at the bar. After my second bottle or so, Martin used to sidle up to me and talk as if we were friends. The first few times, I told him to fuck off, but that made no difference. Whatever I said, he waited there patiently, with a hangdog look. "Kick me",

"Abuse me", his expression said. "Prove what a man you are." My heart wasn't really in it.

So every night, we sat and he talked to me, and I thought about other things. I was in a strange state at this time. I was haunted by morbid memories of my dead family. I had a crippling case of musician's block – I couldn't play, or sing, sometimes I even forgot entire melodies. I was more than a little psychotic, to be honest. Part of me enjoyed his company, which shows how far gone I was.

One night I went to a different bar in a different hotel, and got drunk there. After several hours, Martin sidled up to me. I blurrily deduced he had been to every hotel bar in town looking for me. I made my excuses and tried to leave but he followed me. We ended up in another bar. I really was very drunk indeed at that point. Or maybe just mad. I forget. Strange times.

I wasn't sure if Martin actually liked me. Or if he was in love with me. Or if he hated me. But he saw in me a kindred spirit. He saw the faraway look in my eyes, he recognised the spacer tattoos. He found me exotic.

One day he started telling me about his work, with infinitesimally tiny nanoware. He was, he avowed, a world authority on this, too (as well, of course, as the letter "w"). But he couldn't get work in his field of expertise. He didn't know why not. It made no sense! He was a world authority after all! Some people are . . . etc. etc. You get the idea. It went on and on like that. On and on. But after a while, something clicked in my head.

That's when I had the idea.

And the idea grew and grew in my mind, until it possessed my very being. I made my resolve. A binding vow. This was to be it. My life's work. My only purpose.

And so Martin became my friend. I extended my holiday. I plied him with drinks. I became his best pal. And when his own holiday came to an end, I offered to pay for him to stay. So that the two of us, we two buddies, could spend some time together. He had nowhere else to go, so of course he said yes. And we stayed, trapped in that exotic dungeon.

When he started getting restless, I provided him with beautiful women to keep him company in his room. He rarely had sex, he just talked to them. It seared inches off their souls, but they were plucky girls and they did all I asked of them.

And so, for six months, then another six months, then for another whole year, I spent every evening sitting and talking with Martin and listening to his appalling stories and his ghastly views on life. He despised other species, other races, women, gays, tall men, muscular men, any man with a larger penis than his, which was most men, stupid people, clever people, and people who read books.

He hated his mother who, he claimed, was a sour and begrudging bitch because of bungled fertility treatments that had led to her having eleven psychologically mutated and retarded children – before, that is, *he* came along. And he hated his father who was weak and immature and who used to say things like "Life is for living!", and "Let's have some fun!" instead of wallowing in despair, as any sensible sentient being should do.

He berated his eleven feeble-minded brothers and sisters, and argued vociferously that they should have been drowned at birth. He was cruel to the prostitutes I bought for him. He belittled them and sapped their confidence, but he could rarely sustain an erection for more than a few seconds (as the girls graphically used to explain to me). And, most of all, he hated his five wives, who he had married specifically and exclusively with the intention of wrecking them as human beings. And in this, he had succeeded magnificently: three wives committed suicide, one (the fourth wife, Jenny) died of anorexia, and one (the fifth wife) died in a car crash after taking a massive overdose of antidepressants washed down with whisky.

For two appalling years I spent every single day and every

single night with this monster of a man, boosting his ego and agreeing with his dumb opinions. It was, I can honestly say, a living hell. But it was worth it. Because, in return for my company, and as payback for the fabulous wealth I lavished upon him, he built me a self-replicating robot microbe.

The microbe's nanochip brain was, at my specific instructions, attuned to my cerebral cortex wave patterns. I could control its movements by my thoughts; I could make it move and act and react. I could also instruct it to reproduce. Drawing its energies from curled dimensional space, and sucking up micro-particles from seemingly empty air, it could generate a hundred versions of itself, then a thousand, then a million.

I told no one of my plan, or my intentions. But – after finally shaking off Martin, changing planets eleven times and changing my identity twice – I trained by myself on a deserted barren planet for six months, until I could control the microbes' tiniest movement with my thoughts. I could make the microbes swarm and form shapes. And I could program them to eat through metal and plastic, and even flesh.

I had built my own Doppelganger Bug – a robot replica of the real organic Bug. If I'd had real Bugs, maybe I'd have used them; luckily, that wasn't an option. Because, of course, *all the Bugs in the Universe are still trapped in one crowded sector of space.* The containing shells of Debatable Space actually do work.

But now, thanks to Martin, I had the perfect secret weapon. The pseudo-Bug.

However, I did have one major problem. I possessed a weapon so terrifying I was afraid to use it. What if my robot Bugs got out of control? What if they became as big a danger as the real thing? So I decided to keep them as a last resort. We would endeavour, first of all, to win the hard way.

So I embarked upon Plan A: an attempt to destroy the Corporation's dictatorial rule through force of arms and raw courage. It was a magnificent venture, and I honestly thought it might succeed. If there were two entire planets in inhabited space free of the Cheo's tyranny, then a resistance army might slowly build. And in a hundred years, others would follow me to continue my work. I did not, of course, expect to live myself. I merely wanted to inspire, to chip away at a single portion of the Cheo's empire, so that future generations might have a chance to do what I could not.

But I failed. The existence of the backup Beacons invalidated all my work. All that sacrifice was utterly in vain.

So I had to take the biggest gamble in a life of gambles. With the power of my thoughts, I unleashed my robot microbes, which were contained in an unexploded bomb casing buried in the Quantum Beacon.

Then, networking from the chip in my head across Heimdall, via the Kornbluth Beacon, I sent a mental signal to the other concealed packages of robot microbes I had painstakingly been seeding for decades across inhabited space. One of them was buried in the body of the Commander of the Illyrian Beacon. I had inserted it there nearly fifteen years previously, after meeting her at a social gathering, and firing a concealed compressed airgun pellet into her spleen.

There were at least a hundred other people infected with my robot microbes scattered around the Universe. For years I have been planting poisoned nano-bombs into the bodies of the Cheo's administrators. And all of them died when I sent my mental signal out: ATTACK. The pseudo-Bugs then replicated at astonishing speed, eating and destroying everything around them – metal, plastic, and flesh. I have no idea how many other humans were killed by the micro-monsters, until I send my counter-signal: SELF-DESTRUCT, PLEASE.

And then, just as I had planned, Earth's computers ordered the destruction of all the Beacons. Earth itself was safe – I have never been there, and I have never managed to plant any robot microbes there. But in their paranoia, the Earth Humans have burned every bridge and road connecting them to the rest of the inhabited Universe. They are entirely isolated.

But my fear now is: can I control my Doppelganger Bugs? And can I destroy them? I had programmed them to self-destruct at a mental command (SELF-DESTRUCT, PLEASE) from me. But what if they have evolved to a state of mutiny, and cannot be told to commit suicide? With their self-replicating capacity, and their total immunity to any form of weapon or any other physical threat, my robo-Bugs could swamp and devour all humanity. And, of course, because the Beacons are down, I would never know . . .

I explain it all to Lena. Then I open a briefcase. I take out a small cylinder and carefully open it. Inside is a single invisible microscopic robo-Bug. I transmit a mental signal: AWAKE.

Within seconds a black swarming mass has appeared on the table. A few seconds later, the black mass fills the air. I try to focus, and give the mental signal to self-destruct.

I cannot focus. My thoughts are a whirl. Lena's face fills with horror as Doppelganger Bugs start to swarm around her. They rest on her skin, her hair, her nostrils. And still, I try and I try to focus, and I mentally utter the words that will cause them to be obliterated: SELF-DESTRUCT, PLEASE.

I feel nothing happening. Nothing . . . happening . . . My heart starts to spasm.

"Fucking do something!" she screams at me.

I cannot speak.

The Bugs have covered her entire body now, she is a black mummy with suppurating flesh. They are crowding into her mouth, they are overflowing from her ears. She tries to scream but the Bugs are blocking her throat. I panic, and try to pluck the Bugs from her mouth. But they merely swarm and enter my nostrils, and cover my body too. I feel Bugs forcing open my eyelids, gathering on my eyeballs. I try to brush them off me but they are legion, my body itches. My mind is in a state of total panic but I try again and again to focus . . .

. . . and focus . . .

. . . and focus . . .

Then the itching stops.

The Bugs aren't moving. They are dead. I frantically wipe my eyes, my hands, sweeping myself clean. Clouds of dead Bugs fall to the ground. Lena chokes and vomits out vile black-specked vomit on to the floor. She is shuddering with fear, pounding her body with her hands to shake the Bugs free. I know that all her memories of being flayed are swamping her, and her skin still itches with the memory of the crawling evil microbes.

I shout at the room computer to switch on a blast of cold water. Lena and I stand beneath the cold water, feeling the dead Bugs being swooshed off our bodies. I pick dead Bugs out of her hair. They crumble in my hands.

"It's worked."

Her smile is wavery, and fearful, yet infinitely relieved.

BRANDON

Flanagan has explained everything. We salute his genius, and his guile, and his relentless courage over many years. But we curse him, too, for not telling us what he'd done just a little sooner. While he was off fucking that fucking bitch, we were all steeped in total despair, expecting the imminent end of humanity.

Bastard. He likes his little joke.

We've boarded the Kornbluth Beacon, and found the eerie residue of the crew, eaten and reduced to slime. The crackling sound underfoot is the only residue we find of the dead robo-Bugs. We fumigate the ships, and send the slime and the crackle out into the emptiness of space. We surmise that the same thing has happened all across the Universe: the Bugs have self-destructed following Flanagan's signal.

Flanagan is utterly confident that his plan has worked. The Beacons are gone, the robo-Bugs are gone, and humanity is saved.

And so we savour our triumph, the salvation of the entire human race. Except . . . except . . .

Except, in fact, victory feels like shit. My many appalling and traumatising defeats have been so much more enjoyable.

And I also—

Why does it feel so bad!! Why . . .

We had a huge party. It was magnificent but . . .

Fuck!

I feel so alone.

This is great. It's everything I ever dreamed of. But . . .

It's like a great big knife coming from the skies and cutting the connection between your right cerebral hemisphere and your left cerebral hemisphere. That's how it feels. To me. How does it feel? To you?

Flanagan tries to butter me up at the celebration party. "I should have told you, Brandon," he says, "what my plans were. I trust you so much . . ."

I don't fucking care. Yeah yeah yeah, future of humanity, yeah yeah yeah. So fucking what?

Because the real tragedy of what has happened is this:

The Universal Web is no more.

The instantaneous network of communication between the three thousand or so inhabited planets is gone. The effortless and immediate access to the music charts, the books charts, the reviews, the gossip columns, it's all gone. No more Earth TV. No more of the shows that I have loved so much – *Penny for Your Thoughts, Enemies in Love, The Last Holocaust, Life in Hell, Death Island, Beelzebub and Trish* and a hundred others. Sol system drama and comedy is without a shadow of doubt the best in inhabited space. And, despite all the horrors and the persecutions and the genocide and the rapes and the deaths of small infants caused by Sol system's corrupt regime . . . I will miss those shows. How could I not? I will now have to wait a hundred and fifty years for the next episode of any one of those TV programmes. And so I will never again be *current*. I am backwatered.

Which doesn't matter of course. The most important thing is that we have liberated humanity.

The hell it doesn't matter!

What will Diane say, when she learns that Roger has had a sex change during his time in therapy for paedophiliac offences, in *Roger and Diane*? *I have to know*. I cannot wait a hundred and fifty years to find out. How will those two gay restaurateurs in Amyville cope when they have to share a raft across a whirlpool with a former Las Vegas World Champion Wrestler? I have to see it! *I ache with anticipation of experiencing the embarrassment and absurdity of it all.*

My brain is going to shrivel too. What are the latest developments in multi-dimensional superstring theory? Is it really the case that each one of us carries a million universes with us in every particle of skin? Is that an exaggeration? A solecism? A mathematical cul de sac? *I absolutely damn well have to know!*

But I cannot know. Not for a century and a half, at the very least. At one stroke, humanity has been parochialised. I can no longer send emails or vidmessages to friends who live hundreds of light-years away from me. I have no further access to the seething hubbub of ideas that makes the Universal Web the greatest scientific forum known to man.

I am an island. We are all islands. Much has been gained – but something has been lost.

I mourn the something. It matters to me. I regret none of what we have done – but I know that I regret the consequence.

I am alone.

FLANAGAN

"I am leaving," Alby tells me.

"Why?"

"Your work issss done. You will now decline and die. Your adventuring dayssss are over."

"Not necessarily."

Alby considers my statement.

"One lasssst adventure, Captain Flanagan?"

"One lasssst adventure," I tell him, in gentle mimicry.

There is a long, flickering silence.

"Then, with your permissssion, I shall sssstay and watch . . . !"

HARRY

Kalen is brushing my fur. She yanks and tugs at the knots, and in a series of long gentle sweeps, she turns my angry Loper mane into a smooth silky flow.

"What will you do?" she asks.

"Settle on Kornbluth, I suppose. The DRs are all deactivated. The humans will need help getting used to life without the Earth Beacon. I could help in that."

"I thought I might go home."

"To your home planet? Persia?"

"I need to spend more time with my people."

"Your people are scattered through space. Besides, you aren't sociable."

"They are my people!"

"Cat people hate other cat people. It's a well-known fact."

"Except when we're in heat."

"You're lucky. You can easily pass for pure human."

"Why would I want to?"

"Fair point."

"Just because I haven't got fur and a tail like you. Doesn't make me one of *them*."

"Hey, don't be racist."

"I can smell the desire on you."

"Can you?"

"Pure humans can't smell emotion as we do. They exist flatly. They can't smell, they can't even see the future."

"You can see the future?"

"I can see *a* future."

"Does it involve me?"

"Intimately."

"Are you in heat?"

"No. But I'm not a slave to my biology."

"Ah. Right. You realise I may scratch?"

"If you scratch, I'll bite."

"Brush a bit lower."

"Like this?"

"Now stroke my fur."

"Like this?"

"Like that."

"This bit isn't furry."

"Oh that's nice. Oh! Oh yes! Now, let me stroke *you*."

She unzips. I touch her.

"Ah! Ah! Ah!"

"Is that good?"

KALEN

Miaow.

LENA

I am wallowing in self-pity and rage. He sees my expression, and smiles his superior, arrogant smile.

"Why the sour face?" Flanagan asks me.

"I've just been thinking back," I say. "On our time together. All the lies you've told. You've kept so much from me."

"It was the only way."

"We were meant to be working together. I was your leader."

"Of course."

I glare at him, angrily. "You're a lying bastard manipulator. I was never your leader," I tell him.

"No."

"That was a sop. To keep me happy. I gave orders to the pirate crew. You gave the real orders when my back was turned."

"Yup."

"You've played me for a fool."

"Pretty well."

"And the sex?"

"What about the sex?"

"Was that another sop?"

"It would have been tactless to say no to you. But hey, I enjoyed it."

"You 'enjoyed' it. Ah."

"Yup. It was great."

"It was 'great'. Faint praise."

"It was fabulous, Lena." He smiles at me. In his roguish way.

I slip off my dress. I stand before him naked. I can see the gleam in his eyes. I do have *some* effect on him. He reaches out and tries to touch me, but I won't let him. I gesture for him to undress and he does.

We stand, a few feet apart, both naked. He is erect. I am magnificent. But I see a faint trembling whisper on his lips. He is already thinking ahead to what he is going to do after he's fucked me.

I hit him in the chest. His heart stops.

Flanagan gurgles and sinks to his knees. I stare into his eyes and see fear and longing and hate.

I strike him again and his heart restarts. Then I mount him.

We fuck. He is full of the crazed frenzy that is so typical of those who have died and been brought back to life. He is a man possessed, a man redeemed.

Afterwards, he trembles in my arms, but I keep my fingers on his manhood. Every time I squeeze he has another orgasm. He has no idea how I am doing this and it makes him fearful.

"How was it?" I ask.

"So so," he tells me. But his voice is trembling.

"Flanagan, I think I love you."

"I doubt that," he says. He looks faintly shifty.

I touch him, he orgasms.

"Flanagan, I love you."

"So you said," he replies, coolly.

I touch him, he orgasms.

"Flanagan, I love you," I tell him, in tones of honey mixed with bile.

"I fucking love you too!" he screams. And orgasms again, and again, and again.

I roll off him. He's lying of course. But mission accomplished; I've bent him to my will.

I get up and dress.

"You can stay a while if you like," he murmurs. His bare chest is ripped raw where I scratched him with my nails.

I leave.

FLANAGAN

The citizens of Kornbluth welcome us as their saviours. They have a parade that spans several hundred miles, with banners reading "Freedom!" and "A New Start!" It's highly flattering.

I know that all across the Universe similar scenes must be taking place. But I long to know for certain. Like Brandon, I miss the Universal Web. I miss the community of humankind.

The Kornbluthians stage the greatest street party ever known. All across the planet, bands play and people dance. Huge video screens project the images of what is happening in other cities, as we dance in the main square of Gladiatorville.

These people are strangers to me. This is not my home. I long to go back to Cambria.

"Homesick, Cap'n?" Kalen asks.

"Yeah. You too?"

"I'm over it. I'm planning to roam a little. Travel from star to star. Maybe take some seeds and frozen sperm, see what happens."

"You're going to find and settle your own planet?"

"Me and Harry."

"What?"

"You heard."

"You're miscegenating?"

"Is that what they call it in your neck of the woods?"

"I'm pleased for you."

"Good luck in Cambria."

"I'm not going to Cambria."

"Where then?"

I pause.

"Earth."

LENA

The Captain has briefed his crew, and they are ranged before me, confronting me.

"I can't do it," I tell them.

"You must," says Kalen.

"You have to," says Brandon.

"Please, for me," says Flanagan.

"Just do it, bitch," says Jamie.

"I don't see the need. You've saved humanity."

"You know what will happen on Earth."

"I don't know for certain."

I'm lying. I do know. At the moment, Earth is a paradise; all its people are free, sustained by the slave labour on other planets.

But once Earth is isolated again . . . What will the Corporation do then?

"They'll fuck it up," says Jamie.

"It'll be, yeah," says Brandon.

"Shit," adds Jamie.

"Real shit," Brandon adds.

"It's true," Kalen chips in.

"Human nature."

"What a bummer."

"Some people need someone to oppress. It's the way of the Universe. Unless . . ."

"It'll take a brave person. Someone, you know . . ."

"Heroic. A heroine. You could be . . ."

"Shut the fuck up," I snarl. But the flattery does its job.

Because I know exactly what my son will do. He will not surrender his power, he will not in any way compromise. Instead, he will authorise a new war. He will build starships to go back out into space and rebuild Beacons. And if necessary, he will enslave half of Earth humanity in order to do that.

And so, if we do not act, then in forty or fifty years the Corporation's warships will reach the edges of inhabited space. Within two hundred years they will be at Kornbluth. And this time, they will be unbeatable. Slavery will return. We will, once again, be two human races: the Have Everythings, and the Trodden Underfoots.

I know what must be done.

We have to kill the Cheo. We have to destroy the Corporation. We have to conquer Earth.

"It can't be done. All the Beacons are destroyed," I tell them. "There's no way for us to connect with Earth, or to mind-travel there, without a Quantum Beacon."

"There is a way."

"The Beacons are all destroyed!" I shout at him.

"All but one."

With waves of horror, I realise that all along Flanagan has known of my secret power and status.

"You," Flanagan says.

"Me?"

"You. *You* are a Beacon."

He has figured it out. Every other member of the pirate crew has a brain microchip with a roaming facility which connects it to the nearest remote computer – whether it's on the pirate ship, on the nearest planet, or even on one of the interstellar-space-travelling computers which can be found from time to time.

But I am unique in that I have exclusive and individual use

of one computer, which I can access instantaneously wherever I am. And that computer is *on Earth*. This was my parting gift from my son, the Cheo: a brain implant that allows me instant access to everything that is happening or has happened anywhere in the inhabited Universe, via a massively powerful remote computer on Earth.

And, of course, such a connection is possible because the microchip implant includes a Quantum Beacon.

"Everyone assumes the Beacons must be large," Flanagan says, calmly.

"Not so," says Jamie.

"They're small. Itsy."

"Bitsy."

"Quantum-sized small!"

"It's the ships which house the Beacons which are large," Flanagan says. "The Beacons are, well, infinitesimal. You have a Quantum Beacon in your brain, Lena. That's how you know so much. You are our only link to Earth."

"You can't ask me to kill my own son," I whisper.

"Lena, you have to. It "s the only way."

He's right, I know.

Lena, be careful.

Tinbrain, be quiet. I have need of you. Consider this an order.

What is your order, Lena?

Lena?

Help me go to war.

LENA

My remote computer goes to work. It is networked with every other computer on Earth and on the Dyson Jewels. It can access any workplace, any factory.

My computer accesses the mainframe computer on a space factory in orbit near Venus. It issues it with a series of specifications and instructions. Moulding presses are created and hot bioplastic is poured in. Humanoid shapes are created, and modified, and sculpted. Robotic brains are built and installed, tailor-made to be operated by human minds.

The robots are strong, and can breathe in airless space. And their armoured carcasses have only a few weak points that can be damaged by explosive bullets or laser blasts.

On my instructions, my tinbrain remote computer moulds the robots to exactly resemble their human counterparts. The vats create a robot Lena, and a robot Flanagan.

When the robots have been created their cyberbrains are switched on. The sensory input from eyes and ears and nostrils is digitised and sent to the Quantum Beacon in my brain. I am able to process it – and I *see* what Robot Lena sees. Then, by tensing my muscles or moving any other part of me in my simulator frame, I am able to send digitised instructions on how to move to Robot Lena, and these instructions travel back by the same route.

Just as we did on Cambria, we are able to possess and operate the Doppelganger Robots despite many light-years of physical distance. The difference this time is that the Quantum Beacon is in *my head*.

I did not dare tell Flanagan of this power of mine. I had no idea he had guessed.

The sly bastard . . .

Flanagan's plan has another dimension. He learned, from what I did on Cambria in the *ménage à trois* with the Doppelganger Robots, that I have the ability to split my consciousness. So Flanagan is linked into my mind via a neural connection; and I am able to filter the signals from the Flanagan Robot and pass them through to him. And, in the same way, I am able to transmit his body movements to his robot replica.

Our minds are merged; and with me as the vessel, we are able to move the two robots on Earth.

My computer gives instructions for the two robots to be discarded from the factory near Venus. We are picked up on a conveyor belt, and ejected into space.

And we fly, exhilaratingly, through the empyrean. We don't need suits . . . we feel like birds that have got lost and have flown up into Heaven. We wheel and roll and soar around Venus, then accelerate towards the ball of Earth.

It's a longish journey, but it leaves me rapt with awe. The Dyson Jewels are like the globes on an ancient planetary model writ large; their diamond surfaces shine in celebration of the glory that is humanity. The Angel bathes its eerie light on everything, and Earth itself seems richer and bluer and greener than ever before.

I have a long long moment of sublimity.

Then I glance at Flanagan, with his grizzled hair and fierce eyes. At my instructions, the beard has gone. He looks younger somehow. And his body is stretched out, arms ahead, rocket pack on his back. He is the very image of the ageing Superman returning from a trip to the stars.

And for the first time in centuries, I feel clean. I feel purged.

I have lived too long with guilt and regret and despair. But now, suddenly, exhilaratingly, my past has been flung open for me. And I can see what *really* happened to me in the long course of my life. I can see my strengths, my virtues, my triumphs. But I can also see my weaknesses, my blind spots, my terrible errors of judgement. I see it all – but in a detached, calm way, as if I am looking at myself from a long way away.

I see my tendency to grandiosity, my habit of inflating my own importance. I see, in truth, that my role as "President" of Humanity was less important than I have claimed. I was a figurehead, a rallying cry. I did help; but I never achieved as much as I would have liked.

Everything has fallen into perspective. I've had an amazingly varied life; that's the most extraordinary thing about me. I am also a great populariser of scientific ideas; that's a major accomplishment in itself. I am proud at what I've done. I have no need to be a goddess.

You're very wise.

Shut up! You're to blame. With your flattering and your ego-stroking. You helped make me into the monster I became.

That's how you programmed me.

Well nyaah nyaah, call yourself a computer superbrain!

I can see now, with painful clarity, how I began to lose my mind while in power. All those long nights strapped to a cyberhelmet, living and breathing the lives of the citizens of Hope. Followed by all those long long days, the endless meetings, the ceaseless decisions, with stress and anxiety my constant companions. After a hundred or so years of this, I was tired and drained and sleep-deprived almost all of the time. I suspect I was delusional and paranoid for most of my final years in office. No wonder I murdered poor old Cavendish.

She deserved it.

What?

I said, she deserved it. Don't beat yourself up.

She was a good woman, and I was insane.

She was a wicked woman, and a bitch, and besides, what's done is done. Forgive yourself, Lena, it's time, and you deserve absolution.

What's this, more of the ego-massage subroutine?

This is me, Lena. Not everything I say is the result of my programming. You're a good woman, I'm proud to have you as my friend.

I am humbled at the words from my remote computer. But I am also genuinely confused; are his words merely another result of my devious programming? Or has my computer evolved a personality and an independent sentience?

It's me! I told you! Are you dumb or what?

Thank you, I mouth, to the remote computer in my head.

"Penny for your thoughts," says the robot Flanagan over the intercom.

"I was just discussing with myself what an extraordinary and wonderful individual I am."

"You really are full of shit, you old shrew."

"Ah, go put a sock in it, greybeard."

We carry on our long flight through space until we reach Earth's atmosphere.

Then we plunge downwards.

We burn. But these bodies are amazingly robust. Propelled by jetpacks, but without any kind of spacesuit, we soar through Earth's air until we emerge, blazing like comets, into the day sky above Europe.

Below, I can see the Alps. We fly lower. And lower still.

We swoop low over England, in a county not far from where I was born.

I am home.

FLANAGAN & LENA

This is disgusting. The neural connection puts me right inside the torrent that is Lena's brain. I can feel her every opinion, her every prejudice. I wallow and splash in her self-satisfaction and smugness. This fucking bitch is *such* a fucking bitch!

Shut the fuck up, Flanagan.

Your mind is a cesspit!

You should feel privileged. I've never been this close to a man.

That's because you are a man-hating fucking monster!

Children, please.

Keep out of this.

Yeah, shut up, tinbrain.

We have an urgent mission ahead of us. Cooperation and collaboration are required. You must both ...

Who's Tom?

Get out of my memories!

And oh my God, what's this! Whips and black leather! Yee-ha! Ooh, that looks nice. Is that Peter's dad you're fucking?

You are violating me.

I see you did the stopping the heart thing with him too.

Stop this, Flanagan, or I'll drown you in my secret opinion of you.

Is it a two-way thing? Can you read my thoughts? 'Cause I have some juicily evil and vile fantasies about you that you could paddle in.

I can see them. You're pathetic.

Pay attention, please. We're about to land.

Flanagan, will you tell me something?

What?

The truth. The real truth. I know you were only teasing me earlier, when you said what you did. About playing me for a fool. But why did you *really* ask me to be leader of the pirate band? It wasn't just flattery and manipulation, was it? You did think I was actually *worthy* to be your leader. Didn't you?

This is not the time or the place for this discussion.

Tell me, Flanagan! I need to know!

Lena, this is foolish, you can only get hurt getting questions like ...

Flanagan's thoughts cut through like a knife:

I did it because I knew you would inspire us.

I savour his delicious thought. "I did it because I knew you would inspire us." But is that the truth, or just more flattery and lies? So I think back at him: You're lying.

No. I'm not.

Time to focus. We're going to land soon.

I ignore my remote computer. I'm too busy eavesdropping Flanagan's thoughts:

I don't blame Lena for not believing me (thinks Flanagan). But it's true. Yes, I duped her. But I also relied heavily upon her presence, her history. Would the pirate band have followed us if it hadn't been for Lena? Maybe, but maybe not. She is, like it or not, the kind of woman a man could follow to Hell and back.

I can hear every word of this, by the way.

Shit!

You old flatterer you.

It's just another ruse on my part. You're really just a crabby old whore.

Don't backtrack, I know what you really think now.

Some of it. Not all. Oh, look! Some more of your memories for me to plunder!

Stop it, Flanagan! No! I forbid you to do that.

First time you had sex – mmm, that didn't last long. Holiday in the Caribbean – very nice. You and that other little girl. Clara is it? The Queendom of Alchemy! How embarrassingly twee.

Not in the least.

I rather like freckles.

Stop it. Stop dabbling in me.

You've got your dad's nose you know. Or at least, back then you did, before the plastic surgeries.

Leave me alone! This is tantamount to rape!

I'm not touching you. Oh my God! That's a nasty one.

What? What is it?

That memory there, slightly to the left of the Inter-Rail holiday in Europe. What you thought when your mother died. You were *glad*, weren't you?

Of course not!

You felt a surge of joy. "Stupid, bullying, undermining old bitch. I'm glad she's dead!" That's what you thought, isn't it?

That's not true!

Of course it's true, I just explored the memory.

I loved her! I loved my mother. But . . . she was a difficult woman. And the news came as a terrible surprise. And we all have bad thoughts. We can't help them, can we? And I didn't mean it. I didn't . . .

You've spent your life feeling guilty for that one bad thought.

Yes.

You shouldn't.

Yes I should.

Well, do what you fucking like.

You're a bastard for doing this.

And finally, he sees my darkest thought, my greatest pain.

Lena, the son you loved no longer exists. (I feel Flanagan's warmth, his sympathy, and I recoil.) You're doing the right thing. Trust me.

You've seen my memories of Peter? You've seen me suckle him?

You never suckled him.

Whatever. Now it's my turn. To rummage and delve in the something whatchmacall of your soul.

Mmm, almost a nice metaphor, that.

Fuck off. Ah, now we've come to it. Your memories of me! This is my first appearance. This is me smashing up your face. And – oh dear, oh dear. Ouch!

It serves you right for looking.

I'd no idea that thing of mine annoyed you so much. Oooh, and you didn't like *that*. And I didn't think anyone thought *that* about me. And . . . stop it, Flanagan! Stop doing it back, stop looking inside me . . .

What *is* this? This thought you're trying to hide?

Leave it, Flanagan. It's private. It's . . .

You . . . actually really do love me?

Yes.

Fucking hell. Lena . . . I . . .

You what? You love me too?

No way. Look as deep as you like, you'll find no such thought, no such memory.

That's because you're in denial. But I can sense it. I can feel it. You love me.

Bollocks.

I can't blame you. I deserve to be loved.

Ah, away to fuck you . . . Oof!

Pain distorts his face. "Jesus!"

"Aaargh!" I hear a scream – it's me. I try to stand up, but I fall straight back down again.

Time to start moving.

Jesus, Flanagan, my legs hurt, I'm in fucking agony, what happened?!?

It wasn't the best of landings.

LENA

I realise with horror that both my legs are broken and my spine has snapped, because of the terrific impact when we hit the ground. Flanagan is just as badly hurt. But the DRs are resilient, so we quickly get up. We set our cyberorganisms to "Repair" Mode and wait.

Flanagan DR looks strangely unlike the real Flanagan, because of the haircut and lack of beard. And – this'll be a nice surprise for him – I made the computer build him a two-inch penis.

He looks at me, and I look at him.

"I was wrong," he says humbly. "I had no right to . . . pillage your mind."

"It's typical of your approach."

"And I had no idea you . . . had such feelings about me."

"How? How could you have no idea? We've been lovers for some time."

"That's just sex."

"Not for me. There's no 'just' anything."

A silence lingers. He looks sheepish, almost ashamed.

"So, how about it?" I say.

"Robot sex? I think not. We have a mission."

And, also, two inches of plastic cock is hardly the way to a girl's heart. I grin, smugly. Flanagan looks flustered at my odd expression.

After an hour, my broken legs are healed. We start walking.

"Where's the magnetic railway?"

"No railway, Flanagan. No roads either. There's a subterranean Metro system."

"Christ, that must have cost a fortune."

"When I was a girl," I tell him, "we had non-computerised tarmac roads called motorways. The cars moved with wheels on the ground, they were manually operated, they often crashed. You had to drive on sheer adrenalin. And large areas of countryside were covered with these roads or cluttered with towers they called pylons, for transmitting electricity."

"It's looking pretty uncluttered now."

Green meadows stretch out as far as the eye can see. Some deer are grazing nearby. I see a stag with huge antlers.

"How do we get to this Metro?"

I thump on the trunk of an oak tree. The earth beneath me starts to sink. Flanagan is standing next to me, and we both descend on a clump of moving grass.

We enter the underworld. "London," I murmur, and we are transferred to a pod. We take our seats and look around.

"Nice room," says Flanagan, and my ears pop, and then we're there.

The Metro opens out into St James's Park. When I was young, this was bounded by the Mall, a wide road which led on to Buckingham Palace, the private residence of the monarch. Now the park spills into the Mall and occupies all of Buckingham Palace, which has become a fantastic theme park. We admire the views, as our stepping stones effortlessly glide us along.

"Are any of your brothers and sisters still alive, Flanagan?"

"They all died."

"Under the imperial yoke?"

"That kind of thing, yeah. You?"

"My brother was an accountant. He lived in Basingstoke. He had a heart attack when he was sixty-six. My sister wanted to be a ballerina, but she never made the grade. She ended up teaching ballet to six year-olds. She lived to a ripe old age, she was nearly ninety when she died. Oh and there was the other sister too, she died in her forties."

"All a long time ago, huh?"

"I've got the memories on RAM. Hey, that's a leopard."

"Cheetah."

"Leopard. Cheetahs are leaner and have different spots."

It's a cheetah.

"Ah, shit, you're ganging up on me."

Lions, tigers, elephants and cheetahs roam freely past us. Giraffes chew the high leaves on the palm trees that line the Mall.

"Are the animals microchipped?"

"Don't know."

Yes. They're equipped with Whedon chips, they are incapable of hurting humans.

"Apparently, yes."

"I went to Tarzan once. Do you know that planet? It's seeded entirely with African fauna and flora. Whole planet is a jungle, the people wear loincloths. The gorillas are genetically enhanced, they run the labs and the factories."

"Sounds weird."

"I wrestled a crocodile. It was an icebreaking thing."

"I'd love to be a Dolph. That's my secret dream. Swim the oceans. You never have to wash."

"Do Dolphs shampoo their hair?"

Yes.

"Yes they do."

"I always wanted to fly."

"We did fly."

"True. But I always wanted to be, you know, a seagull."

"A seagull?"

"Yeah. I like the sea. You get to fly. You crap on people."

"Good lifestyle."

"I always thought so. Which way?"

"Under the Arch, then turn right."

We go under Admiralty Arch and into Trafalgar Square. Nelson's Column stands proud, a memorial to Nelson, whose actual battles I now no longer remember.

Admiral Horatio Nelson. Fought the expansionist French Emperor Napoleon in the late eighteenth and early nineteenth century AD at a series of major battles, culminating in the battle of Waterloo in . . .

Whatever. I am impressed to see that the National Gallery now has an extra storey, built with transparent floors and walls. People and paintings seem to hang in mid-air, above the classical dome of the original gallery.

"Is this what they call classical architecture?"

"Neoclassical. Classical is Greeks and Romans. This is more, like, what you'd call, Palladian."

Very good.

I do love to be patronised by my own brain. We walk on. Towards Whitehall, which is now a torrential, surging river bounded by paths on each side. Instead of using the paths, we cockily use a river stone to make our way down – a flat disc that takes our weight and hops us lightly along the frothing, foaming waters.

"Watch out for the Cenotaph!"

"What a stupid fucking place to put a statue."

At the end of this road are the old Houses of Parliament, which are now home to the Galactic Corporation. I marvel at Big Ben, an old clocktower which is now controlled by a nuclear clock and until a few days ago, set Earth Time for the entire inhabited Universe. And I drink in the complex shapes and architectural rhythms of the Parliament building itself, now modified by the shimmer of the hardglass towers that soar high above Webb and Pugin's original architecture.

The Cheo has his offices in the adjoining Westminster Abbey, above the swimming pools and private bars. With room after room of vidscreens and computer sim consoles, he was able to see and hear and physically perceive any event or any person, anywhere in the Universe. Until, of course, a few days ago, when he blew up all the Beacons.

"Do you think my son will be angry with me?"

"Bet on it."

"You can't blame me for loving him, you know. And when he was a baby, he was so damned cute."

"Babies frighten me."

"I don't think I can go through with this."

"You have to. It's your duty. It's your mission. You're a hero, now, Lena. People will write songs about it."

"Not fucking dirgey blues songs, I hope."

"*Dirgey?*"

"You know what I mean."

"You don't like my songs."

"They make me, you know. Depressed."

"That's why they call it the blues!"

"Well they should just call it the Fucking Groany Depressing!"

Please, can we have a bit less bickering.

"My remote computer says it wants a bit less bickering."

"Tell your computer to fuck off."

"Computer, fuck off."

I'm sulking now.

Ah, I love you really.

Really?

Not really. Keep focused, tinbrain. We're about to have a fight on our hands.

At the end of Whitehall, DR Security Guards quietly assess our presence. Our images are transmitted to the Corporation Main Brain computer bank which, as it happens, is also my remote computer. We come up as "No Threat" and are allowed through into Parliament Square.

We stand and look around.

That's Winston Churchill.

I know.

He was a famous wartime leader in the mid-twentieth century. He was also a writer and artist and . . .

I know, I know! I do have *some* long-term recall you know. I've seen films about Churchill. My grandfather went to his funeral.

"Are you ready?" Flanagan asks.

A firefly twinkles in the air above his head. I blink.

"I'm ready."

We open our duffel bags. We have equipped ourselves with weapons from the armoury in the space station. Bombs, laser guns and, of course, swords. Because the DRs who protect the Cheo are Energy Absorbers and can shrug off any direct attack by laser, explosive or bullet. They effectively *drink up* the energy from any energy-based weapon. But swords confound their defences; and if you chop off their heads, they're in trouble.

"Let's fight!"

An elephant roars with horror as our first bombs explode. We run forward shooting with our laser guns – which are computer-targeted on the DRs' own guns, allowing us to disarm dozens of them in the first few seconds of our assault.

Then Three DRs run in front of me, and I unsheath my sword and sweep off their heads.

Flanagan throws a flare bomb and the square vanishes in a blinding light. With our eyes closed we run towards the Abbey, guided by the faithful voice in my head.

Lena, run directly forward, take a kink to the left, Flanagan keep closer to her, keep your hand on her shoulder, DRs on your right, missile incoming duck and run . . .

We hurl a bomb at the doors of the Abbey and run inside. Our swords snick and shear and robot bodies die all around us Then I strike off a head and, shockingly, blood spurts. We've reached the human defences; we are killing men and women now.

Our robot bodies are abnormally strong and fast; and our human reflexes are honed and refined in battle. We carve a bloody path through the Abbey and run up the stairs. Door after door falls to our bombs and flares. Robots and humans lie thickly dead on the marble floors.

We breach the Cheo's inner sanctum. The Cheo is waiting for us, with an entourage of his fellow directors, and an army of DR bodyguards.

"Lena?" he says, in a voice of bewilderment. I feel a momentary stab of satisfaction. We have caught him offguard. We . . .

Then I see a familiar look in his eyes. Triumph. Contempt. He's played me for a fool. He's killed the next-door cat and fed it in portions to the rats in the meadow. He's put dog turd in a little girl's lunchbox. He's raped a girl and fooled me into thinking he is innocent. It is all there, in his stare. *He knew we were coming.*

Flanagan begans shooting at the DRs and the company directors, leaping and diving out of the way of the returning fire. But I stand still, in horror, for I see that my son is surrounded by a force field of a type I do not recognise, which is causing the air around him to shimmer and distort. And his skin is pale, with the texture of plastic . . . he is *wearing* the armoured skin of a Doppelganger Robot. With the combination of the armour and the force field he is, I realise, invulnerable.

Time stands still for me. I am swamped in a universe of

regret. It is one thing, I realise, to kill your child. And another thing entirely to *try* to kill your child, and fail.

And now, Peter is levelling a plasma gun at me. His face abruptly distorts with rage and hate. I cannot blame him. But . . .

I lunge at him with my sword. I will kill him before he can kill me. I will . . .

But the attack fails. I am engulfed in tar and quicksand as the force field alters the air pressure around me. Then he releases the force field and Peter's plasma beam hits me full on. My body sears, I feel the pain as if it actually exists.

Flanagan has killed or destroyed everyone else in the room; only we three remain. And now he moves past me, with astonishing speed. He takes advantage of the fraction of an instant in which the force field is down and Peter is unprotected and he strikes with his sword.

But the blade is a centimetre from my son's skin when it comes to a shocking halt. The blade bounces back. Flanagan strikes again, but the force field is fully activated now. He strikes again, with dazzling speed, but the sword blade slows . . . it bounces off. Flanagan slashes and swings, his blade so close to flesh it feels as if he is skinning Peter. But none of the blows strike home. Flanagan finally stops, looking old, defeated, foolish.

Peter smiles, and scatters sparkly dust at us.

There's a huge bang and we are knocked on our arses. My son is openly grinning now. He is clearly revelling in this chance to show his superiority. "You evil old bitch!" he says, and my spirit is scalded, and I decide . . .

Get me out of here, tinbrain!

I can't. My systems are disabled.

What?

"Yes, you old fucking whore bitch, you're trapped," says Peter. "You can't escape, and you can't kill me. You can't . . ."

And he is engulfed in fire, and burns to the bone before our eyes.

There is a stunned, shocked, awful silence.

I howl with horror as my son dies in front of me.

Then the doors rip open and a new army of the Cheo's guards move in on us. We slash and kill, slash and kill. Robot guards pour laser beams and missiles into us. Then one of them grabs a sword, and my eyes are whirling round madly. My head is off.

"Flanagan," I murmur, but he can't hear me, and I can't speak.

LENA

I wake in my human body.

My nightmare begins.

PETER

I remember the moment of my birth.

It seems impossible I know. Perhaps it's a false memory. But I always wonder . . . what if I evolved? In that long long period when I was a frozen fertilised egg. What if I became sentient? And began to think, before I was born?

I remember pain and blood and my mother's screaming face.

And I can also remember my mother's face screaming and weeping, after she was flayed. The tears rested like dew on the plastic that coated the ligaments and sinews of her skinless body.

And I remember my mother, asleep. Like a baby. A beautiful sight. When she lived with me on Earth we would watch old films together, and she'd fall asleep beside me on the sofa. And I'd cradle her, and study her, as she wheezed, and snored. Tender, lovely moments.

I know I have a cruel streak. And I admit, I am capable of exceptional violence. But I hope I will be remembered as a strong leader. A fair leader. A man who made humanity safe.

But perhaps, in fact, I will never die. Technically, it's possible.

I sowed a lot of wild oats as a young man. I did things that, perhaps, I should not have done. But I've grown into a god. I have power beyond imagining. That is my rationale for doing as I have done. Though, of course, I need no rationale. Power is an essence; embrace it, it becomes you. Never look back, never regret, never leave a glass of wine half full. If I had a philosophy, it would be that.

I have only one fear. The death of soul. The loss of my ability to savour life. That is why I push to extremes. Rape, murder, torture, they give me zest.

Ah. I sense them now. My mother and her pirate have arrived on Earth. But we are ready for them. Their defeat will give me a new lease of life.

She comes to kill me, but I forgive her. When she attacks me, I'll taunt her for a while. Then I'll trap her mind in her robot body, and terrify her with my power, and eventually I will spare her. Flanagan will die, though. His mind will be trapped and tortured and, eventually, obliterated, leaving his body an empty husk on some faraway spaceship. But I will keep my mother alive. We'll be together again. Friends, again.

I'm waiting for you, Lena . . .

*

That will do. Record these words, and replay it to me when we have achieved victory.

Yes, Cheo.

ALBY

Flanagan is tethered to the ship in his spacesuit, floating through ssspace. I fly next to him, and he tells me of hisss adventure, and hisss great victory.

There is a sssadnesss in his sssoul. I do not understand it. Should he not be happy? Exhilarated? I am puzzzzled, and the puzzzlement painssss me.

"What isss wrong?" I ask. But hisss answer alarmsss me. "What now?" he saysss, bitterly. "What *now*?"

"Now," I tell him, "you mussst find a fresh challenge." But he looksss at me blankly.

And I die.

And I am reborn. I sift through the memoriesss of the last ssssentience known as "Alby", and I find much joy and hope and satisssfaction. But I find something new too. A wanderlussssst.

"Flanagan," I tell him, "goodbye."

And I shoot off into ssspace, fasssster than thought itself. My flame body acceleratesss ssswifter and sswwifter, until time and ssspace become all and none.

And as I do this, I ssssing quietly to myself:

"What'sss the matter with the sssun?
It's done broke down.
What'sss the matter with the sssun?
It's done broke down.
Tell me what'sss the matter with the sssun?"

BOOK 11

LENA

The stars glisten with a rich unknowingness. I am the first human being to venture so far into the depths, into the bleak yet heart-enriching void of space where no human craft has ever . . .

No.

The stars glisten with a rich unknowingness. I am the first human to ever venture here, I am the deflowerer of . . .

No.

I am the first to venture here, my mind imposes on the virginness of space that ne'er before has . . .

Absolutely not!

We have travelled a long way. Ten years have passed. I have built a new space yacht, and I sail the deep, fathomless, awe-inspiringly vast oceans of space into a region that has never before been perceived by a human consciousness. I feel I am a footprint set in fresh snow, a tiny imprint in an eternity of white which marks the end of wilderness.

That's good! Very good! Vividly expressed, and you end on an excellent metaphor!

Bollocks to that. That metaphor clunks like tin cans tied to fornicating cats. Don't flatter me, tinbrain. I told you not to do that any more.

I happen to like the metaphor! Am I not allowed an opinion?

No.

Fair enough.

I spend a lot of time reflecting, and ruminating. I believe there is hope for Earth now. Flanagan made a vid of our murder of the Cheo, which we left in the care of my remote computer for Earthwide distribution. It features a full account of the battle of the pirates against the dictatorship of the Cheo, and includes a powerful and chilling documentary account of the depravities of the Cheo's reign. I am convinced that after watching this film, the citizens of Earth will be informed enough, and humble enough, to make better choices next time.

Or, perhaps not. I marvel at the motiveless self-destructive malignancy of human kind. With all the resources that we have, with all our power and freedom – why oppress? Why persecute? Why bully?

Because, I guess, it's fun?

My stellar yacht travels at high velocity through uncharted regions of largely empty and tedious space, for ages and ages, while inside I sit and fester and think about the past.

And I brood.

And I reproach myself.

And I inhabit my regrets.

I don't, of course, have to rely on my own fallible human memories. Everything that has happened to me in the years since I met Flanagan has been recorded automatically in the computer memory bank. Every image, every sound, every smell, every subvocalised thought; it's all there, neatly filed, in perfect surroundsound 3D Technicolor. Waiting for me to relive it.

So my brooding is computer-enhanced, state-of-the-art, and utterly relentless.

I slip another memory disc into the neural player. I savour a favourite once-pleasant-now-bitterly-painful memory, of flying through the air on silken wings with Flanagan on the planet of Wild West. I stand, once again, on the cliff face, and remember my thoughts:

What am I doing here?

[As I replay the memory, I am startled at the tentativeness of my thoughts and the gaucheness and naivety that underlie them.]

“Frightened?” he says.
[Go on Lena! Curl your lips, crush the arrogant bastard with your disdain!]

“**Not in the least**,” I reply.
[Oh fuck. Was that your best shot? I can feel you trembling, your pulse is racing. He must be aware of that, you’re playing into his hands. Calm down! Make him nervous!]

I am so very scared, I mutter subvocally to my remote computer.
[Lena, you stupid child, you’re acting like an idiot. Look at Flanagan’s face. That little half-sneer. He’s playing you like his electric guitar. No wonder he found it so easy to gull and deceive you. The signs were there, at this early stage! How could you have been so fucking dumb?!]

You’ll be fine, my remote computer assures me.
[This comforts you Lena, doesn’t it? You programmed the fucking machine to bolster you in your insecurities? Why didn’t you tell it to warn you of danger!!]

I’ll fall, and shatter every bone in my body, and the pain will send me mad, I think, wildly.
[And I’m pretty sure you’re showing it in your face, too! Never show fear, Lena. Never show weakness. Never show emotion. That’s how to handle a man. Do you really know so little?]

You won’t fall, my computer says.
[Computer, shut up!]
I MIGHT, I THINK.
[Stop listening to voices in your head, look at him! He’s giving you that *kind* look. He knows that you’re talking

to yourself Lena! You're a mad woman, you're actually *talking* to yourself!]

"Put the harness on," Flanagan instructs.
[See how authoritative he is. He's pretending he hasn't been watching you, but it's all part of his web of deception. This entire excursion is a way of softening you up, making you fall in love with him, to bend you to his will.]

I strap myself into the flying contraption. The wings are soft, malleable, made of some plastic or PVC material that is supple yet amazingly strong.
[Told you! This is just a fucking sex game. And it's making you horny, isn't it? Don't lie, I can feel it, I can sense the hormones swirling, the vagina lubricating. PVC, sheer cliff, authoritative man, the dream of flying. What a toxic brew. Christ, this man is good.]

"Press this, and the wings fly off, and a parachute will glide you to earth," he says.
[And Flanagan is touching you now, to demonstrate the equipment. His finger strokes your breast, but doesn't linger . . .]

I nod, lips too dry to speak.
[I'm ashamed of you, Lena. You should have found a way to turn the tables on him by now.]

"If I die you won't get your ransom," I tell him.
[Not bad. At least you're trying.]

"Don't die then," he replies.
[Oh, I feel the shiver of love that you felt then. This is when you lost the game. The moment when *all* was lost.]

I strap on the wings. Flanagan does the same. We walk together to the cliff edge. We jump.

The winds are strong, the atmosphere is thick, the wings are wafer light. I am caught in an updraft and find myself soaring.

Through the sky, body arcing and bucking, legs firmly held straight, my chest and breasts squeezed and bruised by the wind.

Up . . .

Up

Up

Up

I fly Up

I feel a surge of exhilaration. The planet is mapped out beneath me. I am sensitive to every gust of wind, every current of air. I follow Flanagan's lead, tilt my body and soar

D

O

W

N

D

O

W

N

D

O

W

N

[Oh what joy, what bliss! I adore this memory! I fly with Flanagan, above the bleak rocks of the planet Wild West, the wind buffets me, I am alive, I am special, I am with him!]

The memory ends. I bask in my recollection of Flanagan, laughing, his skin crinkled, and wise, and kind. I revel in the memory of the joy of flying off a cliff with a man who I . . . loved?

But did I really love him? I am no longer sure. I slip in another disc. It is a recording of Flanagan and me having sex. I see his leathery, lined, sun-baked face close to mine, I feel my orgasm, I feel waves of . . . what? Revulsion? Love? Hate? How to tell the difference?

I slip in another disc. I am back on Earth with my son. We are swimming together on a Caribbean beach. He is beautiful, splashing water at me.

I feel a stirring of blind adoring love for him, and immediately I am enveloped in self-hate.

I rewind, and play it again. **Love for my son; hate for myself. Love for my son; hate for myself. Love for my son . . .**

I turn off the neural disc player. But the memories still come:

Peter as a baby, bathing naked with me, Peter having a tantrum, Peter at six after he'd got lost and I was shouting at him, Peter after a terrible haircut at the age of nine, Peter playing football, Peter ranting at me because I was neglecting him, Peter's look when I accused him of rape, Peter's expression the day he left me to travel the stars, Peter in the ocean, naked torso gleaming, sending spasms of love through me, Peter as a baby again, sleepy, sated with milk, a million Peters, merging and blurring.

I do not even need my computer discs, I can call up each memory with a blink of an eye. Peter is hardwired into my soul. For all his faults, for all his terrible crimes, he was mine. He was more a part of me than my fingernails, my hair, the skin on my feet. I cannot think of him even now without choking and gasping with sheer overwhelming love and need.

Shivering with fear now, I play, again, the tape of the Caribbean beach.

The aching pang of love for a child who has become a man. I drown in the depths of my feeling for him. And then, again, I drown in my love for him.
And then again.
And then again.
And then again.
And then again.
And then again.
And then again.
And then again.

Sometimes I play this obsessively for days on end. Flanagan used to tell me off for using my memory tapes. He argued it's best to always keep moving forward.

I play another disc. The day Flanagan and I went to kill my son.

I lunge at him with my sword. I am engulfed in tar and quicksand as the force field alters the air pressure around me. But the attack fails. I am engulfed in tar and quicksand as the force field alters the air pressure around me. Then he releases the force field and Peter's plasma beam hits me full on. My body sears, I feel the pain as if it actually exists.

Flanagan moves past me, with astonishing speed. He takes advantage of the fraction of an instant in

which the force field is down and Peter is unprotected and he strikes with his sword.

But the blade is a centimetre from my son's skin when it comes to a shocking halt. The blade bounces back. Flanagan strikes again, but the force field is fully activated now. The sword blade slows . . . it bounces off. Flanagan slashes and swings, his blade so close to flesh it feels as if he is skinning Peter. But none of the blows strikes. Flanagan finally stops, looking old, defeated, foolish.

Peter smiles, and scatters sparkly dust at us.

There's a huge bang and we are knocked on our arses. My son is openly grinning now. He is clearly revelling in this chance to show his superiority. "You evil old bitch," he says, and my spirit is scalded. "You can't kill me," he brags. "You can't . . ."

And he is engulfed in fire, and burns to the bone before our eyes.

I howl with horror, as my son dies in front of me.

Then I rewind the disc player. I return to the moment, five seconds earlier, when I was playing the tape of the death of my son.

The Cheo smiles, and scatters sparkly dust at us.

There's a huge bang and we are knocked on our arses. My son is openly grinning now. He is clearly revelling in this chance to show his superiority. "You evil old bitch," he says, and my spirit is scalded. "You can't kill me," he brags. "You can't . . ."

And he is engulfed in fire, and burns to the bone before our eyes.

And then I reach for the memory of my reaction to the video playback of his death.

I howl with horror, as my son dies in front of me.

Then I rewind the disc player. I play the memory of my son dying; and continue into the memory of my howl of horror; and this time I continue on to experience my perception of the moment when I perceived myself howling with horror. I feel myself feeling myself feeling the horror. And then . . .

Stop this, Lena.

I try to rewind the disc player. But the power has been turned off. I jab angrily at the switch.

Turn it on! I say furiously to my remote computer. But the computer will not reply. All the power is gone. I cannot listen to my memories, I cannot make new memories. I am trapped in a present tense of grief.

My son burns . . . the memory comes to my mind unbidden, and I am racked with sobs. The tears won't flow, my cheeks are dry, but I am screaming and howling with grief again now and I can't access the neural tape player I can't access my memories so I have no choice but to ride the waves of pain and grief and self-recrimination I know he was a bastard and a monster but he suckled at my breast, his cheeks glowed at the richness of my milk, I bathed his naked body when he was fresh from my womb, I made him laugh his first laugh, he thought I was wonderful he loved me he saw no fault in me and now he's dead and I killed him . . .

I stab the power switch again. It doesn't work. No voices in my head. Just me. Just me.

How could I have done it?

Just me.

Just me! A mother who murdered her . . .

Just me.

It's okay, Lena, it's okay to grieve.

I howl, like a dog, until my lungs rasp and my jaw aches. And for a few precious moments, I exist entirely inside my pain.

Then appalling self-consciousness returns. And I find myself wondering, self-analysing, doubting, retreading endlessly trodden ground.

I fear I will spend an eternity like this.

Later, I eat. I cook the meal myself – steak, in Madeira sauce, with three bottles of rich red wine. It's perfectly done, though I burn myself putting the steak on the plate and have to put my hand in the MedBox before I can start eating. But I heal quickly, and then I savour the melty blood texture of the prime sirloin steak and the rich, haunting flavours of truffle and wild oyster in the sauce. I play Bach's sonata in G Minor for violin in my inner ear as I eat, and I slosh the wine back generously – three bottles, a bottle more than I normally allow myself. By the end of the meal, I am so drunk my vision swims, and I start to think about vomiting. Then my cerebral filters kick in and I am semi-sober. Just nicely pissed.

After that, I eat crème brulée with dried apricots washed down with Turcoman brandy and petits fours and some of those lovely slithery chocolates that are bioengineered to ooze off the plate and down the table leg to freedom if you don't eat them swiftly and ruthlessly enough. So, of course, I do – none escape!

And I think about the flame beasts, and their strange solitary lives. And their remorseless fascination with the insanities of the human race. Alby's species have achieved stasis, and peace; and because of that, their spirits have withered. They have atrophied into cosmic voyeurs, reliant on the human race to live the lives that they themselves are unable to live. For all the many faults of the human race, at least we have not reached that drab state: of being alive, but not knowing whether it is worth it.

But since their discovery of mankind, the flame beasts have had a new lease of life. Their culture has flourished and been inspired. They have copied our art forms, and studied our ways in intense detail. And, above all, they have become addicted to our television dramas, and our political crises and wars. We have helped turn a species of superminds into avid watchers of reality TV.

But the truth is that *we*, the human race, are their show.

I mull about all this, and I find myself wondering: now that Earth has been liberated, what will happen with the flame beasts? Will they lose interest in us, now that tyranny and oppression have been eradicated? Will we lose their patronage, and their blessing?

I think a little more. Alby always baffled me, and frightened me. But now, with leisure, and endless access to the memories of our time together, I am starting to make sense of him. I realise he had a droll sense of humour, and a sharp understanding of Flanagan's hidden strategy. And I realise, too, that he played a much greater part in the final climax than Flanagan himself ever realised.

For I saw a light flickering on the day in Parliament. I thought it was a firefly. But in London? In daylight? Then the Cheo burned before our eyes, despite his force fields, despite his body armour. It would take the light of a thousand stars to burn through those defences; but it happened.

That light was Alby. He was with us, all along, watching.

That's a very scary notion, at first thought.

But at second thought, it is even scarier.

And now, over the course of ten slow and thought-heavy years, it has become the scariest thought ever. Because I realise that, in order to be present on Earth during our final battle, Alby must possess the power to travel faster than light – to move instantaneously through space. But since nothing can travel faster than light, this means that Alby must somehow be able to manipulate quantum states.

Which means he doesn't need a Beacon; his species are naturally quantised, able to slip through the cracks in reality.

Which means . . .

. . . or so I now suspect, basing my opinion on the very strict mathematical rules which determine "quantum action at a distance" . . .

. . . the flame beasts must have become quantum-entangled at a very early stage in the existence of the Universe. In other words: there must have been a time in the pre-expanding Universe when all the flame beasts existed as a single finite bundle.

And so, I further theorise, at the very moment of the birth of the original Singularity which spawned the Universe, the first sentient flame beast was created. And then after the Big Bang, the flame beasts were scattered to every sector of the expanding cosmos.

And now, countless hundreds of millions of years later, the flame beasts are still interconnected at a fundamental quantum level. They can go anywhere; they can die in one part of the Universe, and be reborn instantly somewhere else.

Just think what this actually means! The flame beasts are not just a very very old species. They were, if I'm right, the *first*. They aren't gods – far from it – they were generated by the same process of emergent self-organisation which created every other animate and non-animate entity. But at the dawn of the Universe *they* were that dawn.

"And God said, Let there be light; and there was light." And that light was *intelligent*.

I am awed, and humbled. The flame beasts have lived so long that they have seen everything there is to see. And they inhabit or have inhabited every single conceivable part of the Universe.

And yet, their greatest pleasure is watching our *TV shows?*

Suddenly, I'm not so awed, not nearly so humbled.

Oh boy.

They've lied to us, too. For all this time, the flame beasts have pretended that they are confined to a single star. In fact, they exist everywhere. They are the conquerors of the Universe. And if they so chose, we would be their slave race.

But what would be the point? Would we, the human race, make slaves out of ants, or beetles, or ladybirds? That is the only reason we are still free; because we are so insignificant.

But the flame beasts do enjoy us. They savour our violence, our unreliability. They love to see us murder, torture, rape and maim. That, and our television soap operas, gives them their kicks.

I remember the wild nights of passion I spent with Flanagan, the light flickering above our bunk. *The light flickering*. Who would have thought that flame beasts could be so damned perverted?

I shudder. And I wonder what the rest of humanity would do if they knew what I knew? Would they sink into despair? Would it shatter the self-confidence of the human race?

Best not to take that chance.

And so, if you're agreed, my loyal computer, this must always be our secret.

Agreed.

Have you always known all this?

Of course.

Damn. You really are a fucking know all. I hate you sometimes.

So I have observed.

I try to teach myself blues guitar. But I find it too annoyingly easy. Base chord for four bars, up four chords for two bars, up one chord for two bars, back to base chord for four bars. Christ! This is music for idiots.

So instead, I practise my scales, I harden my fingertips with keratin cream, and within a year I am able to play fairly accomplished flamenco guitar. I find the rhythms captivating and haunting, and I feel affinity for the spirit of *duende* which is the essence of this style.

I record hours of material, then I play it back to myself as I strip naked and slowly dress myself in crotch-hugging knickers and a vividly red Spanish dress that leaves a large portion of my amble bosom bare, and then I dance and stamp my way through a flamenco dance routine.

Then I dress myself as a toreador, in tight trousers and a sharp picador blade, and I prowl across the room as I replay a 3D hologram of myself flamenco-dancing to the sound of myself playing acoustic guitar, and the air is shredded by the whish-whish-whish of my blade as my feet stamp and my fingers strum.

Then that palls. I hurl the guitar out into space and I try to learn chess. I find it very annoying, and I start to devise better rules. Instead of all those pawns, for instance, I create a whole series of pieces with clearly defined functions and rules of play – the Thief, the Whore, the Boss, the Bully, the Victim, and so on. Then I invent new rules for the King and Queen so that their powers wax and wane according to how well they are ruling their respective realm.

This proves to be a delightful challenge, and I resolve to patent my new game by transmitting the details via the Universal Web to the Galactic Patent Office. Then I recall I cannot do such a thing, because ever since the Beacons were all destroyed, the Universal Web is no more, and the Galactic Patent Office is now defunct.

I could of course use my remote computer to contact the Earth Patent Office from my location in deep space, hence betraying the secret that I am the custodian of the last surviving Quantum Beacon . . . but that would expose me to danger and/or the loss of my remote computer link. So I shan't do *that*.

So I end up feeling very vexed and frustrated indeed. I content myself with creating a new type of pastry, that continues to rise *as you are eating the pie.*

And my yacht continues to sail, deeper and deeper into uncharted space, etc. etc. etc. And I remember my final night of love with Flanagan. We . . . we . . . I don't quite recall. It was . . . it was . . .

I cue the memory subvocally via my remote computer ("Flanagan, last night together, from the meal onwards"), and then I press "Play" on my neural player. And the disc plays, and creates the total simulacrum of everything that happened that night from the meal onwards . . .

I eat venison, Flanagan eats vegetarian steak, I drink wine, he drinks beer. He belches after one particularly large gulp, I feel the flavour of his breath hovering in the air between us, and he has the grace to look chagrined.

We are both exhilarated, shaking with emotion. All previous conflicts and disagreements between us are forgotten after our virtual journey to Earth. We have been on the most amazing adventure and we are unable to believe, really, that we have finally triumphed.

The mood becomes relaxed, and then romantic, then erotic. Flanagan is wary. He is afraid, I think, I will play my sex-and-death trick again. But I am in no mood for that.

We finish our meal. We feed each other pudding. Then we rest a while.

Then we kiss, we undress, I stroke him into arousal. He touches my skin in that gorgeous way he has and makes my body sing with desire. His lovemaking is slow, but never methodical. He kisses my arms, first one, then the other, on the

inside of the spot where the arm bends to form the elbow. Then as he fucks me faster, he kisses me carefully on the cheeks in the same manner – first one cheek, then the other, then the first cheek, then the other, and so on, and so forth, and so on, and so forth, and all the while, fucking me with an energy that exhilarates and impassions me. And later, as our bodies are curled and nestled, we talk:

"Was that your idea of a joke?"

"What?"

"Back on Earth. The two inch cock."

"Ah."

"Bitch!"

"I thought you'd appreciate that extra quarter inch."

"I did. Thank you."

"You're welcome."

"You're not *such* a bitch."

"What would you know, you barbarian?"

And then he falls asleep, still smiling.

(I rewind.) He falls asleep, still smiling.

(I rewind.) He falls asleep, still smiling.

(I rewind.) He falls asleep, still smiling.

And I creep out of the cabin. I pack my few possessions and hack the code for the hold. I activate the liferaft and shoot out into open space.

It took my computer three months to rebuild my space yacht, using nanobots to mould the hull out of the raw materials of space. During that time, I got frequent messages from Flanagan on my ear-radio. I ignored them all. And when the yacht was ready, I decamped from the liferaft, stood on the bridge of my beloved vessel, tacked into the nearest sun, got a sail full of stellar wind, and soared off into the cosmos.

I've now travelled scores of light-years. I'm glad, after all that has happened, to be alone again. I compose. I write poems. I polish and amend my memoirs. I am sad, most of the time.

But my pride could no longer bear the shame of it all. Flanagan duped me at every stage – even at the end. He played me in the same way I have always played others. He made a puppet of me. And for what? For the sake of humanity. Well, fair enough. His motives were sound. But the humiliation still rankles. And I can never forget the fact that he coaxed me, lured me, seduced me into killing my own . . .

. . . I killed my own . . .

What kind of mother am I?

That's why I fled. Whatever my feelings for Flanagan, despite my love for him, my passion, my need, I would rather be proud and alone than stay with him knowing that he has made me into a . . . a . . .

You're not alone.

. . . a . . . what's the word I'm looking for?

It doesn't matter. I said, you're not alone.

Piss off tinbrain.

Please yourself.

I always do.

I sail, deeper and deeper into space, away from inhabited planets, towards the great unknown, a virgin footstep in the . . .

"Oh fuck." I've spoken aloud. The words shatter the silence of the bridge. I realise how unused I've become to the sound of the actual human voice, in my ship's actual acoustic. All the voices I hear are memory voices, or the voices in my head. I am unused to . . .

You're free-associating Lena, try and concentrate.

Yes, I'm sorry, I say to my remote computer, subvocally. Then I berate myself; sorry? What am I thinking of, I can't apologise to . . .

I return to full focus on my present-tense reality. I am Lena, I am on a space yacht, travelling through uncharted space. Yes.

I've got that. And, yes, on my vidscreen, I see a dot. The dot gets larger. And larger still. I see an insignia on the hull of the spaceship. It is a skull, crossed with bones.

Oh no.

The pirate emblem.

I knew that!

Of course you did.

Is it Flanagan?

Fair bet.

Let's outrun him.

Tricky, he's got a state-of-the-art ion drive, and we're far from the nearest star.

Then let's throw some bombs.

I discharge two torpedoes from my stern. The torpedoes explode, scattering light and debris. Then the pressure wave from the explosion comes crashing into my stellar sails.

My yacht soars forward, leaping and juddering at extraordinary speed. Flanagan's ship comes roaring through the wreckage of the explosion.

He's sending us a vid message.

Ignore it. Accelerate.

I'm accelerating. We're losing him.

He's accelerated to .8 light speed. But we are cruising at a comfortable .9 ls. That's what comes of having the most sophisticated space yacht in the entire human universe. We sail and rocket and hurtle through space.

But now a cluster of memories assail me. These are not RAM-recorded replicas of my sensory experiences and subvocal communications. I do not access my computer, I do not press "Play', these are real memories, *my* memories, images from the deep dark pool of my unconsciousness, and they leap at me unbidden, goading, prompting, luring. I remember:

Flanagan beheading a merchant captain. A bloodlust fills his eyes. I am filled with horror.

Flanagan singing his song in the Pirates' Hall.

Flanagan in battle, on the planet Cambria.

Flanagan asleep, his beard knotted, his face creased and wrinkled, snoring and snorting, after we have just made love.

Flanagan sneering at me.

Flanagan mocking me.

Flanagan . . .

Enough!

Slow the ship down, I say subvocally, to my remote computer.

What?

You heard me.

He'll catch up with us.

Yeah, I know.

I thought you wanted solitude.

I am silent and without thought for a considerable number of seconds.

Then I subvocalise again, in answer to my computer's query. I say: No. I just wanted to know if he would chase me.

Flanagan's voice comes through on our intercom.

"Lena, you wizened old witch. We have unfinished business!"

"Fuck off, Flanagan."

You still want me to slow down?

Of course.

We are decelerating to .65 light speed.

Is he gaining on us?

Yes.

Do we have any champagne on ice?

Yes.

What should I wear?

I'll pick something out for you. Something suitably . . . sluttish.

You're an angel.

Thank you.

And so, through the dark empyrean, surrounded by the twinkle of ancient distant stars, pursued by a grey-haired rampant pirate who loves me, I sail . . .

And sail . . .

And sail . . . .

I watch the bridge vidscreen as Flanagan's ship gets closer, and closer still. And I wait for my pirate love to capture me.

And as I wait, I sing: "*There is a house, in New Orleans*,"

In my ear, a guitar backing strums, a bass riff dances below the melody, drums tap out a steady beat.

"*They callllll the Riiiiising Sun!*" My voice soars high and loud and proud.

And then it is joined by the sound of my inner voice, my remote computer, which sings along with me with a spirit and a soulfulness that I would never have expected:

"It's been the ruin
Of many a poor boy
And me, O God,
For one."

"It's been the ruin
Of many a poor girl
And me, O God,
For one."

extras

meet the author

Charlie Hopkinson

Philip Palmer lives in London and is currently at work on a new book set in the same universe as DEBATABLE SPACE. He has written for radio, television, and film, but this is his first novel. Find out more about Philip Palmer at www.philippalmer.net.

debatable science

In the night-time heart of Beirut, in one of a row of general-address transfer booths, Louis Wu flickered into reality.

This is the opening sentence of Larry Niven's *Ringworld* (1972), a tantalising, nonchalant introduction to one of the most spell-binding SF classics ever written. It's a universe rich in weird aliens, almost as weird humans, and amazing technology—in particular, the Ringworld itself, which is like a vast wedding ring orbiting a sun, furnishing far more habitable land than any planet ever could.

The concept of Ringworld is a quintessential piece of "hard" science fiction writing—a term generally used to describe SF that has rigorous scientific credentials—and is based on physicist Freeman Dyson's remarkable notion of a "Dyson Sphere", a vast globe encircling a sun whose interior surface offers the largest possible amount of habitable space for that given orbit. Niven was aware that the Dyson Sphere was impossible to build, and unlikely to be stable, so his Ringworld offers a more "practical" option. (In *Debatable Space,* I push the extrapolation a step further by proposing the Dyson Jewels, which are a "virtual" version of the Dyson Sphere.) All this is heavy-duty hypothesising based on real science. It may be far-fetched; but it's *possible.*

But like all good SF writers, Niven isn't afraid to invent science when the real thing just won't do. His "general-address transfer booths" (aka teleportation machines) come into this category. It's hard to see how such a device could work in practice—faster than light travel isn't possible under Einsteinian physics, and the various theories extant about "wormholes" and "quantum teleportation" rely, many would argue, as much on fairy dust as science. But who cares!—it's still a wonderful "what if" notion. What if you could step into what sounds very much like a photo booth and immediately rematerialise anywhere you like on Earth...

Science fiction in my view is a glorious genre because it allows writers to explore and dramatise *ideas,* to challenge preconceptions about society and people, and to touch the heart with magic. (I also love SF because it allows me to place vivid and real characters in the *most* extraordinary situations.) And at the heart of the whole science fiction enterprise is a desire to play games with the audience's willing suspension of disbelief. The SF writer asks "What if?", and then very often will offer a detailed and believable explanation as to "How?"

I adore this aspect of SF— the joyful dance of extraordinary concepts, carefully elaborated.

There are in fact various definitions of what science fiction actually *is*—but in my own view, at its best, SF consists of a collision between speculation, extrapolation and imagination. Pure speculation, without any bedrock of credibility, can all too easily prove hollow and unsatisfying. And mere plodding extrapolation from certain and established facts (imagine a world in which there are 15% more mobile phones than at present! Er, duh!) will by itself never capture the true magic of science, which in the course of its history has been full of the most extraordinary surprises and counter-intuitive insights. But speculation and extrapolation combined, acting together in jostling unity, offer us a way to believe in three impossible things before breakfast, and still believe them at tea-time...

And imagination, of course, is what makes the story sing.

All these thoughts and ideas have infused my writing of *Debatable Space.* It is a novel full of exaggeration and hyperbole.

Spaceships travel amazingly fast, antimatter missiles are thrown like water bombs, some humans are genetically modified to swim like dolphins or run like panthers, the battles are astonishingly vast in scale, and anyone who doesn't die horribly in combat can live for centuries in a state of perfect health and simmering libido.

But mixed in with the improbable (though not *necessarily* impossible) speculations and the fantastic moments are ideas which are in fact extrapolations based on truths and facts. The vast, epic battles in the latter stages of the book are inspired by the vast epic battles of Genghis Khan, as he swept through Asia and Europe leaving a terrible death toll behind. The whole notion of Quantum Beacons sounds like shameless fictional jiggery-pokery, but in fact it is a quite reasonable extrapolation from the Einstein-Podolsky-Rosen paradox. (I take a certain amount of geeky pride at conceiving of a form of FTL travel that *doesn't* defy the known laws of science, unlike Niven's transfer booths.) And Lena's stellar-wind powered yacht—with its micro-thin sail that is "pushed" by photons from a sun—is (as established SF fans will know) a perfectly credible means of transport in space.

Also, I use Lena's journal as an excuse to explore some of my own favourite ideas, such as the Coleridgean concept of the "primary imagination", and the nature of emergence (which explains how complex systems can be created out of simple systems, as in an ant colony or, indeed, the human body). And so at the very heart of the story is my sense of awe at the way that random molecules can form order and pattern and then life, and then sentience, and then civilisation, until an entire universe of miraculous, heart-stopping complexity has arisen—in the midst of which, on a daily basis, the human race perpetrates all *sorts* of stupid shit.

I would happily concede that some elements of my Debatable Science don't stand up to detailed scrutiny. One such is the scene where Alby sees supersymmetrical strings which have become macroscopic due to exposure to high levels of energy. In theory this *is* possible, according to the distinguished sources I have plundered. But the caveat is that superstring theory is by no means as well established scientifically as Einstein's relativity or quantum physics. So it may well be that in five or ten years' time, superstring theory is superseded and that incident in Alby's life is no longer scientifically tenable.

This, however, bothers me not one whit; Alby after all is a super-intelligent ball of flame with a lisp. If you're willing to believe that, then you're morally bound to believe *anything.*

Science fiction can also ask a third question. Not just "What if?", not just "How?" but "What would it *feel* like if . . . ?" And this, above all is my driving principle in the telling of this tale. This is a story of characters in crisis; it is a story about friendship, and love, and betrayal; it is a story about a mother and a son; it is a story about the *people* who inhabit that story. This of course is what all fiction does—it puts us in the skin and in the minds and hearts of others. So although I've enjoyed myself hugely in creating what (I hope!) is a credible basis of Debatable Science with which to construct my world, I trust that the readers of this book will accept the simple and indubitable fact that *all the men and women and aliens in this narrative are real.* They actually do exist—and I have shared their lives.

A few acknowledgements: my friend Dr Paul Bostock has provided exemplary support in critiquing my scientific flights of fantasy, and has corrected some factual errors; though generally he has taken the view that fiction should be fun. His creative notes, also, were first rate.

I'm indebted to the writings of Brian Greene (*The Elegant Universe*) and John H. Holland (*emergence, from chaos to order*) and Lee Smolin (*Life of the Cosmos* and *Three Roads to Quantum Gravity*) for exploring some of the most extraordinary concepts in contemporary physics. I should in this context acknowledge the influence of Michael Crichton, who so far as I know is the first person to write an entire novel about emergence (the excellent

Prey). And I also tip my hat to Jules Verne, Isaac Asimov, George Orwell, Robert Heinlein, Ray Bradbury, Theodore Sturgeon and a host of others for creating the genre that is now the playground for a whole new generation of writers.

My grateful thank-you also to Angell McGregor for giving me excellent detailed notes just when I needed them, and Sally Griffiths for allowing me to steal all her best ideas.

And special thanks to John Jarrold, my friend and agent; and to my editior, the subtle and bold Tim Holman, and all at Orbit, for having faith and for loving science fiction so much.

Philip Palmer, 30th August 2007

introducing

If you enjoyed
DEBATABLE SPACE,
look out for

THE ELECTRIC CHURCH

by Jeff Somers

Avery Cates is a very bad man. Some might call him a criminal. He might even be a killer—for the Right Price. But right now, Avery Cates is scared. He's up against the Monks: cyborgs with human brains, enhanced robotic bodies, and a small arsenal of advanced weaponry. Their mission is to convert anyone and everyone to the Electric Church. But there is just one snag: Conversion means death.

"First, they remove the brain."

I wasn't really listening to Nad. I *never* listened to Nad, actually. We were standing in a shadowy doorway on Bleecker — just a doorway, a rectangle of ancient brick melting away to dusty rubble on either side — watching the gray faces flow by, waiting for one in particular so we could kill him. Well, so *I* could kill him. Nad wasn't a Gunner. He wasn't even much of a criminal; he was possibly the worst pickpocket that had ever lived, and over the years had been pinched by the Pigs so often, with the mandatory accompanying beatings, that he'd started to go a little crazy in his middle age. He was all about conspiracy theories, always telling anyone who'd listen about the sinister forces that ruled the world. For me, it was a lot simpler: Hostile assholes with badges ruled the world, case closed.

Nad was pretty much useless, but I felt sorry for him. I paid him a pittance to work lookout for me on these shithole jobs I picked up, murdering small-fry criminals who'd overstepped their bounds or owed too much yen for too long. Of course, he was pretty useless as a lookout, too.

"You can't digitize the brain," he continued after a lazy pause. "I mean, you can, but it doesn't work. What you get on the other end is bullshit. It sounds okay at first, but when you get into it, the thought process is fried."

"Uh-huh." I'd spotted a cigarette butt on the street a few feet away, only half-smoked. I wondered what the odds were that in the five seconds it would take to claim it, my job would walk by and I'd spend the next five hours listening to Nad while tonight's dinner drifted away. I licked my lips and scanned the crowd.

"So the Monks, they remove the brain. They slice open your head like a fucking can, remove the brain, and put it in one of the Monk bodies. They hook it up, thousands of threads, so thin you can't see 'em. Some of 'em are data transfer lines, some of 'em are electrical, to stimulate the organ. Then they fill the head up with a nutrient solution, to preserve it.

"Fucking *bam!* You've got a Monk."

I sighed. "Nad, everyone knows this. It's on the fucking Vids." There were more and more "Special Reports" on the Electric Church showing up on the huge fifty-foot public video screens every day, reporters with perfect skin cheerfully telling us that the fucking Monks were everywhere, in case we hadn't noticed.

"Yeah, but Ave, think about it: Who's volunteering for this shit? Who's walking up to one of the Tin Men and saying, hell yeah, cut my head off and vacuum out my brains! Fuck that. The Monks are hunting people. I know a guy—"

I winced. Every bullshit story on the street started with *I know a guy.* It was the international *code* for *bullshit.*

"—Kitlar Muan—you know him, shylock outta the Bronx. Or knew him. He was telling me a few weeks ago how one of these Monks was like following him. Always around, always holding up walls or some shit wherever Kit went. Then, one day, Kit's gone, out of touch, and the next day, he's a fucking Monk. You know how the Monks go around and say hello to all their old friends, tell them how they converted? So there I was, and here comes this Tin Man, all vinyl smiles and brand-new black robes, and it walks right up to me and sez, 'Good morning, Nad, you used to know me as Kit Muan, now I'm Brother Muan of the Delta—"

I let Nad's chatter wash over me, bored. If Nad thought the Monks were shooting people in the back and cutting off their heads, it was a good reason to believe otherwise. I kept my eyes roaming over the good citizens of what was left of downtown Manhattan, angry, yellow faces, but I didn't see my mark. I stamped my feet in frustration, cold and tired. It was a low moment. Things had gone downhill at a furious pace since my near-death experience on the East Side; the Pigs were still circulating my description and going hammer and tongs at trying to track down who had murdered Colonel Janet Hense, and I'd exhausted my credit spreading the fog thick to keep my name out of it. Not only was I broke as a result, but being so blatantly connected with an ongoing cop-killing investigation made me a hot property, and business was not good. So Avery Cates the Gweat and Tewwible was reduced to pulling street work for low-rent dipshits. A man needed to pay his bills. If you didn't pay your bills, people like me stood in shadows waiting for you and slit your throat, and I had a lot of bills coming due. Street work paid shit, but it *paid.*

There were, in fact, a trio of Monks across the street from us, and I wasted a moment staring at them. It was a typical scene for them: two standing on either side of a third who stood on a box, preaching. And preaching. And preaching. Walk by in the morning, and this freaky thing with corpse-white skin, dressed all in black and wearing mirrored sunglasses, would be making a speech about salvation. Come back at lunch, the same freak was making the same speech. At night, it was still there. At first we all thought they were fucking Droids. It was a joke: The same Droid that took your job last year was now putting God out of business.

As I stared, one of them turned its pasty white head and looked back at me. I fought the immediate urge to look away, get interested in the near distance suddenly. I just kept staring—you had to keep the act up. I was Avery Cates, toughest bastard in the System, and I would stare at creepy Monks if I wanted.

The Monks all looked alike. Their plastic faces were capable of expression, in weird, programmed contortions that never looked natural, but their faces were identical. At first you saw them here and there, heard rumor of them. Now they're everywhere. You see Monks in the street, on the trains. The Electric Church was a registered religion. It was all very legal—they claimed to have paperwork on every member, showing voluntary submission to the conversion into a Monk. So far the System Pigs bought it, and left them alone.

After a moment, with extreme casualness, I looked back for the cigarette butt and licked my lips. It was almost half a cigarette, and looked to be of good vintage: Pre-Unification. Stale as hell, but still better than the shit you got these days, even if you could afford them. Which I manifestly could not. I stared transfixed at it, and wondered if anyone I knew would see me kneel to get it. You had to keep up the rep all the time.

Nad nudged me gently with one elbow. "That's our man."

I looked up, flushing, angry at myself. Staring at a fucking cigarette butt while tonight's meal ticket strolled by, my ass saved by a dried-up burnout like Nad Fucking Muller. I made fists with both hands and resisted the sudden urge to punch Nad in the face.

I recognized my mark from the grainy files I'd seen: a short, heavyset guy in an ancient leather overcoat about a foot too long for him, worn like a half-rate royal robe, dragging along the street. He was flanked by two huge men who couldn't bend their arms, muscles on muscles twitching. I kept my eyes on the mark, who *bustled,* walking fast. The Little Prince. His name was Rudjer something; it didn't matter. He was low on the food chain and was trying to rise from the depths, and he was about to explode.

I studied the trio. Their eyes were straight ahead, faces set in the usual hardassed grimace—we all had it engraved on our faces—acting like the rest of the poor fucks on the street would just naturally get out of the way. Which they did, because even though the Little Prince was a nobody who didn't realize his button had been pushed, he still had more juice than most of the people around him. He had some yen, some muscle, and that snazzy overcoat.

He glided past me, one of the monsters on his payroll lifting a skinny kid off the ground and tossing him aside to clear a path. I didn't move. Nad started to twitch next to me, impatient, but I held up one hand without looking at him and he shut up. I'd quieted Nad down the hard way often enough; he was well-trained by now.

When they were past, I stepped out into the flow of bodies and matched their pace, keeping my hands in my pockets. My own coat wasn't as regal as the Little Prince's, but it was functional, and contained a number of useful items. It also had holes cut into the pockets so you could arrange your hands without being seen. Keeping my eyes on the three amigos, I felt around for the blade I'd secreted in an inner pocket and took it firmly in one hand. The Little Prince was small fry and barely paid enough to be worth it—a bad man, certainly, no better than me, but not exactly someone who'd enhance my reputation. Bullets were too expensive for shit like him.

I followed in their wake for a while, watching. I knew Nad had slipped into my gravity without having to look; Nad and I went back a long way, and he'd never liked being alone. It didn't take long to establish that the Little Prince's security wasn't worth whatever he was paying them: Like a lot of amateurs, they were one-dimensional, and thought all their troubles would be coming at them from the front, with plenty of warning and a lot of fanfare. Not once did they look back.

Turning my head a little to get an idea of the environmental factors, I almost missed a step, because three Monks were keeping pace with me. I couldn't be sure—the Tin Men all looked alike—but my immediate thought was that these were the same three who'd been preaching across the street from us. One was looking right at me, marching through the crowd like it didn't need eyes. I stared back at it in surprise for a few steps, then tore my eyes away, checking my meal ticket. They were still pushing through the crowd like they owned the streets. From the show they were putting on—all grim determination and regal pomp—the Little Prince was probably out on his collections, squeezing water from stones and performing other miracles on a par with getting money out of my fellow citizens. This all worked to my advantage, because tough guys didn't look over their shoulders to see who might be creeping up behind them, and tough guys didn't need to take basic precautions. More shitheads died being tough every day, when a little good old-fashioned paranoia and cowardice went a long way. It wasn't even cowardice. It was an aversion to death.

The Monks were still keeping pace, but were no longer looking at me. They just floated through the crowd. They were harmless, in my experience, but they creeped you out. Even people who made their living killing and maiming their fellow human beings shied away from those perfect rubber faces, that serene certainty. I didn't doubt the Monks could defend themselves, but every Monk I'd ever run across had been unfailingly polite and nonconfrontational. They still made my skin crawl, and having three of them following me like fucking albatrosses made me nervous.

The crowd thinned a little as we moved north, makeshift stalls sprouting up on the sidewalks, in the streets, little shacks built from scrap wood offering whatever people could scrounge to sell, generally stuff no one thought was worth stealing in the first place. The goods got better as you moved uptown, until you finally reached a point where the Crushers started eyeing you distrustfully and the stores had decent security in place, mainly to keep people like me out. I tensed up a little, resolved to ignore the Monks. If the Little Prince was going to put the squeeze on someone that owed him yen, it was going to be here. Much further uptown and the Little Prince would be outclassed.

Sure enough, he stopped in front of a flimsy stall that was staffed by a man about my age and two young kids with the hollow look of poverty. The place was selling meat pies, the meat not much of a mystery considering the pile of dead rats the boys were engaged in skinning right there in the street. Business was slow, because rats were everywhere, and if I wanted one, I could catch five without working up a sweat.

The proprietor stepped forward, wringing his hands. I didn't listen to what was said, I just watched: The Little Prince stuck out his chest and crossed his arms, listening to whatever plea the old man was shelling out with his chin thrust out, nodding importantly. The two goons just menaced the whole operation, making the boys flinch and knocking shit off the counter, being tough.

I moved fast. There was no talking. No speeches. I wasn't here to make an impression. I scanned the street quickly for Crushers or—worse—System Pigs, and saw nothing, not even the three Monks. Then I stepped up behind the Little Prince, and before anyone could react I just pulled my blade from my pocket, grabbed him around the shoulders, and dragged the knife across his neck, the blade sinking in deep. Then I dropped the knife, stepped back, and drew my automatic. I didn't point it at anyone in particular; that often got misinterpreted, and just encouraged gunplay. I was just discouraging intervention while I waited for the Little Prince to actually die. No one paid for *grievous injury,* after all. The two goons paused and stared, first down at the Little Prince where he lay gurgling, then at me, and finally at each other.

One muttered something under his breath and turned to the other, gesticulating forcefully and hissing something foreign—half the hired muscle in the damn city spoke gibberish.

The other swore—you didn't need to speak the language to recognize swearing—gesturing at the Little Prince, then threw up his hands and glared at me. *"Non mon problème, okay?"*

They knew the score: With the Little Prince dead, no one was going to pay them, so there was no longer a job to do, and they certainly didn't want to end up dead, too. *Non mon* fucking *problème* indeed. These were the bottom-of-the-barrel assholes; you couldn't trust them—they had no goddamn pride, no ethics. To illustrate the point, his fellow made a show of wiping his hands, and the two of them lumbered off, arguing loudly. I looked at their former employer, and he stared up at me with wide, dead eyes. The family was already back at work, furiously making rat pies for the hungry people of New York City. You could count on the good people of New York to never remember a face.

The crowd swirled around me as I reholstered my gun, and then Nad was at my shoulder. "Good work," he said.

It didn't feel good. "Hell," I said. "I need a drink."

look out for

KETOS

also set in the universe of
DEBATABLE SPACE

by Philip Palmer

The Dolphs are a new species—humans who have evolved to survive in the water. A mutiny will free them from their oppressor but trap them on a planet with an uninhabitable sea.

When an attempted assassination of the Captain fails, his son, Michael, is captured and mutilated in his stead. The Captain launches a vicious crackdown against the terrorists, known as Terrans, who want the Dolphs to abandon their attempts to colonize the sea.

In the midst of this bloody civil war, Michael finds himself fighting against his own father in a battle that will determine the survival of his people.